I0572273

Jeanne

Sylvia Hornback

Jeanne
A journey from abandonment and abuse
to forgiveness and truth

Author: Sylvia Hornback

All rights reserved. No part of this book may be reproduced or transmitted in any form or by any means, electronic or mechanical, including photocopying, recording or by any information storage and retrieval system, without written permission from the author, except for the inclusion of brief quotations in a review.

Copyright © 2019 by Sylvia Hornback

ISBN: 978-1-7321916-6-2

Library of Congress Control Number: 2019951846

Edited by: William Greenleaf

Design & Layout by: Douglas DoNascimento

Published by: Briggs & Schuster
              BSA.IM

Printed in the United States of America

For the many children who have suffered and been
harmed through abuse, neglect and abandonment.

For the loving responsible grandparents and extended
families who have come forth to give of themselves
in their healing.

Acknowledgments

Influences and events when we are young forge us for the rest of our lives. It is up to us to define who we will be and if we let others determine who we are. This was clearly evident through the hours of interviews I conducted with women about their childhood experiences. Some were reticent and shy at first, but when they began to talk about what had happened to them, they wanted to tell everything. Often, the telling would reveal events they had not remembered for years. The revelation of what one woman said startled her so, she said, "I had completely forgotten that and saying it out loud it sounds terrible. I must have wanted to forget."

We cried together, we held hands and prayed together.

While Jeanne is historical fiction, the story is inspired by true events. The setting is in a different time and place to keep the identity of those who gave interviews anonymous.

When a child feels unloved, it is difficult for them to ever feel worthy of someone else's love. I heard women say this over and over. For those who made it through struggles with joy in their hearts had a common thread. They believed God loved them no matter what, even if their feet and hands were too big, they weren't smart enough or pretty enough.

Thank you, dear ladies for your remarkable courage in sharing your stories. Thank you for trusting me to write it for others.

Foreword

When I met Sylvia Hornback for coffee a few weeks ago I had no idea the treasure I would walk away holding. She handed me a golden box. The exchange felt sacred as the manuscript, Jeanne, was passed from her hands to mine. Sylvia asked me to read her latest book and offer feedback. I was in a particularly busy season and not sure how I was going to add a few extra minutes in the day to read but I made a commitment to do just that because I love my friend, Sylvia.

Sylvia is a leader among her peers. In any crowd, her beauty and her confidence are a shining light. There is a peace and steadiness in her demeanor that is contagious. When Sylvia's eyes meet mine, I know I've been seen. When she listens, I know I've been heard. And when she speaks words of advice, I know I want to follow her.

I brought the manuscript in the gold box home and placed it carefully beside my bed, wondering when the best night would be to lay aside my own work and read Sylvia's manuscript.

I committed in my mind to read two chapters. Wow! I couldn't put it down! It was no longer 'Sylvia's manuscript' but a beautiful story of a young woman finding love, safety, friends, and faith. "Oh, Jeanne, I know you are a fictional character, but I have found such joy in reading about your life."

Sylvia has a refreshing way of introducing us to Jeanne and her dysfunctional family of origin.

The weaving of the story of a young woman coming of age

during war times, abandoned by her parents, but intensely loved by an army of others.

Jeanne is a story of pain and rejection. It is a story of resiliency, strength, and hope.

Sylvia, I am grateful to you for sharing Jeanne with us. What a gift!

-- Wholeheartedly in Hope,

Beverly Ross, MA, LPC-S

Executive Director of Wise County Christian Counseling & Jenny's Hope

May the God of Hope fill you with all joy and peace as you trust in Him, so that you may overflow with Hope by the power of the Holy Spirit.

- Romans 15:13

jeanne
A journey from abandonment and abuse
to forgiveness and truth

Chapter 1

The August morning of 1940 bore a roiling heat that at midday would assault every citizen in the tiny West Texas town of Deep Creek. Mesquite trees with their feathery leaves and clacking beans offered the only shade, weak and trifling in the attempt. The hot, hard-packed red earth continued to simmer throughout the night while it shriveled the grass and weeds alike.

Jeanne Bradshaw squeezed her eyes shut to hold on to slumber before the air in her eight-by-ten box became unbearable. Only a few moments of predawn sleep were possible before the rising temperature encompassed the day. Jeanne wrestled with the thin bedsheet and flopped over like a hooked perch on a riverbank. She didn't understand how her brothers slept in this heat. Maybe it was untroubled minds or simply exhaustion. She was glad for them. She lifted her heavy braid off the back of her neck, allowing a slight breeze to cool her.

Scrabbling sounds alerted her. Jeanne held her young body still and listened to rustling noises coming from downstairs. The pull chain clanked against the light bulb in the kitchen, and instantly a sliver of yellow light raced up the stairs and into her bedroom.

Carefully, Jeanne sat up and leaned across the windowsill's peeling paint to search the mesquite-covered yard. A waning moon was disappearing on the horizon, and filtered shadows made it difficult to see in the dappled silhouettes below. The approaching dawn offered a milky light, and everything was still and silent outside, at least on her side of the house. Nothing out of the ordinary.

Silverware clanked to the floor. A drawer banged shut. Someone was moving about inside the house and had even been bold enough to turn on a light.

Jeanne felt a familiar tightness in her chest, and her breathing quickened. It wasn't the first time she'd awakened to the sounds of this intruder. Jeanne reached between the rails of the crib beside her cot and placed a hand on Robby's back. Protective feelings washed over her as she gazed at her diminutive six-year-old brother, sleeping soundly under his faded blue bunny blanket. She drew her hand away, lifted the thin sheet from her slender legs, and set her bare feet on the cool linoleum floor, readying herself for the inevitable confrontation.

Swallowing was impossible as air waited inside her mouth constricting Jeanne's throat with dread. She licked her dry lips and gulped air to keep her coughing reflex at bay. She pressed her cheek against the sticky facing of the bedroom door and listened to the frantic searching sounds on the first floor. It had to be Betty Ann, her wayward and sometimes present mother. Betty Ann, the beautiful, sought-after mother who hypnotized everyone who knew her. Her mother materialized and disappeared in their lives on a whim. Her presence or her absence never surprised Jeanne. Betty Ann coming home before daylight and making a racket was not a good sign for Jeanne or her two brothers. Usually, her mother slept on the living room couch at the front of the house. This time, she had returned home for a specific reason. The disturbance was coming from the kitchen.

Easing the door open, Jeanne tiptoed across the dusty hall to the top of the stairway facing her older brother's bedroom. Waiting there was futile, so she moved on toward the sound. The old wooden steps creaked loudly enough for anyone to notice. Betty Ann would know someone was coming.

Jeanne pushed slightly on the closed door, just wide enough to see slender hands with long red varnished nails picking through the drawers in the kitchen. There was no mistaking those hands: small, well kept, soft, white, and terrifying.

"I know you're standing there," Betty Ann growled through gritted teeth.

Jeanne noticed an open red leather purse with a silk rose embroidered on its side on the edge of the table, ready to gobble up any treasure her mother could find.

"Get yourself in here," Betty Ann ordered, never looking up from her task. "Where's that money hid? You and Eli do your best to keep it from me, but I'll have it before I leave."

There was no need to pretend she hadn't heard the demand, so Jeanne stepped through the door, shielding her eyes from the garish light. She eased the door closed behind her, hoping the wooden barrier would subdue the sound and not wake Robby. Waiting for a response was torture, and self-consciousness incapacitated her. Thin arms and legs stuck out of a voluminous dingy white undershirt that hung to her bony knees. Her golden-brown hair was a twisted rope resting on her back, and wisps of it clung to her damp neck and the sides of her face. She was acutely aware of her gangly form and her disheveled appearance. She knew her presence alone was enough to inflame Betty Ann.

Jeanne went to her silent place, her dark sable eyes alert and shining, her sharp mind racing to escape the impending battle. She didn't dare speak for fear of triggering the violent temper that prowled just beneath Betty Ann's thin skin. Sometime last year, around Jeanne's thirteenth birthday, her mother's viciousness toward her had intensified. Since then, Jeanne had tried to become smaller, invisible.

Betty Ann stopped searching and looked at her. "My God, look at your big feet! You're taller than I am, and you've got the feet to match. You take after your daddy, for sure. Where are those new shoes I got you?"

Attacking Jeanne drew attention away from the money search, but by this time, Betty Ann had worked herself into a frenzy. She was smoldering, and Jeanne was the target.

Jeanne felt helpless as she tried to respond. "I just got up, Mama. I haven't had time to dress." She followed a familiar script by responding to her mother with logic. It never worked, especially when Betty Ann believed it made her appear foolish. Jeanne understood that the expected answer should be, "I'm sorry, Mama, I'll put the shoes on right now." Some apology and nothing less than complete compliance to Betty Ann's will.

Betty Ann's fury exploded. She drew back and slapped Jeanne hard across the cheek. "Don't you sass me, you little slut! Go get those shoes and put 'em on. You hear me?" Betty Ann grabbed the front of Jeanne's cotton T-shirt. Her mother ripped the shirt from top to bottom, leaving bloody tracks from those perfect nails across Jeanne's pale chest and budding breasts. Left around Jeanne's neck was a remnant of binding, a faded cloth necklace encircling her throat like a white noose. Trails of blood dribbled down her torso and splattered the checkered floor red. Jeanne grabbed the two sides of torn fabric and attempted to cover herself, but Betty Ann clamped her hand on Jeanne's arm, dug in her sharp claws, and shoved her across the kitchen. Jeanne slammed into the table, stumbled across a dinette chair, and crashed against the wall.

"Stay there!" Betty Ann screamed.

Clutching the scraps of shirt together proved useless as Jeanne sat there numb, emotionally and physically, to this abuse. She didn't look at her mother. She couldn't. Jeanne rubbed her cheek as she wondered what made her numb to the blows her mother rained on her. *Why does she explode into these horrific rages?*

Jeanne remembered when she was younger how much it had hurt. The red welts and dark bruises lasted for days. She cried every night, and even her father would leave the house when Betty

Ann began one of her tirades that often ended in beatings. Today, however, Jeanne's expression showed nothing. She did not let the pain affect her. Only later would she experience the soreness and see the bruises that testified the attack had taken place.

Jeanne sat there frozen, turning off every emotion to protect herself. She would not let Betty Ann see her cower and cry and say she was sorry. That wouldn't happen. It hadn't happened for a long time now.

Her mother switched to other tactics to inflict pain. "You're an icy bitch, Jeanne Bradshaw," Betty Ann shrieked. She closed her eyes as if she were imagining an unspeakable horror entering the kitchen to torment her.

Jeanne caused her mother's fury. Betty Ann had told her often enough how disrespectful and judgmental she was. Her mother's anger was a razor-sharp stiletto piercing her skin. She blinked at the stinging wounds and held her outside shell calm.

"What's wrong with you?" Betty Ann derided her. "Don't you feel anything? I don't understand you. I will never understand you." Betty Ann ran her fingers through her blond hair and shook it in place. She straightened her emerald-green pencil skirt and flicked the ruffles on her lacy white blouse. She justified her anger with each movement, primping and smoothing her guilt away.

The only way to change the direction of this confrontation was to turn Betty Ann's attention back to the money. Jeanne didn't want the violence to escalate again because she hadn't put on the shoes.

While Jeanne seemed tough and unmoving on the outside, her mother's scathing comments had rendered her helpless on the inside. Even if Jeanne were the most verbose person in the universe, she would always stop short of telling her mother what was on her mind. Jeanne tried to understand what she had done to make her mother despise her so.

Betty Ann leaned against the icebox, gasping for breath after her harangue. Her hands shook as she tidied her hair and again straightened her skirt, preening until it tranquilized her.

Jeanne tried to decide if her mother's actions were calming or building steam to blow up again. Did she still have enough venom to continue berating her? Jeanne silently willed her big brother to wake up and come into the kitchen. She needed him now. She hoped Eli could soften the anger emanating from Betty Ann. However, the commotion had disturbed neither Eli nor Robby. Unlike Jeanne, her brothers were sound sleepers.

She had to acknowledge the too-small loafers. The shoes that hurt her feet and crushed her toes were still in the store box. They hadn't fit from the beginning. Her mother had told her she was not buying shoes any bigger than a size six. She wouldn't have a girl in her family who had feet any bigger than that. Betty Ann told Jeanne that she would get used to the shoes, and all she had to do was break them in. Jeanne had tried. Walking in the shoes rubbed blisters on her heels within an hour, and that made wearing the shoes impossible, so she had lied and told her mother she was breaking them in just fine. She hoped her feet would heal before school started. She worried how she would get real shoes for school. If the weather stayed warm, she would go to school barefooted like many of her classmates.

Jeanne sat on the cracked chair nearby and reached for the shoebox under the kitchen table. She pulled out the shoes and crammed one foot into a brown leather loafer as her mother began her search again. Betty Ann seemed to have already forgotten the madness that had overtaken her a few minutes earlier. Jeanne wavered between thinking her mother was insane and believing her outbursts were unadulterated hatred toward Jeanne herself.

During different times—the good times—Betty Ann would draw her into her perfect fantasy world. Jeanne trusted her hypnotizing words, and she would crave her mother's attention. Then, snap! Betty Ann would turn on her and say, "Why are you hanging on me? Get away from me. Leave me alone." Then Betty Ann would abandon them. Sometimes for a few hours, and sometimes for days. Even now, Mama lured her back into her web of adoring charisma. Jeanne hated herself for believing the good or the bad coming from her mother's cutting remarks. When Jeanne sat alone considering her life, it didn't matter what mood Betty Ann was in. All her moods were destroying her. She wondered how she would survive.

Betty Ann was so intent looking for the money that Jeanne was able to ease a long-sleeved shirt from the back of another chair and cover herself. She stood to make her mother aware of her presence. "I have the shoes on," she said to her mother in a soft, compliant voice. She immediately realized her mistake.

Betty Ann whipped around and looked at Jeanne's feet. "Don't you look like a silly ass. That damned shirt on that skinny body, and now look at you. You're almost fourteen, for God's sake. Big hands, big feet!" Betty Ann laughed hysterically. "No wonder your daddy left."

"You said I favor Daddy, and I'm glad I'm like him."

"He was handsome, all right, but not good looks for a girl. Why, when I was fourteen, I had every boy in high school after me. Even a teacher or two. You have nothing. They wouldn't pay any attention to"—she gave a dismissive wave—"whatever this is."

"Why did Daddy leave, Mama?" Her need to have the information was greater than her fear of reprisal for asking the question.

Betty Ann's eyes flashed. She stepped forward and then stopped. "You never mind. He did, that's all. He told me he still loved me."

Betty Ann's words were clearly intended to inflict pain, and it worked.

Daddy had shown them love in his quiet way. For the years he'd been present in their lives, Jeanne recalled happy moments. "What about us?" she pressed. "What about Eli, and Robby, and me?" It had been two years since her father had gone on one of his trips and never come back. She was afraid of the truth.

Her mother's shoulders sagged, and her face clouded. A penny fell from her pale hand, which was fat with stray coins, and rolled under the stove. Then Betty Ann straightened and directed her icy gaze at Jeanne. "There is no *us*," she hissed. "You were a sickening disappointment to him."

Jeanne shrank from her. She tried to become stone, not to listen. Every word stung, and every word bore deep into her soul.

Betty Ann slammed open the pantry door and rummaged through the mostly empty shelves. She pushed aside the few cans of beans left on the shelf. "Here it is." She smirked as she reached to the back of the shelf. "Finally." She grabbed a pale yellow envelope and ripped it open.

"Don't take it, Mama." Jeanne sounded weak and pleading, even to herself. Eli had hidden the few dollars behind the last jars of green beans.

"You can't keep this from me! Not a chance on your life. What's yours is mine. Don't you forget that, Jeanne." Her eyes narrowed. "I can still beat the hell out of you. It's my right."

"Eli works hard at the grocery store for that money." Jeanne's voice trembled. She had to say something.

Her mother stood still as she fanned the dollar bills and counted them out loud. "Is this all? I need more than this!" Betty Ann's face contorted. "Seventeen dollars?"

"That's all of it. We have nothing else. You have it all." She clenched her fists at her side. She wanted to rail at her mother.

"How dare you talk to me like that, Jeanne Bradshaw. You're lucky I've got to go." Betty Ann stuffed the cash into her red purse.

"We need food for Robby," Jeanne said as she stepped back against the cupboard. She was afraid of her mother. In this state, she was capable of anything.

"Go to the church. They'll give you something." Her mother, now wild-eyed, clutched the purse to her chest. "Take Robby with you. They'll feel sorry for you." She glanced nervously at the opening to the living room.

"Are you afraid the boys will see you've taken the money?" Jeanne asked. If Eli appeared, Betty Ann would be troubled with a twinge of guilt. But it didn't seem to matter to her mother one way or the other when Jeanne was the witness.

"I'll take care of you another time," Betty Ann snapped as she pushed past Jeanne. She looked distraught and panicked. Her heels clicked haltingly as she hurried out the back door. The screen door slammed shut.

Jeanne followed her mother to the already sweltering front porch. She glimpsed a blur of green as her mother disappeared around the corner of their little gray house on Bent Street.

Jeanne turned back to the house when she heard Robby crying. She kicked off the offending too-small shoes and ran upstairs, slamming into Eli on the landing.

"Hey, what's going on?" Eli asked.

"Gee," called Robby.

"I have to see about Robby." She pushed by Eli. "There, there. I'm here sweet boy."

Chapter 2

Robby quieted when Jeanne stepped into the tiny bedroom.

She turned sideways to slide around the crib and unclasp the side rail. "Good morning, sweet boy." She smiled at the innocent face topped with unruly beige hair. "Let's get that diaper changed." Jeanne saw Robby's gently slanting eyes following her every move with complete trust. She would always be kind to this innocent angel, even if she was churning with anger and hurt.

Regardless of the troubling circumstances in this family, Robby was always the essence of love.

"That's a good boy, my Robby baby. Are you hungry?" Jeanne patted his soft warm back, and Robby patted her in unison.

He put his arms around Jeanne's neck when she gathered him to her. He weighed nothing at all, so she carried him. He was too weak to walk more than a couple of steps without falling or becoming too tired. His lips and the tips of his fingers would turn blue. The doctor had said it was his heart, and he probably wouldn't live to be over five or six years old. He had already lived that long.

Jeanne couldn't stand to think of anything happening to Robby, so she carried him everywhere, hoping she could circumvent something catastrophic. "Sit here while I get dressed." Jeanne put Robby on her cot and gave him Gus, his brown bear, to play with while she got dressed. After she put on a skirt and blouse, she headed back to the kitchen with Robby balanced on her hip.

Eli stood over the stove, cooking bacon. "Ouch!" He jumped back and rubbed his bare chest while he turned the sizzling meat over in the skillet. "You'd better do this. It pops on me every time."

Jeanne put Robby in his high chair and took the fork. "Is the burn bad? You have to turn down the fire."

"Nah, just stings." Eli scratched his head and backed away from the stove and the hot skillet.

"Your shirt is on the chair," she said. "I wore it earlier this morning." She leaned over to watch the flame under the bacon while she turned the knob on the burner.

"Morning, Robby." Eli slipped on the shirt and tucked it in his jeans. "What did Mama say?" Eli asked as he sat at the table and poured Robby a glass of milk. "Her yelling woke me."

"She didn't say anything worth repeating." Jeanne knew she was being short with Eli, but she couldn't help it. Her nerves were still on edge, and she had faced her mother on her own. It wasn't that easy to handle Betty Ann by herself. She stared at the eggs in the pan and stirred them absent-mindedly.

"What about her being here to take care of Robby when school starts Tuesday?"

"She didn't mention it." Jeanne hadn't thought of it either. Her feelings had filled her up like a balloon ready to pop. Emotions had stifled her ability to think.

"Then why did she come?" Eli asked as he ran his fingers through his black hair. "Did you ask her?"

"Eli, I didn't have a chance," she snapped. "She was in and out of here so fast, and she was in one of her moods." Jeanne put the fried bacon on a plate and scooted it across the table in front of Eli. She always prayed for strength to survive. She guessed she had done that. Survived. Her prayers were always so desperate.

"Okay, okay," he said.

Their conversation lagged while Jeanne scrambled eggs. Eli drew glasses of water for them and Jeanne buttered bread for oven toast, Robby's favorite. The ordinary routine of the morning soothed them. The trio was surviving, with two brothers who were completely different from her. Grateful for this bit of peace in the aftermath of conflict, Jeanne sat and folded her hands, not hearing a word of Eli's rote blessing as he prayed.

While they were eating, Jeanne finally talked about Betty Ann's visit. "Mama found our money. She took it all. This time she even took the loose change she found in the kitchen drawers."

"What about our food?" Eli asked. "Do we have enough?" He raked his long black hair out of his face as if he were ridding himself of the obstacles in his way.

Robby was always their first priority. She and Eli had agreed long ago that when Betty Ann left, they would assume she wouldn't be back. Jeanne hoped she would be, and so did Eli. Even with her screaming and violent temper, life was predictable when she was there. It was familiar chaos.

"I can stretch the food to last at least a week," Jeanne replied. Robby didn't eat much. If she could get eggs, she could scramble them for him.

"What about Robby?" Eli reached over and put his big paw of a hand on Robby's brow and gently smoothed his hair.

Robby adored his big brother and gave him a loving smile.

"I love you too," Eli said, answering an unspoken communication between them.

"We need the right kind of food for Robby," Jeanne said. "I have to mash his food so he can swallow. He can always drink milk, though." She went to the pantry, pulled out the meager remains, and positioned the food on the table among the breakfast dishes. The sight was sobering with only one can of evaporated milk, a half-empty tin of crackers, a container of peanut butter, and three cans of beans.

"Milk is thirty-five cents a gallon at the store," Eli said. "A whole gallon will spoil if we can't get ice to keep it cool." Eli opened the door to an empty wooden icebox, waiting for a block of ice to help it do its job. "We can't afford it."

"What if we get a quart bottle or canned milk?"

"That'll cost us more. One quart is fourteen cents."

"I'll ask for my babysitting money," Jeanne said. "She owes me for a week and one extra day that I worked in May."

"Aren't you babysitting anymore?"

"I've worked my last week," Jeanne said. "Their grandmother from Abilene is here. Everybody's having money problems, and she came to help."

"I don't get paid at the grocery store till Saturday afternoon," he said. "I can get leftover food for us at the store. It will be odds and ends as usual, but it won't cost us anything."

"We can make it till Saturday when you get paid."

"I'll go to the store this morning and work all day today and tomorrow. That will bring another day's pay."

"Mama said for us to go to the church to get food if we needed it." It was bad enough with their mother coming and going as she did. The whole town gossiped about it.

"Only if we have to. I get looks in the store now as it is. Mr. Benson comes in every day asking about Mama." Eli's face scared her. He was more than hurt. He was angry.

"What did you tell him?"

"Nothing. I nearly hit him yesterday."

"Don't hit him, Eli. Then you would be just like her."

Eli sat there with his head in his hands. "I won't. Don't worry, Jeanne. I know what a temper and jealousy have done to this family already."

❧

Jeanne decided to collect her babysitting money after supper that evening. Eli had gone that morning and returned that afternoon. Now that he was home, she wanted to get her money. She had three dollars coming. The children were a handful, but she didn't mind. They were nice to Robby, and they ate lunch there. She had calculated that her earnings would pay for Robby's milk for two weeks.

The high-pitched whine of cicadas dominated Jeanne's afternoon trek. She stopped on the cracked sidewalk to locate one loud culprit grasping a stout limb above her head. She liked their familiar sound in the hot summers. However, the noisy insects would soon be gone. The days were getting shorter, and the nights were getting cooler.

The cicada flew away to another tree to continue its courtship song, its whirring faded. Jeanne was still smiling when she knocked on Mrs. Alison's screen door.

"What are you doin' here?" Molly Alison said. The eight-year-old girl looked at Jeanne through a hole in the screen panel and didn't offer to unhook the door. "Mama's here and it's near suppertime. We don't need no babysittin'." Molly cocked her head and glared at Jeanne.

"I'm not here to stay with you," Jeanne explained. "I want to talk to your mama."

Jeanne kept the four children while their mother worked as a cashier at the grocery. Molly thought she was old enough to watch her brothers, so she didn't warm up to Jeanne as the boys did.

"Molly, why didn't you tell me Jeanne was here?" Mrs. Alison said as she walked up behind her daughter. "Come on in, Jeanne." She didn't sound welcoming. The buxom Mrs. Alison opened the screen door and motioned Jeanne in the house. "What brings you here?" She wiped her brow with a red-checkered dish towel. Sweat was pouring off her brow, and her freckled face shimmered in the low light of the house.

Jeanne's stomach did a flip. She hated asking for the money, even though she had earned it. She screwed up her courage. "I came to get the sitting money, Mrs. Alison."

"Well, come have a seat. I'm in the kitchen frying chicken. Mr. Alison will be home shortly."

Jeanne followed her to the back of the house. Mrs. Alison

pointed to the table where one chair was open for sitting. A bowl of potatoes and a paring knife greeted her. Jeanne obliged, and she began to peel the potatoes.

Mrs. Alison turned her back to Jeanne and tended to the frying chicken. "I don't have your three dollars," she said, never facing Jeanne.

The words bounced off the grease-splattered wall and hit Jeanne like a fist. It was just what she was afraid might happen when she asked for her pay. Mrs. Alison seemed to be too ashamed to turn around and face her. Jeanne felt sorry for the woman in the sweat-soaked dress and wanted to help her regain her dignity.

Jeanne finally said, "I can come back later or take partial payment now and the rest later."

Mrs. Alison's rounded shoulders slumped, and the hot lard bubbled in the frying pan as she moved the chicken about. "How about two bits? Maybe I can spare that much."

Jeanne stopped peeling the potatoes. She didn't think she would get any more of her wages than that today, so she gave in. "Yes, ma'am."

At once, a chubby arm reached up and retrieved a coffee can off a shelf above the stove. With her other hand, Mrs. Alison deftly switched off the gas burner. The soft rattle in the can said there was no paper money inside.

Jeanne held her breath.

Mrs. Alison faced Jeanne, counted out two dimes and a nickel, and placed them in a row on the table. The telltale rattle stopped. "There you go. I need to finish dinner now."

"Yes, ma'am," Jeanne picked up her coins and hurried out of the house. She darted over the sidewalk as she ran and didn't slow until she reached the shed behind the house. Leaning against the shaky wall with her heart beating out of her chest, Jeanne wrestled with her feelings. She was angry because she didn't have all the money she'd earned. They were close to desperation. *How can I feel sorry for Mrs. Alison too?*

Inside the shed, a weak light filtered through dried boards.

Jeanne found an empty glass jar, carefully wrapped the money in a small square of cloth and stuffed it in the jar. She found a lid and ring that fit, screwed it on, and then hid it behind an old kettle. If she was lucky, Mama wouldn't find the money, piddling as it was.

∽∞∾

The next day after work, Eli strode through the back door with a burlap tow sack slung over his shoulder. "It's not much, but it's something," he said with a big grin. "Daniel let me have the sack so I could bring it home."

Jeanne left the stove and riffled through the assortment of food in the sack. "I didn't know your friend Daniel was working there. Is this okay with him?" Jeanne pulled out a can of milk, a real treasure.

"Yep, he put that in the bag."

"Did he drop out of school just before graduation?"

"No, he got his diploma. He decided to graduate with eleven years instead of the new requirement of twelve. He's already in training to be a manager."

"Have you thought about that? Going ahead and getting your diploma, I mean."

"I've thought about it," Eli said as he left the room.

Jeanne knew he was struggling with the decision. Eli had a chance to get a scholarship, or he could take his diploma and go to work. At least they had food for a few days. Eli would get paid tomorrow, and she had her twenty-five cents.

Chapter 3

Jeanne gazed across the yard toward the black thunderheads on the horizon. She hoped the rain would come their way and cool the sweltering, sticky afternoon. Tree leaves hung limp with their undersides folded upward, giving in to the blistering sun. The house had been stifling, so she and Robby spent the afternoon outside. This shady side of the house offered a modicum of relief.

Their worn quilt pallet stuck to the indentions in the sparse grass and provided a thin bit of insulation between them and the cooked ground. While the sun slid across the sky, they had been able to remain in the shade of the house and the lone chinaberry tree. Jeanne leaned against its trunk and closed her eyes. She was drunk with the warm stillness, and the clink of Robby's toy cars and trucks lulled her into a fretful nap. Her mother was digging red nails into her arm when her eyes flew open. It had only been a few days since Betty Ann had been there, but Jeanne couldn't get the ugly encounter out of her mind. She turned her face south as a small breeze began to whirl across the yard. She looked toward the storm clouds as they drew closer.

"I thought you two might be out here," Eli said as he rounded the corner of the house.

Jeanne looked up and saw her brother with a broad smile plastered on his face. "You look happy."

"I am." Eli beamed. "I've been talking to Coach. He says scouts from Tech are coming to Deep Creek again to see me play at the scrimmage next week."

"That's great news." It was exciting. Jeanne felt a thrill for Eli with his good luck coming their way.

Eli sat on the quilt and patted Robby on the back. "This may change everything for us. Coach says I could go ahead and graduate or wait another year for the college offers. He thinks I could have more than one college give me a football scholarship."

"Where else could you get a scholarship?" Jeanne's insides were churning. She wanted this for him, but at the same time, if Eli went away, what would she do? What if Betty Ann didn't come back? Where could she and Robby go? She wouldn't spoil the moment for him by asking those questions, but she knew they were on his mind.

"MacMurray and Decatur Baptist College are coming," Eli said. "Decatur Baptist is only a junior college, but I could go to a four-year school after I graduated from there."

"That's far away."

"Decatur Baptist is farthest. Tech is the closest, but regardless of where I go, I would only come home at the end of the year."

His words hung in the air. Jeanne tried not to look upset. She wanted this for him, but she was afraid for Robby and for herself. She had been scared this day would come. Eli had always wanted to leave this place. Of that she was certain. He had to know the impact of his words on her.

"I'm glad for you," Jeanne finally said. "It's your chance of a lifetime, and you must take it. Otherwise, none of us will get out of this town. You have to go and make a life for yourself."

"There are possibilities for you too," he said. "I can help. We'll think of a way."

Jeanne didn't know what that way was. She had pushed the

thought of Eli leaving out of her mind for a long time, and now the reality was looming before her. She loved learning and wanted to finish high school. She didn't even dare dream of going to college.

A door slammed shut in the house as the wind howled. Sudden gusts of sand stung their skin.

"We'd better go in," Jeanne said. "A storm is coming." She started gathering the toys.

The sky was covered in gray clouds pitching angrily over the rooftops. Eli grabbed Robby, and Jeanne snatched the quilt. Fat drops of rain splashed on their heads as they ran to the house. Eli was in the back door first, and Jeanne slid in just as a loud clap of thunder boomed. They laughed, delighted from the cooling race, then halted abruptly. Groceries covered the countertop and the kitchen table.

Before they could say a word, Betty Ann's voice rang out. "Children, why don't you help your mama put away this food?"

Jeanne was stunned. She had wanted her mother to return and be responsible, but Betty Ann was always unpredictable. The groceries suggested she might stay for a while. The timing was right, since school would be starting in a week.

Jeanne automatically started putting away the food and helping with dinner. She gathered cans and arranged them on the shelf in the pantry. She busied herself cutting up carrots as the familiar scene unfolded.

Eli had put Robby in his high chair and was talking. Jeanne could see that he was still on cloud nine about his scholarship chances. She listened again to the news Eli had delivered to her minutes earlier.

"Mama," Eli related, "Coach said the scouts from colleges are coming for the scrimmage next week."

"Why, that's wonderful, Eli," Betty Ann said. "You are something special."

As Eli began his story with breathless animation, his joy eased tensions in the tiny kitchen. His words spilled out, every syllable tingling with excitement.

Betty Ann hurried over to Eli and hugged him. "Did you hear that, Robby? Your big brother is going to college." She clutched Robby's soft hands and clapped them together, making him laugh and squeal with delight.

The impact of Eli's news wasn't as disturbing to Jeanne this time. Was it because Mama was here, time had passed, or had she adjusted? She didn't know. She covered the carrots with water and put the pot on the burner to cook. She allowed herself a small smile, admitting the conversation was a happy one. She felt comfortable being ignored. *A football scholarship is as good a topic as any*, she thought. She let their talk drift into the background while she set the table. Eli and her mother looked normal. Smiles on their faces. Mama cooking and teasing. Eli folding his arms with his chest puffed out. Jeanne was on the outside peering at her family. *Maybe I can start school on Tuesday*. The chances were promising.

∾

The rain came in a rush, slashing sideways at the house. Waves of the heavy deluge were deafening, but calm reigned in the kitchen as the storm raged around them. They ate their dinner while darkness covered the windows. Then, as quickly as it had come, the storm subsided and passed on to the next county, taking the violent winds with it.

"I'm glad that's over," Betty Ann declared. "I was afraid the rain would keep me from going out tonight."

"Where are you going?" Eli asked. "You just got here." He stepped back and turned to look at Betty Ann squarely.

She ignored his implied accusations. "Oh, I'll be back, Eli, my boy. Don't you worry, and don't wait up for me."

Jeanne could see the mixed emotions taking hold of her brother's face. He wanted to believe her. He had been mesmerized by her warm presence and her generous affections. She had enticed him with her words as sure as Coach had convinced him he would get a scholarship.

"Come on, don't look so dreary," Betty Ann said. "Let's listen to the radio. Edgar Bergen and Charlie McCarthy are on tonight. Leave the dishes, Jeanne. We'll wash them together later."

Betty Ann rushed into the living room. Jeanne heard the click of the dial, and suddenly laughter from the show's audience rolled into the kitchen. Mr. Bergen was playing Mortimer Snerd. He was yucking it up as his goofy character, and Jeanne stopped to listen. She put away the leftovers and picked up Robby from his high chair. When she stepped into the living room, Mama took Robby on her lap, and Jeanne sat on the floor next to Eli. They laughed, even Jeanne. At the end of the program, Jeanne gathered a sleeping Robby in her arms and said good night. She heard the theme song of *The Chase and Sanborn Hour* as she carried him up the stairs to bed.

Despite how tired she was, Jeanne couldn't sleep. Writing always helped, so she took out a worn leather journal and began to write. Her father had given the old journal to her. He said someone left it at one of his jobs. No one claimed it, and he had cut out the few pages the former owner had used and given it to her. She looked at Robby and penned a poem. Writing about Robby always felt sweet.

Later that night, Jeanne looked out her bedroom window at the steam rising off the rocks from the earlier rainfall. She was grateful for the cool air the brief storm had left. She lay atop her sheet and soaked in the freshness floating into her room. She wondered how long the idyllic family facade would last. She prayed out loud: "Dear God, give me the strength to endure whatever is to come." How many times had she said these words? Grandma Biddy had told her he would answer her prayers, and sure enough she had endured.

A man's voice fractured the quiet evening. "Come back here, you crazy bitch!"

Jeanne scrambled to the window to listen. She strained to get a glimpse of what was happening, but grunts and panting noises were all she could hear.

"Let go of me!" Betty Ann screamed. Her mother was arguing with someone at the front of the house. They sounded closer to the road than the front porch.

Jeanne had to see what was happening. She grabbed her shirt and pants from the end of the bed and dressed as she ran down the stairs. She stopped at the screen door, and when she saw movement, she burst through the door. "Mama!" she yelled. She cupped her hands around her mouth and shouted louder. "What's wrong? Who's out there?"

"Go back in the house, Jeanne. I don't want you here."

"But Mama, who's there?"

A slap and crying sounds echoed from the road. Jeanne could just make out a car parked in the shadows.

"Don't you come out here."

Jeanne could hear her mother sobbing, but she couldn't see anything except the silhouette of the car. She was torn. Should she wake up Eli to come help? She strained to hear. Now it was totally quiet. Jeanne's bare feet floated over the wet grass as she inched closer to the car.

"I want my money," the man said. "Give it to me, or you'll get worse."

"I don't have it," Betty Ann shouted back at him.

Jeanne could see them standing in front of the car, facing each other. Black outlines of anger and drunken posturing circled one another. She felt a touch on her shoulder.

Eli stood close to her. "What's the noise out here?"

"It's Mama and Mr. Morrison from the feedstore."

Another slap rang out. Jeanne could see the man swing and hit their mother. Betty Ann fell to the ground, and Eli flew past Jeanne before she could react. The man at the road staggered back and turned just as Eli tackled him to the ground and started beating him with his fists.

Jeanne ran to her brother. "Eli, Eli, stop!" She tried to grab Eli's arm, but he slipped out of her grasp as if she were not there. "Eli!"

Her mother stood up and darted around to face Eli. Betty Ann knelt in front of Eli, and in between blows, took her son's face in her hands. "Eli," she said.

He looked up, saw his mother, and let his arms fall slack.

"You go back in the house. I'll take care of this."

Jeanne tugged on his arm and got her limp brother off the ground. She grabbed his arms and guided him back a few paces. Jeanne listened to his ragged breathing, saw his eyes close and tears streak his gritty face. She turned and stood between the man and her brother.

The man in the dirt groaned.

"Get up, Melton," Betty Ann said as she bent and took his arm. "Get up. Get in your car and go home." She kicked him in the side when he didn't do as she told him.

Melton Morrison moaned and slowly sat up. He leaned to the side, and Betty Ann steadied him. His head flopped forward.

"Get up! Get up! You have to leave here," Betty Ann said. "Go home to your wife."

"I want my money back," he blubbered. Now he was crying. He stood up and staggered up the slight incline to the road.

His words were garbled, but Jeanne understood. There was no money. Mama had spent it to put food on their table.

Betty Ann grabbed a jacket off the ground and swung it at the man staggering toward the car. "Don't you ever come back here, Melton Wayne Morrison. Look at you! In front of my kids, in front of my house." She threw the jacket at him, and it landed on his head.

Melton stumbled into the grill, pulled the garment off his head, and grabbed the bumper to keep from falling.

Eli's breathing slowed, and Jeanne could see that his rage was subsiding.

"Let's go back to the house," Jeanne said. She took his bloody hand. "We need to take care of your hands."

"It's nothing. I'm waiting here till he leaves." Eli pulled his hand back and stuck it in his pocket.

"I'm staying with you," Jeanne said. She stood beside her brother while the man pulled himself along the side of the car, opened the door, and fell into the front seat.

Their mother turned and walked away from the scene. She trudged past them and went into the house without saying a word.

The car engine roared to life, lurched forward, and jerked along the road heading away from town. They stood there listening to the fading car sounds until silence overtook them.

Jeanne and Eli walked to the house. Eli went straight to his bedroom and shut the door. Jeanne found her mother asleep on the couch, fully dressed. The living room was silent, except for her mother's gentle snoring. Bone-tired, Jeanne climbed the stairs to her room.

Chapter 4

"Wake up, sleepyheads," Betty Ann called from downstairs. "Breakfast is ready."

It was the first day of school. Jeanne turned over and saw that Robby's crib was empty. It wasn't often Mama could come in her room and get Robby without her knowing it.

Jeanne quickly got dressed. She decided on a white blouse that buttoned at the neck. She wanted to hide the trail of brown scabs that were scattered across her chest. She didn't want her mother to see a reminder of what had occurred a few days ago. She pulled on her last year's gathered gingham skirt. While the waistband still fit her, the skirt was too short, but not above her knees yet. Grandma Biddy had made it for her and put in a deep hem so she could let it out when she grew. The material was sturdy and hadn't faded, so she could wear it to school until December.

As she brushed her hair, the incident from last night kept going through her mind. It was as if each pass of the brush eliminated bits of the debacle with Melton Morrison. She pulled the brush through her thick mane, and it soothed her emotions. Her thick, long hair was heavy and hard to tie, but today she gathered it in a ponytail at the nape of her neck to stay cool. She used strips of cloth Grandma Biddy had cut for her to make a bow. She was ready to face the morning. Jeanne left the offensive shoes in her closet. *Maybe Mama won't notice.*

She descended the stairs and headed into the kitchen. She was the last to arrive. Plates of bacon with eggs piled high were on the table. Betty Ann carried stacks of toast and pancakes on a big yellow platter and proudly placed it in the middle of the table. Jeanne looked carefully at her mother. There was no hint of the blows from last night. Her mother looked fresh and rested while she, on the other hand, was exhausted.

"There, that should do it," Betty Ann said. "Isn't your mama the best?"

"Yes, ma'am," Eli said. He was beaming as he dug into the feast.

Betty Ann looked at Jeanne expectantly.

"Yes, ma'am," Jeanne echoed. She didn't want to ruin the carefully planned breakfast reunion. Jeanne had to admit that she was relishing the food and was falling into the microcosm of happiness swirling around the kitchen table. She opened the jar of molasses and poured out a healthy serving. Robby sat in his high chair eating scrambled eggs and drinking his milk.

"Pancakes, your favorite, Jeanne," her mother announced.

"Mine too, Mama." Eli grinned as he stuffed a whole pancake in his mouth.

"Eat all you want, honey," Mama said. "You're the man of the house, and soon you'll be going to college. Just think, the first one."

⌘

Two Saturdays later, Jeanne left the house while Robby and Mama were napping. She walked five blocks north to the Methodist church. They had a small library in their basement, and Jeanne checked out books from time to time.

She waited for her eyes to adjust to the dim light before she descended the worn steps into the cool, quiet room. A miniature lamp—the only light in the basement—illuminated the area around the desk where Mrs. Williams sat reading. She was a mite of a woman whose feet barely touched the floor when she was seated.

"Hello, Mrs. Williams," Jeanne said.

She scooted forward in her chair to greet Jeanne. "Why, hello," Mrs. Williams said, then cleared her throat. She cleared her throat often when she talked, but Jeanne had learned to ignore the irritating habit.

"I've come for more books."

"Finished already?"

"I have. You know I loved *Gone with the Wind*."

"Yes, all the ladies do. I always have a waiting list."

"Yes, ma'am." Jeanne put three books back on the desk. She wanted to read them again, but she was eager to read the new books too.

Mrs. Williams looked at the books. "Are you sure you don't want to keep *The Story of Ferdinand* to read to Robby?"

"I think I want something new for him."

"I have just the thing. How about a colorful Mother Goose book?"

"He would love that."

"We just got this one. You can have it, if you can get it back in a couple of days. I have a waiting list, you know." Mrs. Williams showed her the new book, *Rebecca*.

Jeanne had heard of the book. She smiled. "I would love to read it." Jeanne left with *Rebecca, The Yearling*, and a Mother Goose book. She was excited to have new books to read. She had read everything else in the small church library. Even with school starting, she never had enough to read. She had spent a long time in the library and hoped Mama and Robby were still asleep.

"Where have you been?" Betty Ann demanded. "I've been stuck here while you've been out gallivanting all over town." Her mother marched across the living room, looking directly at Jeanne. Then she pivoted and shambled back toward the kitchen. She seemed distracted.

Jeanne ran up the stairs and put away her new books. She didn't want any conversation to focus on the fact that she read all the time. She set the books on her bed and looked at Robby sleeping in his crib. "Can I help with dinner?" she asked when she went back downstairs. She passed her mother sitting on the divan and walked into the kitchen. It was clean. No food was out. Nothing was cooking. Jeanne turned back and looked at her mother.

Betty Ann's hair had been freshly washed. A loose robe was carefully draped across her shoulders, and her makeup was applied perfectly. Betty Ann jumped up and started pacing and wringing her hands.

"Where are you going?" Jeanne asked.

Betty Ann ignored her question. "Get upstairs and tend to your brother. He's calling for you."

Jeanne knew that tone, so she escaped up the stairs to her little brother. Their room was a haven, and Robby was always glad to see her. He never criticized, never judged. His love was unconditional. She hugged him close. He still had that baby smell.

She and Robby were sitting on her bed near the window when the crashing sounds began. She hummed a song to Robby to keep them both distracted from the scene downstairs. Then she opened the Mother Goose book and started reading aloud. She sang the rhymes to him, and they played patty-cake. Her distraction strategy worked for Robby but not for herself.

Jeanne hoped Eli would be home from work soon. Eli's presence could change their mother's erratic behavior. He was a boy, after all, and ever since he had reached puberty, Betty Ann insisted that he was the man of the house. She wanted his approval, the opposite of when he was a boy. When their father, Robert, was away on one of his trips, Betty Ann would beat him with a belt too. Jeanne was sure her brother remembered this, but also knew that he wanted to avoid conflict.

Jeanne believed her father had loved her mother. Robert had traveled most of the time when they lived together as a family. His homecoming was always a grand reunion. They laughed and hugged, and he shook Eli's hand. During one of her father's visits, Robert had slid his hand down Betty Ann's back, curled his fingers over her backside, and pulled her to him in a fierce embrace. Even as young as she was then, Jeanne had realized that her parents had a bond different from anyone else in the family. He loved her. He must have. Until that moment, Jeanne believed everyone's love was the same: one big lump, one word, one pool to drink from.

The house became quiet again, and Jeanne gathered Robby in her arms and slowly walked down the stairs. Stopping on the last step, she leaned against the wall to listen. Robby rested his head on her shoulder.

"Eli, didn't you get paid today?" Mama said as she held out her hand.

Jeanne clutched Robby tighter. She watched helplessly.

"Yes, ma'am," Eli said. He hesitated only a second before he dug in his pocket and deposited the cash on her open palm.

Eli had always defended their mother and made excuses for her. Their pretty mother, who spent their money on clothes, shoes, and hats for herself, was always impeccably dressed and told him how wonderful he was. He believed it, but this time he looked defeated. She fooled him every time. People in town told Eli what a good-looking mother he had. They wanted him to put in a good word for them. The comments made Eli angry, but Betty Ann soothed him, telling him to not pay attention to those old men. Then she asked him to tell the story again, about what each man had said. Eli retold the stories she wanted to hear.

Jeanne hesitated for a moment, then walked into the living room. Mama was dressed up to go out. The robe was gone. She didn't bother to look at them as she stood there and counted the money Eli had given her.

"You look nice, Mama," Eli said. "Where are you goin'?"

She snapped her purse shut. "Of course I look nice, honey," she cooed. "Don't you have any more money for your mama?"

"That's all of it," Eli said. He sounded crushed.

Jeanne's heart broke to see him disappointed, yet again. She had experienced their mother's selfishness many times, but it was seldom directed at her big brother. Eli believed she screamed and spent their money on herself, but this blatant cruelty was different for him.

"Well, okay then," Betty Ann half-heartedly answered her firstborn. A flicker of regret crossed her beautiful face.

A horn blasted from the dusty road, twice staccato and then one long sour whole note. She and Eli looked toward the window.

Betty Ann moaned. "I've got to go." She picked up a small brown valise stowed beside the sofa.

"Don't go, Mama," Eli pleaded.

Dread closed in when Jeanne saw the leather suitcase in her mother's hand. She had never planned her times away. She simply left. Jeanne hadn't noticed it earlier. She had been in a hurry to get away from her before she exploded. Mama had been irritated because she was leaving.

Jeanne moved into the room, switching Robby from one hip to the other. "When are you coming back, Mama?" She glanced at her older brother standing there with his arms folded. Her sweet, helpless baby brother hugged her neck. *Poor Robby senses something is wrong*. She was determined to survive and make it through this tirade one more time. *Maybe the last time*.

"Will you be back to take care of Robby?" Eli asked.

"I have to go," Betty Ann insisted. "You don't understand. I have to go. This is my last chance to get away from this hellhole. I've decided you and your sister are old enough to take care of yourselves. You're a grown man, Eli, and Jeanne can take care of Robby. You'll be all right."

"Mama," Robby intoned, reaching out for his mother. Jeanne let him lean as far away as she could without dropping him.

"I love you, baby boy," Betty Ann said, but she didn't move closer to take him from Jeanne. Betty Ann didn't answer Eli's question. She backed away from them and moved closer to the door.

This frightened Jeanne. She had never seen Mama resist kissing and hugging Robby before. Suddenly, the cruel insults, the slaps, the whippings she had endured weren't as painful as this. Mama was truly abandoning them. Jeanne was sure of it. Tears streamed down her face. Her reaction twisted the life out of her. Jeanne took a step forward. Her stone facade cracked open, and her heart was exposed beyond repair.

Robby began to cry. He didn't understand what was happening.

Betty Ann opened the screen door and then hesitated in the doorway. She looked back at them.

Jeanne studied her mother, who was adorned in sparkling crystal jewelry and a fancy new red dress with matching purse and high-heeled shoes. Her hair was newly permed. *Who is she leaving with this time?*

"Don't go, Mama," Eli begged again. Surprise, anger, and agony creased his tanned face.

Another honk blared from the street and punctuated the scene. Mama turned the screen door loose. It banged shut with a *whap*, and Mama hurried to the waiting automobile.

The images burned into Jeanne's memory—her mother's blondined hair, too stiff to move in the breeze, the back of her red dress, high heels sinking into the sandy soil on her way. She never glanced back at her children.

Chapter 5

Jeanne sat on the worn-out dinette chair and looked at a list of options she and Eli had talked about last night. A week had passed since her mother had stormed out of their little gray house on Bent Street, leaving them with little food and taking Eli's earnings from the grocery store. Their supplies were running out.

Her pencil lingered on *Go to Grandma Biddy's house*. This should be their choice. Her father's parents. But if they could figure out a way to survive in Deep Creek, she would stay with Robby and try to make it for Eli's sake. He deserved the scholarship to college, and he had a good chance to improve his life.

Taking care of Robby was easy, though Jeanne hated that she was having to miss school. Each afternoon they waited for Eli to come home from football practice at the high school. Jeanne got up and began to pace the floor. She was anxious to go over the list of options. Maybe he had more ideas than they had thought of last night. Texas Tech coaches had told Eli he might have a chance for a full scholarship if his senior year playing football was as good as his junior year had been. Eli's reputation leading the six-man football team to the state playoffs had attracted college scouts. He was that good.

Jeanne was hopeful one of them could get out of this town and away from Mama for good. It wasn't only her mother. It was everything. The gossips in town, the women looking over the tops of their glasses, the nasty comments from the men. Jeanne tried to ignore the ugliness. She could see the judgments written on their faces easily enough. Deep in her heart, she knew Mama would show up again, the same as she always had. But when?

She was willing to stay at home with Robby if there was no other choice. Eli had to finish school and get his scholarship. The problem was money for food and utility bills. She couldn't work if she kept Robby, and Eli could only work on weekends with his football practice every day. That wouldn't be enough. Even now, she had food for supper, but she didn't know what to do after breakfast tomorrow. Maybe she could stretch the food another day.

Robby was napping on the sofa, barely moving in the dangerously high temperature. The extreme heat wave had lasted for a week, at a time when the weather should be cooling. The living room was the coolest part of the house, especially now that Jeanne had moved the box fan from upstairs to blow directly on him. A shallow pan of water quivered in front of the blowing fan, adding moisture in the air and lowering the temperature.

She looked at the clock on the wall. It was getting late, and Eli was still not home. She remembered he had a scrimmage against the team from Andrews today. Maybe that was the reason he was late. She paced the floor in the kitchen and tracked the time. Another fifteen minutes had passed. Still no Eli.

"Gee, Gee," Robby called. She could hear the need in his soft voice.

Jeanne walked into the dimly lit living room and picked up Robby. "I'm here, sweet boy," she said, holding his limp body in her arms. She sat on the edge of the sofa and rinsed his warm face with a damp wash cloth. Every few minutes, she dipped the warmed cloth in the cool water and bathed his face.

"Gee." Robby patted her on the shoulder.

"Want supper?" Jeanne carried on a detailed conversation with her little brother while he listened to every word. "I have it ready. We're going outside under the 'skeet' tree to have a picnic."

Robby patted her on the back and smiled up at her.

Jeanne spread out an ancient worn quilt on the ground under the largest mesquite tree in the yard. She placed Robby in the middle. "There you are. Now you stay put, and don't move. Here are your cars and trucks. Play with them while I go in the kitchen and get our supper. I have a hot dog and red Kool-Aid for you." Jeanne kissed him on the cheek.

Robby clapped his hands, picked up one of his toy cars, and managed to lie on his stomach to roll the car across the patchwork quilt into a shoebox garage. He did this over and over until Jeanne was satisfied that he was occupied. She walked over to the faucet and turned on the water sprinkler. She positioned the spray mist so a few drops splashed on Robby.

"Gee, Gee." Robby laughed and tried to catch the drops as they fell on his face.

Jeanne and Robby were finishing their meal when she spotted Eli walking up the drive, head down, dragging his feet.

"What happened?" Jeanne shouted as she jumped up and ran toward him. She noticed one arm swinging by his side, but the other arm was up next to his body, bent in a sling and covered in a white cast. "Your arm, it's broken! What happened?" She couldn't fathom the horrible twist of fate and didn't want to accept this crushing blow and the impact it would have on his college plans.

His eyes were watery as he silently stared into the distance.

Jeanne moved aside and let him pass. She knew his heart was broken.

Eli sat down next to Robby and his cars, and Jeanne followed suit. The sun slipped away, and a breeze picked up, pushing the temperature down a few degrees.

"I broke my arm in the scrimmage," he finally said. "The doc says I'm out for the season. I've been at the hospital getting it set and put in this cast."

Jeanne listened as Eli told the story of the play and the guy who had broken his arm.

"I'm sorry, Eli. I'm so, so sorry. What did the coach say?"

Eli sighed. "He said I don't have a chance for a scholarship now that I can't play. I think he was mad at me for getting my arm broken. He told me I let the team down, and we wouldn't have a chance to win the district championship now."

"Surely, Coach Baker didn't mean it. He was upset. Maybe you can concentrate on basketball now and get a scholarship that way."

"Maybe." Eli looked stricken.

"What about your job at the grocery store?" Jeanne asked, knowing the answer.

"It's the same," Eli said. "I can't carry heavy boxes of produce, and they let me go. They said come back when I have the cast removed. That's five weeks." Eli got up and walked into the house.

❧

The next day, Jeanne and Robby were playing a game with cards on the sofa when she watched Coach walk up the porch steps.

"Anybody home?" Coach Baker yelled through the front door. "Eli, I came to check on you."

Jeanne was still upset that he blamed Eli for getting injured. She approached the front door and shaded her eyes as she looked into the morning sun. She could only see the outline of the thin man in a hat standing on the other side of the screen door. "Coach Baker, Eli isn't here." She didn't know whether to let him in or not. It was hot on the front porch, and she was forgetting her manners. Still, she hesitated.

"I came by to talk to Eli," Coach Baker said.

"He's gone to town to look for a job." Jeanne backed up as the coach opened the screen door and walked into the house.

"Is your mother here?" He looked around the living room. He paused to stare at Robby sitting on the sofa holding Gus. His expression was one of judgment.

"Gee," Robby said.

"No, not right now," Jeanne said as she sat by Robby and put her arm around him. Coach Baker looked different. He had a sneer on his face, and he squinted in the dim light of the house. People reacted strangely when they met Robby for the first time. Jeanne struggled to keep from shivering at the coach's belligerent attitude.

"So, this here is the feebleminded boy," he said. "I've heard about this mongoloid and your mother." He crossed his arms and didn't take off his hat. Contempt burned on his face.

Jeanne didn't answer. She sat perfectly still, glaring at the stranger in her home. She wanted to will this hateful man to leave. She had seen ugly looks before when she had Robby with her in town, but never this disgusted blatant aversion to Robby's condition.

He looked up the stairs and continued to examine the house, measuring every corner. His bony fingers gathered the edges of the curtain and rubbed the fabric together as he looked out the window.

"What do you want? I told you Eli wasn't here."

He turned his head to face her. "You'd better alter your tone. You're talking to your betters." He nodded toward Robby. "You and that abomination."

Jeanne bounded to her feet and doubled her fists. "Shut your mouth! Don't talk about my brother."

Coach Baker sneered at her. "Doc told me about his condition. He said it happens sometimes, but I don't believe it." He leaned forward and pointed at them. "Something needs to be done about this freakish situation."

"You need to leave—right now." Jeanne stood between Robby and the vile man, ready to fight.

"I'll come back later to talk to Eli. Tell him to expect me." Coach Baker strode out the front door in a hurry and let the screen door slam behind him.

Jeanne rushed to hook the latch. She didn't want any more

unwelcome visitors barging into her home. The man's threats had scared her. He had done nothing to them, but she felt exposed and vulnerable. She picked up Robby and patted him.

∞

The next morning, Jeanne carried Robby outside where it was cooler. The back of the house was pleasant before the sun reached midday. Eli sat on the steep back porch and swung his legs under the edge, clicking his heels on the support post underneath. He leaned on the ornate wrought-iron railing with his good arm, humming a pleasant tune. Jeanne sat on the steps and looked up at Eli while she held Robby in her lap. Eli seemed content, even after what had happened. She only told him that Coach had come by asking for Mama. It was too difficult to explain her feelings about Coach's obvious disdain for Robby.

"I've tried everywhere," Eli said. "The hardware store and the feedstore said the same thing. Come back when I get the cast off my arm. And that's more than a month."

"I'll go to the church," Jeanne said. "We don't have a choice this time. The preacher should be at his office by now." She gave Robby a kiss and handed him to Eli before she lost her nerve. Eli bounced Robby on his knee playing ride-a-horsy as she stepped onto the sidewalk.

Jeanne took her books with her to the church library and slipped them in the slot for returns. She hated giving up the Mother Goose book, as Robby had enjoyed it so much. Jeanne found the front entrance locked, so she sat on the steps and waited for someone to show up.

Soon after, Pastor Beaumont approached. "Hello, my dear. You're here early. What can I help you with?" He stood there waiting for an answer.

"I came to see if I could get a few canned goods from the food pantry, Brother Beaumont." Jeanne didn't look him in the eyes.

She couldn't. She was too embarrassed.

"I see," he said as he unlocked the door and walked into the dark hallway. "Did your mother send you?"

"Yes, sir." Jeanne stood and followed him into the church.

"Why didn't she come?" He walked past the office and the choir room and opened a door at the end of the hall.

"She's not home right now." Jeanne was afraid she had said too much. Mama had told her to never trust anyone, never let them know she wasn't home. People were too nosy and would come and take Robby.

"Let's see what we have here," Pastor Beaumont said. He seemed distracted as he pulled dented cans off the shelf and stuffed some potatoes and onions in a small box. "Here you go." Stacked on top was a loaf of white Wonder Bread. "You tell your mama to come next time."

"Yes, sir." Jeanne walked out the front door with the preacher behind her. He locked the door as soon as she left. Jeanne turned back and waved, but he had already disappeared inside the parsonage next door.

It was early afternoon when a Deep Creek entourage knocked on the front door. Jeanne could see them through the screen walking up the sidewalk. She had called Eli by the time they reached the front porch. Eli went to the door this time. Coach Baker, Pastor Beaumont and his wife, Dr. Comstock, and the banker, Mr. Zorn, came inside.

"Have a seat, please," Eli said.

The preacher and his wife sat on the sofa alongside Coach. The doctor sat in one of the living room chairs while Mr. Zorn sat in the other one. Jeanne stood in the kitchen doorway. Robby was in the kitchen eating. Jeanne felt she needed to stand between him and the group in the living room. Eli had moved to the other side of the room and stood near the staircase.

"Is your mother here, Eli?" Dr. Comstock asked.

"No, not right now," Eli replied.

"Well, we've come to help you decide what to do about your predicament," Mrs. Beaumont interrupted. The stiff woman scooted forward on the sofa and looked at Eli.

"What *predicament* is that?" Jeanne said.

"We'll talk to your brother, missy. He's eighteen, not you," the preacher's wife informed Jeanne and looked back at Eli.

"Let Doc handle it, Jane," the preacher said as he patted his wife's hand. She nodded to her husband and sat back against the cushion.

Dr. Comstock eyed the group. "You kids are living here by yourself."

That knowledge hung there without either party acknowledging or denying the fact.

He continued with authority when there was no argument. "Eli, I know you've lost your job because of your broken arm. The church won't always have food to give you. Jeanne was lucky today. We can help you with a few things, but one problem is bigger than the others."

"What's that?" Eli asked. "What do you mean?"

Mr. Zorn spoke up. "Your mama hasn't made any payments on the house in a year, and the bank has repossessed it. It belongs to the bank now. We have a buyer for the house, including the contents. You'll have to move out in two weeks."

"What! You can't take our house," Jeanne protested. "Our daddy bought this house. He paid for it." She was distraught. They couldn't move.

"That's true, young lady, but your mama took out a loan and used the house as collateral," said Mr. Zorn.

It had to be true if the banker, Mr. Zorn, said it. She couldn't believe it. Mama walked out and never told them what she had done. She must have known that the house was being repossessed by the bank.

"We have a job waiting for you, Jeanne," the pastor said. "Mrs.

Fordham needs a maid, and she will give you room and board and two dollars a week for your services. She said Eli could live in a room above the carriage house for helping with the yard work."

"I can't do that," Jeanne said. "I have to take care of Robby."

"We have a solution for that too," Mrs. Beaumont said. "Tell them, Doctor."

"We can send him to the state school. I have a friend in Austin who works there. He could get him admitted right away."

"We would never send Robby away from home," Eli said. "You know how frail he is, Doctor. He would never survive a trip there."

"We won't do it," Jeanne asserted.

"You may not have a choice," Coach said. "He's old enough to go to school, and it's against the law to keep him at home."

"That's enough of that," Dr. Comstock said. "This is too much information for you to comprehend right now. We'll go and let you discuss this, but you'll have to make a decision soon."

⌘

Later that evening, Jeanne faced her big brother from across the dinette table. "We have to do something, Eli. We don't have any money, and I cooked the last of the food today." She showed Eli the piece of paper with their options written on it.

"I know," Eli said. "Mama hasn't come back yet. Do you think she will?"

Jeanne ignored Eli's question and tried to read his face. She had to say what she thought, now that his chances for college had been ruined in one afternoon. "Even if Mama came back, the bank has sold the house. We're going to have to leave. Staying here is not an option, Eli. You know that. I will not let them take Robby to a state home." Jeanne waited.

"Yeah, you're right," Eli admitted. "We need to go to Grandpa and Grandma Biddy's farm. What will they think, having three more mouths to feed?"

"Grandma always says to take care of family."

"They've done that more than once for us. I remember Grandma Biddy coming and cooking and cleaning when Mama was gone. You were too little to remember."

"Would you help on the farm?"

"Sure, and Grandpa is still stronger than most men I know, even though he's over sixty."

Jeanne smiled to herself as she remembered sitting in Grandma's lap while she rocked her to sleep. Their daddy used to tell them there was always enough to eat on the farm. Was her hope too good to be true?

"You can finish school. That should make you happy."

"It does," Jeanne replied.

"It's a long way, and we'll have to walk."

"I know," Jeanne said. "We have to get ready tonight so we can leave in the morning."

"What food do we have to take?"

"We have half a loaf of bread and a partial jar of peanut butter from the church that you know Robby can't swallow." She had a plan in her head, but she had to give Eli time to accept the inevitable.

"Okay, let's go to the farm in the morning," Eli said. "I'll get the wagon out of the attic. We can use that."

Jeanne was relieved that Eli had made up his mind. She wanted to believe Grandma and Grandpa would be glad to see them. She was exhausted worrying about having enough food and clothes, and she was terrified of the authorities taking Robby away. That night Jeanne tossed and turned, thinking of the eighteen miles they had to cover the next day.

Chapter 6

Before daylight, Jeanne and her brothers were packed and ready to leave their home on Bent Street. Robby sat in the wagon in front of the house with extra clothes stuffed around him. He was patient, watching his brother and sister scurry in and out of the house.

Eli shut the front door and ran down the steps. "That's that, I guess."

"Let's take turns pulling the wagon," said Jeanne. "I've put the food and water on top of the clothes with Robby."

Eli led the determined little caravan out the front door and down the sidewalk. With an umbrella on top of his cast and a canteen of water slung over his good shoulder, he set a steady pace. Jeanne followed, pulling the wagon to the sidewalk barefooted. When the roads heated up later in the day, she knew that she wouldn't be able to stand the torture to her feet. She had brought the leather loafers, even though she despised them.

"Let's go through the middle of town," Eli suggested. "It's the shortest way."

"All right. I think we can get through town before folks wake up and start moving." Jeanne didn't want people in Deep Creek to see their pitiful little caravan. She could picture Mrs. Campbell at the Mercantile rushing out in the street and admonishing them for taking Robby out on a hot summer day. Or even Mr. Crockett at the bank coming out and wanting to know where their mama was. Hopefully, they could finish their trek on Main Street before anyone was up for the day.

Unfortunately, early risers popped up on every street. Clanking milk cans greeted them when they turned off Main Street to head west toward Grandma Biddy's.

Daniel Karlson was unloading milk for the grocery store and spotted them immediately. "Hey, Eli." Daniel waved and trotted over to them. "Are you okay? I heard about your arm."

"Yeah, we're good," Eli said.

"Where you headed this time of day?" Daniel looked at the stuffed pillowcase with their meager belongings.

Jeanne's cheeks burned when he noticed her bare feet. They looked like the destitute orphans they were.

"Hello, there." Daniel knelt to talk to Robby. "How're you doin', little fella?"

"Sorry, Daniel," Jeanne said. "We've gotta go." She pushed on the small of Eli's back and pulled the wagon forward. "Good morning to you."

"We'll miss you working at the store." Daniel stood to let them pass.

Robby waved to Daniel as the three walked off down the empty road. Daniel looked disappointed, and Jeanne had mixed feelings about cutting the conversation short and leaving.

"What was your hurry back there?" Eli asked. "Daniel was only being nice."

"I know, but I'm uncomfortable and embarrassed," Jeanne confessed. "Look at us. I don't want anyone feeling sorry for us, that's all."

"Pride goes before a fall, Jeanne Bradshaw." Eli was half-teasing and half-preaching, and Jeanne knew he was right.

"Hey, wait up a minute," Daniel called from the back of the

truck. "Take this with you," he said when he caught up with them. "It's not much. Maybe it'll help." He shoved a blue forget-me-not flour sack in the wagon with Robby, and by the time Jeanne looked up, Daniel had run halfway back to the milk truck. He turned around, saluted, and disappeared around the corner.

Jeanne opened the bag. "Oh my," she whispered as she found a bottle of milk, apples, and a tin of crackers. She felt guilty that she hadn't been nicer to Daniel.

Jeanne was in trouble by the time they got to the other side of town. Her feet were cut and bruised from the rough streets. She could not make it the next sixteen miles in this painful condition. A short time later, they had reached the creek for which the town was named.

Jeanne finally gave up. "Eli, I have to stop. My feet are killing me." She slid down the incline and dipped her feet in the flowing water. The temperature in the creek bottom was at least ten degrees cooler, and the water was heavenly.

Eli left the wagon up by the road, picked up Robby with his good arm, and joined her at the creek bank. "We just got started. We have to go on before the day gets too hot."

"I know, but I only have those awful shoes that are too small, and I can't even think of putting them on again."

Eli placed Robby on the cool grass. He dug around in the pillowcase Jeanne had packed and pulled out the shoes. He pitched the make-do suitcase at Jeanne. "Get your socks on. I'm going to fix these shoes."

Jeanne did as she was told.

Eli took out his pocketknife and made quick work of cutting the toes and heels out of the brown leather loafers.

Jeanne worked her feet into the odd remaining strips of leather. She walked around to test the altered shoes and quickly adjusted to the flapping soles. Soon her feet stopped hurting, and she was able to keep up with Eli.

It wasn't long before Jeanne had to open the umbrella and hold it over Robby, but she had to change sides every five minutes to ease her aching arms. They were halfway to Grandma Biddy's when she heard a screeching sound, and a wheel came rolling off the wagon. Robby went flying out and landed face down in the ditch.

Forgetting her mangled feet, Jeanne scrambled over the rocks toward her little brother. "Robby, Robby!" she screamed. She reached Robby before Eli had a chance to backtrack and make his way down the ravine.

"Gee, Gee," Robby cried.

Jeanne scooped him up and held him in her lap. "There, there, Gee Gee is here. Don't cry, sweetheart. Where are you hurt? Let me see." Jeanne found a few cuts on Robby's arms and a scrape on his cheek.

Eli fell to his knees and gently ran his big hand over Robby's limbs. "I don't feel anything broken. No blood on his head." Eli sat on the grass and wiped the sweat from his forehead. "I'll check the damage to the wagon."

Robby whimpered but didn't cry.

"He's more frightened than hurt," Jeanne said, "but I need to get him out of the sun."

As they sat in the shallow shade of a brushy fence line, Eli delivered the pillowcase and a glass jar full of water. "This was still intact," he said.

"At least we have something."

"The wagon is totally wrecked and can't be fixed," Eli said as he crouched beside them. "The side is broken, and Robby wouldn't be able to hold on to the wagon. Even if we fixed the wheel—which we can't—it's too dangerous and might fall apart again."

"I'm sorry, Eli. We shouldn't have come. It's too hard." Jeanne looked at Robby, who had fallen asleep. *At least the cuts have stopped bleeding.*

Eli stood and walked up to the road. The pavement had ended, and now they were traveling on gravel and dirt. He looked up the road for a ride, but they hadn't seen a car or truck the entire day. When Eli picked up the flour sack, milk dripped from the bottom. He pulled the tin of crackers from the soggy bag and held it in his hand. They had eaten the apples but had saved the milk for Robby. Now, they had nothing for Robby to eat.

"Eli, come back," Jeanne called.

Eli hurried toward them. "What's wrong?"

"It's getting terribly hot here." Jeanne handed Robby to Eli. "Help me put Robby on my back. I can carry the umbrella with one hand."

Robby's arms were slack and dangled against Jeanne's back, so she placed her left arm under his bottom to hold him secure. Settling against Jeanne's back eased Robby's fears while the steady motion of walking lulled him into twilight sleep.

"Let's look for a shady place," Eli said. "You and Robby can rest there while I walk on to the farm and get Grandpa. I should have gone by myself in the first place and left you and Robby at the house."

"I thought we could make it too."

"Surely, a car will come along," Eli said. "All morning and nothing on the road."

"We'll find a place to stop." Jeanne began scanning the roadsides and countryside beyond, but there were only fields of cotton, fuzzy white heads waiting to be baled. They walked on in the heat, passing clumps of prickly pear and scattered thistle that offered no shade and cast an angry threat with their spines. Halting for a few minutes to drink the last of their water was the only break for the next two miles.

"I can take him now, if you want," Eli said.

"I'm doing fine, and your face looks like you're in pain. Is your arm hurting?"

"A little bit," he admitted. "The river is not too far. Can you keep going?"

"I have to. No choice." Jeanne shifted Robby. "Let's go."

They walked for another hour before the trees emerged on the horizon, marking the curve of the river ahead of them.

"I see the river, Eli." Jeanne picked up her step. The thought of the trees and the water ahead gave her the energy she needed.

Eli shaded his eyes and kept moving. "That's it!"

⸎

The cooling shade washed over the trio as they entered the treelined river bottom. A ribbon of live oaks and pecan trees skirted the banks and offered a permanent invitation to rest. Jeanne and Robby settled under a giant pecan and listened to the water flow by while Eli filled the glass jar to bathe Robby. They took time to wade in the chilly stream before Eli began his hike to the farm.

Although Eli felt better after eating most of the bread and cooling down, Jeanne was apprehensive about him leaving. Eli told her he was dizzy before they reached the river. His newly broken arm had to be hurting. He was determined to make it, and she and Robby were counting on him. He had to get to the farm for help. Before he left, Jeanne dunked his shirt in the river and tied it around his neck for the hot trip ahead.

Eli trudged off, taking measured steps as he climbed the riverbank. When he reached the road, he stepped over the brittle ruts and walked on the smoother middle toward their grandparents' farm. The dried mud crunched as he made his way west into the sun. Jeanne gazed into the distance until she could no longer hear his footsteps or see his silhouette on the horizon.

The comfort of the soft breeze cooled Robby and Jeanne while they rested in their damp clothes. They laughed at the squirrels jumping from limb to limb in the thick branches above their heads. They were frantic in their nut gathering for the winter, even though there were more than enough pecans for them. The squirrels were silly and delightful at the same time. The lingering summer cicadas droned a lullaby, and soon Jeanne and Robby were asleep above the muddy riverbank.

Something bumped Jeanne in the side and awakened her. Robby had kicked her in his sleep. She realized he was having a seizure. The trauma of the day had been too much for him. His frail body jerked and twisted. Jeanne got on all fours and used her body to protect Robby from injuring himself against the tree. She had to keep him from rolling off the bank into the water. She grabbed the pillowcase and surrounded his head with clothes while he was thrashing in the grass. His flailing movements knocked into Jeanne, but she didn't notice the blows in her fear. Robby's jerking soon became smaller and less violent until finally, he stilled.

Jeanne panted as she released Robby. She slid her hands under his limp head and back, steadying her grasp as she moved him back to the makeshift pallet. She checked his pulse and found it rapid and erratic, so she sat beside him and watched him breathe. Grandma Biddy called these episodes "spells." Jeanne couldn't believe she and Robby had survived this scary spell. She held out her hands and saw they were steady. One thing was for sure: she had to be strong for Robby, and she was. She and Robby had been through a few seizures before, but never one this severe.

Jeanne leaned back on the tree trunk and continued her vigil and whispered her prayer. *God in heaven, I am yours and You are my God. Help me, Be my strength.* She sat, she observed, she paced, she waded in the shallows again, and she bathed Robby when he awoke.

Robby was thirsty, and Jeanne didn't know how to calm him. He cried, and then his cries turned to moans. Finally, she distracted him with his little trucks and a song. He loved "You Are My Sunshine," and she sang it over and over until Robby became exhausted and fell asleep.

Twilight was fast approaching as the heat of the day dissipated. Jeanne rummaged through the clothes and put on a sweater. She covered Robby with Eli's spare shirt. Darkness descended quickly in the river bottom, and Jeanne felt the dampness surround them. She wanted to move to a drier spot, but it was too dark to see where she was going. She kept checking Robby and decided to wait before she attempted a move, since he was sleeping peacefully. She didn't want to chance falling in the dark while she was carrying Robby to the top of the embankment.

Finally, Jeanne relaxed, curled her body protectively around Robby, and fell asleep to the river's night sounds.

Jeanne was startled awake. Her heart beat wildly, and her eyes opened wide. She held her breath and strained to hear what had disturbed her sleep. Moonlight filtered through the swaying tree limbs and cast shifting shadows across the water, which added to her dread. Dim rays of the moon crawled down the embankment, and soon the pale light would reach the spot where she and Robby lay on the pallet.

Jeanne propped herself up on her elbow to get a better look at her surroundings. She wished she had memorized the landscape before they had fallen asleep, but it was too late now. She had never been afraid of the dark, but she couldn't predict Robby's reaction to this unfamiliar place if he awoke. She dared not leave him alone and walk to the road to look for Eli and Grandpa. She decided to wait again and listen.

She lay there looking up toward the stars and tried to adapt to the evening noises. Soothing rhythms played across the fields, over her skin, and on to the river. Occasional chatter from the trees punctuated the night song, and Jeanne calmed. She shifted her slim body away from Robby, settled against the trunk of the sprawling pecan tree, and kept watch. The moon moved higher in the sky, and Jeanne estimated the time to be around midnight.

Has something happened to Eli?

She stood up and sidestepped around the giant tree, keeping her back against the trunk. She froze. Rustling sounds echoed from the plowed field beyond the band of trees along the river. Jeanne checked on Robby. His small frame was outlined beneath the plaid shirt still in the same position since he had fallen into his deep sleep. His small chest moved steadily beneath the cover. Jeanne breathed deeply, willing him to take the next breath.

Something rustled in the grass behind the tree, which made Jeanne edgy. She picked up a stick and held it ready. She could hear swishing and chatter. Smiling to herself, she recognized raccoon prattle. She decided to scare them away from the pallet, and when she stood, the family of furry bandits skittered down the embankment and disappeared into the night along the river.

Jeanne checked Robby's breathing and sat again by the tree. He was barely visible. She was about to put more cover on him when she heard footsteps in the grass. A pale light came from the field, and Jeanne looked up to see Grandpa walking into the clearing holding a lantern. Eli followed, carrying a blanket and paper sack.

Relief flooded over her. She hadn't realized how tense she had been until that moment. "You made it!" Jeanne cried as she ran to them and threw her arms around Grandpa's neck. He lifted her off the ground in a fierce hug. Jeanne was comforted by his strength. His air of control gave her confidence that their hardships were over. She wasn't alone.

"I didn't get a ride on the road," said Eli. "I'm sorry you had to wait so long." He handed Jeanne a paper bag. "Grandma Biddy sent sandwiches."

"Robby had a seizure," Jeanne said. "Be careful with him."

Grandpa held out the lantern to Eli. "You carry the lantern. I'll carry the little boy." Grandpa stooped over Robby and gathered him in his arms. Gnarled hands braced a bobbing head as he placed him gently on his shoulder.

Eli started back across the field with Grandpa following. Jeanne hurried to stuff their belongings in the pillowcase.

"Let's go, Jeannie girl," Grandpa said. "Grandma Biddy's waitin' for us."

"I'm coming." Jeanne fell in behind Grandpa, his silver hair shining from the glow of the lantern. She had a beacon to follow.

Sylvia Hornback

She held the sack and the pillowcase in one hand and a sandwich in the other as she dodged clumps of dirt. She was thankful. Tonight, she had food, and in less than an hour, she and Robby would have a place to sleep.

Chapter 7

The afternoons were cool on Grandma Biddy's lazy front porch. Autumn breezes sailed across the dried wooden boards and made the chore of snapping fresh green beans pleasant. Grandma's weathered hands *whooshed* atop her starched dress as she tirelessly addressed the bushel of beans at her feet. As she sat in her rocker, strands of gray hair escaped her tightly wound bun and drifted back and forth in the wind.

Grandma brushed the wisps off her cheek, scooped double handfuls of beans from the basket, and dropped them in her lap. This routine began the snapping process. "Ends go on the newspaper, and the snaps go in this dishpan," she said.

Jeanne smiled and took the pan. This was fun for her. Preparing their food for winter was satisfying. She, too, piled green beans high in her pan and started removing the ends. "Did Daddy sit out here on this porch?" she asked.

"He did. I think it was his favorite place." Grandma stopped rocking and gathered more beans into her lap. "Those were dear times." Her green eyes sparkled. Happiness creased her face, and smile wrinkles appeared at the corners of her mouth. The expression erased any harshness caused by the difficulties of farm living. A bit of the girl she had once been revealed herself.

Robby sat in the swing nearby, playing with the homemade pinwheel Grandpa had given him. Earlier that morning, Jeanne held paper corners together while Grandpa tacked them to a whittled stick. The pinwheel whirred perfectly as Grandpa blew on it for a test run. The afternoon breeze was perfect for Robby to hold it in the wind and watch it go around. Not only did Jeanne learn how to prepare beans, but she learned about a magnetic tack hammer too.

Old Dog lay under the swing with velvety ears spread on the porch as he slept. The graying basset had taken the responsibility of watching Robby from the moment they arrived. Rarely did Old Dog leave Robby's side. It was a great comfort for Jeanne to know he was there.

Grandpa had liberated Old Dog from poachers on the farm who were illegally hunting game at night. Grandpa had run them off with his shotgun and made them leave one of their hounds. They had mistreated the sad-eyed dog and had been on the verge of killing him. Grandpa carried him back to the farmhouse, and Old Dog stayed. Jeanne had learned a strong sense of right and wrong from her grandparents. Rescuing Old Dog was only one example. She was relieved to be on the farm with them. She felt a kinship with Old Dog.

Grandma's toes tapped the planks to continue the motion of her rocking chair.

Jeanne's slim legs and bare feet hung over the edge of the porch, swinging with the constant rhythm. She had stopped snapping and held the dishpan in her lap.

"I see you're dreamin', Jeanne," Grandma Biddy said. "You have that faraway look. I used to be that way sometimes."

Jeanne smiled. "I was thinking about what has happened since we've been here. Robby is healthy, Eli is working with Grandpa, and I even have shoes to wear to school." She stuck her legs straight out and wiggled her toes. "I even have socks to wear with them."

"Are you getting used to the attic room and being by yourself?"

Jeanne looked over at Robby. "I still wake up at night looking for Robby."

"He's better off being downstairs with Grandpa and me. You've had that burden long enough."

"I never thought of Robby as any trouble. He's been by my side his whole life."

"It's time you two made a change. I'm here to help you, and it's too hard for me to go up and down those narrow stairs."

"Yes, ma'am." She missed having Robby with her. A loneliness engulfed her. *How can I let him go?*

Grandma rocked back in her chair, popped the long green bean in two, and dropped it in her apron. "You still need dresses for school. The schools in Readfield aren't a one-room school like the one in Deep Creek. The newspaper reported the high school alone has over four hundred students this year. It'll take getting used to the large numbers."

"Why did Readfield survive the Depression and Deep Creek didn't?" Jeanne wanted to get her mind off Robby not being near at night. She supposed Grandma was right, but she was having a hard time making the transition.

"It's a crossroads, and it's the county seat. Travelers are always coming through, and the whole county goes there for business. We're lucky we live close enough so we can buy what we need. We'll stop at the dry goods store tomorrow when we go into town. They have nice gingham there. You can take your pick. Now go on in and check the corn bread for me."

"Yes, ma'am. I'll take Robby with me." She scooped Robby up and took him to the kitchen. She still needed him to be where she could see him. Old Dog followed. Robby was still small enough for the old high chair, and Jeanne slid him in without having to take off the tray. He was full of glee as he slapped the top of the tray with both palms. Jeanne put a tin cup full of milk in his hands. His answer was a nod and a smile as he took his tiny sips. Old Dog slept by his chair.

Jeanne was efficient as she did as she was told, but she continued her contemplation. There had been so much change that she hadn't taken the time to understand what had happened in her life. She had yet to make friends at school, and a girl named Sandra made her life miserable. On her first day, Jeanne had met the snooty Sandra in the school office. Sandra was quick to tell Jeanne that she was not welcome in Readfield. She was a year older than Jeanne and seemed more sophisticated. Thankfully, the bell rang, and Jeanne rushed out to find her first class, leaving the haughty brunette with her nose in the air. Jeanne retreated to her studies to escape her troubles at school and at the farm.

"The corn bread should be done," Grandma said as she came into the kitchen and dumped the snapped beans in the sink.

"It is." Jeanne plunked the heavy iron skillet on top of the stove and slammed the oven door shut. "Perfect again, Grandma." Jeanne's brow furrowed as she reconciled herself to the fact that Eli had given up his dreams of becoming a coach. He had decided to accept his eleven-year high school diploma and work with Grandpa on the farm. The town of Deep Creek was still making the transition to twelve. Eli had the choice to get his diploma rather than continue for one more year. She was as disappointed as he was when he made his decision. His arm had healed, but his broken heart had not.

"What are you worrying about, Jeanne?"

"Eli, I guess. He had lots of dreams." Jeanne didn't share her own worries or the hostile atmosphere of the new school with anyone. One girl had made it her mission to make her life miserable with a snide remark at every meeting. However, Jeanne was resolute about ignoring comments at school and getting her education.

"Don't worry about your brother. He'll make it in this world. You'll see. Things come easy for him. If not college, it'll be something else. Everybody loves Eli. It's another story for the women in this family. Life's hard, but we are tough. So are you, Jeanne."

Grandma Biddy had spent her egg money to buy material for

Jeanne to have enough dresses. She told Jeanne that she wouldn't have her going to school in flour sack skirts and blouses. Grandma was certainly tough but good to her. What did it matter what people said?

The next morning, the family piled into the old pickup. Eli and Jeanne sat in the back, and Grandpa, Grandma, and Robby were inside the cab. Old Dog stood on the porch and watched them find their places.

"Wear this bonnet," Grandma said as she handed it to Jeanne. "I don't want you burning that face and looking like a farm girl."

The bonnet was stiff with starch and checkered blue and white. "Isn't that what I am, Grandma? A farm girl?" Jeanne dutifully put the homemade bonnet on her head.

"Well, you never mind," Grandma said. "You'd have gloves for your hands too, if I had any."

Jeanne looked horrified and glanced at Eli, who pulled his hat over a stupid grin. She sat beside him. "Don't you say a word, Eli Bradshaw."

The town of Readfield was five miles away, but the rain-washed roads made the Saturday journey to town take thirty minutes. Readfield was three times larger than Deep Creek, and Jeanne was excited despite herself. She had only been to the high school on the bus, but she caught glimpses of downtown in the early morning light. She was curious about the stores there, and today she would see for herself. Readfield was the county seat, and a huge, boxy, limestone courthouse had the place of honor in the middle of the square. Storefronts lined the streets in four directions and spilled onto the side streets toward the hospital and the movie theater. The First Baptist Church and the First Methodist Church were prominent structures only a block off the square. Jeanne couldn't see everything before Grandpa had angled his truck to park in front of the grocery store.

"Eli and I are going to the feedstore to talk with Mr. Ingram," Grandpa said over his shoulder. "We'll either meet you back here or at the Jot 'Em Down Store."

Grandma waved that she understood.

Jeanne climbed out of the bed of the truck and took Robby. She pushed the bonnet back off her head and let it dangle there on her back. "What's the Jot 'Em Down Store?" she asked as she shifted Robby.

"What you might think. You get what you need, and the clerk jots down the goods to keep track of your bill until you can pay. The Jot 'Em Down has a big variety and helped us make it through the Depression."

"Oh."

"Now then. I'm going into the grocery store first. I need flour and salt."

Jeanne balanced Robby on her hip and followed Grandma into the enormous A&P. Jeanne couldn't believe what she saw. She could barely take it in. She started with the produce and carefully read the names written above each one. Most she knew. They had the biggest apples she had ever seen, and her mouth watered when she spotted a large crimson fruit called an elephant heart plum. She dared not touch one, though she wanted to.

"Luscious, aren't they?"

Jeanne jumped back and hugged Robby closer to her. She whirled around to see Daniel Karlson standing there.

Daniel wore a white apron stained green, and he was holding a bundle of collards. "I didn't mean to scare you." A big grin lit up his whole face.

Robby clapped his hands and reached toward Daniel.

Jeanne smiled despite herself. "What are you doing here? I mean, here in Readfield. You were in Deep Creek."

Robby left Jeanne's arms and settled in Daniel's, the same as he often did with his big brother.

"I was, but my uncle owns the store here and the one in Deep Creek. He has three others, but I'll be working here for a while.

This is the biggest one. Uncle Fred says he wants me to learn the business."

"Is that what you want?" Jeanne wanted to know if people got to do what they wanted in life, or if they took what came their way.

He nodded his head with a smile. "I do. I like it. I think it's the organization of everything. I don't mind the hours, and I enjoy meeting people. I'm lucky to have the chance. Especially since Papa died."

"I'm glad you're happy, Daniel." Jeanne meant it. Daniel was a nice person. She still felt guilty remembering their last meeting.

"Thanks. Here, this is for Robby." Daniel offered a box of animal crackers.

"You don't have to . . ." Jeanne tried to refuse, but Robby was gripping the box by the string handle and shaking it.

"I better get back to work," Daniel said as he gave Robby back to his sister. "Good to see you and your family are doing so well."

Jeanne looked around and saw Grandma walking out the door with her purchases in her arms. She and Robby caught up with her on the sidewalk.

"There you two are," Grandma said. "Jeanne, I'm going to put this package in the back of the pickup, and I'll meet you at the dry goods store."

Jeanne walked around the square and looked at every shop and storefront. When she finally stepped into the Watkins Dry Goods store, she was mesmerized by the colorful cloth choices. She inhaled the lemon yellows, the rose pinks, and the crisp blue cottons. She hoped she could make up her mind. She walked past the shoes, toiletries, and handbags and straight to the tabletops piled high with new materials. The left side of the store held ladies' items, and the right side carried men's clothing and sundries.

No one was attending the women's side, so Jeanne began to look around in the quiet of the store. She stopped and inhaled the delightful lavender sashay bags and perfumed soaps on the shelf. She inspected the two mannequins that wore the latest style—for West Texas. One was a paisley dress shorter than she had ever seen.

The other was a red coat. Jeanne touched the coat and decided that as stylish as it was, it wouldn't protect her in their bitter winters. She searched through the folded fabrics on an oblong oak table in the middle of the room. It was a garden of choices. Larger bolts of material were stored on shelves behind the counter, but Jeanne preferred to drift by the samples, touching and admiring each one. Even Robby was fascinated with the colorful squares.

"Well, who do we have here? Miss Smart Aleck." A familiar whiny voice pierced the calm of the lovely silence.

Jeanne recognized the voice of Sandra Crawford from school. She pretended not to hear her and kept on staring at the material pieces, even though she no longer saw patterns or colors. Her anxiety filled her insides and radiated to her fingertips. She had encountered Sandra before, but she had managed to mostly avoid her. She had to think. Robby was not aware of the cruel person hovering behind her. She moved to put him on the floor so she could knock Sandra into the middle of next week.

"Don't you ignore me, you little tramp," Sandra spewed. "You're just like your mother. I've told the girls to hold on to their boyfriends. If you're around, they better watch out."

Jeanne's fury churned inside her. She spun around and looked Sandra square in the eye. "You shut your filthy—"

Someone snatched her bonnet from her hand, and Jeanne saw two other girls standing there. A bony, dishwater-blond girl with red splotches on her face held Jeanne's bonnet in her hand, laughing hysterically. "Look at this! You're dirt poor." The girl held the bonnet by the long ties and banged the starched blue checks against the wooden counter until Grandma's creation was limp.

Jeanne grabbed for the bonnet, but the girl jumped back. Then the third tormentor on the other side of the table started pointing at Robby and screeching, "Imbecile! Freak!"

Jeanne held him against her chest, the bonnet forgotten. She was in protection mode. When she tried to leave the store, the three girls blocked her way. They stood shoulder to shoulder and crowded Jeanne back against the counter, pinning her there. She desperately looked for a way to escape when they joined their hands and trapped her inside their circle. They began hissing and chanting "imbecile" in a singsong voice, and Robby began to cry. He buried his head on her shoulder.

"What's going on here?" a man bellowed as he walked over to the scene in his store. "Girls, it will not sit well with your parents when I let them know how you've behaved here today. Now get on home."

The girls stumbled backward and tried to leave the store at the same time. Finally, they pushed through the door and scurried out of sight. The front door banged shut.

A ringing quiet settled over Jeanne, Robby, and the man who had rescued them. Jeanne looked up at a giant of a man. She had never seen anyone so tall. He had a pair of men's trousers hanging over one arm and several ties draped over the other. Straight pins were scattered over both lapels, and he held a tape measure in his left hand.

"Well, my goodness, that was unpleasant," he said. "I'm sorry, young lady, that you had to endure the harping of those three vultures. They're a nasty bunch."

Jeanne retrieved her bonnet from the floor. "Thank you, Mr....?"

"Watkins, Mr. Watkins." He looked at Robby. "Hello there, little guy. Are you all right?"

Her little brother stopped crying and stared at the giant towering over them. His small, purple-tinged fingers still clutched her as he began to hiccup.

Jeanne was stunned and stood there speechless. She heard a man call for Mr. Watkins from the back.

"Miss Mary is at lunch, and she'll be back to help you shortly." Mr. Watkins gently patted Robby on the back. He walked behind the counter on the right side of the store and ducked through the door where the voice had summoned him.

Jeanne walked over to the ladies' counter and set Robby on the edge. His lips were dark. She checked his fingertips. They were tinged blue and purple. Jeanne hugged him and wiped his tears away.

Grandma Biddy came into the store, dabbing her brow with a white handkerchief. "Be glad you're in here, Jeanne, where it's cool," Grandma said, seemingly unaware of Robby's tear-stained face. "It's a hot one out there today." She took a few steps toward Jeanne.

Mary Watkins entered the women's area through a thick black curtain at the end of the shelves. While Mr. Watkins was a giant, his wife was tiny. Jeanne didn't think she weighed ninety pounds and wasn't even five feet tall. However, she was no less formidable, and she took charge at once. "Good afternoon, Mrs. Bradshaw. What can I get for you today?"

The two women exchanged pleasantries. Neither was aware of the horrifying scene that had taken place only minutes earlier. Robby's hands were pink again and wrapped around his box of animal crackers. Before Jeanne had a chance to react, she faced two determined women with cloth spread out before her on the counter. By this time, colors or patterns didn't matter to her. The thrill of picking out material for a new dress was not important. Jeanne struggled to smile and appear appropriately happy and grateful. She ended up with a lavender piece that Miss Mary preferred and blue cloth with white flowers that Grandma liked. They were both delighted.

While Grandma and Miss Mary pored over McCall's latest patterns, Jeanne took Robby to the truck for a nap. She spread a quilt out in the bed of the pickup near the cab, eased next to him, and placed her hand on his back. She leaned back and rested her head on the window. For the first time, Jeanne relaxed in the shade of the tall storefront of the A&P.

Silently, her tears came. At first, she didn't even notice the salty drops as they wet her face. She blinked into the scattered rays filtering through the clouds and cried for Robby, for Eli's lost hope, and for herself.

Chapter 8

Sounds of the courthouse square crawled their way to the forefront, and Jeanne heard chatter at the truck tailgate. She wiped her face with the shamed bonnet and shoved it on her head to hide her humiliation. The emotional release of her tears allowed Jeanne's mettle to return and kept her from disintegrating in public.

"Pa got the seed we needed to plant the winter wheat," Eli said as he loaded the huge flour sacks and the wheat seed. "We have to plant the seeds tomorrow. If we don't, chances of them sprouting are less every day."

Jeanne hustled to help stack the supplies around their sleeping little brother and make room for the three of them to ride home in the back. "I thought we had plenty of time."

"We did too, but Pa heard the men at the feedstore talking about the weather, and he's afraid a storm will come and keep us from getting in the fields."

Assisting Eli gave Jeanne something to take her mind off the events of the day. Before Jeanne told Eli she had seen Daniel in the A&P grocery store, two girls stopped at the tailgate to talk. They reminded Jeanne of two preening geese as they stood there laughing and smoothing their hair back. Her tall, handsome brother sat on top of the stacked seed bags and smiled at them. She had to admit that more than one girl back in Deep Creek had wanted to be Eli's girlfriend. The female population in Readfield conducted themselves the same way, so she sat back and watched their romantic notions fly around like chaff. At least someone in her family was liked in this town.

By the time Grandpa headed back to the farm, Jeanne had composed herself. She recovered and listened to Eli jabber during the return trip.

Eli paused and took a breath. "You're unusually quiet, Jeanne. What's wrong with you? I expected you to be full of news and excited to come into town. Didn't you enjoy buying your new material with Grandma Biddy?"

"Oh, sure I did. I'm tired after the excitement of the day, I guess." She wondered how she could ever confide in anyone about the terrible confrontation in the dry goods store. Repeating those hurtful words would pierce her heart the same as the first time they were spoken. She did not want to rekindle her anger. The fury inside scared her. She had seen her mama go into rages and knew the unspeakable damage it caused. Nausea engulfed her as she remembered the three girls in the store. She decided to change the subject. "Are you calling Grandpa 'Pa' now?" Jeanne didn't want to shorten Grandpa's name. It shouted they had given up on their father and admitted that he was never coming back.

"I am. We're both men," Eli said. "He doesn't mind. He likes it, and I remind him of Dad."

"What will Daddy think when he comes back?" Jeanne didn't want to put Eli on the defensive. She loved Grandpa too. No one compared to him, and she was glad Grandpa and Eli got along so well. Eli was getting over his disappointment. She mentioned her daddy because she wanted to get her feelings in order.

"I'm eighteen, Jeanne. Dad left us a long time ago, and it won't change if he comes back. He'll always be our dad, wherever he is."

"Yes, he will." Jeanne's voice cracked when she answered, and she coughed. She struggled to regain her composure after grasping the finality.

"Grandma says it's all right if I call her Biddy," Eli said. "She smiled when I asked her."

"I don't know if I can, but it's natural for you to do it."

They sat back in silence for the ride home. Jeanne was lost in her thoughts. Robby sat in her lap and watched the countryside.

The torrent of the day's events swirled in Jeanne's head. Here she sat, bumping along on the trip back to the farm with two new dresses, Eli calling their grandparents Biddy and Pa, and three full-blown enemies waiting at school. Jeanne had no friends at the high school, and the new teachers didn't understand her level of achievement. They assumed the small Deep Creek school was inferior to the larger Readfield one, but she had had excellent teachers at her former school.

∽

That night they had a cold supper, but not one person in the family cared, for they were famished. Grandma took corn bread off the back of the stove as their main course, and they crumbled the thick chunks in a goblet and poured milk over it.

"Corn bread and milk are my favorite," Grandpa declared. "We've had many nights on this farm when corn bread and milk kept us from going to bed hungry."

Grandma Biddy smiled. "But not tonight." She placed a bowl of stewed apples on the table. "This dish will add some flavor."

They shared the events of the day as they ate. Eli continued to be talkative, but Robby dozed in his chair. Any outing exhausted him.

"I'll put Robby to bed," Jeanne said. Old Dog padded along behind them and took his place beside Robby's cot.

Robby opened his eyes as Jeanne guided his flexible arms through the sleeves of his pajamas. "Gee," he said when he lay back on his pillow and closed his blue eyes again.

"Let's say our Lord Jesus, sweet boy," Jeanne said. The routine centered Jeanne when she recited the familiar plea for God's love. She smoothed Robby's small hands between her large ones and looked at his curved little fingers before she pressed them together in prayer and whispered in his ear. With a bowed head, Jeanne prayed, "Lord Jesus." Tears dripped onto their clasped hands. An ache throbbed within her, but she sensed a presence encircling them that comforted her. Jeanne composed herself and opened her eyes.

Robby was nestled in the covers, completely relaxed and asleep. Old Dog looked up at her as if to say, "He heard you." The dog rested his head on his front paws and sighed. He was at his post.

After Jeanne returned to the supper table, Grandma talked about her visit with Mrs. Watkins at the dry goods store. "Jeanne will look lovely wearing her new dresses," Grandma said. "Miss Mary showed me the latest patterns, and after I saw how they looked, I can sew it to look like the picture. It's the latest style."

"You're a wonder, Beulah," Grandpa said. "I imagine you can make anything you set your mind to."

"Which of the piece goods do you favor, Jeanne?" Grandma asked her. "I'll make that dress first."

"The blue one, I guess."

Grandma looked at Jeanne. "I thought you'd be excited."

After what had happened today, Jeanne's swallowed rage still overpowered her. Her anger burned because of her mother, and at her father for not being there. It was too much. Her spoonful of soggy corn bread halted midway to her mouth. "Where is our daddy?" she blurted. "Don't you have any idea where he is?" She laid her spoon back in her bowl.

Startled faces in varying stages of eating stared back at her.

Jeanne wanted to regret asking, but she couldn't. Tight-lipped and red-faced, she waited for her answer.

"Claude, she's old enough to see the letters," Grandma said.

Grandpa's shoulders dropped, then he nodded in agreement.

"All right."

Grandma Biddy's chair screeched in protest when she got up and left the kitchen. Jeanne stared at the empty chair, wondering what she had disturbed with her questions. She didn't have enough time to ask anything else before Grandma returned with a cigar box clutched to her chest. A faded ribbon bound the lid to the box.

Jeanne fixed her eyes on her grandma's wrinkled hands as they placed the box on the kitchen table and loosened the faded ribbon. Grandma Biddy took out a bundle of letters, caressing and patting them before she passed them across the table to her. Jeanne could feel the pain emanating from the yellowed envelopes. Her pain. She understood the letters had come from Daddy.

"Girl, you read those for yourself," Grandpa said. "Ask your grandma if you have any more questions. I ain't talkin' about it no more. That's it." Grandpa pushed his chair back from the table and walked out the back door.

Jeanne looked at Eli. "You've seen these before, haven't you?"

Eli stood, picked up his bowl and spoon, and took them to the sink.

"Why didn't you tell me?" Jeanne's head was spinning. She didn't understand this.

"Grandma said you should read them for yourself," Eli said. "Give me time." He followed Grandpa out the back door.

"Finish your supper," Grandma said. "That's enough talk. Keep those letters in this box, then put them in the secretary when you're through reading them." She handed the crumbling box to Jeanne.

Jeanne put the bundle of letters back inside and slid it under her chair. She ate her food and helped wash the dishes. All the while, the box under her chair was screaming at her. Would there be answers or more questions?

⟲⟳

That night, Jeanne sat on the edge of her cot with her fingers curled over the side of her thin mattress. A cold front had blown in, and she had closed the window for the evening. Nevertheless, the chill in the air pressed against her skin, even though she was wearing her new soft gown with long sleeves. She crossed her arms, held on to her elbows, and smoothed the heavenly fabric over her legs. Jeanne hadn't been able to make herself open the letters that sabotaged any enjoyment she might have had that evening. The errant box was perched on her night table like a menacing crow, daring her to look inside.

She took the box from her night table, put it on her lap, untied the ribbon, and lifted the letters out. She held them in her hands and read the outside: *Mr. and Mrs. Claude Bradshaw, Route 1, Readfield, Texas*. Only one of the letters had a return address, and it was too faded to see in the lamplight.

As she held the envelopes, Jeanne shivered, and a wave of exhaustion poured over her. With shaking hands, she returned the letters to the rickety box, slid it under her bed, and clicked off the dim light. Maybe she could face her father's words tomorrow.

Jeanne lay on her back beneath Grandma Biddy's handmade quilts and stared at the ceiling. She couldn't see the letters in the dark, but she could sense them burning a hole through the bottom of her cot.

❧

"Jeanne, I need you to come downstairs," Grandma yelled up to her the next morning. "Robby has a fever."

Jeanne finished buttoning her blouse on her way down the stairs. "How bad is it?"

"He's tired from yesterday," Grandma said. "He has a fever. Come to the table and eat breakfast. I need you here so I can go to the barn."

"Are we going to church?" Jeanne asked.

"Not today. Grandpa needs Eli to help deliver a calf."

At least if she stayed home and helped with Robby, she wouldn't have to risk meeting more new people. And if the men were busy, she and Grandma were stuck there anyway because neither of them could drive.

"Robby is asleep," Grandma called. "Rest is what he needs right now. You keep an eye on him. I'm going to tend to my chickens." She grabbed her bonnet and dashed out the back door.

"Yes'm," Jeanne answered as she left the kitchen to check on her sleeping brother. When she was satisfied Robby was resting peacefully, she ran up the stairs to her room. She had been waiting all morning to read the letters.

The bright sunlight shining through the tiny attic window gave her plenty of light to see the postmarks. She counted three. Two were yellowed. She checked the dates and found those two were older than she was. Spread out on the quilt, they looked ordinary, but she knew that couldn't be the case. Otherwise, why would Grandma have made such a fuss about giving them to her, and why wouldn't Eli talk about them? Jeanne sorted them by dates across her bedspread. The span of time was twenty years. The last and thickest one was stamped a year ago. Jeanne resisted reading it first. Perhaps it could tell her where her father was. She hoped.

Instead, she picked the oldest one. It was postmarked 1919. It was addressed to Mrs. Beulah Bradshaw. Jeanne was overwhelmed seeing her daddy's handwriting. Emotion welled up inside her and spilled out in sobs of loneliness. She managed to stop crying and unfold the thin paper.

Dear Mama,

Today Betty Ann had her baby. It's a boy. He doesn't have a name yet. Betty Ann is not acting right. She cries all day and won't pick up the baby. I wish you were here to tell me what to do. Please come to Deep Creek if you can.

Your son,

Robert

Jeanne gently folded the page, slid it in the envelope, and sat back against the wall with the letter in her lap. Eli was born in 1921.

Chapter 9

"Jeanne, hurry or you won't make it to the bus stop on time." Grandma continued to fuss at her. "I don't know why you're so poky getting down the road this morning."

"I'll catch the bus in time. Don't worry." Jeanne kissed Robby, grabbed her books, and ran down the muddy road to the mailbox that doubled for the bus stop. When she boarded the bus, she found an empty seat where no one would bother her. It was hard going back to school to face Sandra and her two lackeys. She wasn't in the mood to talk to anyone. She loved school and was fortunate to be able to finish high school now that Grandma Biddy took care of Robby. She truly was grateful, but she dreaded the inevitable conflict.

Soon she exited the bus along with the hoard of noisy kids. She stood at the entrance to the new Readfield Theodore Roosevelt High School.

"Come on now, get to classes," a man said. He waved his arms in the air and shooed the talkative teenagers toward the front door. "Stop lollygagging out here."

Jeanne recognized the football coach, Mr. Hayden. He taught

her world history class. The crowd started moving, and Jeanne scooted in the long white building unnoticed behind a group of girls. She carried all her books with her to each class. She didn't want to stop at her locker in the middle of the hallway. It was too far away from the teachers who stood at their doors between classes. Her locker was just the place to be cornered, and she could manage to hurry by other students when she changed classes.

That strategy worked for the first half of the day. Jeanne had managed to avoid contact with Sandra—so far. Lunch was a different story. Jeanne considered skipping it altogether. The cafeteria was full of students and she was alone, the perfect target, but she would not flinch at the challenge. All classes were required to eat lunch in the cafeteria, and she was a rule follower. The loud chatter funneled up the staircase as one class left and another clamored to claim its place. Hungry kids quickly crammed around eleven tables.

Jeanne looked ahead for a space near the teacher on duty. Finally, she located a table close to the cafeteria monitor and started in that direction. As Jeanne walked down the flight of stairs toward the tables, someone pushed her from behind. She grabbed the rail to keep herself from tumbling down the last four steps. Her books and lunch went flying. She crashed down violently against the concrete floor, her knees taking the brunt of the fall. The three girls she had been dodging all morning stormed by her, laughing and kicking her books while she tried to recover.

"Someone is clumsy," Sandra announced to the passersby.

Students stepped around them, embarrassing Jeanne even more.

"Maybe she's an idiot too," the blond girl called Ida taunted.

Someone stood behind Jeanne and pulled her back by the waist of her skirt. The button snapped off and tore the seam. She stumbled and went flying against the railing and smashed the back of her head.

"Oops, is this your lunch?" Sandra sneered at her.

Jeanne felt red anger creep up her neck and onto her face as Sandra twisted the ball of her foot squarely on her brown paper bag.

The three girls walked off, laughing and congratulating themselves while Jeanne picked herself up off the concrete floor.

"Those horrible creeps!" said a pretty girl with a long black ponytail. "I'm Becky."

Becky offered Jeanne a hand and kept talking. The constant gab made it easier for Jeanne to recover and regain her composure. Whether it was nervous energy or a genuine attempt to help, Jeanne didn't know. Either way, she was appreciative.

She stood quickly and peeled the greasy mess of a lunch off the concrete floor and dumped it in the metal trash barrel outside the cafeteria door. She gathered her skirt and twisted the waistband together, holding it at her side with one hand so it wouldn't fall off. When she turned around, Becky stood there holding her books.

"Come on and sit with me," Becky said. "You can join my bunch. Believe me, sitting by yourself is an open invitation for punishment. We'll go to the office after lunch and get a safety pin for that skirt." Becky moved forward with determination and confidence. She sailed by boys and girls alike and paid them no attention whatsoever.

Jeanne was encouraged and slipped in with Becky and her friends. She didn't know the "bunch," but she had to believe it would be better than Sandra's gang. She followed Becky to a table in the middle of the cafeteria and slid in beside her. She still held her skirt waist closed as she sat there and assessed the crowd. Becky talked to her matter-of-factly and didn't make a fuss over the incident. The girls at her table looked like regular people.

"Ladies, this is Jeanne," Becky announced. "Meet Nancy and Barbara."

Jeanne nodded to the other girls and shifted her books in front of her. Behind the barrier, Jeanne felt her knee. She let go of her skirt waist and rubbed a large knot that had popped up below her kneecap. It began to sting, but she covered the injury with her skirt and tried to listen to the table conversation, which of course was about her. She would check her knee later when she was alone.

"The Twaddle Squad struck again and ruined Jeanne's lunch,"

Becky said. "So, cough up a donation to the cause."

Before Jeanne realized what was happening, parts of lunch appeared in front of her. She had half a sandwich, an apple, and a small square of corn bread.

"Hold on a minute," Barbara said. She left the table and came back with butter and sorghum. "You can put that on your corn bread."

After lunch, the girls in Becky's circle stayed together, and Jeanne walked along with them. Becky seemed to know everyone. Jeanne stood to the side when she made a quick run to the office and came back with a safety pin.

"I think this will hold till you get home," Becky said, handing the pin to Jeanne. "Mrs. Nobles raised her eyebrows like she always does when I asked for it, but she gave it to me anyway."

"I need to get to English class," Jeanne said as she pushed the large pin through both sides of the waistband. Her three new friends stood around her until she was finished making the repair.

"Carry your books on that side and maybe no one will notice," advised Barbara.

Jeanne smiled. "Thank you for lunch today."

"I have English next too," Nancy said. "Come on, let's walk together. There's an empty seat behind me."

"We go down the other hall to math," Becky said. "See you at the pep rally."

Jeanne and Nancy made it to their seats as the bell rang. Mrs. Chaney was passing out their graded papers and stopping to talk to each student about their work. Praise was not the norm. Jeanne fidgeted in her seat and took deep breaths while she waited her turn. This was the first paper she had written for this teacher.

"Miss Bradshaw, I want to talk to you about your paper," her English teacher said. "I suppose you had help in writing this composition." Mrs. Chaney placed Jeanne's essay face down on her desk and stood there with her arms crossed, waiting for an answer.

"No, ma'am," Jeanne answered. She had always done well in

English. One thing her mama had demanded was that her children speak proper and correct English. Jeanne learned her lessons well. She did not want her mother's wrath to ignite because of her mistakes.

"Well, the next time you write a paper for my class, you can write it during study hall so someone can watch you. This is a temporary grade till then."

"Yes, ma'am." Jeanne turned her paper over and saw an A+ written on the top. She tried not to grin, but a small one spread across her lips. *First, I make three new friends, and now teachers are noticing that I'm smart.* She would have to prove herself to Mrs. Chaney. Here in Readfield, she had seventy other students in her class, while at Deep Creek, she only had ten. She looked forward to the challenge. This was a good day despite the earlier debacle on the cafeteria stairs. When she looked up from her desk, Nancy was smiling at her.

∽

Her daddy's letters waited for Jeanne after school. She had only read the first one.

She raced upstairs and retrieved the cigar box from under her bed. Then she placed the box next to her. She wanted to savor the letters, so she decided to write about the day's events first. The dramatic confrontations stirred a thousand emotions in her. When she felt this way, she wrote poems. For a time, she destroyed what she had written because her mother searched her room and read her journal. Jeanne was careful not to write anything about Mama except something flattering. Poems camouflaged her true feelings, so she wrote poetry. Since moving to the farm, she had been more open writing in her journal. Today at school had been a doozy, and she wanted to pour out her feelings on paper. She whispered prayers as she wrote. She had gotten through many trials this way. Afterward, she would read the letters.

Jeanne postponed completing her homework until she had a chance to read the next letter. She took the envelopes from the cigar box one by one and placed them on her quilt. She took the time to reread the first letter about the boy her daddy mentioned. Then she picked up the second letter. The postmark was dated 1921, the year Eli was born. When she pulled out the thin paper, a small black-and-white photograph fell to the quilt top.

Gingerly, she picked it up and held it in her hand. The picture was fuzzy, but it looked like a child about three years old. This couldn't be Eli. It was a boy with blond hair and blue eyes. Jeanne turned the picture over, but there was no writing on the back. The paper crumbled easily, and a corner was gone. To keep from damaging the photograph, Jeanne put the tiny picture between pages of her journal and stored it in the drawer of her bedside table. She hoped the next letter would give her a clue to the identity of the child. Jeanne opened the second one.

Dear Mama,

Betty Ann is gone again. Mrs. Belknap won't keep the baby anymore. This week I had to stay with him, and I lost my job because of it. Jobs are so scarce here. I need help. I know Pa will say I told you so. What he said about Betty Ann turned out to be true. I am coming home with the boy. I can help Pa with the farming and you with the garden too. At least we will have food on the farm.

Your son,

Robert

P.S. He's a smart kid and won't be any trouble for you.

Jeanne sat back and held the faded paper in her lap. There was no mention of Eli, and Betty Ann had walked out. Jeanne assumed the picture was of the mystery boy. Daylight faded, and she remained there contemplating the information she had read.

"Jeanne," Grandma called out.

Jeanne carefully put the letters away and went downstairs to help with supper. She was frying the potatoes when Grandma Biddy noticed her skirt.

"What have you done to your skirt, Jeanne Bradshaw?"

"I had an accident today. I'll fix it. I'm sorry, Grandma."

"You need to be more careful with your clothes, young lady."

"Yes, ma'am." She didn't know why she hadn't told Grandma what happened at school. She didn't want any more battles today, and the last letter was waiting for her. Maybe it would reveal the mystery about her mother and the blond boy.

"Put the skirt in my sewing basket. I'll mend it tomorrow. Now, set the table. Dinner's nearly ready, and Pa and Eli will be in soon."

Grandpa and Eli came in the back door, and Jeanne hurried to get the table ready. Eli's face was contorted in pain, and he clutched his arm. He would not look at her, even when she put his plate in front of him. They ate in quiet contemplation. Jeanne tugged her skirt closed and thought about the day at school. She would look for her new friends tomorrow. Surely, she would have a better day.

"I'm going to turn on the radio," Eli said. "I want to hear what's happened in Europe with the Germans and the Soviet Union." He stuffed the last bite of potatoes in his mouth, left his plate on the table, and walked into the living room.

"I'll be right there," Grandpa said. "I want to hear the war news as well."

Jeanne went through the motions and helped clean the kitchen and take care of Robby. She wanted to ask Grandma about the picture and the little boy that wasn't Eli, but this evening wasn't the right time.

Chapter 10

Music bounced around the four walls of the Sycamore Evangelical Baptist Church. In a week, it would be Thanksgiving. Tiny Mrs. Mary Watkins sat on two hymnals to play the church piano from a proper angle. Sometimes Miss Mary stood so she could reach the foot pedals. When she did rise from her elevated perch, the pace accelerated. Miss Mary really got carried away. She was one with her music. Instantly, Jeanne was swept into the lively singing of the choir.

The country church opened its arms to all faiths. They even had a few Catholics sitting in the pews. On this frosty morning, everyone was bundled up against the blue norther that had struck in the night. Most of the congregation sat on the right side of the church, close to the potbellied stove trying its best to fill the space with warmth. When the service was over, no one lingered to visit. It was too cold.

"Hello, Bradshaw family," the pastor said as they all filed out of the church.

Grandma Biddy nodded a greeting to him, then hurried down the rock path carrying Robby. Jeanne knew she wanted to hop in the pickup before he got chilled.

"Got to start the truck, Preacher," Grandpa yelled over his shoulder as he ran off behind his wife.

Jeanne and Eli were left at the door to howdy with Brother Wilson.

Eli stuck out his hand. "Thank you for that fine sermon, sir. This is my sister, Jeanne. She can really sing."

"My goodness, what a wonderful gift, young lady." The rotund Brother Wilson smiled at Jeanne. "I'll tell Miss Mary. She's always looking for good singers."

Jeanne was horrified. *What is Eli thinking?* She had never been in a choir in her life, and she sure wasn't going to get up and sing in front of all those people.

"How about you, young man? Do you sing as well?"

"Oh, no, sir. Jeanne got all that talent. I'm tone-deaf. I move my lips so I feel like I'm participating."

"Bless your heart, son." Brother Wilson looked stricken. "I'm sure you can do other things."

"Glad you could come to our church," the pastor called after them when they rushed away.

"Are you crazy?" Jeanne said when they were out of earshot. "Telling the pastor I could sing!"

Eli grinned. "You need to be singing, Jeanne."

"You can sing too. Now Miss Mary will come looking for me to join the choir."

"What's wrong with that? It'll be fun. You know it will be."

"I don't know," Jeanne said. "I'll think about it."

They all crammed into the front seat of the truck.

Grandma chuckled. "We look like a double-decker sandwich."

"At least we're all staying warm," Grandpa said as he put the truck into gear.

Robby giggled, and they all laughed. When they reached the farm, they popped out like squished marshmallows. Jeanne took Robby from Grandma Biddy, and they were the first ones to get to the house. Old Dog was agitated and stood by the front door barking. He hurried in the house when Jeanne opened the heavy wooden door and walked into the main room where they could warm themselves by the fireplace.

"Mama!" Robby cried.

There stood Betty Ann facing the fire. Robby reached for his mother, and Betty Ann whirled around, full of smiles. "My baby boy," she said. "Come here to your mama. Whose darling boy are you?" She took him from Jeanne and went back to the fire, cooing and fussing over Robby.

Eli walked in. "Mama? What are you doing here?"

"Eli, my handsome son! Come give your mama a kiss. I love you so much."

Eli smiled and walked over. He picked up Betty Ann and Robby and swung them around, holding them off the floor. "I'm so glad to see you," Eli said as he put his mother down. "We've missed you, Mama."

Betty Ann smoothed her hair from the lively whirl around the room, and Jeanne noticed the dark roots making shadows on the blond head. Jeanne's eyes moved down her mother's slender frame to find a wrinkled dress and scuffed shoes. Her red fingernails were chipped and uneven. Jeanne had never seen her mother look this unkempt. *Where has she been, and what happened to her?*

"I know you have, sugar," Betty Ann cooed. "I can only stay for a short time, though. Then I have to get back."

"Get back where?" Jeanne shot back.

"She speaks!" Betty Ann glared at Jeanne, while Old Dog continued to bark. "That's my business, Jeanne Bradshaw. Eli, don't pay her any mind. She's not going to ruin our visit. What is wrong with this dog? It won't shut up."

"Odie," Robby said.

"What?" Betty Ann asked. "What is he saying?"

"It's what Robby calls the dog," Eli told her. "His name is Old Dog."

The dog started howling when he heard Eli say his name.

"I declare, Betty Ann!" Grandma said when she walked in.

"How did you get here, and what's wrong with Old Dog?"

"I walked in the front door, Mother Bradshaw." A familiar haughty look shot across to Grandma and then melted into smiles again for the boys. Old Dog kept howling.

Jeanne saw Grandma Biddy smoldering behind her glasses. She was blinking fast while her neck and face turned red. "Jeanne," she instructed, "go set an extra place at the table for your mama. I'll warm up the beans and bring Old Dog in the kitchen. I know what's wrong with him."

When Jeanne went into the kitchen, Grandma sent her to warn Grandpa that Betty Ann was in the house. She was too late. He walked in the front door to find Betty Ann and the boys laughing at a wild story she was telling. Jeanne could see Grandpa's surprise, his anger, and then she saw his control. He didn't say a word to anyone and purposely walked through the front room into the kitchen. Jeanne had never seen him show resentment until now. Her grandparents had never talked about Betty Ann. They seldom talked about their son, Robert, either. *My father, my missing father.* She thought about the letters, and fear drained the blood from her face. Betty Ann had a way of unearthing secrets. She would find out somehow.

Jeanne ran up the stairs to her room to hide the box. She searched, desperate to find a good hiding spot. She couldn't believe she had not read the last letter. *How stupid of me!* She grabbed her journal and the box, wrapped them inside a pillowcase, then stowed it out of sight. Just in time. She heard footsteps outside. Soon her door swung open and banged against the bare wall.

"What have you got, Jeanne?" Betty Ann asked. "Eli told me you had some letters. He said Biddy gave them to you."

Jeanne was stunned. "I don't have them anymore." *Why would Eli tell her about the letters?*

"They're from your daddy," Betty Ann said. "What did he say about me?"

Jeanne didn't know what to say, so she stayed quiet, knowing that her silence would only inflame Betty Ann more. Jeanne backed up against the slatted wall with her hands clasped together at her waist. Her tight grip choked her fingertips white. She cast her eyes down at the floor. She dared not look anywhere in the room and give away the hiding place.

"You better give them to me." Betty Ann sounded hollow and desperate. "They belong to me."

"Those letters belong to Grandma, not you," Jeanne spit back.

Betty Ann jerked the narrow drawer from the table and shook it upside down, scattering papers across the floor. She stepped to Jeanne's bed, grabbed her pillow, and threw back the quilts and the thin mattress.

The letters did not belong to her mother, but her mother claimed everything: their money, their belongings, their souls. Jeanne's throat closed, and she felt her skin prickle as her mother searched her bedroom.

"Nothing here?" Betty Ann asked. "You must have them in another rathole. Only a pitiful cot and a rickety table." She paced across the rag rug, then kicked it aside. She looked toward the rafters. A growl of frustration escaped her milky white throat.

Jeanne watched her through hooded eyes, afraid she would give away the hiding place. Betty Ann was waiting for Jeanne's reaction, but Jeanne remained still and stoic.

"So, you thought you could leave my house, and I wouldn't find you. How did you convince Eli to go with you?"

Jeanne remained a soundless gong. The vibration rang from outside in. She didn't want to start a row but being homeless and having no food for Robby flashed through her mind. Did she forget that she signed away the house? Jeanne was incredulous that her mother could still claim the house. "You left us with no food, that's how," Jeanne finally said. "Eli couldn't work after his broken arm, and we really didn't have a choice. We could have starved, and you wouldn't have cared."

"You think you can find out something about your daddy by coming here?" Betty Ann hissed. "Don't bet on it, missy. You've gone and got Eli upset. Who do you think you are with that sneer on your face? I'll knock that look off. You hear me?" Betty Ann raised her hand.

Jeanne stood her ground and prepared for the blow, daring her mother to hit her.

Betty Ann's face transformed from a distorted mask of disgust to one of shock.

She remembered where she is, Jeanne realized. *Mama can't hit me where my grandparents or Eli can witness her rage.*

"I can't stand to look at you," Betty Ann railed at her.

Jeanne was familiar with her mother's threatening tactics. The harsh words would not break her. After all the years of cruelty, she expected her mother's sarcasm.

Betty Ann took a step toward her.

"Come down for dinner," Eli yelled. "Biddy has the food ready."

"Don't think this is over," Betty Ann snarled. "I'll get those letters."

Jeanne quickly stepped around her mother and headed downstairs while she had a chance to get away. She waited at the bottom of the staircase until she saw her mother's high heels appear on the top step and start down. The letters were safe for now.

"What's taking you women so long?" Eli said from the kitchen. "Come on."

Jeanne listened to the cheer in her older brother's voice, and her heart sank. He was hopeful again, and he would be hurt again. *You women? Good heavens! Does Eli think Mama and I were having a friendly girl talk?* Jeanne headed to the kitchen, settled into her chair at the table, and bowed her head for her grandfather's mealtime prayer.

Thank you, God, she repeated in her head. *For what? Where is God? I've never seen him.* Jeanne glared at her older brother, who looked away. She was furious. She couldn't help it. It would always be a terrible battle between her and Mama.

∽

When it was time for bed, Jeanne was nervous about where her mother would sleep. She hadn't been able to get back upstairs to check on the hidden letters. Her mother's eyes were following her wherever she went. Jeanne suffered her scrutiny throughout the afternoon, and before Grandma could make up a pallet that evening, Betty Ann issued her own orders.

"I'll take Jeanne's cot upstairs. She can sleep with Robby on his cot. I have everything I need in my purse." Yellowed hair bounced up the stairs. The same high-heeled shoes, the same searing voice, the same Betty Ann.

Jeanne didn't mind the pallet on the floor next to Robby sleeping peacefully on his cot. Old Dog was next to her on the floor. He had settled down when Robby fell asleep. Jeanne couldn't sleep, though. She lay there staring at the coals in the fireplace in the next room. She had turned over a dozen times, but sleep wouldn't come.

It was close to daylight when she heard the creaking steps. She was alert and listened without moving. She put her hand on Old Dog's head, and he relaxed. He seemed to understand. Rustling sounds moved into the living room. Jeanne recognized the sound of the secretary drawers being opened. Her mother was looking for the letters. Then Jeanne saw a shadow in the doorway.

"What do you think you'll find there, Betty Ann?" Grandpa asked. His deep voice rumbled across the room. Jeanne had been so intent on watching her mother that she hadn't heard her grandpa approach.

"Claude. I was just . . ."

"I know what you're doing," Grandpa said. "You back away from my business, right now. You're going to leave this house and never come back." Grandpa moved toward Betty Ann. "If I see you again, I'll tell Eli everything."

"Don't worry yourself," Betty Ann said. "Why would I want to come back to this hovel? I have someone picking me up at dawn." She slid her purse up on her shoulder and walked past Grandpa. Her footsteps clicked across the floor as she went to the front door and slammed it on the way out.

Old Dog's bass voice rolled in his throat at Jeanne, and he went back to his post near Robby. Grandpa went back to bed, while Eli and Robby continued sleeping on their cots, undisturbed.

∞

The boys were excited the next morning. Eli lingered, waiting for Betty Ann to come down the stairs. The morning was even colder than the day before, and tree branches crackled from the heavy layers of ice. A loud shot rang out.

"The ice is breaking the big limbs," Grandpa stated as he slipped on his boots. "We may lose trees. I haven't seen a storm like this since the night Robert was born. It was like this then."

"Pa, are we going out to work today?" Eli asked, hurrying to the fireplace for warmth.

"We'll wait awhile," Grandpa replied. "The machinery won't operate in this weather anyway, but let's load up on firewood." Grandpa was already out the door and back with an armful before Eli made it to the door. "Stack it closer to the door and bring a load in for Biddy in the kitchen."

Jeanne saw how Eli kept glancing up the stairs, but he put on his heavy coat and hurried to gather more wood. She wrapped Robby up tight in a quilt and carried him closer to the fireplace.

"It's getting cold up there, Grandma," Eli said on his second trip for firewood. "Should I go check on Mama?"

"No use in doing that," Grandma said. "She's already gone. Your mammy left early this morning, when she thought everyone was asleep."

Eli dropped the wood and walked out the front door into the cold.

Jeanne knew Betty Ann had it all planned. She was looking for money. Jeanne remembered the letters. Had her mother found them? Jeanne ran up the stairs two at a time. It looked like the bed hadn't been slept in at all. She pulled the cot over to the high porthole and tried to open it. It was stuck. It had frozen shut in the storm. She shoved with all her strength, but it wouldn't budge.

She sat on the edge of her cot with her head in her hands. She took a deep breath and held her head up, then tramped downstairs. She was warming her hands when Grandpa walked in carrying the frozen pillowcase.

"Is this yours, Jeanne?" Grandpa said with an expressionless face.

"The north wind must have blown it off the roof," Jeanne said. She took the cold bag and walked up the stairs to her room.

Jeanne shivered, partly because of the cold temperature in the tiny loft and partly because of anticipation. Her daddy had written the letters. This time she would not miss her chance. She would read them all.

She took a deep breath and pulled the letters out of the pillowcase. There was nothing left of the cigar box. Six cardboard rectangles remained to protect her father's words. Her slim fingers traced the edges of each envelope. She waited a while longer before she read it. She didn't want the anticipation to end. It seemed foolish to her now. She tried to imagine what could be in that last letter. She fantasized that her father owned one of those oil wells he talked about and had made a million dollars. He wanted her and her brothers to join him in Dallas where he had a mansion waiting for them.

She looked down at the thick letter. Her father must have had more to say in this one.

Sunday, March 1938

Dear Mama,

Eli has a job now that he is sixteen. He's working at the grocery store. I am proud of that boy. Jeanne tries to cook and clean after school. Betty Ann is in one of her states and stays in bed all day because of Robby.

Two weeks ago, Dr. Ellison told us about Robby. He has always been a sweet baby, but he hasn't grown like Eli and Jeanne did. The doctor says he's not right and sickly and that he won't live to be six years old. He has a bad heart. His lips turn blue when he has trouble with his heart. Betty Ann cries all the time. Jeanne takes care of Robby when she is not in school.

I leave for work on Monday. I am taking the train to Oklahoma City. Please come if you can and check on the kids. This is getting too much for me to handle by myself. The truth is, before Robby was born, Betty Ann told me he wasn't mine. Then she told me she lied. I don't know what to believe because she went ahead and named him after me anyway. Mrs. Billings next door said that Betty Ann took little black pills that made Robby turn out this way. Could that be true?

I know you have work to do on the farm, but I worry about the kids when I'm gone. Write to me at the address on the back of the envelope.

Your son,

Robert

Jeanne flipped the envelope over and read the address. *P.O. Box 15, Oklahoma City, Oklahoma.* Was he still there, or had he traveled to another oil patch to find work?

⚬⚬⚬

Jeanne finally returned to school a week later. The storm had devastated the entire county. The fact that Betty Ann had walked out and escaped the ravages of the storm was conflicting for

Jeanne. She didn't know if she wanted her mother to be on the farm with them or to be out of their lives for good. Robby barely realized Betty Ann had been there, the visit was so short. On the other hand, her big brother was hardly speaking to anyone. He still believed Betty Ann's words of love and her outpouring of affection. Jeanne only trusted her mother's actions. After all, she had heard the conversation between Grandpa and Betty Ann. She felt guilty about loving and hating her mother at the same time.

Will I always feel this way? And what do the letters mean?

Surely, Grandma Biddy knew she would come asking questions.

Chapter 11

The December morning was cold and clear as Jeanne made her way to church for choir practice. She pulled her wool scarf close and tied it tight under her chin as she walked down the dirt road. She had forgiven Eli. He didn't know Mama like she did. He viewed the letters as news and not life changing, and she felt better when there was peace between them. Jeanne listened to the soughing in the junipers that rose up beside her as she walked. She imagined their dark green would have disguised winter had not the temperatures been so frigid. Grandma Biddy's knitted socks and muffler kept her warm for the two-mile jaunt to the Sycamore Evangelical Baptist Church.

Singing with the church choir occupied Jeanne's Saturdays, but most important of all, she had made another friend, Maggie. She made Jeanne feel comfortable and at ease as the newest member of the choir. Jeanne smiled to herself when she thought of the smorgasbord of choir members. Maggie's clear soprano voice carried the whole section of five in the church choir, while

Jeanne's raspy alto blended well with the middle-aged ladies, who themselves had been in the choir for years. She learned the songs with ease if she stood next to Cora, Carol, and Carrie. The three Cs had been singing in the choir for longer than anyone could remember. The only time Jeanne would miss a note was when Director Mary would sing along with the sopranos or the tenors instead of sticking to directing. For the most part, Jeanne performed acceptably. The Christmas program was only five days away, and she and Maggie were singing a duet during the live Nativity performance. Jeanne was on her way to the last practice before the real performance. She practiced "Silent Night" as she walked.

Grunting noises in the bushy junipers interrupted her singing. She slowed to find a stick for protection. Animals were usually scared of humans and avoided the road, but something in her hands would comfort her. A few steps away, Jeanne found a sharp cedar branch lying in the gully beside the road. The brown spiny leaves stuck into her skin and made her hands sting, but she felt safer holding it.

Snorting sounds burst through the brush while she was standing in the ditch with the stick, and black javelinas rushed across the road toward her. She was halfway up the embankment when a dozen adolescent peccaries led by a large sow raced by Jeanne on both sides. She didn't move till they had disappeared into the thorny brambles behind her.

She took a deep breath and climbed out of the ditch onto the road. When she reached the edge, she faced an enormous boar eyeing her on the other side. A main part of the family had scrambled on to safety and left this old man to guard the rear. His frightening tusks rubbed together and made a chattering noise, warning her not to get too close.

Jeanne wrinkled her nose at the powerful smell emanating from across the road. She had heard Grandpa call them skunk pigs because of that smell. Looking directly at Jeanne, the boar stood his ground and grunted. Even being a much smaller-sized hog, this javelina male was no less scary. Jeanne didn't move and grasped her makeshift weapon harder. More of the skunk pigs gathered behind the boar. One by one, black youngsters ventured across the road single file, slow walking in the road, then hurrying into the underbrush. Finally, the old boar seemed satisfied his brood was safe. He snorted again at Jeanne, angled across the road, and vanished into the squatty, dark green forest.

Jeanne still held the scratchy stick. Fresh air blew against her face, and she heard the birdsongs begin again. She smiled and walked down the dusty road, swinging the stick. The exhilaration of the javelina confrontation stayed with her all the way to the church.

∽

Jeanne pushed open the church cemetery gate at the same time Maggie bounced out of the rumble seat of a black Model T Ford. A stranger stepped out on the driver's side. Jeanne waved at her friend, and Maggie ran to greet her.

"Jeanne, I have someone to help with the choir," Maggie said. "This is my cousin, Jameson. He can sing tenor."

The stranger walked up behind them as Maggie pulled her toward the church.

Jeanne glanced over her shoulder at Maggie's cousin. "Hello, Jameson," she said.

Miss Mary rushed around them into the church to escape the cold. Jeanne turned on the steps to look at the young man who had driven the car. Jameson was a tall, lanky boy with unruly beige hair. While his clothes were rumpled, his shirt appeared to be clean. He stuck his hands in his pockets and looked away when he spoke to her. Jeanne hoped his singing was better than his manners.

"Come on, you two." Maggie held the door and waved them in. "Miss Mary and the rest of the choir are waiting."

Jeanne hurried through the door, and Jameson followed them into the warm sanctuary. Inside the cozy church, an evergreen fragrance filled the air.

The sanctuary was a cloak of safety for Jeanne, and the faces of the older women in the choir were always welcoming. They were already warming up and singing the scales. The last she saw of Jameson was when he went to the back row to stand with the men. He looked rather lost. She opened her hymnal to "Silent Night" and smiled about the skunk pigs running across the road.

⚬⚭⚬

Jeanne was vigilant watching for the pigs on her way home. She wouldn't walk that way again without thinking of the rush of piglets and the protective boar. She hurried, for the day had turned cloudy and dreary, and it was getting late.

She composed the letter she wanted to write to her father over and over in her head. She was going to send it to the Oklahoma City address from the last letter he had sent. She hoped the effort wouldn't prove futile. By the time Jeanne walked in the front door, it was the middle of the afternoon. She wanted to write a letter to her father before it got dark.

The room's heat was overpowering. Robby was lying completely still on a cot in front of the fireplace. Grandma Biddy was sitting in a kitchen chair pulled up close to him, bathing his flushed face. He didn't look at Jeanne when she entered the room.

"What's wrong, Grandma?" she asked. Fear gripped her heart as she rushed to the cot. Robby looked terribly sick.

"Robby has a fever again," Grandma said. "Eli's gone to fetch the doctor."

Jeanne sat on the floor beside Robby and felt his warm face. "I'm here, Robby boy." She took his limp hand and held it in hers. He looked at her, and she saw pain in his watery eyes. Jeanne started singing Christmas carols to soothe him. She didn't know what else to do.

"Sit here with him," Grandma said as she stood. "I need to tend to supper." She handed Jeanne the damp cloth.

Jeanne dipped the cloth in the pan of water and continued to sponge his face. The cool rag absorbed the heat from his brow, but the fever continued to burn.

Robby seemed to get weaker and weaker by the hour. He was asleep when Dr. Hadley finally arrived. Grandma greeted the doctor and guided him to the sickbed by the fireplace. Jeanne stood and moved away for the doctor to sit in the chair to examine Robby. He leaned forward and brushed his long fingers along Robby's face. He looked into her little brother's eyes.

"Let me help," Grandma said as she unbuttoned Robby's pajama top. Her hands quickly opened the front and exposed Robby's pale chest. He looked over at Jeanne, and she moved closer and put her hand on his shoulder. His eyes closed.

Dr. Hadley cupped the stethoscope in his hands to warm it, and then gently placed it on Robby's chest to listen. Jeanne followed the instrument as it traveled over his fragile body. She tried to interpret expressions from the doctor's face, but it was expressionless. She was sure he was practiced at concealing bad news from his patients and their families. Dr. Hadley examined Robby's torso, but mostly, he listened to his heart. When the doctor removed the stethoscope and put it away in his bag, he remained quiet for several minutes.

Jeanne suffered through the silence. The clock on the mantle was a hammer pounding out the seconds. If the doctor didn't say something soon, she would scream. She felt Old Dog's cold nose against her arm, consoling her. She automatically smoothed the fur on his back while she waited.

"He's got a high fever and his throat is red, Mrs. Bradshaw," the doctor said. "Not sure what it is, but the boy may not be able to fight it. He's so fragile. It's not pneumonia . . . yet." He sat there in the chair looking at Robby, and not facing Grandma. Then he stood to go.

Grandma spoke first. "I've done everything I know how, Doctor. Don't you have something to give him?" She stood ramrod straight and looked the doctor in the eye. She remained steadfast between the doctor and the front door.

"He might have a chance if his fever breaks," Dr. Hadley conceded. He inched toward the door and looked at Jeanne.

Jeanne moved to the chair and began bathing Robby's face. She was desperate to do something. She watched the standoff unfolding between her grandma and the doctor.

"We know what to do for a fever, Dr. Hadley," Grandma said. "What would you do for any other child who was this sick?"

He looked down at the floor and said nothing.

Robby's barking cough split the silence lingering in the room, causing worry to crease Grandma's face. Dr. Hadley finally knelt, digging in his black bag. Grandma waited in front of the door, and Old Dog moved over to wait with her.

When the doctor stood and faced Grandma, he had something in his hand. "Give him a teaspoon full of this every six hours." Dr. Hadley held out a slim brown bottle with a cork stopper.

Grandma stepped forward and took the medicine. She nodded to him.

The doctor nodded back, then walked around her to the door.

"Wait," Grandma said. She handed the bottle to Jeanne and picked up her handbag from the rocking chair. She pulled a dollar from her purse and handed it to the doctor. "Like any other patient, we pay our way, Doctor."

The doctor took the money and looked at the floor again. "Yes, ma'am." He turned around and looked at Grandma, at Jeanne, and then at Robby. "Don't you ladies get your hopes up." He then disappeared through the door.

Jeanne could hear his engine rumble to life and move off down the driveway to the county road.

"Get a spoon, Jeanne," Grandma said. "Let's give Robby his first dose."

Jeanne hurried into the kitchen and came back with a spoon. "What do you want me to do?" She looked at the vial of black medicine in Grandma's hand.

"You sit behind Robby and lift him up so he doesn't choke."

Jeanne straddled the cot and eased in behind Robby. She lifted his frail body into a sitting position. "Come on, Robby, open your mouth," Jeanne whispered to her little brother. She tenderly held his head with her hands.

Grandma poured the vile-smelling syrup into the spoon. "Here you go, Robby. Open up," Grandma coaxed. Robby moaned and twisted his head away from the spoon, but Grandma held his chin with one hand and got him to swallow the first bit of medicine. "His next dose is at ten."

Jeanne looked at the clock on the mantle. She prayed he would be better before that. When she eased Robby back down on the cot, he began gagging. Before Jeanne could do anything, Robby threw up. Jeanne quickly sat him up again.

"Oh, no!" Grandma exclaimed. "He has to keep the medicine down. I'll get a pan of warm water to clean up the mess. Carry him to the chair, and I'll change the sheets."

Jeanne wiped his mouth and face and changed his shirt. She wrapped him in a blanket and held him in her lap while Grandma changed the bedding.

This same routine continued through the night, and finally Jeanne fell asleep on the floor by the fireplace. She woke up to Grandma talking to Robby.

"All right, my darling Robby, open one more time for Grandma." She dribbled a small amount of the medicine in his mouth, and he swallowed.

Jeanne sat up and stared at Grandma dipping her fingers in a bowl of water. Robby would begin to gag, and Grandma would flick water in his face. He would catch his breath, and it would hold the reflex at bay.

"I'm making a Methodist out of you tonight, Robby, my sweetheart." She sprinkled him with water again when she could see the insistent urge rise in his throat.

"What are you doing, Grandma Biddy?"

"Why, I'm making a Methodist out of Robby. He's had two full doses, and his fever is less."

"Go lie down for a while," Jeanne said. "I can baptize Robby with sprinkles."

"I'm sure you can, honey." Grandma smiled up at Jeanne. "You watch his throat. That tells you when he is about to throw up. He should be able to sleep now. That will be the best medicine for him." Grandma Biddy got up from her chair and left Jeanne in charge.

Jeanne loved her grandma, the woman who took on the world for her family. She felt guilty that she had slept while her grandma stayed up to take care of Robby. She noticed for the first time Grandma's white hair was loose from its tight bun. Dark, sunken eyes looked at Jeanne, and tired wrinkles creased her face. Heavy burdens weighed on her grandma. She had been too caught up in her own worries to realize the toll it was taking on Grandma. For now, Robby was resting, and he was cool to the touch.

Chapter 12

"Look what I've got," Eli shouted as he banged the door open and hauled in a fat cedar.

Or is it a juniper? Jeanne wasn't sure which.

"You've cut a Christmas tree," Grandma said. Her smile brightened the whole room.

Eli tugged the green limbs inside, and instantly the room filled with the wonderful evergreen fragrance that reminded Jeanne of the church.

"You bet. I've already hammered a cross stand to the bottom of the trunk." Eli stood it in the corner, and everyone admired the tree and the joy it brought to the room. Jeanne breathed in the pungent fragrance of Christmas. Old Dog howled in celebration with them.

"Hurry up, you two. Let's start decorating," Grandma said. "Auntie Boots will be here with her four young'uns any minute."

"I haven't met Auntie Boots," Jeanne said. "What's she like?"

"I know Eli has," Grandpa said. "Get him to tell you."

Grandma started laughing, and Grandpa ducked out of the room. Jeanne turned to Eli. "Well?"

"She's not like anybody you've ever met. I don't remember

much. I was pretty young."

"I'll say this," Grandma said. "She has stars in her eyes. She loves anything Hollywood."

They decorated the tree with garlands of popcorn and chains of colored paper glued together. Grandma Biddy made them milk tea. She and Robby liked the milk tea instead of coffee. Jeanne was not able to down a cup of coffee yet. Grandma said it was an acquired taste.

Grandma opened a can of condensed milk, added water, and heated it in a boiler on the stove. "Jeanne, measure two tablespoons of brown sugar and stir it in the pot," she said. "I'll get the cinnamon."

It was the best Christmas drink ever. She was washing the cups when a whirlwind of cold air, laughter, and noise burst through the front door. *Auntie Boots!*

"Christmas Eve gift, y'all!" Auntie Boots yelled as she slammed the door. "We gotcha on that one."

"You sure did," Grandma said. "Come on in. Take off your coat and warm yourself by the fire."

Jeanne stood there drying her hands with her mouth agape. Before her stood a woman at least six feet tall. She had flaming orange hair and was wearing cowboy boots. On top of that, she had on pants. The blouse she was wearing was bright pink. Jeanne had heard Miss Mary at the dry goods store say that redheads should never wear pink. Apparently, Auntie Boots didn't give a hoot about following any fashion rules.

"Where are James and the kids?" Grandpa asked.

"They'll be along this evening at the pageant. He dropped me off and then stopped to visit with his mama. You know how she and I get along." She paused and looked at everyone in the room. "We don't." She laughed. "We're like oil and water. It's best if we don't get into a squabble. Especially around Christmastime."

Jeanne couldn't believe Grandpa and Auntie Boots were related. They had different mothers and were twenty years apart, and Auntie Boots was about the same age as her own daddy. She had always heard stories about her, and she believed the wild tales she'd heard, now that she had met her notorious aunt.

"Well, aren't you a pretty thing," Auntie Boots said. "I guess you're Jeanne. Why, honey, you could be a model for one of those fashion magazines."

"Stop that, Bootsie," Grandpa said. "Jeanne doesn't need her head full of Hollywood dreams. There's already enough of that in this family. You and her mammy are all we need."

"She is that pretty, Claude," Auntie Boots said. "You don't want her running off in a few years is all."

Grandma chimed in. "She's smart too. She's going to amount to something."

Jeanne stood there while they discussed her future like she wasn't there. Her grandparents were proud of her. It was a nice feeling.

"Where's my present?" Auntie Boots asked.

Grandpa grinned. "She did say 'Christmas Eve gift' first. I guess we'll have to give her something. You know that's the custom. Whoever says 'Christmas Eve gift' first gets a present."

Grandma went into her room and brought out a gift wrapped in red tissue paper and tied with a silver ribbon. When she presented it to Auntie Boots, she made a little bow.

Jeanne detected a sparkle of mischief in Grandpa's eyes, while Grandma Biddy sat down in her rocker and folded her hands in her lap.

"Why, Claude," Auntie Boots said. "You shouldn't have. You know it's fun to be the first one to say 'Christmas Eve gift.' You don't really have to give a present."

Grandpa stood there and rocked up on the balls of his feet, looking pleased with himself.

The bigger-than-life woman sat down on the hearth and tore into the package. She held the box in her hand and carefully lifted the lid. Out jumped two tightly held springs. One smacked Auntie Boots on the nose, and the other went flying across the room into Grandma Biddy's lap. Grandma clapped her hands and laughed till tears streamed down her face, and she couldn't say a word. Jeanne had never seen either of her grandparents so tickled.

"I was ready for you, Bootsie." Grandpa guffawed and slapped his knee.

"Oh, no! I've been had!" Auntie Boots said through gales of laughter. "Just you wait, Claude Bradshaw." Orange hair bounced up and down, and her face turned into fun itself.

Jeanne was so surprised that it took her a minute to realize what had happened. "I think you got me too, Grandpa."

Everyone looked at Jeanne and started laughing all over again.

Jeanne relished the frosty air cooling her hot cheeks outside the church on Christmas Eve. After the applause and congratulations, the warm church had closed in on her. Her family had ambled out of the sanctuary and on toward Grandpa's pickup. Auntie Boots and her clan were piling into their old jalopy. Everyone was ready for Christmas Day.

"Hey, Jeanne," Maggie called. "Ride with us. We can make the wonderful night last a little longer."

"I don't know." Jeanne wanted to go home. She had planned to read the letter she had written to her father one more time tonight. After Christmas, she was taking it to the post office to mail it. She had waited for the right time. The pillowcase of letters was like poison, reminding her of Betty Ann's visit. She wanted to rid herself of that terrible feeling. She hoped mailing the letter to her father would give her a new beginning.

"Come on, Jeanne," Maggie said. "Eli is going to ride in the front with me. You can ride in the back with Jameson. It's not terribly cold. Besides, Jameson is a good catch. That car he was driving is his when he graduates this spring." Maggie's voice was pleading.

"All right," Jeanne relented. "I'm coming." She wanted to please her friend. Maggie liked Eli, as most girls did. He was handsome and kind. She decided to give in and go since it wasn't that far to the farm. However, she didn't like this boy. She didn't care how many cars he owned. She wasn't impressed.

Jameson leaped up in the bed of the pickup Maggie's dad was driving. He offered her a hand as she climbed in. She didn't want to take his hand, but she glanced at Maggie through the back glass in time to see her wink. Maggie was a little boy-crazy. Even though Jameson had a blanket over their laps, Jeanne envied the riders in the warm cab.

"Your song was really good in the pageant," Jameson said.

"Maggie has a pretty soprano voice. I was glad I could be a part of it." Jeanne didn't know how to take compliments. It made her nervous. She noticed Jameson had scooted closer to her, and she inched away from him. There was something about him. She wasn't comfortable, and her stomach was in her throat. She didn't know how to act around boys.

The road was bumpy, and they were tossed around in the back of the truck. Jeanne held on to the side. Around the next bend, Jameson slid close to her and yelled, "My curve!"

When the washboard ride ended and they were going over the bridge, Jameson put his hand on her thigh. Jeanne froze. She wasn't sure what to do. Was it an accident? He didn't say a word, and Jeanne looked straight ahead.

They bumped off the bridge, and the truck swerved to miss the potholes in the road. Jameson and Jeanne bounced about, but his hand was back on her leg and higher on her thigh. This was no accident. They would be at the house in a couple of minutes, but a lot could happen in two minutes.

She swallowed and grasped his hand to remove it. He wouldn't budge, and his hand moved inside her thigh. She grasped harder. He grabbed the inside of her leg and squeezed. By the time the truck stopped in front of her house, she had to use both of her hands to tear his hand away. Jeanne scrambled out of the pickup and ran into the house. She heard Jameson laughing as she closed the front door.

The warmth of the room welcomed Jeanne from the cold. Around her, all sizes of bodies were stretched out on the floor, creating a calm of their own. It was a stark contrast to what she had just escaped.

"My goodness, what a look," Auntie Boots commented. "Come over by the fire." She was all wrapped up in a colorful shawl, smoking a long black cigarette. She took a long draw and held in the smoke.

Jeanne stepped over pallets of sleeping children. She ducked under the long row of socks bulging with fruit hanging from the mantle and sat beside her aunt. Auntie Boots let out her breath slowly, and a trail of smoke floated up the chimney. Jeanne looked at the red-tipped cigarette, a snoring Uncle James, and the sleeping children.

Before either of them could say a word, Eli burst in the door with a gust of freezing wind. "Jeanne, you didn't even thank Maggie for the ride. Did you forget your manners?"

"Close that door," Auntie Boots ordered.

Eli saw the floor covered with people and quickly shut the door. "Sorry," he whispered as he walked gingerly to his room.

Jeanne let out a heavy sigh.

"I've seen that look before," Auntie Boots said. "What happened to ruin your Christmas Eve? Boy trouble?"

Jeanne burst into tears, and a soft arm hugged her close. She wanted to hide. *What did I do to make Jameson think it was all right to touch my leg? Did I encourage him? Do other boys think I'm that way? What has Maggie told him?*

"It wasn't your fault, honey," said Auntie Boots. "So, don't go blaming yourself. Who was it? That Jameson kid?"

Jeanne nodded. Her aunt had read her mind. She was mortified, but she wanted to hear what her aunt had to say.

"I figured. He was sniffing after you all night. I could tell you didn't even know he existed. Little bastard."

Jeanne was startled a bit at the language, but the description suited him fine. "I didn't know what to do."

"Find your voice, girl." Auntie Boots sat straighter and looked at Jeanne. "Tell them in no uncertain terms: 'Get your hands off me!' Then, if he doesn't get the message, kick and scream till he does. Remember, you don't take shit from anybody."

"Auntie Boots, I froze up inside and couldn't say anything."

"I've never had any trouble speaking my mind," Auntie Boots said. "But I didn't have a childhood like yours either."

"It seems like I'm always surprised by what happens. I don't expect people to be cruel, even though . . ." Jeanne stopped before she said something about her mama. Auntie Boots was family, but when she talked about her mama to someone, it always felt like she was betraying her. Betty Ann said to never talk about what went on in their house to anybody. Her mama said they would suffer for it if they said a word.

"Honey, you don't have to explain. I've known Betty Ann a long time. That green-eyed monster will eat her alive someday. Combine that with her temper, and you have a horribly destructive person." She gave Jeanne a sympathetic smile. "I know it eats at you too, honey. If you can accept your mother for who she is, then you can forgive her."

One of the boys whimpered in his sleep and began thrashing and throwing off the covers. Auntie Boots flicked her cigarette in the fireplace and put her finger to her lips. Their conversation stopped as they waited for him to go back to sleep.

"We can talk again," Auntie Boots said. "Go on to bed now. Tomorrow is Christmas."

Jeanne felt courage rise within her and take root as she quietly ascended the stairs to her room. She wanted to hold on to this feeling and savor it for a while. She wanted it to grow and make her brave and not afraid anymore. She despised Jameson for making her feel weak and insecure. She felt dirty. She could still hear him laughing, but she would not be a joke. She would remember her aunt's words of advice. She had to find her voice.

⌒∞⌒

The next morning was chaos. Even Robby felt well enough to smile and enjoy watching their aunt's children buzz around the house. Jeanne was dressed and ready to help with breakfast when she came downstairs, but kids were already jumping up and down and gathering around the Christmas tree.

"Jeanne, grab Robby," Grandma Biddy said. "Let's get the stockings down."

When Jeanne carried Robby in and sat on the divan, Uncle James was already passing out the stockings. Each Christmas morning stocking held an orange and an enormous peppermint stick.

"Uncle Claude has a hammer and a cup towel in the kitchen so you can break up your peppermint," Auntie Boots told them. "Go on in there if you want to break off a few slivers."

"I want to look at mine, Mama," the youngest girl said.

"You go right ahead, Doris. The rest of 'em will be sorry when theirs is all gone."

"This one is yours, Jeanne," Uncle James said. He stepped over the mass of arms and legs in the middle of the floor and handed her a sock with a familiar lump in it.

Jeanne rested the stocking on Robby's lap and took out the orange. A piece of paper fell out. She saw her name on the folded note, so she opened it.

Merry Christmas, Jeanne!

Free driving lessons on Christmas Day.

You need to learn how to drive, girl.

Your Auntie Boots

Jeanne looked up at her aunt, who was grinning back at her. She jumped up and, still holding Robby, ran to her aunt and hugged her. "Thank you, Auntie Boots. This is the best present ever!"

"Well, come on then," Auntie Boots said. "Let's get started.

We're driving Claude's pickup. It's a stick shift, and you might as well learn how to work with a clutch."

Jeanne handed Robby to Grandma and ran out the door. Auntie Boots was right behind her. The truck was parked out front waiting for them, but before Jeanne climbed into the driver's seat, she looked back at the house. Everyone had gathered on the porch to watch: all the kids with sticky red faces, Old Dog barking, all three men standing shoulder to shoulder with their arms crossed, and Grandma Biddy holding a waving Robby.

Jeanne waved back and slipped into the truck behind the steering wheel. Before she started the old truck, Auntie Boots gave her instructions. There was no doubt who was in charge, but Jeanne was about to become independent.

Auntie Boots leaned out the window and yelled, "Yee haw! Here we go!" Her orange hair blew back, and she stuck out her arm and waved at the crowd on the porch. "Keep it between the ditches, Jeannie girl."

Chapter 13

Jeanne sat at the kitchen table trying to warm up after she and Eli had spent the afternoon watching Polkadot pace uncomfortably in the corral. The spotted Jersey didn't want to cooperate with their birthing timeline. The calf would come in its own time. Eli had penned Polkadot in one of the stalls so she wouldn't wander off and have her calf in the bushes somewhere. Grandpa had told Jeanne and Eli to watch her for signs of calving, but so far, she and Eli had suffered the cold for nothing.

Jeanne left Eli at the table and went upstairs to get the letter she had written to her father. She wanted Eli to read it. Reluctantly, Eli took the letter from her and glanced over it quickly.

"Your letter is fine," Eli said as he handed it back to her. "I don't believe you'll hear from him. He's been gone a long time."

"I want to try at least," Jeanne said. "You knew him better than I did. Mama always said he was weak and had the spine of a jellyfish. Do you believe that?"

"I stopped thinking about it a long time ago. I don't believe anything, but you send it if you want. I'm tired of disappointments and broken promises. That's why I'm staying here on the farm. At least I can depend on Pa and Biddy." He left her sitting at the table.

She stared at the pitiful attempt to communicate with her father.

Grandma walked into the kitchen. "You can drive me into town in the morning. Then you can mail that to your daddy. You'll need this to buy your stamp." Grandma put a nickel on the wooden table and slid it across in front of her.

"Have you tried to write to him?" Jeanne asked.

"I did write him once. You have the only letters from him. That doesn't mean you shouldn't try."

∽

It was Jeanne's first time driving. Grandma didn't seem nervous, and she acted like it was the most natural thing in the world for Jeanne to be driving her into town. Eli stayed with Polkadot. The contrary cow was still pacing with no sign of a new calf. Jeanne didn't get nervous driving until she drove inside the city limits and encountered other cars and trucks.

"Stop here at the grocery, and I'll get out. I'll be through shopping by the time you get back from the post office."

Jeanne parked and ran up the post office steps with hope in her hands. When she opened the door, Sandra Crawford was standing in the line. Jeanne wanted to turn and run back out the door, but her aunt's advice stopped her. She marched up and took her place in line, ignoring the girl two people in front of her.

"Well, look who's here, Miss Smart Aleck," Sandra taunted when she walked away from the window. "Whatcha got there?" She reached for Jeanne's letter.

Jeanne moved back, and her nasty opponent staggered in front of her. Jeanne held the letter close and moved to the window.

"Yes, miss, what can I do for you?" the clerk asked.

Jeanne focused on the man and kept her back to Sandra. "I would like a first-class stamp for this letter."

"That'll be three cents."

Jeanne passed the nickel to the clerk. She dared not look around for Sandra while she waited for her change. She boldly walked out of the post office and to the parked truck. She saw Sandra gawking from the curb as she drove down the street to the grocery. Jeanne smiled and said out loud, "Thank you, Auntie Boots."

It started to snow on the way home, so Jeanne drove to the barn and parked inside before she and Grandma got out of the pickup. Jeanne found Grandpa in the stall tying Polkadot to the rail. She could see the head of the calf and two legs sticking out. Eli dashed around and began tying a rope around the calf's ankles above the hooves.

"What are you doing?" Jeanne asked. She gathered their packages in her arms and stood looking at the bellowing cow.

"We're going to pull the calf," Eli explained. "The calf's too big. She's been in labor too long already. We don't want to lose them both."

"Where's Robby?" Grandma asked. "He shouldn't be in the house by himself."

"He's over there by the haystack," Grandpa said. "He's asleep, and Old Dog is with him."

Grandma hurried to Robby, gathered him in her arms, and folded the blankets around him. "We'll be in the house. We can't stay out in this weather."

"Come around here, Jeanne, and hold her head," Grandpa instructed. "Talk to her and see if you can keep her calm."

Jeanne set the packages down, squeezed into the stall, and stood at Polkadot's head. She attempted to hold her head, but the cow would have none of it. Polkadot easily shook her big head out of her grasp, so Jeanne simply talked to the cow until she saw the calf fall on the ground.

"Untie her and let her clean up her calf," Grandpa said. "She needs to bond with her baby."

Eli untied the rope, and Jeanne edged along the side and stepped around the newborn. Polkadot was licking the baby clean, and Jeanne stood outside the stall watching while mama and baby introduced themselves.

"Let's go in the house," Grandpa suggested. "We can check on them after supper."

In January, after school had started again, the Agriculture Cooperative scheduled a meeting at their farm to make decisions about spring crops. The cooperative was a collective of tenant farmers who worked for Mr. Barry Ledbetter, an attorney in Readfield. The seven-member cooperative met twice a year to discuss the best cash crops for planting. Grandpa discussed what was on the agenda at the dinner table with Eli, so Jeanne and Grandma were privy to the topics and what Grandpa wanted. Mr. Ledbetter would be in attendance for the final decision only. The men wanted a united front when they discussed what crops they would plant in the spring, so they came early for the meeting.

Jeanne was helping Grandma prepare tea cakes—lightly sweetened cookies that Grandma said went well with tea.

"Remember, Jeanne," Grandma explained, "don't call them tea cakes. The men are drinking coffee, and they might not even eat one if they thought these were served at a woman's tea."

Jeanne sprinkled sugar on top of the last batch and put them in the oven. "How could they ever resist eating one when the whole house smells so delicious?"

"Exactly."

The farmers arrived at one o'clock, and Old Dog sniffed each one. He followed them to their seats and kept an eye on them until Grandpa called the hound back to sit by the door. The hardened, leathery men filed in with somber faces, nodding to each other in a subdued manner. The atmosphere gave Jeanne the feeling that something dreadful was about to happen. She shivered and couldn't help peeking in the room from time to time to study the somber faces. She tried to catch a word or two about the discussion.

Eli and three other boys about his age were standing in the back of the room against the wall, listening. The crowded room amplified the chatter and elevated the noise to a deafening din by the time Mr. Ledbetter arrived. Jeanne pressed her ear against the kitchen door and stood motionless to listen. Grandma didn't ask her to move away but nodded to her and left the room.

"Men," she heard Mr. Ledbetter begin. "I have news from the president of the company. I'm afraid two of you did not produce what the cooperative needed this year." Mr. Ledbetter paused. "You know who you are, so I won't go into that, but the executives in Dallas are willing to give you one more year to prove yourselves, if you can show you have enough help at harvest."

"I'll go first, Tom," Grandpa offered. "We know this has been coming. You and I recognize the problems we've had are not from our lack of working. Drought and boll weevils are to blame. If you don't provide a way to control the weevils, then cotton's not the best crop to grow."

The men nodded in agreement, and the chatter stopped. They waited for Mr. Ledbetter to respond.

"I understand, Claude," Mr. Ledbetter said. "That's what I've told the Dallas bunch. This year they have agreed to corn and wheat. It seems we are sending more and more of our wheat to Europe. The war is destroying the wheat production, and they need to feed their armies."

"What are you saying about help, Mr. Ledbetter?" Eli asked. "I'm going to be on the farm to help my grandpa."

Jeanne didn't want Eli to stay and work the farm. She felt there wasn't a future for him to be a tenant farmer, and Grandpa's days were limited on the farm. Physically, it was harder and harder for him to handle the labor-intensive work. Jeanne could help, and maybe they would manage till she finished school and got a job.

"I'm glad you brought that up," Mr. Ledbetter replied. "I can't promise this, but the need is so great that we may be getting help from the government. They're sending people to work on the farms to help bring in the crops. The farms nearer the cities will most likely get the most help. I've talked to Texas legislators, and the word from Washington, DC, is that we can let kids out of school early to come help with the harvests. That's an idea they're kicking around at the moment."

"If people come from the city, where would they stay?" one of the farmers blurted out. "We don't have facilities for them."

"I think they want the nearby towns to help out," Mr. Ledbetter said. "Remember, this is only a rumor so far, but we must have experienced farmers who know what they're doing to raise the best crops."

The men began talking in small groups, but Grandpa and Mr. Ledbetter stood to the side and had a conversation of their own. Jeanne left the door and retrieved the tray of cookies when loud chatter signaled the end of the meeting. It was time to serve the tea cakes.

With Eli helping Grandpa, they would be able to stay at least one more year on the farm, maybe more. Jeanne couldn't picture Eli as a farmer, but that was the choice he had made. She had always believed he would get a college education and better his life. Survival meant changes for all of them.

Jeanne still had enough daylight to read her letters by the time Grandpa's friends and Mr. Ledbetter left. She raced up the stairs and opened the old pillowcase under her bed. She would be up late finishing her homework, but she had to read the letters again before she asked Grandma Biddy questions. She wanted to ask Eli what he thought first.

∽

Jeanne had her chance that evening when she and Eli went to the barn to check on Polkadot and her calf. The new heifer was nursing when they reached the stall. Eli forked fresh hay in the

128

stall and filled the trough with water.

Jeanne had brought the picture with her to show Eli. "Do you know who this boy is?" She handed the photograph to Eli.

Eli leaned the pitchfork against the side of the stall. He took the picture and held it closer to the lantern's light to get a better look. He stared at it for a long time before answering. "I don't know who this is. I've never seen him before. Where did you get it?"

"It fell out of one of the letters Grandma gave me. You must have read them."

"No, I couldn't. I didn't want to know. I don't want to know now." He handed the picture back to Jeanne. "Why can't you forget about this and leave it alone?"

"Because we have a brother out there, and we need to find him. It's important to me."

"It could turn out bad if we found him."

"I'm willing to take that chance. Why aren't you?"

"I don't want to talk about it anymore, Jeanne." Eli tromped off, climbed in the pickup, and drove out of the barn and down the road.

Jeanne had pushed too hard. Eli was tenderhearted, and he was still recovering from his losses. First his arm and college, and then their home. He ran away from the pressures. Like Betty Ann, like their father. Jeanne turned and observed the sleeping cow and calf. They were exhausted, and she was glad someone was at peace. She picked up the lantern and walked back to the house.

Chapter 14

For the next two months, drizzle, heavy rain, or heavy gray clouds dictated the days. Jeanne was about to go crazy. School was even dull to her. Classes had settled into a blur. She had extra work writing for the school newspaper, and she had finished her three assigned articles.

The roads had become so bad they couldn't chance driving the truck into town or even going to church. She had to walk an extra two miles to catch the school bus. She didn't mind the walk, but her shoes and socks were constantly wet and caked with red clay. Anyone who rode the bus had the same problem. The kids had stopped complaining, tired from whining about their misery.

Today was Saturday, and thunder and lightning rocked the whole house early in the day. Eli had built a fire to take the chill out of the air.

While Jeanne's spirits were low, her grandparents paraded around the house with huge smiles on their faces. Jeanne had heard the Depression stories but was too small to remember the worst of it. Grandpa said that this was the first good rain in three years.

The drought had ruined farmers in the Midwest. It was also

the reason Grandpa and his neighbors were tenant farmers. The cooperative had come in and bought all the land around when times were hardest. The crops shriveled on the stem, and grasshoppers ate whatever managed to grow. While the cooperative purchase saved the farmers and their families from starvation, they didn't own their land anymore. This rain meant crops would grow again, and the land would be saved from becoming part of the Dust Bowl. Farmers farther north had plowed their fields and exposed the topsoil to ready it for planting, only to have it picked up and blown away by fierce winds. Those high winds, the drought, and the farming techniques ruined farmers. Desperation ripped across the United States. Grandpa said half of Texas and Oklahoma was in New Mexico now. This rain gave them hope.

"Jeanne, when this storm lets up, go to the cellar and count the number of jars we have left," Grandma said. "I'm worried about the canned vegetables lasting us till we can start gathering vegetables from the garden."

"Yes, ma'am. I'll go right away."

Jeanne was distracted. Rain pelted the window and made little rivers slide down the pane. She traced her finger down one then another. She had finished reading the books she had checked out of the school library and was trying to read the family Bible that Grandma had given her to occupy her time. Robby was taking his afternoon nap, and Eli and Grandpa were in the barn. Now was the perfect time to interview Grandma about her father's letters and the picture. There had always been something going on so that she and Grandma were never alone. Today she would have that chance.

Grandma was sewing on her Singer machine, her pride and joy. Her shoulders were bent over the machine, and her head moved up and down with the movements of the treadle.

"Grandma, would you teach me to sew?" Jeanne had tried before to mend a few of their clothes, and it turned out to be a sorry lot. They wore the patched clothes anyway. It was what they had, but the dresses Grandma Biddy had made for her were nearly perfect. She wanted to sew like that.

"I want you to start with hand sewing first." Grandma pulled the material away from the sewing foot. "Come over here and let me measure this skirt on you. Then you can learn how to sew a proper hem in your own skirt." Grandma's starched cotton dress made a soft crackling noise when she turned from the sewing machine.

Jeanne left the chair by the window and took the garment from Grandma. She slipped the blue skirt over her head and wriggled it down to her waist. She remembered the day they had purchased the cloth at the dry goods store. She didn't deserve this new dress. She backed up to let the waist be adjusted.

"Don't expect this waist of yours to always be so tiny, little girl," Grandma counseled. "When you grow into a woman, things change."

"Mama has a small waist. How does she keep her waist so small?"

"Betty Ann has more up top, and that makes her waist look smaller," Grandma explained matter-of-factly. "She's always cared more about how she looks than anything else."

"I guess that won't be the case for me, since I take after my daddy." Jeanne sighed.

"There could be worse things. Your daddy is a handsome man, and you're a pretty girl, though you don't know it yet. No more of that down-in-the-mouth talk. Now, be careful when you take that skirt off, and don't lose the pins where I've marked it."

"Grandma, who's the baby in the letters that Daddy is talking about?" Jeanne asked outright. "The letter is dated before Eli was born. Where is he? Is he my big brother?"

"I wondered when you were going to get around to asking about that." Grandma took the pins out of her mouth and slowly stuck them in the red pincushion on top of the machine. She smoothed the loose wisps of hair back into her bun and looked up at Jeanne. "He's your half-brother." She let out a long sigh.

Jeanne gasped. "So he's alive. How could I have not known till now?" She backed up and stood there with the pleated skirt hanging on her arm and bare legs shaking. The room had gone silent. The fire had become ashes, and the rain had stopped. Jeanne took time to gather her thoughts and rein in her emotions. Though her grandmother's withdrawal from the conversation suggested a certain resignation to things as they were, Jeanne remained hopeful she might offer something—a clue perhaps—that would lead her to the brother she had never known.

"No reason for you to know," Grandma Biddy asserted. "Your daddy didn't want you or Eli to know. He thought it would be better that way."

"Where is he?" Jeanne asked.

"Put your clothes back on before you catch your death." Grandma tossed Jeanne's old skirt back to her and turned to her sewing machine.

"What's his name? Daddy only called him 'boy' in the letters." Jeanne could feel her anxiety rising.

"We all called him Sonny," Grandma said, not looking at her. "Betty Ann wouldn't ever name him or tell us if she did."

The cruelty stung Jeanne as if it had happened to her. She sat down with her spine against the ribs of the rocking chair, not angry at Grandma, but at her mother. *How could it be? Mama wants to punish everyone around her, and what a way to do it.* "Did you ask her?"

"Of course we did." Grandma Biddy raised her eyebrows, blinked at Jeanne once, and returned to her sewing.

While Grandma pumped the machine treadle with her right foot, Jeanne sat back and felt a little sheepish. She hadn't meant for her tone to sound so sharp. She listened to the steady rhythm of the needle pumping in and out of the fabric and tried to comprehend not giving a child a name.

Grandma sewed the pleats in place, then attached the waistband to the skirt with a precision that most people could only imagine doing. Jeanne rocked back and forth until Grandma finished the skirt. Then Grandma faced her.

"I'm ready to sew, Grandma." Jeanne wanted to make up for

lashing out at her grandma, who wasn't to blame.

"I see you are. Take this thimble. You might as well learn to use one from the beginning. It'll save you a lot of sore fingertips."

Jeanne had put in hems before, but Grandma gave her detailed instructions anyway. Jeanne moved to the chair by the window with plenty of light pouring through now that the sun was shining. She settled in and began her questions again, this time making sure to keep her voice calm. "What happened when Daddy came back to the farm with the boy?"

"That's a good place to start." Grandma nodded. "Things went along fine for a while. Pa and your daddy worked together every day, and Sonny stayed with me. He was a good boy, and like your daddy said in his letter, the child was smart."

"What did he look like?"

"Not like your daddy or your mother, if that's what you're thinking. He had blond hair and blue eyes. Under all that bleach, Betty Ann's hair is brown, like yours."

"Are you positive he's not my full brother?"

"As sure as I can be and not be the Lord up above. I don't know who the father is. No one else does either. Your mama and daddy never did speak of it. There are things you don't talk about, girl."

"Will you talk to me about the boy?"

Grandma took a slow, deep breath—the way she did when she was getting ready to say something important. "I loved the child. He was easy to love, but I knew it wouldn't last. He was calling me Biddy, and your grandpa, he called Pa. We called him Sonny. I was on the front porch shucking corn when Betty Ann came walking up to the front door. That was about six months after your daddy and the boy came back to the farm. She sat on the edge of the porch and started talking about the crops and Robert. She said, 'I'll get my baby. He's such a good boy.' Then she got up and fetched the boy from inside the house."

"Why didn't she stay away?" Jeanne asked. "She didn't want us kids. I can't tell you how many times she's come in and out of our lives just like that." Jeanne felt the anger well up inside her.

"Acting like she had been there all the time. Pretending she had talked to you just that morning."

"She has a conscience, Jeanne," Grandma Biddy remarked. "It sneaks up on her sometimes and gets so strong she has to do something to change how she feels about herself. Her pretending is how she copes with her guilt."

"When she came back that time, why did everyone here let her get away with acting like that?" Jeanne couldn't believe no one ever held Betty Ann accountable.

"We all knew what she was doing, and we were afraid she would take that sweet boy away."

"She did it anyway, didn't she?" A scripture Jeanne had read ran through her head. You had to repent to be forgiven. There was never any repentance in Betty Ann.

"Try to take it with a grain of salt," Grandma said. "You're young, and you have your whole life ahead of you."

"She takes her guilt out on me," Jeanne said. "It's hard to take that with a grain of salt."

"It was more than guilt that brought her back to the farm," Grandma explained. "She was pregnant with Eli. That was the only reason she came back. She had nowhere else to go. The next week, Eli was born here on the farm."

"What happened to the little boy, Sonny?"

A gamut of emotions appeared on Grandma's face. It seemed painful for her to dig up these old memories. "Your mother stayed here on the farm for another year after Eli was born. Then one day she went into Readfield and took Sonny with her. When she came back, she didn't have him. Wouldn't talk about it afterward. Said the boy was her son, not ours, and she'd do with him what she pleased."

"I'm sorry, Grandma. Do you think Daddy knows what happened?"

Grandma shrugged. "Maybe he does. Betty Ann was tight-lipped, and your daddy never talked about it. We didn't have a chance to find out about what happened to Sonny. Before we understood what was happening, your daddy got a traveling job, and he and Betty Ann took Eli and went to live in Deep Creek. They moved into that house you were living in there."

Chapter 15

"Beulah, we're hungry," Grandpa yelled when he came in the back door.

Jeanne heard laughing and the door banging.

"What's that commotion in there?" Grandma inquired as she got up from her sewing and went to the kitchen. Jeanne hopped up and followed.

"Well, Javier. My goodness! You're back." Grandma rejoiced with a broad smile. She went over and gave a short, wiry stranger a hug.

"His family's outside," Grandpa said. "They're in a truck and have been camping all the way here from Mexico."

"Javier, this is our granddaughter, Jeanne," said Grandma.

Javier smiled and nodded his head in Jeanne's direction. She smiled back. She had heard of Javier but had never met him or his family.

"Go on to the cellar," Grandma said, "and after you count the jars, bring in extra beans and beets. We're going to have a big dinner with Mr. Cantu and his family tonight." She hurried outside to see Javier's wife and children.

On her way to the cellar, Jeanne stopped and peeked around the corner of the house. She saw a tiny woman standing by the truck, holding a baby in her arms. She had the most beautiful black hair Jeanne had ever seen. Two girls were standing next to their mother. One was six or seven, and the other could have been Jeanne's age. Two boys standing in the back of the truck looked to be younger than Eli. Old Dog was making friends with all of them.

Jeanne ran on to the cellar, trying to stay on the tufts of grass and not step in the mud. With seven more people, their food wouldn't last long, but Jeanne was excited to have the Cantu family there.

She could hear Grandma Biddy say, "We'll manage. Don't you worry."

The cellar had a tiny square of light coming in from an inset of thick glass at the top of the wall—enough light for Jeanne to see the canning jars after her eyes adjusted. The curved cement ceiling was a few inches above Jeanne's head when she stood in the main part of the cellar. She didn't have to bend over when they hid in the cellar during a storm. She imagined adding seven more people down there, then dismissed the idea because Grandma Biddy would see to it that they would manage. Jeanne grabbed a basket at the bottom of the stairs, then swatted the cobwebs and dust away to get to the shelves. As she wiped the sticky web from her hand, spiders hurried to reconstruct their intricate webs and repair the damage.

Jeanne counted and stacked the extra jars in the basket and ran up the stairs to daylight. When she approached the front porch, Mr. Cantu and his family had pulled the loaded truck into the barn. The entire Cantu family were stacking boxes and pieces of furniture near the storage room, and Grandpa and Eli were hammering boards on the cracks in the walls. They had wasted no time in preparing a place for the Cantus to stay.

"What's happening?" Jeanne called to Eli. She hurried to the barn and set the basket down. The frenzy of activity was welcome after the days of idleness.

"Pa is fixing the storage room," Eli responded, "so Mr. Cantu and his family can have a place that's dry and out of the weather. Mr. Cantu and his boys are going to help us on the farm." Eli went back to his hammering.

"Jeanne, bring that basket to the kitchen," Grandma yelled from the back porch.

Jeanne picked up the basket and ran to the house. When she opened the kitchen door, Robby was sitting in the oldest girl's lap, and the younger girl was playing patty-cake with him. The mother was nursing her baby, and Grandma was in a cooking flurry.

Grandma smiled. "Don't just stand there. Come in and meet Mrs. Cantu. Her baby's name is Felipe, and the girls are Ana and Isabel. This is Jeanne."

"I'm Isabel. Can I help you?" The tiny girl stood on a chair to reach in the basket. Jeanne judged her to be younger than she had previously thought. She towered over her.

Together they unpacked the basket and lined the jars on the table. Isabel pointed toward a burlap sack of peppers the Cantus had brought with them.

"Rosa is going to make one of her dishes for us to go with supper tonight," Grandma said.

Rosa nodded and smiled. She said something in Spanish, and the older girl, Ana, took the baby from her mother and laid him down on a pallet in the living room.

From that time on, the women worked together like that, shoulder to shoulder, chatting constantly with a mix of English and Spanish. Rosa was like a daughter to Grandma Biddy, and Jeanne suddenly had two sisters.

The Cantu men continued to sleep in the truck bed, but the girls and the baby had beds inside. The storage room had been transformed into a rainbow. The colorful blankets spread across the beds brightened the room. It was no longer a dingy barn. Shelves on the walls held their clothes, but the cooking supplies and food were left in the truck. A firepit was built for cooking, and most evenings Jeanne and Eli joined the group around the fire.

The rain stopped long enough to get the fields planted. With the extra help, Grandma was able to enlarge her garden to twice the normal size. That next Saturday was garden-planting time. The garden was a rectangle of red dirt turned and ready for seeds. Jeanne stepped off the length and estimated the garden to be a hundred feet long. At the end, she jumped from row to row and counted the twenty furrows Eli had plowed for the day's planting.

"Jeanne, grab the wheelbarrow, and you and Ana get the seedlings off the front porch," Grandma ordered. She was all business, and everyone was excited to get the garden planted.

Grandma wore an old pair of Grandpa's bib overalls and had them rolled up to her knees, but she still wore her regular shirtwaist dress underneath. Grandma provided a bonnet for each of the girls, and they took their bonnets with loud protests and giggled all the way to the garden plot.

Jeanne was stuck with old black rubber boots to walk in the muddy parts of the garden. She tucked her long trousers inside the boots and tied her shirt at her waist. She was ready. She hung a seed bag over her shoulder that she had sewn herself. The strap angled across her body so she could be hands-free. The others had similar pieces of cloth tied across their bodies with an open pouch to carry seeds. Robby and Felipe were anchored in an improvised pen made of chicken wire. Robby had his cars to play with while the others worked.

"You and Ana take these green bean seeds to the far end of the garden and work your way back," Grandma instructed Jeanne. She poured the seeds in their pouches and sent them on their way.

The girls walked two rows at a time, planting the seeds along the trellis the plants would eventually climb. Then they retraced their steps and covered them. Grandma Biddy inspected their work, so the girls paid attention to the details to get it right the first time.

Volunteer cosmos were blooming along the border of the garden, each flower brighter orange than the last. They were Jeanne's favorite. The fresh dirt smell made her want to stop and mix mud pies like she did when she was little. That was a happy time. Her daddy was home then.

"Girls, come in for lunch," Grandma announced. Rosa was sitting with Felipe and Robby, and Grandma was headed to the shade.

"Let's go, Ana," Jeanne said.

The girls walked to the edge of the garden, jumped over the thick stand of cosmos and larkspur, and raced to the orchard.

"Ana, you're so fast. I can't catch up with you," Jeanne declared, laughing and out of breath.

They grabbed tortillas filled with meat and sat on the edge of the quilt.

"Mama is going to show us how to make pozole this afternoon when we finish planting," Ana said.

"What's pozole?" Jeanne asked. So far, she had loved the spicy dishes Rosa prepared. They all did.

"We have to make what you call hominy first," Rosa explained. She had a pile of dried ears of corn stacked on the quilt. She picked up an ear and began twisting the corn in her hands until the kernels fell into a wooden bowl.

They all started twisting till they had a stack of slim white corncobs and a bowlful of yellow kernels.

"You girls go get ashes in this bucket," Rosa said.

Jeanne and Ana shoveled ashes from the fire pit into the bucket and hurried back for Rosa to show them the next step. Ana had made hominy many times before, but they were having fun showing Jeanne.

"We'll sift the bits of charcoal out of the ashes," Rosa said. "Then we'll soak the ashes in water overnight. Tomorrow afternoon we can finish preparing the hominy to use in the pozole."

"I love pozole," Isabel squealed as she fell back in the grass and gazed at the sky.

"The peach trees are about to bloom," Grandma observed. "They love this rain. It'll be nice to have a good crop of peaches. The past few years, they've been shriveled, and we got very few of them."

"Peaches are my favorite," Isabel proclaimed.

"Everything is your favorite," her mama teased, and she tickled Isabel till her giggles echoed up through the budding peach tree branches.

⸙

Jeanne was sitting on the front porch reading under the last vestiges of light when Isabel skipped up the steps and stood by the newel post. Isabel held the edge of her skirt in one hand and wrapped the other around the spiral column. She swung back and forth in a semicircle, never taking her eyes off Jeanne. Jeanne patted a spot on the porch, and Isabel hopped over and plopped down next to her.

"What's in that book?" Isabel asked as she leaned forward with her elbows balanced on her knees.

"This is a story about a wizard and a girl from Kansas," Jeanne said. "Would you like to read it? I've read it several times."

"I can't read," Isabel said.

"I can teach you, if you want."

Isabel's face brightened. "Do you think I could learn? We move a lot, you know."

"Of course you can," Jeanne told her. "Let's make a trade."

"A trade?"

"You teach me Spanish, and I'll teach you to read," Jeanne offered. "We'll have a lesson every day when I get home from school. Then you can practice while I'm gone during the day."

"Sí, señorita." Isabel laughed. "That's your first lesson."

"We have a bargain then?" Jeanne asked.

Isabel stuck out her hand, and Jeanne took the small one. With big smiles and a handshake, they sealed the deal.

Isabel jumped up, gave Jeanne a quick hug, and ran off toward the barn. She then turned around and ran backward, shouting, "I'm going to tell my mama!"

⸙

Rosa was standing over a black cauldron of boiling water before dawn the next morning. Violet wispy clouds streaked the sky when Jeanne joined her by the crackling fire.

Jeanne looked in the pot, expecting the hominy to be ready. "How long will it be before we can eat the pozole?"

"This is only water. I need to add the strained lye water to it," Rosa told her. "Then we'll add the corn. Then stir and stir and stir and stir some more. A few hours." Rosa added more wood to the open fire.

"What's lye water?"

Ana joined them at the fire. "From the ashes we soaked last night."

"Help me with the bucket," Rosa said.

The girls lifted the bucket and poured it slowly into the black cauldron.

"I heard you made an agreement with Isabel last night," Rosa stated.

Jeanne smiled. "I did."

"She's excited about it." Rosa picked up a bowl filled with corn and added it to the mixture.

"If we go to church, who's going to stir the hominy?" Ana inquired.

"Roberto is staying here," Rosa explained. "He said he wanted to help. He can go to second mass."

Roberto joined them barefoot and shirtless. "I'll take the paddle," he offered. "You can get ready."

"Where are you going to church?" asked Jeanne. "You could go with us."

"Gracias," said Rosa, "but we go to the Catholic church in Readfield."

The Catholic church was tiny compared to the Methodist and Baptist churches in Readfield. Jeanne had seen pictures of St. Peter's Basilica in Rome. The Cantus were the first Catholics she had known. Maggie had said Catholics were going to their community church, but she didn't know who they were. She decided she would see if she could find a book about it in the library.

After Rosa and Ana left, Jeanne stood with Roberto and helped stir the corn and lye mixture. "Roberto, my father's name is Robert too."

"I know. I was named for him. He and my father were good friends. They worked on this farm together. The same as Eli and I work together now." Roberto handed Jeanne the wooden paddle so she could take her turn at stirring. He picked up a flat strainer and skimmed debris and hulls off the top.

"Did you know him?" Jeanne asked.

"I met him only one time, and I was very little."

"It's been a long time since I've seen him," Jeanne said.

"You miss him," Roberto said.

Jeanne could hear the understanding in his voice. "Yes, I do." She barely noticed that full daylight had come.

The sun was warming the morning nicely, and Jeanne was still stirring the swollen corn and skimming hulls when Grandma called her to come in and get ready for church.

Chapter 16

After school the following week, Jeanne was waiting in line to ask the librarian for primary books when Sandra Crawford strolled in and stood by the counter. Jeanne ignored her, but she caught Sandra looking at her. Jeanne didn't want trouble. She wanted to get a book for Isabel.

She told the librarian what she needed, keeping her voice low so Sandra wouldn't hear, and Miss Beatrice showed her a row of beginner books. "I think you can find something here. Take your time, dear."

After the librarian left the primary section, Jeanne kept an eye on Sandra. Her nemesis didn't have her friends with her today, but neither did Jeanne. She knelt to select a primer from the bottom shelf. Any one of these would do.

"Are you getting books for that idiot brother of yours?" Sandra's voice twanged from the shelves above. "I don't know why you're wasting your time."

"Leave me alone, Sandra." Jeanne selected a book and moved over a few feet to get away from Sandra's harping. She wouldn't be baited.

"You're the one bothering me by being here. You're nothing but trash." Sandra moved down the aisle closer to Jeanne. "Maybe you're taking our library books to those Mexicans at your place. I'll tell the principal how you're treating school property."

"Sandra, you're pathetic. What do you want? A fight with me, or a library book? Make up your mind. These shelves are protecting you now, and I don't see any of your so-called friends."

"I don't need any protection, but you will. Everybody says that simple brother of yours should be in an institution."

"You don't know what you're talking about."

"A simpleton and poor. Trash!"

Jeanne's face turned red as she stood up and stared at Sandra through an opening in the books. "That's the last time you'll open your mouth about my family," she said through gritted teeth. She slammed the readers down on the nearest shelf and tore around the rows of books toward her enemy. She ran straight at Sandra and pushed her backward over a table. The noise was startling, but Jeanne stood there glaring with her fists by her side and fire in her eyes.

Sandra sat up and quickly scooted off the edge of the table. She went running down the aisles and out the library door.

Miss Beatrice stood speechless behind the counter.

Jeanne hurried to pick up her tossed books. She marched to the counter and signed the cards inside. When she gave the cards to Miss Beatrice, Jeanne looked over her shoulder and saw that the encounter with Sandra had been hidden by the rows of bookshelves. Miss Beatrice's bewildered look verified her confusion. While Jeanne waited for her books, the librarian didn't utter a word as she stamped the books with a return date.

On the bus ride home, Jeanne sat by herself and pressed her head against the window, watching the lime green of spring flash against the pane. Perspiration trickled down the sides of her face. She rolled her cheek against the coolness of the glass. This was what anger did to her. Sandra deserved the push, but Jeanne didn't feel good about it. She had become her mother. How could she be so dreadful? Her constant desire was to not be like Betty Ann, and here she was becoming her. Would praying help her? Jeanne vowed to herself to never be that way again. She hated herself for what she had done. She was out of control. *Is it better to do nothing and let that vermin get away with her vile remarks?*

When she stepped off the bus at the mailbox, Jeanne had recovered to the point that she could walk to the farmhouse and seem normal.

"Did you get a book for me?" Isabel greeted her as she ran up the steps on the front porch.

"I did. Let me see where that is." Jeanne set her books down and spread them across the porch.

The mite of a girl jumped up and down and squealed. When Jeanne handed her the book she had checked out, Isabel threw her arms around her and hugged her with all her might.

Jeanne forgot about the encounter with Sandra and her temper. *How can I stay distraught when Isabel spreads so much joy?* Jeanne loved teaching Isabel her letters and words just as she had taught Robby numbers from cards and dominoes.

Isabel was quick to learn, and Jeanne was thrilled when Isabel's letters became words. Then words made sense and became reading. There was no stopping Isabel after that.

Jeanne continued checking out books for Isabel, and she never saw Sandra in the library again. Sandra's Twaddle Squad stayed clear of Jeanne and Becky. Jeanne had told her friends about the clash in the library. They approved, clapping and squealing at her triumph. She accepted their accolades but felt she didn't deserve any of it. She didn't share her feelings of shame with them. They wouldn't understand. How could they?

Grandpa had taken the new calf away from its mama so they could milk her for the families to have more milk and cream. Grandma churned the cream into butter. They needed all the milk they could get now that there were several more mouths to feed. It was Jeanne's responsibility to feed the calf twice a day. She went to the barn before and after school. Soon the little heifer, Daisy, followed Jeanne around like a puppy.

Their second cow, Lady Bell, was due to deliver another calf any minute. Jeanne didn't see her that afternoon around the barn, but Lady Bell would show up when it was feeding time. Jeanne finished her chores and went upstairs to complete her homework.

"Jeanne, I need you to go out and find Lady Bell," Grandma called from downstairs. "She's wandered off to have her calf, and we need to get her in before that storm gets here."

"I'm on my way," Jeanne answered as she bounded down the stairs. She grabbed her bonnet before Grandma could remind her to take it.

The minute Jeanne was out of sight, she pushed the bonnet off her head and ran down to the creek to find Lady Bell. She looked in places out of plain view where cows went to have their calves. When cows walked away from their normal grazing pastures, it was a sure sign they were going into labor. Jeanne wanted to get Lady Bell back to the barn so they could help her with the birthing. It had been a close call with Polkadot, and she had given birth several times. Lady Bell, however, was a heifer, and Grandpa had told Jeanne that a cow having a calf the first time could have problems. They needed to be nearby to help if necessary.

The day was turning dark. At first Jeanne thought it was getting close to evening and sundown, but when she looked up, a thick cover of trees blocked her view of the sky. She heard rustling in the underbrush. "Lady Bell, come out," Jeanne yelled. The brambles scratched her arms, but she found the cow's hoofprints and continued through the brush. Jeanne came out on the other side and saw where Lady Bell had walked into the creek and gone up the opposite embankment. Soon the wind picked up and it started to rain. The air around her looked green, and a chill ran down her spine. She needed to hurry and find Lady Bell and get back to the barn.

Jeanne climbed the steep incline following the errant cow's tracks. Something stung her arm and hit her on the head. White balls of hail started pelting Jeanne, and she ran for cover under a hackberry tree on the ridge. As suddenly as the hail began, it stopped. Jeanne used her high position to search her surroundings and spotted Lady Bell back across the creek trotting toward the barn. Apparently, she didn't want to be caught in the storm either. They shouldn't have worried.

The wind had died down, but the sky seemed closer and darker. Jeanne studied angry clouds churning above her head. She was sliding back down the creek bank when she was pelted with debris. Sand stung her skin. She pulled the bonnet down and tied it tightly under her chin. She started to run when she heard the roar. The roar turned into a terrible screech that came at her from the southwest. Jeanne was in the creek bottom, which was the best place she could think of for protection.

The howling surrounded her, and she fell to her knees and grabbed at a tree trunk. She wrapped her arms around the oak far enough to grasp each wrist. A black wall loomed over her. The noise was deafening. More sticks and sand beat against her body, and she could hear branches breaking. The crack sounded like gunfire. Jeanne gripped tighter.

She ducked her head and shut her eyes. Her legs flew out from under her and flapped in the wind like clothes on a line.

"Oh, God. Oh, God. Oh, God. Help me," she cried. The bonnet was stuck between her head and the trunk of the slender oak. Its ruffle blocked half her sight.

Abruptly, the wind stopped. Jeanne's legs crashed to the ground, and she slid down the tree trunk still clutching her arms. She heard her own sobs when the tornado hit her from behind. The force of the cyclone rotated her body like a human weather vane. She closed her eyes and prayed again. "Help me. Please save me from this storm, Father."

The tree glowed as if it were on fire, but Jeanne was not burned. The light surrounded her, and she floated effortlessly to the ground.

She felt the wind subside and the bright light disappear. The terrible roar moved away from her.

In the distance, she heard the cracking and breaking of tree branches. Slowly, she lifted her head and looked around her. She was holding on to the only tree still standing along the creek. Limbs and leaves were scattered everywhere. Trees were uprooted and broken in half.

With numb hands and wrists, Jeanne pried herself away from the trunk. As she stood on wobbly legs, torrents of rain beat against her. She had to move before a flash flood threatened her. With added debris from the storm, she was still in danger in the creek bottom.

Jeanne climbed the slippery embankment and started walking. Her bonnet fell back as the rain soaked her clothes. She headed home the same direction as Lady Bell when the storm hit.

Jeanne couldn't stop shivering. She was cold to the bone. Bit by bit she made her way over the downed trees and limbs. Then she heard her name.

"Jeanne! Jeanne!" Grandma Biddy was calling her.

Jeanne could see a line of people across the field. They were searching for her. She tried to call back, but the heavy rain made it impossible to see or hear. Water filled her mouth and ran into her eyes. Jeanne blinked through the rain. Finally, she could see Eli and Roberto running in the field, but when they reached her, they stopped. There were no hugs. Jeanne searched their shocked faces.

"Don't touch anything, Jeanne," Eli yelled through the downpour. "Keep walking. Don't sit." He pointed the way.

Jeanne didn't know what he was talking about, but she kept walking like he told her. Eli and Roberto walked beside her until she reached the others. They had the same shocked expression. Rosa held her rosary to her mouth and prayed. Isabel and Ana were crying.

"Jeanne, you're going to be all right," Grandma Biddy reassured her.

"Of course I am." Jeanne was confused. "What's wrong with you all?"

"Just keep walking," said Eli from behind her.

It was heaven in the barn, all warm and dry. Jeanne saw Lady Bell chewing her cud in the far stall. "Do you want me to check on Lady Bell, Grandma?" Jeanne asked.

"No, child," Grandma answered. "Stand still while Rosa and I help you."

Jeanne looked down at her arms and her hands. "My goodness, I look like a porcupine." Long, thin splinters were stuck in her arms and the backs of her hands. She was bleeding from each prick. Blood dripped from her fingertips and splashed on the straw. "I didn't notice."

"You are in shock," Grandma said. "Your back and the backs of your legs are worse. We have to get you cleaned up and warm."

Jeanne stood shivering as the women removed the largest splinters with their fingers. Grandma used tweezers to get to the smaller ones.

"We have to take out the splinters before we can get your wet clothes off," Grandma said.

Grandma called Grandpa in to set up a makeshift table for Jeanne to lie down on her stomach. He placed two planks side by side for Jeanne. When she was in place, the women continued their work. As soon as they finished with her arms, they began on her back. The shock was wearing off, and Jeanne started feeling the pain. Rosa, Ana, and Grandma Biddy made fast work of removing the splinters from her back. Isabel collected them as they were removed and put them in a bowl. She counted 573 splinters.

When Jeanne's clothes were cut away, the women used the tweezers again. It was midnight by the time they finished and covered her with a soft blanket. Grandma gave Jeanne a dose of laudanum for the pain and to help her sleep. She fetched Eli and Roberto to carry Jeanne into the house on the board where she lay. Grandma had them put her in the living room near the fireplace so she could look after her.

The next morning, the creek was running beyond its banks and prevented any work on the back forty acres. However, there was plenty to do on the main section of the farm. Daylight had the men out digging ditches to drain the flooded fields.

"Grandpa, the fields are draining," Eli said, "but the water is going into the creek. That'll make it impossible for us to cross. We won't be able to get into the field across the creek."

"It can't be helped," Grandpa stated. "We don't have a choice. We have most of our crops on this side. We'll replant that back forty."

"There's only one tree left down by the creek," Eli said. "All the others were ripped away in the tornado."

"Don't get in the water," Grandpa warned. "All those downed trees are hiding in that muddy water and will kill you."

Eli nodded. "We won't. Roberto and I can finish the main fields by ourselves. You can get Juan to help drain Biddy's garden if you need him."

Half of the garden the women had planted had washed away in the storm. The larger plants had held on but needed soil added to cover the exposed roots. Grandma Biddy was going into Readfield to see if she could get replacement plants at the feedstore.

In two days, Jeanne was able to climb the stairs and sleep in her own bed. Isabel visited her and spent more time with Jeanne reading. Robby sat with them and listened to Isabel read the Dick and Jane books. The living room was a one-room schoolhouse on the farm. Old Dog and Robby never tired of listening to the stories, and Isabel never tired of reading them.

"When do you think you'll be able to go back to the library and get the next book?" Isabel asked Jeanne. "I'm ready for the next reader."

"Grandma Biddy said I could start back Monday. I'm afraid you'll have to make do with that book until then."

The punctures on her calves were beginning to itch. Jeanne picked up a brown bottle, poured a drop on her finger, and spread pink calamine lotion over the wounds on her legs. She had to lie face down and wait for the medicine to dry before she could go downstairs. Grandma had given her a small bottle, and it helped. She could at least wear heavier clothes on her back and move around more. She was healing.

Jeanne had gone back to the creek and looked at the devastation surrounding the lone tree where she had held on with all her might. She had not forgotten her prayer. She had asked for God's help, and he had answered. Jeanne had not talked to anyone about surviving the tornado, and her family had not pressed her.

Chapter 17

Jeanne bounced out of bed on a clear and bright October morning. Today she was fifteen. No one had even remembered her birthday last year, and neither had she. So much had happened around her birthday that turning fourteen hadn't mattered to her. It seemed so long ago that she and Robby had spent that night by the river. She wasn't going to let anything sidetrack her birthday this year.

Last night at the dinner table, Eli had stood up, cleared his throat, and announced with a big grin, "Since tomorrow is Jeanne's birthday, I'm taking her to see *Gone with the Wind*." He waved the tickets in the air and looked at Jeanne. "It's in color, little sister."

Jeanne looked around the table at everyone smiling and watching her. She jumped up from the table and gave her big brother a hug. "Thank you, Eli. I don't know what to say."

She had stared at the ceiling in her room way into the night, but she was up early. She wanted to be sure her favorite blue dress was pressed perfectly, and she would take a bath and wash her hair early so her thick mane would have time to dry. Grandpa was taking her into Readfield to meet Eli at the movie theater after he got off work at five o'clock.

Readfield had a wonderful building for movies, the Majestic Theater, a perfect name. Burgundy velvet covered the seats. Two aisles ran down the sides, dividing three sections on the main floor. There was a balcony that Jeanne had hardly noticed, but Becky had told her that section was reserved for the older kids who were out of high school already. They went up there and smooched. Her friend Maggie was out of high school, and Jeanne would ask her about the balcony. She guessed that put Eli in that category. Had her brother gone up those back stairs and watched the movies from up there? Jeanne was curious about the balcony, but she didn't want that experience today. She was going to sit with her friends, smack in the middle of the main section. She didn't want to miss a thing.

Past Saturdays when the Bradshaw family made their weekly trip to Readfield, Jeanne had strolled down the street past the Majestic Theater and read the posters out front. *Gone with the Wind* was coming. Even though movies ran several months later in Readfield than they premiered in larger cities, it didn't matter to people in West Texas. It was a first-run movie to them.

Jeanne had only been to the Majestic Theater once before, and that movie was a Western, *'Neath the Arizona Skies* with John Wayne. She fell in love with the whole experience, the characters, the story, the action, the dialogue. The screen was black and white, but she didn't care. When the lights were turned down, she was immersed in the story. Jeanne was there suffering with the half-Indian girl, Nina, looking for her white father. She was the one rescued by Chris Morrell, the handsome cowboy. Jeanne forgot everything else while the movie was playing.

Grandpa parked on the square, and Jeanne walked the block to the movie theater. Becky was in line with Barbara and Nancy. All three waved and motioned for her to come stand with them.

"I'm waiting for Eli," Jeanne said. "He already has my ticket. He got it for my birthday."

"You lucky girl!" Becky exclaimed. "Do you think Eli will sit with us? He's so handsome."

"Don't be so forward, Becky!" Nancy scolded. "That's Jeanne's brother."

"It's not like you haven't told me a million times how cute you think he is," Becky fired back.

Nancy turned beet red. "I know," she admitted, and they started giggling.

Jeanne laughed with them. Eli always had girls interested in him. He wasn't only tall and good-looking. He was a good person.

"What are you girls laughing about?" Eli startled them.

The girls were struck dumb and stood there wide-eyed. Nancy put her hands over her mouth as if she might say something she shouldn't.

"Oh, I'm glad you're here," Jeanne said. She whirled around to see Eli and Daniel standing there.

"Hello, Jeanne," Daniel said. He nodded to the girls behind her. "Hello, ladies."

Jeanne considered the two young men standing before her. They were a contrast, and they had become good friends working at the grocery together. Her brother's dark features, black straight hair combed back, and eyes as black as a moonless night were only highlights to his smile that brightened the day. He stood six feet four, and his presence commanded attention when he walked into a room. No wonder the girls were crazy for him. On the other hand, Daniel was much more serious. He was close to six feet, and his hair was a curly golden blond. He had more of a little-boy face with dimples and a scattering of freckles. His best feature was his eyes. They sparkled. Sky blue twinkled at everyone. Yes, it was Eli's smile and Daniel's eyes. One day, some girl would be lucky to get either one as far as she was concerned.

"We need to go in and find a seat, since we have our tickets," Eli said. He waved them in the air and walked to the line with people who already had tickets.

Jeanne waved to her friends and followed Eli and Daniel to the ornately carved front doors. They both stepped back and bowed.

"After you, birthday girl," said Daniel.

Eli led the way into the dark theater and located three seats in the middle. Jeanne went in first and stopped at the center. She sat and leaned back in the chair, closed her eyes, and breathed in the heavy aroma of popcorn. When she opened her eyes, she could see in the dim lighting. A heavy velvet curtain hung in front of her and stretched across the screen. It matched the upholstery on the chairs. Huge sconces hung on the walls and gave enough light to see on the far sides of the aisles.

There in the dim light she saw her friend Maggie, and Jameson was walking behind her. Jeanne's stomach did a flip. She would not let that creep ruin this day. She wouldn't ignore Maggie, but she didn't have to speak to Jameson. The friendship with Maggie had cooled since the Christmas program nearly a year ago. She missed her friend, but she couldn't bring herself to confess what had happened with Jameson. Maggie had tried to set up another date with her cousin, but Jeanne always said she had to study. Maggie finally gave up.

"Have some popcorn." Daniel sat down on the other side of her. He passed the sack of buttery goodness, and they all had their mouths full when the music started. The story of the Civil War unfolded in front of Jeanne in extravagant Hollywood-style. She was mesmerized by the beautiful people, loving and suffering, whirling around her.

In just over three short hours, the movie was over. For days and even weeks, Jeanne figured she could escape her world by daydreaming about Rett and Scarlet, the land, and the terrible war. She could hardly wait to tell her grandma about the dresses and how everything was in color.

Jeanne listened to the crowd talking about the movie. They were pouring out of the theater in a buzz. Eli and Daniel stopped to talk to two other guys. Jeanne turned when Becky and the girls ran up to her and started speaking all at once.

"Jeanne, you can wait here and talk to your friends," Eli told her. "Daniel is going to take us home. We'll be back in a minute with his car. We have to take care of business at the grocery first."

Eli and Daniel took longer than she expected. The movie crowd had dispersed, and Jeanne waited with her friends.

"Will you be all right, Jeanne?" Becky asked. "We have to get home. I told Mama we would be home right after the show. She'll be getting worried."

"I'll be fine. You all go on now," Jeanne said. "Eli said he would be back, and if he said it, he meant it."

"If you're sure?" Nancy said.

"I'm sure." Jeanne laughed. "It's not dark yet. This is Readfield, after all."

Jeanne's friends walked down the street and around the corner out of sight. She returned to the movie poster behind the glass windows and read the names of the stars again. She wanted to memorize the names and didn't mind waiting alone. It gave her a chance to daydream about the movie.

A few stragglers were still filtering through the front door of the theater. Conversations were quieter but nevertheless happy. Jeanne was smiling to herself when she sensed someone standing next to her.

"Hello, Jeanne," Betty Ann said. "Did you enjoy the movie?"

For a moment Jeanne didn't recognize her mother when she turned to look at her. Rumpled and dirty, her mother reeked of alcohol and body odor. She recognized the voice all right, but the woman who stood before her barely resembled the Betty Ann she knew.

"Hello, Mama," Jeanne said. "I did enjoy it." She waited for her mother to make a cutting remark.

"How did you get money to come to the movies?" Betty Ann asked. "Your grandma and grandpa don't have any money."

"Eli brought me." Jeanne wasn't going to mention that today was her birthday. Her mother would find a way to ruin it. She watched Betty Ann's eyes searching wildly for Eli.

"I've seen Eli working in the grocery store," Betty Ann said.

"He gives me money sometimes. Did he tell you he talked to me?"

Jeanne was too hurt to respond. *Why didn't he tell me about seeing Mama in town? He even gave her money.*

Betty Ann smirked. "I can tell by the look on your face that he didn't say anything to you. He's my good boy. He did just what I told him."

"Are you living in Readfield? I haven't seen you around on Saturdays when we come into town." Jeanne's attempt to talk about something else didn't work.

"I was walking by and saw you sashay out of that movie door," Betty Ann said. "You were really having the time of your life talking to those girls. Who are they?"

"Friends from school," Jeanne answered. She looked for Daniel's car, but there were no vehicles on the street.

"You should have a boyfriend by now." Betty Ann sneered at her. "Why, I had three or four boyfriends when I was in high school. Everybody wanted a date with me, even one of the teachers. You should have a boyfriend taking you to the movies, not your brother. You're pathetic."

Jeanne didn't react to Betty Ann's familiar tirade about how Jeanne fell short. She looked at her mother now. Her hair was so yellow and dyed, half the hair on her head had broken off in places. Jeanne scanned the rest of her mother to find a dirty dress and shoes and stockings with holes in them. Soiled gloves covered her hands, and a black shawl with fringe was thrown around her upper body. While they were standing there, Betty Ann pulled the shawl tighter and tied a faded scarf around her head. She patted her head while she tried to push stray hairs underneath the scarf and out of sight.

Jeanne felt sorry for her. "Are you all right, Mama?" She tried not to wince at the strong sour smell coming from her mother—the same smell when she had been drinking and hadn't bathed in some time. Jeanne had always been the one to sober her up and get her back on her feet. *Should I try to help her?*

"Don't you give me that look." Betty Ann pulled the shawl

close around her neck. "I can still teach you a lesson or two. I ought to slap you silly." Betty Ann flexed her gloved fingers and moved toward Jeanne.

She backed away from her mother and started walking toward the town center. She had to get away from Betty Ann.

"Don't you walk away from me!" Betty Ann screamed. "I'm your mother. I can do what I want. Come back here!" She took a few steps toward Jeanne and then hurried away from the movie theater.

At the corner, Jeanne looked back over her shoulder and saw that her mother was gone. No one was standing in front of the Majestic Theater. Jeanne continued on and stopped at a streetlight that had just come on. She waited there to catch her breath. The square was quiet. The shops were closed, and the sky was a darker blue. Evening would come down in minutes. Jeanne walked to a bench in front of the courthouse and sat down just as a car drove up beside her.

Eli jumped out of the passenger side. "Hop in, sis. I thought you were going to wait at the movies."

"My friends were expected at home and left, so I decided to walk on to meet you." *I wonder what happened to Mama.* Betty Ann's remarks were empty and had no power, and for the first time, Jeanne was not shattered by her mother's insults.

She sat back in the seat and let the new feeling wash over her on the bumpy trip home. She let the conversation between Eli and Daniel drift into the background and tried to recapture the euphoric aftermath of *Gone with the Wind.*

Chapter 18

Ears of corn had dried on the stalk, and the wheat swayed golden in the fields. Harvest was upon the farm. Grandma Biddy stood on the back porch with a wooden spoon in her hand and waved at Grandpa Claude and the kids in the back of the truck. They were the corn crew. Three boys and three girls were working the corn rows.

Grandpa dropped the six at one end of the field so they could work their way to the other end pulling the ears off the stalks. "Take your time and don't miss any ears," he said. "We need every one of them." Then he drove to the other side to wait for them.

"Let's get started," Eli shouted. "The sun is coming up and we can see."

They wore big sacks over their shoulders and gloves to keep the dried husks from cutting their hands to pieces. When they made it to the end of the row, they dumped the ears in the back end of the truck. When the truck filled, Grandpa took the load back to the barn and dumped the load in the bins to dry. The same routine was repeated from morning till night.

Right away, little Isabel struggled to reach the top ears. One of her brothers or Eli went back to help her when he finished his row.

"Hey, squirt," Eli said. "Need help?"

Even little girls loved her big brother. Jeanne didn't tell Eli that she had seen Betty Ann. *Like Eli didn't tell me about giving Mama money.*

The youngsters worked in the cornfield while Mr. Cantu pulled the cutter with Grandpa's horse, Buck. The speckled gray had a comfortable life most days, but he worked hard during planting season and harvest, and it took a couple of weeks for Buck to get used to pulling. The cooperative shared a horse named Pretty Boy who was in better shape than Buck. Pretty Boy worked every day. The glimmering chestnut was a pretty boy, and old Buck was jealous. He turned to biting when they were hitched together. It took a strong hand to control the two horses.

Mr. Cantu was firm and was able to harness the horses to the cutter and walk them to the wheat field without trouble. While he cut the wheat, Jeanne and the others worked the cornrows till the middle of the afternoon. All except Isabel would then walk to the wheat field to stack the shocks of wheat. The older kids could catch up with Mr. Cantu's cutting by the end of the day.

Jeanne and Ana worked with Juan in one row building a stook from the sheaves, while Eli and Roberto teamed up on the next row.

Jeanne could see they were keeping a similar pace. "Let's beat them to the end," she whispered, pointing to the finish.

Juan nodded and elbowed his sister to pick up the pace. At first, the two older boys didn't notice their hurrying until Eli saw Jeanne begin to run.

"You're energetic for the end of the day," Eli observed.

"Oh, just stretching," Jeanne replied nonchalantly.

"Be sure you have eight sheaves stacked over there." Eli stopped to watch the trio hurrying to fix the bundles of wheat into A-frames. "What are you doing?"

"I think I know," yelled Roberto. "Come on, Eli. Pick up the pace!"

"I see what's going on here," said Eli. "The battle's on now."

Ana squealed and started running. They raced down the row building stook after stook. Eli and Roberto, carrying a sheaf under each arm, overtook their younger siblings. They sat at the end of the row laughing and waiting for the others to finish.

"Nice try, but it will be a long time before you can beat men at their job," Eli bragged.

"We almost had you," said Jeanne.

"Not a chance," Eli asserted. "The losing team gets to finish up. Come on, Juan. You need to be with the winning team. Let's go to the barn."

The girls waited for Mr. Cantu to finish the last row. They didn't mind stacking the few sheaves left. Jeanne and Ana liked to watch the blades slice the wheat near the ground and pass the stalks back to be tied before being thrown to the ground behind the machine.

Scooping up the rich black dirt and letting it sift through her fingers, Jeanne looked at the golden glow of the approaching sunset and thought of the land. Is land that important? Grandpa was a tenant farmer, a sharecropper. The words sounded derogatory, but she had never been ashamed. Grandma Biddy had told her no one was any better than anyone else, and if you did a good day's work, you should hold your head up high and be proud. Jeanne believed that too. It felt good to look back and see the work she had done that day.

Mr. Cantu waved to the girls and turned the horses back toward the barn and the house. Jeanne and Ana walked to the last row to stack the last wheat teepees to dry.

Jeanne and Ana wanted to clean up before dinner and decided to take a bath in the creek. Grass and wheat were in their clothes, and Jeanne couldn't stop itching. They told Rosa they were going to the creek, but Rosa insisted Juan go and keep watch for them.

"Hurry up," Juan kept yelling over his shoulder. "I'm starving."

"We just got in," said Ana. "You're not going to die."

"We won't be long," Jeanne assured him. "It's freezing in here."

The minute the sun had set, the girls had privacy, but the temperature had dropped. In a few minutes, they had had enough and got out and dressed.

"It's about time," said Juan when they appeared on the trail with their hair dripping. They carried their shoes with them.

"Something could have eaten us, for all you care." Ana dashed around her brother and on to the barn.

"Not so fast," he said as he raced after her and disappeared into the barn behind her.

Jeanne ran up the steps to the back porch and through the kitchen door. She was greeted by her family gathered around the table.

"Have a seat," said Grandma Biddy. "You're in time for the blessing. Why don't you say it tonight?"

"I don't know what to say." Jeanne was still shivering and wanted to slip into her seat and start eating.

"Sure you do," Eli encouraged. "You've heard it a million times."

"Okay then." Jeanne stretched out her hands and held on to Robby's hand with one and Grandma Biddy's with the other. "Lord, thank you for your bounty, and bless this food to the nourishment of our bodies, and our bodies to your service. In Jesus's name, amen."

"See there," Grandma said. "You did just fine."

"Next time, we need to pray for those poor souls at war in Europe," Grandpa said.

"Is it that terrible over there?" Eli asked while he spooned a heap of potatoes onto his plate.

"Be thankful that we have enough to eat," Grandma said, looking at the mounds of food on Eli's dish.

"I am, I am," Eli assured everyone as he looked around the table. "Is that why the Cantus are worried? Their families in Mexico are suffering. They don't have enough food."

Jeanne couldn't believe she had said the blessing at the table. Adults were supposed to pray in front of people. She was learning to do things she would have never done if they had stayed in Deep Creek. She was beginning to sew. Grandma was letting her put the hems in things now. Soon she would be able to make a whole garment. Rosa had taught them how to make hominy for pozole, and today she built a stook. *What will I learn next?*

The diners were quiet.

Jeanne looked up from her plate to see her family busy eating. "How long does it take for the wheat to get dry enough?" she asked.

"That depends on the weather," Grandpa said. "I hope it stays dry for a few days. Threshing shouldn't take too long."

"I have news for everyone," said Grandma. She looked at Eli and Jeanne. "I got a letter today from your daddy."

Jeanne was so surprised by the news that she couldn't speak.

"What did it say?" Eli asked.

"It's been a few months getting here to the farm," Grandma said. "Why don't you read it out loud, Jeanne?" Grandma handed the letter to her.

Everyone gathered in the living room around the fireplace. Jeanne sat on the hearth and removed the delicate paper from the envelope. Her hands trembled from anticipation. She looked out to see eager faces staring back at her. Even the Cantus had joined them. Jeanne began.

August 9, 1940

Dear Mama,

I'm sitting here on a cot with thirty other men in the bunkhouse. We are working on a construction site in California. You should see the Pacific Ocean. It beggars description, so big and so blue. I'm sorry I haven't written in a long time. I hope you and Pa are all right on the farm. I guess you have canned a lot and put up food for the winter. I wish I could have a big piece of your corn bread. Ha! Ha! Have you heard from Betty Ann and the kids? I miss everyone. The good news is, I can be home for Christmas.

Your son,

Robert

"Well, we'll see," Grandma Biddy said as she got up and walked into the kitchen.

"He hasn't gotten my letter," Jeanne said with dismay. "He's in California, and I sent mine to Oklahoma." She wanted to will her letter to find her father, but she had no control over it. *What can I do?*

"It might catch up to him if the post office forwards it," Grandpa said. "It hasn't been returned to us, so there's a chance he'll get it."

Jeanne looked at Grandpa. "Do you think he'll come for Christmas?"

"Maybe he will," Grandpa said as he got up from his chair.

Quiet talk lingered in the room. Eventually everyone drifted out and went to bed.

Jeanne still struggled with her disappointment. It crushed her spirit, but finally she folded the letter and slipped it back in the envelope. She picked up Robby, already in his pajamas, and sat in Grandma's rocking chair. Jeanne held him on her lap and sang a lullaby until he was asleep. She looked at his sweet face. He wouldn't even know Daddy, if he did come for Christmas. Grandpa had said he might come. That was something. She nodded in the chair with Robby close and warm. She opened her eyes when Eli took Robby and carried him to his cot.

"You can go to bed now, Jeanne," Eli said.

She smiled at her two brothers, rocked forward, then rose from the chair. She was tired. She climbed the stairs to add her father's latest letter to the others. This was a letter of hope.

Jeanne walked into the kitchen still in her gown. "What's happening? What's that noise? It's not sunrise yet."

Grandma was taking biscuits out of the oven.

Jeanne went to the back door to see the Cantus loading their truck.

Rosa came up the steps and met Jeanne at the door. "We're going back to Mexico," Rosa said, "to be with the rest of my family for Christmas."

Jeanne was stricken. "When are you coming back?"

Nobody answered. Neither Ana nor Isabel had mentioned leaving. *Maybe the girls are surprised too.* They were part of her family, and she hadn't even imagined them leaving. She fought off tears.

"Go get dressed, young lady," Grandma ordered. "You can't say goodbye in your gown tail."

"But . . ."

"No buts. Get," Grandma said. "You need to help me pack food for their trip." She turned and put another batch of biscuits in the oven.

Jeanne nodded to Grandma and ran up the stairs. As she dressed, she grabbed a book and writing paper from her bedside table. She scribbled notes and stuffed them in her skirt pocket.

Back downstairs, everyone was rushing in the early dawn. Jeanne could feel the excitement, but she was still in shock. She and Grandma had packed biscuits and ham, along with apples and pears from the cellar.

"What's in the barrels?" Jeanne asked. Giant wooden barrels were tied on the sides of the truck.

"That's our water," said Ana. "It should last us for the whole trip."

Roberto walked up and tied gourd dippers to the iron handles on the lids. They looked worn and perfect for their job. "Hand up that tow sack," he shouted from atop the loaded truck bed.

Eli tossed the stuffed burlap bag to his friend. The truck couldn't possibly hold one more thing, much less people. Then the motor rumbled to life, and the Cantu family began piling on the heavily laden truck.

"Here's something for you along the way." Grandma handed food to the boys on the back, then she passed another sack to Rosa and the baby riding in the cab.

"Gracias, señora," Rosa replied.

Jeanne saw their hands clasped together through the window. She felt the strong bond of love and friendship the women shared, and she suddenly remembered her letters and the book. "Wait! Isabel, I want you to have this book." Jeanne handed it up to the tiny girl she had taught to read.

"Thank you, thank you!" Isabel reached out and clutched the book to her chest.

"It may be hard for you now," Jeanne explained, "but you'll be able to work out the words. Keep practicing."

Isabel wrapped her arms around Jeanne's neck and gave her a fierce hug.

"Isabel, let's go," her father said. "You need to sit down."

Slowly Isabel let go and found her place among the boxes. Still hugging her book, she scooted in beside her sister.

Jeanne pulled out the notes she had written and handed them to Ana. Ana smiled at her and waved goodbye with the pale blue paper flapping in her hand. As Jeanne backed away from the truck, it rolled forward. She heard the gears grind into place and watched the small band leave through the gate and roll down the road with a curl of orange dust trailing. Jeanne stood there hanging on to the farewells. She had endured so many. She waited till the powdery cloud from the road had completely settled before she turned away and went back into the house for breakfast.

Chapter 19

Only three weeks remained before school was out for Christmas vacation. Jeanne was still melancholy and missing the Cantu family, especially during Thanksgiving. She hoped her daddy would be home for Christmas.

The day was sunny and pleasant as Jeanne walked home from the bus stop. A black Model T was parked in front of the house. A gold emblem on the car door shone in the afternoon sun. As Jeanne got closer, she could make out a star with *Sheriff* written across the middle. *What's going on?* she wondered.

A man in khakis stood on the front porch. He clutched his hat to his chest with his head bowed as he listened to Grandma. Her face was oddly twisted in concern.

Jeanne began to run, her heart pounding. She skidded to a stop, and both adults looked at her. "What is it? What's wrong?" she asked, out of breath.

"I need to get goin', ma'am," the officer said. "Tell Mr. Bradshaw to come to the office this evening. I'll be there." The man dipped his head first to Grandma, then to Jeanne. He stepped off the porch and got in his car.

Jeanne was nervous. "What's happened?"

Grandma raised her palm toward Jeanne to wait. "Come sit on the porch with me."

Jeanne followed, wiping the perspiration off her forehead. She sat on the bench with her books and looked at her grandma for an answer.

"That was about Betty Ann. She's in the jail in Readfield."

"What happened? Why is she in jail?" Jeanne remembered the night Mr. Morrison was in front of their house. Was he the cause? She hadn't spoken of the incident to Grandma or Grandpa.

"The sheriff said she was picked up last night with a bunch at the juke joint north of town."

"Did I hear someone say jail?" Grandpa asked as he stepped onto the porch.

"Sheriff Brown came by this afternoon," Grandma explained. "He says Betty Ann's got herself in trouble and thrown in jail."

"Why did he come *here*?" Eli asked.

Jeanne hadn't noticed that Eli had walked up until he spoke. She was sick at the news and leaned against the wall for support.

"He wants your grandpa to come and pay her fine before she gets charged for a crime."

"What crime?" Jeanne asked, sitting up straight again.

"I don't know," Grandma said. "Claude, we need to at least find out what trouble Betty Ann has gotten herself into this time."

"I'll go," Grandpa stated.

"I'm coming with you," Eli said. "I'll bring the truck around."

"How much money you got in the coffee can, Beulah?" Grandpa asked. "We may have to pay a fine or post bail. I don't know how much that might be."

Grandma got up from her rocker and went to the kitchen to get the only cash they had. "Jeanne, come and get Robby," she called from the house. "He's up from his nap."

In minutes Jeanne and Grandma joined Grandpa on the front porch.

Grandma reached out and put folded bills in Grandpa's hand. Then she placed her hand over his closed fist and gave it a final pat. "Do what you can. That's fifty dollars. I'm afraid that's all we have."

"I don't know what the sheriff expects us to do." Grandpa ran his fingers through his thick gray hair. "I really don't." He stormed across the yard to the truck.

"I want to go too," Jeanne begged. She balanced Robby on her hip and looked at her grandpa.

Grandpa hesitated at the pickup door. He looked at Grandma.

"Let her come, Pa," Eli said. "She has a right to know."

"Come on, then." Grandpa held the door.

Jeanne handed Robby to Grandma and ran to the truck. She slid to the middle of the seat. She was penned in between Eli and Grandpa. It was tight but better than riding in the back.

Even though Eli had lobbied for her to go, Jeanne had to sit in the truck while Eli and Grandpa went in the jail. They had been in there for half an hour. She was getting antsy, and it was getting dark outside. The lights were coming on in the jail. She saw silhouettes and recognized Eli.

Jeanne jumped out of the truck and walked up to the jail door. She could hear voices as she eased the door open. There was a small foyer before the main room opened, so she slipped through the heavy outside wooden door and stood back behind the inside door. She eavesdropped, hoping to get some answers.

Jeanne heard her mother shouting. "I'm not going with you, Claude Bradshaw."

"Suit yourself, Betty Ann," Grandpa responded. "You have to go somewhere, 'cause if you don't, you'll stay here in this jail."

The sheriff spoke next. "He's paid your fine, but if you don't have a home to go to, then you're considered a vagrant."

Through the slit in the doorway, Jeanne could see her mother's back and the sheriff. If she tried to open the door farther, they would certainly see her standing there. She consciously stepped back instead of giving in to the urge to go into the office and make a spectacle of herself.

"Do you know anyone in town?" the sheriff asked.

"Nobody I'd stay with," Betty Ann said. "Let me get on the train and leave this place."

"Where will you go, Mama?" Eli sounded worried. "How will you take care of yourself?"

"Don't worry, son," Betty Ann said. "Just get me on that train out of here. I don't care where."

"There's a nine o'clock train leaving Snyder for Roscoe," the sheriff said. "From Roscoe, she can catch the Texas and Pacific to El Paso."

"We could drive her to Snyder and make it by nine o'clock," Eli suggested. "I'll take her."

The group started moving toward the door. Jeanne left the foyer, ran to the pickup, and waited. The three men and Betty Ann filed out of the jail and walked toward the truck.

Betty Ann stopped. "What is Jeanne doing here? I—"

"We'll have none of that," Grandpa snapped. He faced Betty Ann, looking her square in the face. "We're doing you a favor, woman. You can stay here, remember." He paused, his angular body standing erect. No one moved, but the wind howled around the corner, adding its snarl to Grandpa's iron will.

The gust blew his thick hair into a prickly crown that made Betty Ann step back. "All right," she acquiesced, then mumbled, "I didn't want her to see this."

Grandpa ignored her and continued to the driver's side of the truck. "Eli, grab the quilt from the cab. You and Jeanne ride in the back."

"Yes, sir," Eli responded.

Jeanne didn't speak. She followed her brother, who climbed in the back with the quilt. She looked back at Betty Ann as her mother was closing the passenger door.

∾

Eli didn't talk on the drive to Snyder. Jeanne understood why, and she sat quietly with her own thoughts thrashing about on the way. Even though the quilt was large enough to wrap around them and over their heads, Jeanne was freezing by the time the truck slowed coming into Snyder. Nevertheless, she peeled back the top and looked up to see the railroad tracks running beside the highway. The pickup finally pulled into the depot, and Jeanne hopped out and looked at the station sign. *Roscoe, Snyder and Pacific Railway Station.* Her mother walked into the station without saying a word. Eli followed her. Jeanne waited in the freezing weather until she could stand it no longer.

Inside the warm ticket office was heaven. Jeanne rubbed her hands together while she searched the nearly empty room. The only other travelers were a couple and their baby who sat on a wooden bench near the door. Jeanne looked at the mother, whose youthful face was childlike. She was Jeanne's age. Her own mother peered out of the side window, staring at the platform where several passengers waited. They were dressed in their Sunday best. Betty Ann tugged on her jacket. She stood to the side and faced away from Jeanne and the ticket window, looking out at the train. Her fancy red purse hung on her arm, and the same black shawl hung on her shoulders. Jeanne was embarrassed for her.

The clock above the station clerk said 8:50. Just as Jeanne read the time, a deafening blast from a train whistle blew. The black giant thundered into the station, snorting and blowing. The sleeping baby began to cry.

Grandpa shouted for the clerk to hear him. "Yes, to El Paso." Grandpa shoved the money across the counter and checked the station for Betty Ann.

Jeanne walked over to her mother. "I heard you say you didn't want me to see this. What did you mean by that?" She, too, studied the enormous steam engine instead of her mother.

Betty Ann turned her head away. "Don't go making anything out of it."

"What happened? Why were you arrested, Mama?"

Her mother took a deep breath and sighed. "You know I don't answer to anybody, especially you. You're my kid, and you should be answering my questions." She wasn't nasty, but resigned in her remarks.

Jeanne saw a flood of defeat wash over her mother. "I know," she said. "I'm not judging you, but I need to know."

"It was the same as other nights—drinking and dancing and such. Two men got in a fight over me, and I ended up in the middle of a knife fight. One was wounded. I think he's in the hospital."

"Why did the sheriff let you go?"

"He went to school with your daddy. He was doing a favor for him."

Jeanne contemplated whether to tell her mother about the letter from her father. At the last minute, she decided to let her know. "Daddy may be coming to the farm by Christmas."

"How do you know that?"

"Grandma Biddy got a letter from him. He's in California."

"Don't count on it. He was always good at making promises and not keeping them."

"I read the early letters Daddy wrote to Grandma." Jeanne's words hung there.

The look on her mother's face told Jeanne what was coming. Betty Ann's mouth spread into a thin grimace, and her eyes squinted through the steam's mist.

Jeanne gathered her courage. "Who is Sonny, Mama?"

"You don't need to know."

"But I do need to know. Is he my brother? My half-brother?"

"I think you know that he's your brother," Betty Ann said. "I won't tell you who he is."

"Why not?"

"He has a good life, and at least one of my children will have advantages. I won't tell you. You would go and ruin everything for him. Let it alone."

"Here's your ticket," said Grandpa. "The train leaves in five minutes. Let's go."

"Do you know anybody in El Paso, Mama?" Eli asked.

"I do, sweet boy." Betty Ann smiled at him and ruffled his hair. She turned and faced Jeanne, her smile fading. She touched Jeanne's shoulder, then walked past the conductor and nodded to Grandpa. She stepped on board and called to them. "Don't you worry, now. I can take care of myself." She vanished into the passenger car.

"All aboard!" announced the conductor. The train whistle blew, and Jeanne covered her ears. The steam hissed, and the iron monster began to turn its wheels. The trio waited there on the wooden platform until the engine moved down the track toward Roscoe. Jeanne scanned the windows passing by, but Betty Ann didn't appear.

Chapter 20

The old pickup bounced along with silent riders on the way to church the next morning. Robby napped in Grandma's lap. He was the only content member of the family. Jeanne was in the middle, straddling the gears as she had on the road the night before. Eli sat in the open truck bed with the food Grandma had cooked for the church potluck dinner.

Grandpa leaned over the steering wheel, slumping against it while he drove. Exhaustion nagged him. "Polkadot didn't give much milk this morning," he said. "I hope she isn't going dry." He awkwardly ground the gears, having trouble shifting in the crowded cab.

"I can shift for you, Grandpa," Jeanne said. She reached with both hands and moved the gear shift into place when Grandpa stepped on the clutch.

"Can we buy that Jersey cow from the cooperative?" Grandma asked. "I could use more cream than we get from Polkadot's milk."

"I'll see Mr. Ledbetter at church this morning. I'll ask him." Grandpa stared ahead, concentrating on something in the distance.

"Do we have enough hay for another cow?" Jeanne asked.

"We have plenty of hay," Grandpa said. "I'm more worried about finding a bull when Polkadot and Lady Bell come into heat."

Jeanne glanced up at her grandpa. He had dark circles under his eyes, and he looked even thinner than he usually did. He had gotten up early and milked both cows. He had let Eli and her sleep. Last night was an ordeal that had taken its toll on all of them.

"We're lucky the weather is warm enough for us to have dinner outside," Grandma said. "It's a mess when we have to eat inside and hard to clean."

"December is the latest we've ever had a church potluck," Jeanne said, "but I'm glad. I'm starving."

Grandpa parked on the far side of the church between the Watkinses' forest-green Dodge and the cemetery gate. Grandpa and Eli always stopped to behold the sleek, four-door sedan with the wide white walls and the ram hood ornament. Jeanne loved to look at the car too, but she couldn't linger today. She heard the piano playing the opening. She rushed in and made her way to the back of the church just in time to line up with the choir before they were seated. No one looked askance at her. Hopefully no one knew of their nighttime jaunt to the train station in Snyder.

"Why were you late this morning?" Maggie whispered. "Jameson is back in town. He wants to see you. What do you say? Want a date?" Maggie hurried to the other side of the church with the sopranos before Jeanne could answer.

Jeanne shrugged and shook her head in the direction of her friend. She hadn't thought of Jameson for months, but the mention of his name sent chills down her spine. She had sidestepped Maggie's questions about him. It seemed Maggie didn't want to give up on her matchmaking. *She's going to keep pestering me until I give a definitive answer.* If Jeanne had a boyfriend, maybe the questions would stop, but she didn't. Maggie didn't go to Readfield High School with Jeanne, so she only saw her at choir practice and Sundays. Jeanne didn't know where Jameson lived and why he visited Maggie's family at Christmas. He was early this year.

Miss Mary tapped on the lectern, and Jeanne snapped to attention. The choir sang "Blest Be the Tie That Binds." The men's quartet harmonized on several old gospel songs. When they were finished, Jeanne tiptoed to sit with her family. She glimpsed Jameson watching her on the way to the pew. Feeling his eyes on her throughout the service made Jeanne miserable and anxious to leave.

The potluck dinner was well underway when the crowd heard a siren blaring on their country road. Forks and spoons stopped midair, and groups of men turned to look in the direction of the sound. A black car with a red flashing light came tearing up the dusty road at full speed. The car slid to a halt, and Sheriff Brown jumped out and marched toward the crowd, obviously in a panic. A loud buzz arose from the tables, and Pastor Wilson walked toward the sheriff as he rushed forward.

Jeanne's heart sank. She was sure it had to do with Betty Ann. She looked for Eli, but she couldn't find him anywhere. Then she spotted Grandpa standing with a group of the elders on the opposite side of the tables, as far away from her as he could possibly be. She wanted to run to him. The sheriff was headed straight for the group of men. Eli was standing with them.

"Afternoon, Sheriff Brown," the preacher said. "What's wrong?"

"I need to talk to you," the sheriff said. They stepped into the circle of men.

Jeanne left the food line and eased her way over to Grandma Biddy. Grandma was seated near the men. She was holding Robby on her lap and helping him with his dinner. Conversations had ceased. The crowd was waiting for the sheriff to tell them what had happened. The children began to play and run around on the grass. Other men left their places at the tables and walked over to join the group.

"Where's your plate?" Grandma said. "Aren't you hungry? It's after two o'clock."

Jeanne pointed to the men. "I came to see why the sheriff is here."

The men leaned in to hear what the sheriff had to say. Shouts and loud voices shocked the crowd, and they stopped eating and stared at the group. The pastor placed his hand on the lawman's shoulder as they walked to the front of the congregation. Fear and anguish clouded their faces, forecasting bad news.

"Can I have your attention please?" the preacher announced. "Sheriff Brown has something to say to you. Please find a seat."

The sheriff stepped back, crossed his arms, and waited.

Jeanne wove her way through the mass of people and inched close to the front to hear.

Sheriff Brown looked as if he hadn't slept since she had seen him the night before. He cleared his throat, and when he began to speak, not a sound could be heard from the crowd. "Folks, your pastor here says to go ahead and tell you the news I heard on my radio. NBC News in New York said that President Roosevelt told us today the Japanese have attacked Pearl Harbor in Hawaii from the air. They have bombed our military bases there."

A woman screamed. "My boy is there! He's in the navy." Her husband hurried over to her and put his arm around her, and they looked to others for answers.

Sobs broke out among the crowd. Shock and surprise covered their faces, and cries rose from the congregation gathered there on that December afternoon.

"Maybe they didn't bomb the ships." The pastor tried to soothe the hysterical woman. "You said it was on the island."

"Where is Pearl Harbor, Sheriff Brown?" a man in the congregation shouted.

Chatter broke out. Many didn't know where this place was. Jeanne listened to people asking questions with no answers.

"I looked it up," the sheriff said. "It's an island in the Pacific Ocean. Pearl Harbor is on that island."

"What about my boy, Sheriff?" the woman interrupted again.

Tears were streaming down her face. "Why bomb us?"

"We don't know any more than that, ma'am. My advice is for you to go home and listen for more news on your radio. President Roosevelt hasn't made his speech yet, so go home and we'll keep alert."

"Are they going to attack the United States?" a man said.

"They already have," Grandpa pointed out.

"I mean here," the man stressed. "Not in the ocean. Does this mean war?"

"We don't know," Sheriff Brown repeated. "Please go home. We must stay ready. Listen on your radios. Come to the office in town if you don't have a radio. You can hear the news in several places. They're setting up in the Majestic so folks can hear."

The pastor stepped up and took control. "Ladies, put the food away, and men, store the sawhorses in the basement, then join me in the sanctuary. We can return to our homes after that. Let's get started."

Pastor Wilson had given people a job to do, and the frantic effort to get home began. Jeanne wanted to go into the church. The need to pray together was overwhelming. It was hard to understand her people being killed by an enemy they didn't even know. Jeanne prayed as she always had for God to help them.

"Take these dishes to the truck, Jeanne," Grandma said. "I'll take Robby in and get a seat."

"Yes, ma'am." Jeanne ran to the truck and hurried back to the sanctuary.

An unusual apprehension accompanied everyone as they scurried through the doors—opposite to the normal calm they experienced entering the church. Muted sobs were scattered throughout the pews as folks rushed to take their seats.

The pastor took his place behind the lectern, opened his Bible, and in his booming voice began to read to them. "Brothers and sisters, from 2 Corinthians 1:4, 'Who comforteth us in all our tribulation, that we may be able to comfort them which are in trouble, by the comfort wherewith we ourselves are comforted of God.'"

The words whirled around in Jeanne's mind. She remembered this scripture. She had at other times been touched by the messages in Corinthians. *Am I comforted?*

"Let us pray to God, for we need him," the preacher said. "It is written right here in the Good Book."

Tears dropped on Jeanne's hands as she bowed her head to pray. Intense feelings welled inside her. She opened her heart to be comforted.

Robby reached over and patted her shoulder. "Gee," he whispered.

∽

Jeanne listened to her grandparents on the ride home. They were trying to understand the severity of what had happened. As comforted as they had been in the church, the reality was terrifying her family. She had heard of the Japanese, and she was as confused as anyone, wanting to know why they had attacked the US.

"I thought we'd fight the Germans, Beulah," Grandpa growled.

"I'll be glad to get home and turn on the radio," Grandma said. "We can hear for ourselves what's happening."

Grandma and Jeanne unloaded the pickup while Eli fed the animals and milked the cows.

∽

Jeanne could hear the crackling and whistling in the living room. Eli turned the dial on the radio. The Zenith sat on a table near the front window for better reception. Jeanne dried her hands with a dish towel, grabbed her notebook and pencil, and sat cross-legged on the floor in front of the radio.

"It's on," Eli announced as he turned up the volume.

They were waiting for Mrs. Roosevelt to begin. Jeanne had written down speeches the First Lady had given on many occasions. She wrote *Over Our Coffee Cups* across the top of her notebook.

Under the show title, Jeanne penciled in and underlined twice, *December 7, 1941.*

Eli backed away and sat in a chair next to the radio. Grandma and Grandpa huddled together with Robby on the sofa to listen to what had happened to their nation that day. Old Dog sat at their feet.

The announcer said, "And now, *Over Our Coffee Cups*, with First Lady Mrs. Eleanor Roosevelt."

There was a pause on the radio, and Grandpa sat forward on the sofa.

"Good evening, Ladies and Gentlemen," Mrs. Roosevelt began. "I am speaking to you tonight at a very serious moment in our history. The cabinet is convening, and the leaders in Congress are meeting with the president. The State Department and army and navy officials have been with the president all afternoon. In fact, the Japanese ambassador was talking to the president at the very time that Japanese airships were bombing our citizens in Hawaii and the Philippines and sinking one of our transports loaded with lumber on its way to Hawaii."

"Oh!" Grandma cried. "They tricked us!"

"Shh," Grandpa hissed and held up his hand for quiet.

Mrs. Roosevelt's words kept pouring into their living room. "By tomorrow morning, the members of Congress will have a full report and will be ready for action. In the meantime, we the people are already prepared . . . I should like to say just a word to the women in the country tonight. I have a boy at sea on a destroyer. For all I know, he may be on his way to the Pacific . . . We are the free and unconquerable people of the United States of America."

Jeanne wrote as much of Mrs. Roosevelt's speech as she could.

Grandpa sat back and rubbed his chin with his thumb and forefinger, as was his habit when he was deep in thought about something.

"What action will Congress take?" Eli asked.

"It means war, son." Grandpa got up and walked into the kitchen. "Let's get a cup of coffee."

Eli followed him.

"What will they be asking us to do?" Jeanne asked Grandma. "Mrs. Roosevelt said we would have moments when our strength would be tested. What does that mean?"

"Farms were important in the last war, and they will be again," Grandma explained. "We'll all have to work extra hard to make the farm produce what is needed."

"Will we be all right?" Jeanne hadn't been alive for the last war. Her threats had always come from within the family. She didn't know what to think of an outside danger to her life.

"We fought for less than two years. It seems so soon to be in a war again. We'll be fine. Mrs. Roosevelt said that she was standing on a rock that was her fellow citizens. That means we are that rock. There's no doubt we'll be tested."

In the first days following the bombing of Pearl Harbor, the whole family stayed close to the radio and even took turns listening so they didn't miss any news.

By the beginning of 1942, the newness of the war had worn off and the pressing responsibility of planting the spring crop took over Grandpa's daily activities. Christmas had been somber, and there had been no word from their daddy. Another disappointment, but Jeanne still had hope he would come.

Late January was mild—a nice break from the icy roads and the bitter cold nights when Jeanne came downstairs to sleep by the fireplace. She bundled up and went outdoors to the front porch.

"That looks like the postman, Beulah," Grandpa said. "The roads must be clearing."

"I'll go meet him." Jeanne already had on her boots, so she jumped off the porch and sprinted down the driveway to the mailbox. When she was halfway there, the mail truck stopped and the postman deposited something in the box. He waived at Jeanne and was out of sight by the time she got to the road.

The metal door to the mailbox was hard to budge and screeched at her efforts. Jeanne had to take off her gloves to open it. She found two letters. Her hands shook as she pulled out the letters, one white and the other blue. The blue one was from Betty Ann. It was addressed to the Bradshaw Family. How long had it been since the train left the station with Betty Ann on it? Only two months.

The other letter was addressed to Claude and Beulah Bradshaw. Jeanne recognized Auntie Boots's handwriting. Tears dripped on the open mailbox door and splashed on her hands. She wiped her face with her gloves and recovered enough to take the mail back home. She was through crying.

When Jeanne made it back to the house, she handed the letters to Grandma Biddy and asked her to read them to the family. "We have two letters, one from Mama and the other from Auntie Boots."

Grandma nodded. "Let's go in the house then. I'll make hot tea, and we can sit around the kitchen table."

Once they were inside with steaming cups in hand, Grandma read the letter from Auntie Boots.

Dear Folks,

We are here in Abilene, shivering in the cold. We had a nice Christmas, although it wasn't as memorable as last year's holiday with our whole family on your floor. The kids are growing like weeds. You wouldn't know them. Of course, we've had the regular colds and such.

This war has interfered with a lot already. The good news is that my lovely husband has a job building a new military base here in Abilene. They call it Dyess. At least for now he doesn't have to join the army. He may be too old to join anyhow. Tell Eli not to do anything foolish like join up. He needs to stay right there. Tell Jeanne to remember what I told her, and Claude, you and Beulah take care of yourselves.

Sylvia Hornback

Love both you ol' coots,

Bootsie

Grandpa chuckled. "Leave it to Bootsie to put a smile on your face. We may have to read it again after we read this next one."

Grandma held up the blue envelope. "Let's see what Betty Ann has to say." She picked up a paring knife and slid it along the top. Her worn fingers pulled out the delicate blue leaves and unfolded the pages.

Dear Children,

I wanted you to know I made it to El Paso. I met a man on the train that gave me a job and a place to stay. I didn't want you to worry, and you all know that your mama will always find a way. This job is in a factory and requires that I be sober, so I guess you could say I'm dried out by now. You'll see me again someday.

Eli, I miss you. Jeanne, take care of Robby and give him a kiss from his mama.

Betty Ann

Grandma carefully folded the paper and put it back in the envelope. "Now we know."

"At least she made it to El Paso and she's all right," Eli said.

Jeanne pushed her chair back and walked out of the kitchen. *Nothing has changed.*

Chapter 21

"Over here," called Eli. He waved his arms and directed the students unloading from the school bus to the field where Grandpa was handing out gardening tools.

Jeanne was part of this work group. There were ten high school students assigned to help tend the fields and crops on their farm. The day before, their county superintendent had come to the school with war news from the state. Grades eight through twelve filed into the auditorium to listen to the first direct action of the war effort that affected them. They were all to help on the farms. The superintendent told them the crops were so essential that they would release the students to help plant, tend, and harvest the local crops. The buzz around the high school was instant from students and teachers alike. Courses had to be adjusted to be covered in the new schedule, and not all were thrilled to be participants in the new venture.

"Show the kids which plant is a weed," Grandpa instructed Jeanne. "We don't want them to mistake wheat for weeds."

Jeanne hurried to the nearest field and stood in front of the group. "These are the young plants. Don't hoe these. Leave them to grow."

"We've got it," one boy said. "I've used a hoe many times." He walked off, followed by others. Some were grinning, but Jeanne noticed somber, aggravated looks from most. *So much for patriotism.* She stared at the rows of wheat as each boy and girl took a hoe in hand and began the grueling work of weeding a field.

At the end of the day, the bedraggled gang sat at the edge of the field, bemoaning that they were not in school.

"This was supposed to be fun. I'd rather be in English class," one girl complained.

"Not me," an older boy named Seth said. "Let me be outside any day."

The group laughed.

"Besides, I want to help the war effort until this summer. Then I can enlist."

"What branch are you joining?" Jeanne asked.

"The marines, of course," Seth said. "They're the best."

Tad, one of the younger boys, spoke up and tried to impress the older boys talking about joining. "My daddy was in the army in the last war, and he wants me to be in the army when I get old enough. When school is out, he may even go down to the recruiter and sign for me."

"Would he really do that?" Seth asked.

"Sure, he said so already. He says that makes a real man, one that fights for his country. He says I could be a hero, and all the girls would like me."

"Time for the bus," Eli shouted.

The workers from town ambled to the bus.

Grandpa stood by the bus door and shook hands with each one before they stepped inside. "Thank you, son," he said to each boy, and to the girls he said, "Thank you, young lady."

On the way back to the house, Eli commented, "They did a fair job today."

"How long will it take them to finish our farm?" Jeanne asked as she sat on the edge of the front porch.

"They're learning now," Grandpa replied, "and every day will be better. Maybe two weeks. It'll sure improve the yield and the quality without weeds in the harvest."

Eli lingered by the door. "I'm going to turn on the radio and check the news."

He seemed melancholy to Jeanne. All the boys were anxious to join the fighting. Her brother was no exception, but he was committed to staying on the farm. His work there was vital to winning the war. Grandpa had said as much over the dinner table many times.

⤳

The next day, more people from town accompanied the students from Readfield on the school bus. Maggie was among them, as were several other young people already out of high school. Jeanne didn't know everyone getting off the bus today. Then a boy with dark curly hair and a crooked grin stepped off the bus and greeted her.

"I guess I'm it," he said. "Hello, pretty girl. What's your name?" He waved to the driver and turned to face Jeanne.

"I'm Jeanne." She was mesmerized by his smile and the sparkle in his eyes. Jeanne had never met anyone so magnetic. She wanted to be around him, and he had called her a pretty girl. She didn't believe him, but she wanted to believe him.

"You must be Eli's sister. He didn't tell me you were so gorgeous."

"Come over here, Billy, and work with us," a circle of girls called to the boy standing next to Jeanne. She heard an echo of giggling come from the group and saw them point in their direction and shove each other with even more laughing. It was obvious they were after Billy.

"I guess you heard." He winked. "My name is William Laird. They call me Billy."

"I did." Jeanne smiled.

"Well, off to work. See you later, pretty girl." He grinned and walked backward, saluting her. After a few steps, he turned around and ran to the bunch of girls, grabbed a hoe, and led the group toward the fields. He cocked his head to the side and whistled as he steered the group toward the work site.

Jeanne felt as if a light switch had been turned off when Billy was gone and out of sight. She fought that disappointed feeling the rest of the day, hoping to get a glimpse of him again.

However, she did glimpse Maggie spending the day near Eli. She followed him everywhere. Her big brother didn't discourage Maggie either. They laughed and talked. She caressed his arm, and Eli would smile down at her. Jeanne understood the game they were playing. It was the same one the group of girls was trying to use on Billy. Jeanne eyed Billy more than she worked. She tried not to let anyone catch her looking, but she couldn't help herself.

At noon, when the workers stopped for lunch, Billy put both hands out, palms toward his female entourage to stop them from following him. Then he walked over to join Eli and the other boys to have his lunch.

"Good-looking, isn't he?" Maggie whispered to Jeanne as she walked up behind her.

Jeanne jumped. "Well, all the girls are crazy for him, that's for sure."

"He's not as handsome as Eli," Maggie said. "Oh, he's a pip, all right. He's a big tease, that's all. The girls love him because he's a flatterer. Watch out for him. He's trouble. My Eli is mature. He'll amount to something."

"You seem a little starstruck yourself," Jeanne replied, not liking the familiar way Maggie referred to her brother. "Are you and Eli getting serious?"

"I wish. Give me time. I'll win him over." Maggie sighed and looked toward the group of males laughing and talking in their own world.

Billy left the group of boys and started walking toward Jeanne, but one of the girls ran over and grabbed his arm. He looked at Jeanne and shrugged his shoulders. Then he walked away.

⚬◦⚬

"Jeanne, come in the house," Grandma Biddy called the next morning from the back porch. "I need you, honey." She was holding Robby and waving.

Jeanne ran. Fear always gripped her when she thought something might be wrong with her baby brother. "What is it, Grandma?"

"I want you to help with the cooking today."

Jeanne followed her into the house.

"We have to feed this bunch," Grandma continued, "and I have the wash to get on the line." She handed over Robby. "This one's fussy and has a runny nose."

Jeanne patted Robby on the back, and he lay his head on her shoulder. "What do you want me to cook?"

"Watch the beans on the stove." Grandma gestured to the simmering pot. "Add water, if need be, and don't let 'em boil down and burn. Peel enough potatoes for everybody and slice the ham. I also need you to go to the garden and see if anything is ready that we can add to the table. They'll be hungry when they take their lunch, and I want to have enough."

"Yes, ma'am."

Jeanne carried Robby with her to the garden, but only a few new sprouts had poked their heads out of the ground. When she returned, Grandma was stirring clothes in the steaming cauldron.

"I'll put Robby down for a nap and come back to help."

"You go on and finish the work in the kitchen," Grandma said. "I can do this. Come help me hang out the clothes when I finish."

"There's nothing in the garden yet. Everything is still too young to pick. Maybe in a couple of weeks."

"All right. We'll make do with what we have. Go on then."

"Good morning, ladies." A familiar voice greeted them. "I thought I might find you back here since I didn't get anybody when I knocked on the front door."

Jeanne and Grandma Biddy turned and saw a big smile above the sacks of groceries standing on the back porch.

"Daniel, what in the world are you doing way out here?" Grandma said.

"I wanted to help by bringing food." Daniel's blond hair sparkled in the sun, and his blue eyes lingered on Jeanne. Daniel was like a brother to her, but she suspected he liked her.

"Well, my goodness!" Grandma said as she dried her hands on her apron. "Thank you, son. Jeanne, go show Daniel where to put the groceries. I have to stay with this boiling pot."

"You're welcome, Mrs. Bradshaw." He came in through the back door and was unloading canned goods when Jeanne walked in with Robby.

"Let me put Robby down to nap and I'll be back." Jeanne didn't even try to think of what to say or do. She merely went through the motions.

Jeanne took a deep breath and walked back into the kitchen, but what she found was a table filled with everything she needed. There were enough apples to make pies, green beans, canned peaches, and a jar of pickles.

She hurried to the back door and looked for Daniel to thank him. "Did you see Daniel, Grandma? I wanted to thank him." She walked down the steps.

"He went over to see Eli. I think they're talking by the barn."

Jeanne walked to the corner of the barn and stopped. Daniel, Eli, and Grandpa were huddled in conversation by the door. She decided not to interrupt. Maybe she had been mistaken about Daniel's feelings for her. He was a good person and was more like a brother. She headed back to the kitchen. She had to hurry to make the apple pies in time for the noon meal.

The men and boys gathered to talk about the war. Daniel stayed and helped Eli. The long table set up in the yard was segregated between the men and women. The girls all watched the cluster of men talking among themselves. There were no loud voices and no laughter. Jeanne didn't want to think about it.

"I guess I'll have to run around screaming to get any attention here," Maggie said. "All they can do is talk about the war." Just like that, Maggie brought the war to the forefront of their conversation, as well.

The youngest one there, Sharon, started crying.

"Now look what you've done," one of the girls said. "Her daddy and brother joined the army this morning."

"Everybody says the war will be over by the end of the year," Maggie said. "Most of the men won't even get a chance to fight."

"Don't be naïve, Maggie," Jeanne chided. "That's what they said in the last war, and look how long that lasted and how many were killed."

"How do you know?" Maggie fired back. The girls' faces turned toward Jeanne, expecting an answer.

"Because I told her," Grandma Biddy said. "I lived through it." She had walked up to the table with a pitcher of tea and set it on the table. "You ask your families. They'll tell you the truth. There's nothing romantic about it. It's going to be hard. You girls better get tougher. We don't know what we might have to endure. Now, it's time to get back to the work at hand. Bring your plates to the back porch." Grandma turned around and walked back to the house.

The table was quiet. The men had listened too. Slowly, each rose and carried their plates to the porch. The afternoon flew by and Jeanne didn't see Daniel before he left, nor did she see Billy till the end of the day.

Before Billy jumped on the bus that afternoon, he sauntered over to Jeanne. He brushed a wisp of hair back and whispered in her ear, "This trip out here is not just for biscuits, dollface. We'll get together, you'll see."

Jeanne's face burned.

Billy walked down the aisle of the bus, with the girls begging him to sit by them. He didn't wave goodbye or look her way.

His words were ringing in her ears as Jeanne walked back to the house with the dust from the road floating over her shoulders.

The youth farm helpers came for another two weeks just as Grandpa had predicted. Jeanne saw Billy every day. He was bigger than life to Jeanne. She realized after he left each day that he had done all the talking and that she had held her breath most of the time. She had never liked a boy like this. The boys in her class were a nuisance. Yes, Billy was different, and of all the girls there, he seemed to have picked her. That was the biggest shock. *Why?* She didn't wear makeup, and she was not as fashionable as the girls who knew the latest thing to say.

"Is that Billy boy the reason you're up so early, child?" Grandma asked.

Grandma knew everything. Jeanne should have known there would be no secrets in this house. "I guess so. He told me he likes me and that he thinks I'm pretty."

"Don't let flattery go to your head," Grandma advised as she stirred the red-eye gravy.

"I won't."

"You are a pretty girl. You're smart too. Don't you forget that." She opened the oven and took out the biscuits.

"He's asked to take me to the movies. Do you think I can go?"

"I don't know him, Jeanne. I'll talk to Pa and Eli about him. We'll see."

"This is the last day for the workers to come. Can you ask them today?"

Grandma nodded. She didn't look happy about it.

Jeanne was excited about the possibility. She heard the bus arriving and ran outside to see everyone get off at their stop. There he was. The first one off this morning. Still the perfect smile. She didn't want to seem too eager, so she waited by the barn where they would collect their tools.

"Can you go?" Billy asked.

"I don't know yet."

He put his hand on the wall by her head and leaned close to her. "You find out and meet me at the theater at two o'clock Saturday. I'll wait fifteen minutes. I don't want to buy tickets and my date not come." He winked at her and grabbed a hoe.

"I should know today."

"Great! I'll talk to you at lunch." Billy squeezed her hand and ran to catch up with the others in the field.

Jeanne opened the back door to find Eli and her grandparents standing in the kitchen. "Are you talking about me?"

"We are, and we've decided to let you go to the movies on Saturday," said Grandpa. "Eli will take you to town and let you off at the movies."

"What? I can't believe it. Thank you!" Jeanne clapped her hands and smiled.

Robby clapped with her, and they all laughed.

"Come to the store after the movies," Eli said. "You can wait for me there until I get off work."

The last day the bus made a run to their farm was Monday, and then it was back to school for everyone. Jeanne thought Saturday would never come.

"We worked on the Morgan place the whole time," Becky shared as she joined Jeanne at the table in the cafeteria. "It wasn't too bad."

"Everybody at our place hoed weeds in the fields," said Jeanne. "What did you do?"

"Babs and I planted pinto beans. Mrs. Morgan and her little girls helped."

Barbara joined them and sat next to Becky. "That's true, we did, but nothing happened to us like I just heard happened to you!"

Jeanne could feel the red creeping up her neck and burn her face.

"It must be true!" Becky said. "Tell me. What is it?"

"She has a date with Billy Laird!" Barbara exclaimed.

"What! You have to tell us everything," Becky demanded.

"We're going to the movies Saturday," Jeanne replied. "That's all."

"That's all? How did this happen? What did he say? Isn't he just the cutest?" The girls bombarded her all at once and didn't stop the questions till Jeanne held up her hands and started laughing.

"Hold on a minute. I haven't even been yet," Jeanne breathed. "Give me a chance to find out if he's nice, then I'll tell you."

"Come on, Jeanne," Becky moaned. "You really know how to make us suffer. Later, we want every detail. You have to tell us about his curly hair, his dreamy eyes, and his sexy smile."

Barbara sucked in her breath and slapped her hand over her mouth at Becky saying the word "sexy." Jeanne couldn't believe it either. They started giggling and attracting the attention of the other tables, but they couldn't help themselves. Jeanne looked at the stares, and they started laughing all over again.

Finally, when they composed themselves, Becky said, "Well, what about it, kiddo?"

"We'll see, we'll see." Jeanne would keep details of her date with Billy to herself, but the anticipation for all of them was fun.

Jeanne stepped out of the pickup and walked toward the Majestic Theater. It was only a half block away from where Eli had dropped her off. She didn't see Billy, but she was a little early. Dressed in her periwinkle-blue dress, Jeanne felt she looked her best. Her hair was smooth and shining. She wore it loose, and it fell to her waist in beautiful waves. She had pulled strands back from her face and held them in place with a tortoiseshell barrette that belonged to Grandma Biddy. Her shoes were practical leather lace-ups. She was comfortable in them as she strolled over to the posters outside the theater. She wanted to read about the coming films. A new animated movie from Disney called *Dumbo* was coming next month. It had been released last year, but it took a long time to get a showing in Readfield. It was all the kids could talk about, and Jeanne wanted to see it as well. She and Eli had talked about bringing Robby to see it. She could imagine Robby's delight.

"Hello, pretty girl," Billy greeted from behind as he touched her shoulder.

She whirled around to glimpse that mesmerizing smile. "Hello, Billy." Jeanne's heart was beating out of her chest.

"Let's go in and see this movie. Do you like Westerns? I hear Errol Flynn and Olivia de Havilland are good in this one."

"I saw Olivia de Havilland in *Gone with the Wind*. She was wonderful."

"I liked her too. She was loyal and true. You remind me of her."

"I do?" Jeanne couldn't believe Billy thought she was like Melanie in *Gone with the Wind*. They walked up to the ticket window, and Jeanne stood by his side, not believing this moment.

"Sure you do, babe," he said as he faced the window. "Two tickets for *They Died with Their Boots On*. Honey, I want the best seats for me and my girl here." Billy smiled at the woman in the booth, and Jeanne could see the lady was taken with him.

"Well, sir, you just pick out what you want when you go in." Her fingers lingered on his when she gave him the tickets. "Enjoy." She smiled.

"We will, sugar." Billy winked at her and took Jeanne's hand.

Jeanne and Eli bumped along on the road home, and all she could think about was Billy. How he put his arm around her in the movie, held her hand when he walked her to the store, and waited with her until Eli got off work.

"You're quiet. Didn't you have a good time?" Eli asked with a grin.

"I did have a good time. Just thinking, that's all." Jeanne heard how she sounded. She couldn't fool Eli, so she changed the subject. "How about you and Maggie?"

"She's all right. I know she's your friend, but she's too forward. I want to make the first move when I ask a girl out."

"There's no doubt she likes you, Eli. I don't know what to tell you. She's determined."

"I'll take care of the Maggie situation. Don't worry. You be careful you don't get your heart broken with Billy. I know you haven't missed how all the girls hang around him, but I'm not sure how I feel about your date with him. I went along with Grandma Biddy. She told us it was better if we said okay to you going than forbidding it. But be careful. He's been around the block, and you haven't."

Jeanne sat back and looked out the window at the fence posts going by the rest of the way home. She understood everything he was saying, but it rankled her, even if she hadn't been around the block. She had a bad feeling in the pit of her stomach about how this would turn out between her and Billy. She wished Auntie Boots lived closer. She understood better than anyone.

Chapter 22

It was Friday, and there was only one week of school left. Jeanne would be a senior soon. She sat on the front seat of the bus and stared out of the window, waiting to get off at her stop. Summer had arrived in May, and it had already begun to get hot. Becky was talking about going swimming in the tank at her place, but Jeanne had to think seriously about her life. One more year for her and she had to decide about becoming an adult. She wanted to be a teacher, but she was needed on the farm. She had always enjoyed teaching Robby, and she especially loved teaching Isabel to read.

Times were hard for everyone because of the war. The crops on the farm would yield more this year, and Grandpa was hopeful every day about the profits. He hoped to get out of debt, and so did the other farmers in the cooperative. They had a meeting scheduled after church on Sunday to get prepared for the harvest. Jeanne had two more final exams to take next week. She would be finished early and could be home to help Grandma in the garden and make soap.

But Jeanne's packed days did not prevent her from fantasizing about Billy. She had butterflies in her stomach all the time. She had trouble concentrating on her studies, and she was looking forward to Sunday. He had told her he would be at church, so they could be together.

"This is your stop, young lady," the bus driver called back to her.

"Thank you, Mr. Reed." Jeanne jumped up and hurried off the bus, embarrassed that she was caught daydreaming. She automatically checked the mailbox. Empty. She started down the long drive to the house. Once inside, she announced, "I'm home, Grandma."

"Gee," Robby called from the kitchen. He was playing on the floor with his toy car and a shoebox.

Jeanne picked him up and swung him around, making him giggle. When she stopped, she hugged him and sat down at the table with Robby in her lap. She reached down and patted Old Dog. His tail slapped the table leg as he wagged back at her.

Grandma Biddy was rushing around the kitchen. "How was school today?" She fumbled the kettle full of water and dropped it on the floor. "Oh, my. Now why did I do that?"

Jeanne scrambled to get a towel to wipe the water off the floor. "Sit down, Grandma. I'll take care of it. What's wrong?"

Grandma slumped down at the table and sighed. "Nothing, child. I'm hurrying too much. I need to slow down a bit. You know my motto of how I have to get everything done in one day and don't leave it for tomorrow."

Jeanne finished the floor, refilled the kettle, and set it on the stove to heat. "Let's have tea. I'll make a sweet cup for Robby. Sit for a minute."

Grandma sighed and relaxed her shoulders when she took the cup of steamy tea. The three of them sat around the table, sipping their beverages. Robby finished his tea spiked with honey in record time and quickly returned to his play. Conversation was safe, the usual daily questions and answers. The women skirted troubles and insisted on normal behavior in a world at war and full of uncertainty. Finally, a curtain of calm worked its way around them, and Grandma became herself again.

"You go up and study for that English test," Grandma said. "I can finish supper."

"I'll take Robby up with me. I can read out loud for him and study Shakespeare at the same time. He loves hearing the Old English."

Grandma smiled and waved her on, then stood and gathered the teacups. Old Dog followed them to the living room and lay down near the stairs. Jeanne carried Robby up the stairs to study. She only had English and history tests to take, and she was confident she would score high grades in both. She loved both subjects, and she was a good writer. Nevertheless, she studied and read Macbeth aloud to Robby.

"Come to supper," Grandma called a while later. "Everybody, come to the table."

Jeanne and Robby settled in their places. Grandma and Grandpa were already at the table.

"Where's Eli?" Jeanne asked her grandparents. "He's usually the first one here." She noticed an extra plate set at the table. "Who else is coming?"

Eli opened the back door and walked in, and behind him came Daniel. "Sorry we're late, Grandma. Things took a bit longer."

"Good evening, Mr. and Mrs. Bradshaw, Jeanne, Robby," Daniel said as he walked over and shook Robby's little hand. "Thank you for inviting me to supper."

"Have a seat, boys," Grandpa said.

Jeanne didn't know what to think. This was the first time Daniel had come to have a meal at their house, even though he and Eli had been friends for a long time. Grandpa said the blessing, and Grandma started passing the bowls of food around the table. Dinner buzzed with healthy appetites and pleasant conversation.

After a lull, Eli stopped eating and deliberately put his fork down, which got everyone's attention. "Daniel and I went to Snyder today," he stated solemnly. "We joined the navy."

Jeanne could tell Grandpa wasn't surprised, and now she

understood why Grandma Biddy had been so anxious this afternoon.

"We talked about this before Eli went to enlist," Grandpa said. "We'll be fine here at the farm because we've been assured that we'll have the youth help. The government is helping during the war, and when the war is over, Eli will be back to help out."

Jeanne's mind raced with anxiety. There was so much wrong with that. *What if Eli doesn't come back? How long will the war last? What if the workers don't come back?*

"When do you leave?" Grandma asked.

"We catch the bus in Readfield next Thursday," Eli said.

"That's less than a week!" Jeanne exclaimed. She stared at both young men. Eli had just turned twenty, and Daniel was a couple of years older. They looked so young, even to her. "Daniel, what does your uncle say about you leaving?"

Daniel's blond head dipped, and he put his fork down on his plate. "What you would expect," Daniel said quietly. "Neither Aunt Cheryl nor Uncle Fred were happy about it."

"I thought you liked the grocery business," Jeanne said. She remembered when Daniel had told her how much he loved it.

"I do, and it'll be waiting for me when we get back from the war."

"The farm will be here when Eli gets back too," Grandpa assured. "You can count on that."

"We can finish this talk on the porch." Grandma took charge, dismissing the men and standing to clean the table. "Jeanne, you go put Robby to bed, and I'll finish cleaning up here."

By the time Jeanne returned to the kitchen, Grandma Biddy had finished the dishes and put away the food.

"Come on, let's join the men," Grandma suggested. "It's a nice night, and you've already done your studying."

The night sounds harmonized with the low voices on the porch. Jeanne wanted to remember everything about it: the faraway owl calling in the dark, the frenzied crickets responding to the warm day, the occasional bat swooping above their heads. She could make out silhouettes from her spot on the edge of the porch when she looked back toward the house.

Grandma bent forward in her rocking chair with her hands folded in her lap. She, too, was drinking in the images of the two young men sitting there until finally she tired. "I'm going to leave solving the world's problems to you youngsters. It's time for me to go to bed. Spend the night, Daniel. Jeanne will make up a pallet for you."

"I'm going too," Grandpa said. "Good night." He closed the screen door with a soft swish.

The rising moon cast a sliver of light on the east side of the porch, illuminating the faces still present.

"Where will the bus take you on Thursday?" Jeanne asked.

"We make stops along the way till the bus is full," Daniel explained. "We're supposed to be at the naval base in San Diego by Sunday at the latest. They call it boot camp. We'll be training there for six weeks before we're assigned to a ship."

"What made you join the navy?" Jeanne asked. "Neither of you has been on the water, much less the ocean."

"I can swim." Daniel smiled. "And the recruiter who came through Readfield convinced us to pick the navy. He said they had the greatest need because so many men were lost at Pearl."

Eli yawned. "I've already answered these questions. I'm going to bed. I'll see you in the morning."

Once they were alone, Jeanne asked the real question that had been worrying her. "Why did you do this, Daniel? You didn't have to join the navy and fight in this war."

"I did, though. I've heard the talk, and I want to live in Readfield. I can't live there if people think I'm a coward because I didn't fight."

"You're not a coward! You're a good person."

Daniel smiled at Jeanne. "Not everyone is as kind as you are. People are changing. They are frightened, and food supplies are becoming scarce. The men are gone from most of the homes, and they can't see the enemy they're supposed to hate. I don't want to become their target. I want to go. People understand that Eli and I have gotten our business in order and now it's time for us to go. Uncle Fred and I have had lengthy discussions about it."

"I guess it's settled then, isn't it?"

"I'm afraid so. It was settled when I signed those enlistment papers." Daniel paused. "I do have one more thing before I leave in the morning. I want to know if you'll write to me."

Jeanne was surprised and hesitated as she considered his sudden request.

"I mean we're friends, and I know Aunt Cheryl will write, but Uncle Fred is not a writer, so I don't expect much from him. I don't have a girlfriend or anyone else."

"Of course, Daniel. I'll write to you. I would be honored."

"Tell me about what's going on in Readfield and here on the farm. You and Eli are like family to me."

Jeanne reached over and took his hand. She didn't know why, but it seemed like they both needed human touch. They sat there watching the moon climb higher and then slide behind the barn. Neither spoke, but they knew this memory would be with them always, no matter what the future held.

The next morning, a terrible sadness overcame Jeanne. The world was changing too fast. The silly gossip on the school bus was inconsequential compared to Eli and Daniel going to war. She finished finals at school and volunteered to help count books in the library. Yesterday, she had said goodbye to friends she might not see again. Today the school was almost empty. Three of the seniors left to join the army the day after graduation.

When Jeanne finished inventorying the textbooks, she walked to the Greyhound bus station. It was already Thursday.

She walked past the brick side wall of the Dumar Drugstore, then across the square to the bus station two blocks away. As she approached, a crowd was gathering to say their goodbyes to the young men going off to war. Although the station had a large awning on the front, no one stood there. They clustered in intimate groups in the street, on lawns nearby, and on the sidewalk leading to the loading area. Jeanne searched familiar faces to find her own family. First, she spotted Daniel and his aunt and uncle. They stood in a somber slump, not saying anything to anyone. Daniel held his aunt's hand, and when Jeanne got close to them, she saw his aunt's tear-streaked face. Daniel waved.

She waved back and joined them in the sorrowful huddle. "Hello, Daniel," she said, then nodded to his aunt and uncle.

They nodded back. Nothing needed to be said.

"Have you seen Eli?"

"They're not here yet," Daniel said. "Cars are parked behind the station. You might find them there, but everyone must come here to get on the bus. It's due in about ten minutes."

"I'll check the parking lot." Jeanne couldn't stand there and wallow in this sadness.

"I have something for you," Daniel said.

Jeanne delayed the hunt for her family and looked at Daniel. "For me?"

"Yes. I know you said you would write to me, and I wanted to give you this." Daniel handed her a small package wrapped in tissue and tied with a narrow satin ribbon.

"Thank you."

"It's stationery. It has pink flowers on it. I'll know when a letter is from you."

"I've never seen anything so pretty." The yellow ribbon was tied in a perfect bow, and she could see the pink flowers through the thin tissue paper. It was lovely.

"Just keep your promise and write."

"I will. I will. Thank you again, Daniel." She gave him a quick hug. "I'm going to look for my family behind the station." She moved away awkwardly, wondering what Daniel's intentions were.

It was quiet at the back of the station but crowded with pickups and cars. The emptiness of the unmanned vehicles added to

Jeanne's dismay. Then she heard sobbing coming from behind a green pickup. Jeanne stopped.

"You can't leave me like this!" a girl cried. "You said you loved me."

The voices were only a few feet away, much closer than she'd thought, so Jeanne waited before she interrupted the private conversation. She backed behind a rusty pickup near the back door of the station.

"Wait, wait!" the girl screamed. "You can't go off to war without marrying me."

Jeanne recognized one of the girls from the work group at the farm. Footsteps crunched the gravel closer to her. She backed up farther and crouched at the wheel, staying out of sight. The footsteps stopped, and Jeanne peeked over the side to see the back of a head with curly black hair. She ducked down again, her stomach in her throat. *Surely, that can't be Billy. My Billy.*

"Girl, I know you sleep around," Billy accused her. "You can't blame this on me. I can get three more boys to say they've been with you."

"That's not true and you know it," she whimpered between sobs. "You were my first, and you know that too."

"You were more than willing," Billy chided. "You're nothing but a little tramp. Shut up, just shut up! I don't want to have anything to do with you. Leave me alone!"

Jeanne couldn't believe what she was hearing. She stood up to see the two with her own eyes. They were facing each other, engrossed in their argument and unaware of her presence. Jeanne recognized the girl as Cindy. She had met her several times, and Cindy was always hanging around Billy.

"You have to make this right, Billy," Cindy demanded.

"You'll have to find another patsy. It's not going to be me."

"See this!" Cindy grabbed Billy's hand and placed it on her bulging abdomen.

He drew his hand back as if he had touched a hot coal. Cindy dropped to the ground on her knees, sobbing, and buried her face in her hands. Billy left and headed to the back door of the bus station. Suddenly he stopped and looked directly at Jeanne. She looked at his contorted face and knew that everything Cindy had said was true. He hesitated only a moment, then rushed into the station. Jeanne walked around the pickup to help Cindy, but she was gone.

"Hey, Jeanne, we're around front," Eli called, waving from the corner of the building.

The bus was late, which added to the nervous turmoil around the station. Jeanne was no exception. She and her older brother stood around, failing at small talk. Her mind was focused on the scene she had just witnessed. Her dreams of marriage, a house of her own, and her darling Billy had evaporated in a few horrible minutes in a gravel parking lot.

About a hundred people were standing and waiting for the familiar blue-and-silver bus to pull into the station. At least thirty were men and boys from the county who had enlisted. Eli and Daniel weren't alone. Jeanne observed her family. Her grandparents were stoic, as were many of the older folks waiting with their families. Jeanne searched for Billy in the crowd, but he was nowhere to be seen.

Eli held Robby. She looked at her brothers and wanted to remember this image forever. Eli wore a white shirt and khakis. His long black hair was combed back, but an unruly wave fell across his forehead and into his eyes. He brushed the curl back with two fingers, as was his habit. Robby's fine brown hair fluttered in the wind while he patted Eli's browned cheek with one hand and wrapped the other around his neck. Overwhelmed, Jeanne put her arms around her beautiful brothers and held them tight.

"Mama," Robby murmured.

Jeanne pulled away. "What did you say?" She looked around the moving crowd, this time searching for Betty Ann.

"She was here a while ago," Eli said calmly. "She came to tell me goodbye. I don't know how she knew."

"Where is she?"

"She said she couldn't stay, so she left. She was only here for a minute."

First Billy, now Mama. Betty Ann was somewhere in the crowd. Jeanne kept looking, but she didn't spot the telltale blond head.

The waiting crowd turned in unison when they heard the bus roaring down the road. They backed out of the way to let the blue-and-silver Greyhound bus pull into the station for its stop. The whoosh of the brakes halted the conversations as reality jolted them.

The door swung open, and a man in uniform stepped out before the driver. The military man looked over the anxious faces. "Men," he said in a deep baritone and walked into the station office. There was no doubt who was in charge.

"We leave in ten minutes, folks," the driver announced, standing by the bus door. "Have your tickets ready." The crowd parted again when he, too, headed to the office.

The voices of the crowd surged with farewells. Scattered embraces varied from long and sorrowful to brief and embarrassed hugs. Jeanne gathered Robby in her arms, and Eli said his final goodbyes. Jeanne looked across heads to see Daniel staring at her. She managed a smile and waved. She would write to him.

Maggie was in the throng and cried as she said goodbye to her cousin Jameson. Then she walked over and hugged Eli around the waist. She was truly a mess. Maggie liked Eli more than Eli liked her. "Don't forget me, Eli." Maggie hiccupped through her tears while Eli patted her on the back.

"Those going to San Diego, line up!" the driver called out over the crowd.

A man holding a clipboard talked to each recruit and said he was thankful to see every branch represented. He glad-handed every family, slapping the guys on the back while he politely took the hands of the women. Jeanne heard him say the United States appreciated their sacrifice. Women smiled at him, but not Grandma Biddy.

"I have to get in line," Eli said.

Grandpa shook Eli's hand. "We'll be fine, boy. You come back to us."

Grandma Biddy hugged Eli and handed him a box of food to carry on the long trip. Most of the boys had something similar their families had prepared for them. Jeanne knew every person standing in that line. Eli and Daniel were taller than the other young men. Jeanne could see them over the tops of heads pushing toward the bus. Families backed away as their son or brother stepped onto the bus. Many of them rushed to the other side to hold hands through the windows or to say one last goodbye. Jeanne waved at Eli and Daniel when their turn came, and the driver punched their ticket. They sat midway on the bus, and Billy was seated behind them. His head was down, and he never looked up as the blue-and-silver Greyhound rolled away and disappeared down the road.

"Come on, Jeanne. Let's go home," Grandpa said.

He took Robby, and they quietly made their way downtown where the pickup was parked.

Chapter 23

Jeanne walked down the road to the house with a package under her arm. Eli's name was on it. They had not received a letter from him since he had departed for basic training. She was excited and worried at the same time. She ran the last hundred feet and skipped up the steps to give the package to Grandma Biddy.

"It's from Eli!" she shouted as she ran in the house. "Grandma, where are you?"

"I'm in the kitchen. Goodness, what is it, child?"

"A package from Eli," Jeanne announced. She placed it on the kitchen table in front of her grandmother.

Grandma Biddy sat down and ran her hands across the brown paper. "It is from Eli. Go out back and get Pa so he can see this too."

Jeanne skipped out the back door and took off running to find Grandpa. It was the middle of the summer, and she had been working in the field with Grandpa all day getting ready for the next planting of winter wheat. She searched the barn first, guessing that he had come in when she left the field. Then she went to the back and looked down the rows of corn, but she didn't find him. She stood still and listened. She could hear the motor of the cooperative tractor in the distance. He was still working, so she decided to go back to the house. She wanted to see what Eli had sent.

"I couldn't find him," Jeanne said, "but I heard the tractor down near the creek. Do we have to wait?"

"I guess he's trying to finish up before dark so he can get the cooperative's tractor to the next farmer waiting. We can go ahead and open it." Grandma had her sewing scissors ready and cut the string. She made fast work of removing the brown paper and opening the cardboard box. Grandma Biddy handed the lid to Robby, who sat in his chair. He banged the lid on his tray and dropped it on the floor. He bent over the edge to look down at his handiwork.

Inside the package, neatly folded, were the clothes Eli wore when he left that day on the bus. Grandma lifted each piece of clothing from the box and stacked it on the table. "Here's a letter," she said as she retrieved the khakis from the bottom of the box. "Read it out loud for us."

Jeanne gently placed her hand on Robby's forearm. "It's from Eli," she whispered excitedly.

"Ee-I," Robby cheered. Grandma handed Eli's shirt to Robby. He took it in both hands and buried his face in the folds. He looked up at Jeanne and beamed. "Ee-I."

"Yes, Eli." Jeanne smiled back. She opened the plain white envelope and unfolded the letter from her big brother. At first glance, Jeanne could see that it was short.

Dear Family,

We arrived in San Diego just fine. It was a long trip. By the time we got here, the bus was packed with boys who had enlisted. They told us we were in the navy now, so no need for us to have civilian clothes. They had us send the clothes back home. We go out for training tomorrow. That's all I can tell you. Jeanne, Billy was on the bus, but he hasn't said much the whole trip, and I haven't seen him since we arrived. He wasn't put in the same group as me and Daniel. The weather is nice here, and the ocean is an amazing thing. I wish you could see it.

I'll write more when I can.

Sincerely,

Eli

"At least we know he got there," Grandma said. "Pa will be glad to see the letter. Well, I need to start the chicken." She went to the drainboard and floured the chicken for frying. "Grandpa will be here in a minute, so go clean up for dinner."

∽

The table was set, and Grandma was feeding Robby when Jeanne entered the kitchen. Still no Grandpa. The days were long in July, and the glow of sunset lingered. Jeanne walked over and leaned on the doorframe, shading her eyes to watch for her grandpa. Old Dog was asleep under the table but woke up enough to lick up the scraps Robby had dropped on the floor.

"I don't see him," Jeanne said. "I don't hear the tractor either. Maybe it broke down, and he's walking home."

"Robby is nodding off," Grandma said. "I'll put him to bed while you go out and look for Pa before it gets pitch black out there."

"Do you think something's wrong?"

"Take Old Dog with you. He'll be of help to you when it gets dark."

The old hound jumped up and ran outside as soon as Jeanne opened the screen door. She had to run to keep up with the short-legged dog in front of her. The sun was down, but a glow still illuminated the sky. She could see the ruts from the tractor leading down the narrow road to the creek and the north field. She could smell the freshly turned earth as she approached the large rectangular field she and Grandpa had been preparing all day. It had to be one of the most pleasant scents in the world. It made her think of the Cantus, Grandma Biddy's garden, and harvesttime. She walked down the crooked path to the creek with Old Dog, but she didn't see or hear anything.

Jeanne stopped on the edge of the plowed dirt. "Grandpa!" she yelled. She waited and listened.

Old Dog howled and started running, then disappeared in the dark. Soon after, Jeanne heard him howl and bark. She followed the sound, hoping he had found Grandpa. A faint light showed Jeanne the narrow path. By this time, Old Dog's bark had turned into constant baying. Jeanne stopped and called again. She waited for an answer, but all she heard was Old Dog.

She continued toward the howling until a tractor silhouette appeared on the horizon. The tractor was turned over on its side. Fear struck Jeanne's heart, and she started to run. She found Old Dog standing by Grandpa trapped under the tractor.

"I'm here, Grandpa, I'm here." Jeanne knelt beside Grandpa and touched his forehead.

Grandpa's eyes fluttered open. "My legs are pinned under the tractor," he whispered.

Jeanne leaned closer to hear. Her knees sank in the mud when she tried to push the tractor off Grandpa. She moved to the tire and pushed. It didn't budge. She fell on her knees by Grandpa, frustrated at her helplessness. "I can't move it. I'm sorry, I'm sorry."

"Listen now, Jeannie girl. You'll have to go get help. Drive over to the Sweeney farm. They have workers there."

"I hate leaving you, Grandpa." Jeanne took his cold hand and rubbed it in hers. She checked him for bleeding, but she saw none on the top of his body. Jeanne's eyes had adjusted to the dark, and she could see the large back tire of the tractor covering Grandpa to his waist. The mud on the creek embankment was what had saved him. His body was pressed into the mud. Both of his arms were free, but it was impossible for him to push the giant wheel off his lower body. Just as it was impossible for her.

"You gotta go. Now git."

Jeanne nodded, her heart pounding. "Stay, Old Dog. Stay with Grandpa." The faithful hound lay down beside Grandpa and licked his hand.

Jeanne kissed Grandpa on the forehead, then stroked Old Dog. She took a deep breath and stood up. "I'll be back. I promise, Grandpa." Then she ran.

"Grandma Biddy!" Jeanne yelled when she got to the back door.

"What is it, Jeanne?"

"Grandpa is trapped under the tractor. He's hurt. I have to go get Mr. Sweeney." Jeanne grabbed the keys to the pickup.

"Where is he? I'll go to him. Robby's asleep."

"He's all the way to the end of the north field by the edge of the creek. Take the lantern. The path is dark." Jeanne raced out the door and headed to the truck.

She saw Grandma Biddy disappear behind the barn with the lantern swinging in the night as she drove away down the drive. Jeanne bumped over ruts while she fumbled for the headlights. She had them on by the time she reached the county road. She had never driven so fast, and still the trip to the Sweeney farm took her ten minutes. Fortunately, the whole family was on the porch when she slid to a stop in a cloud of dust.

"Mr. Sweeney," Jeanne yelled. "Grandpa's hurt! He's trapped under the tractor. I need your help." Jeanne jumped out of the truck and looked up at the people on the porch. Then she burst into tears. She put her face in her hands and sobbed. She felt a comforting arm around her shoulder.

"We'll help you, Jeanne," Mrs. Sweeney comforted.

"Don't worry, we're coming right away," said Mr. Sweeney. "I'll get the men in the bunkhouse. Mrs. Sweeney will come with you and stay with Robby. Wait for us at the house to show us the way."

"Yes, sir." Jeanne wiped her eyes and climbed back behind the wheel and waited for Mrs. Sweeney to get in the passenger seat.

☙

Jeanne stood by Grandma Biddy while the men hooked up chains to their truck and pulled the tractor off Grandpa. He had made an imprint in the mud and was stuck there. Grandma had brought a quilt and covered his chest, but now the men were using it for a stretcher. Jeanne and Grandma held lanterns while the men dug Grandpa out of the creek bank. His thigh was broken, and blood was seeping through his pants. Grandpa screamed when the men lifted him onto the quilt.

"Claude, we're going to lift you on the quilt into the back of your pickup," Mr. Sweeney explained. "You have to go to the hospital."

The men grabbed a corner of the quilt and slowly raised him to the tailgate. Then one of the men jumped in the back of the truck, gripped the quilt corners, and pulled until he was secure in the bed of the truck. The same man folded the sides of the quilt over him like a cocoon.

"I have to go with him," Grandma insisted. She blew out her lantern, and the men took her by the elbows and set her on the tailgate. She scooted back until she was sitting by his head. "Let's go, Jeanne. We're ready."

"Yes, ma'am." Jeanne eased the old pickup slowly down the path until she made it to the road. She kept looking back, afraid they would bounce out of the truck bed.

Jeanne drove carefully over the familiar road into town. She went as fast as she dared. The slow pace made the trip seem interminable. When they pulled into the emergency entrance, no one was there. Jeanne sprinted down a white hall and found a nurse who ran with her back to the truck. Mr. Sweeney pulled up just as the nurse and Jeanne rushed out the door.

"I figured you could use help getting Claude out of the truck," Mr. Sweeney said.

The men carried Grandpa in the hospital wrapped in the quilt matted with mud. Grandma and Jeanne followed them. A nurse directed them to a cubicle where they put Grandpa on a metal platform. Grandma gripped his hand, and Jeanne stood close to his head with her hand on his shoulder.

When a doctor and two other nurses walked in, Jeanne and her grandma were asked to leave. "Come with me," one of the nurses urged, gesturing toward the door.

Grandma hesitated. She didn't let go of Grandpa's hand.

"We need room to work," the doctor explained, "and we'll come get you when we know something."

"All right. Come on, Jeanne." Grandma exchanged Grandpa's hand for Jeanne's, and they left together.

Back outside, the men stood beside the trucks waiting for news.

Grandma walked toward them. "It'll be a while. Jeanne and I'll wait here."

"I'll go on back home now," Mr. Sweeney said.

"Thank you for helping us." Grandma patted him on the arm. "Thank you."

"That's what neighbors are for. Let us know if you need us. Times are hard when the men are off at war."

Jeanne and her grandma retreated into the back door of the hospital. They were directed to the front of the hospital to wait for the doctor to give them the news about Grandpa. The stark waiting room was empty. A long wooden bench faced a line of ladder-backed chairs that formed a funnel for the patients and visitors to follow to the reception desk. Jeanne was covered in mud, and Grandma had blood on her skirt, but Jeanne didn't mention it and Grandma didn't notice. They could have been coming in for treatment themselves, as wretched as they appeared.

They sat in the last two chairs near the desk and waited. After two hours, a doctor approached from the far end of the hallway. His gait was steady but not hurried.

"The doctor is coming, Grandma." Jeanne saw her grandma unfold her hands and grip the chair arms to stand. Grandma and Jeanne stood shoulder to shoulder when the man in the white coat entered the waiting room.

"Mrs. Bradshaw?" he asked.

"Yes."

"Mr. Bradshaw is stable, but he has several injuries. His right foot and ankle are broken in four places. We have repaired his ankle and foot, but he has a bad break in his left femur. It's in a cast."

"Will he be all right?" Grandma asked.

"He won't be able to walk for quite a while. We'll see as he heals. He may also have a hip fracture. We'll know more tomorrow."

"We have to see him before we go home," Grandma insisted.

"He's heavily sedated for the pain. He won't even wake up if you go in there now. It would be best if you come back in the morning."

"We must see him, even if he doesn't wake up."

The doctor nodded. "Come with me then."

They followed the doctor down the tiled hallway and into Grandpa's room. He was pale and still.

Grandma talked to him like he was sitting across the dinner table. "Claude, the doctor tells us you have a few broken bones. Broken bones heal, and you'll be back plowing that field in no time." She picked up his hand and patted it. "Well then, you need sleep, so Jeanne and I are going home for the evening. We'll be back tomorrow." Grandma leaned over and whispered in his ear, "God has hold of you. We're going to trust in him. Remember, I love you." She touched his cheek and gently kissed him on the lips. Grandma wiped her eyes and waited at the door.

Jeanne was afraid she was going to cry again. She could only whisper, "I love you, Grandpa." She hoped he heard her.

❧

The next morning, Jeanne sat on the milking stool, leaning against Polkadot's side while she milked. The sun was up by the time she finished with Lady Bell and fed the animals. Grandma and Mrs. Sweeney were drinking coffee. Both women were haggard but thankful. Stacks of pancakes waited for Jeanne on the kitchen table.

"I can drive you home when you're ready, Mrs. Sweeney." Jeanne sat down at the table and poured herself a much-needed cup of coffee. "Thank you for staying with Robby."

"Thank you, dear. Eat your breakfast and then we'll go. Robby was no trouble at all."

After the meal, Grandma and Mrs. Sweeney hugged each other on the porch. They were outfitted in their everyday flour sack dresses. Mrs. Sweeney was much younger, but Jeanne could see the deep creases in her face from the hard farm life. Most of the women looked much the same. Grandma was stronger than most. She had a determination and will unmatched by anyone. But some wore out early. Jeanne took after her grandma.

"Thank you, Martha," Grandma said. "You've been a big help."

"I'll let Mr. Sweeney know about Claude. I'll pray for his healing."

Jeanne drove Mrs. Sweeney home and was back in thirty minutes. While Jeanne changed clothes, Grandma and Robby settled in the truck. Somber faces focused on the road as they sped to the hospital.

"Let's stop at the post office," Grandma said. "I want to mail a letter to Bootsie. I've told her about the accident."

"Are we going to write to Eli?" Jeanne asked. She wished he were here to help. She was already up early every day and tended the animals before breakfast. The wheat had been harvested, but the corn was still in the far field, and it had a month to go before it would be time to be picked. This would be her routine while Grandpa was in the hospital. She didn't know how she was going to handle the work when school started. Grandma said not to worry, and they would figure it out. *We have to talk about it soon, though.* Jeanne silently worried. *School starts in two weeks.*

Chapter 24

"Beulah, help me up," Grandpa shouted from his bed. "I want to sit at the table."

Grandpa had been home for a week. Jeanne and Grandma had fixed up a bed in the living room. It had been a month since the accident, and Grandpa was making progress, but orders like these were becoming the norm. Jeanne wasn't sure how long it would be before Grandma had had enough.

"I'll help you." Jeanne stood beside the bed and helped Grandpa sit up. She quickly stuffed a pillow behind his back to stabilize his sitting position.

"Wait a minute," Grandma yelled from the kitchen. "I'm coming. I can't leave anything on the stove."

Jeanne lifted his broken foot while Grandma scooted the broken leg into position over the edge of the bed.

"Move my leg a little at a time," Grandpa instructed through gritted teeth. "Don't break my leg again."

"I know how to do this, Claude. Try and be patient."

Old Dog ran to the head of the bed and started to bark. The front door banged open.

Auntie Boots stood in the door with her arms akimbo. "What in the world is going on in here? Another war! Why, Claude Lee Bradshaw, are you giving everybody a hard time?" She threw her head back and howled with laughter.

Jeanne was startled. "Auntie Boots!"

The early morning sun shone behind Auntie Boots. She filled the bright opening with a silhouette of boots, a full skirt, and a broad-brimmed cowboy hat.

"Bootsie, am I ever glad to see you!" Grandma exclaimed.

"When I got your letter, Beulah, I could read between the lines," Bootsie declared as she burst through the door. "I'm here to help."

"Are the kids with you?" Grandma asked.

"No, they're in school, and James can handle things for a while." She looked at Jeanne and winked.

"How'd you get here?" Grandpa asked.

"I drove Old Sacrifice," Bootsie said. "She still runs. That old jalopy got me here all the way from Abilene."

"I thought it was broken down," Grandpa said.

"James fixed it. You know how handy he is. When we got Beulah's letter, he started working on it."

While Boots was talking, she moved Grandma out of the way and shooed Old Dog to the kitchen. Jeanne relinquished the injured foot she held to Auntie Boots and backed up to let her take over. Jeanne put her hand over her mouth to stifle a giggle. Even Grandpa was about to smile when Auntie Boots sailed to his side.

"Now, Claude, let's see if we can get you to the kitchen."

"Be careful, Bootsie," Grandpa fussed.

Auntie Boots ignored him and practically carried Grandpa to the kitchen. She dwarfed his wiry frame. Her strong, big-boned, six-feet-tall physique made lifting Grandpa look easy. Moreover, his body was shrunken due to the month in the hospital. Jeanne had worried he would waste away. Auntie Boots being there lifted her spirits. She and Grandma followed the two into the kitchen where they sat down for breakfast. Grandpa ate more that morning than he had in a week.

"I have a surprise for you, Claude," Auntie Boots announced. "I'll be back."

In a few short minutes, she stormed in, and Jeanne looked up to see bicycle wheels coming through the door.

Auntie Boots clanked the strange contraption to the floor. "James fixed this up for you." Auntie Boots stood there beaming.

It was an improvised wheelchair made from a dining-room chair with armrests. Large wheels were attached to a frame on the sides, and there were plank footrests on the front. Small caster wheels in the back held the chair steady.

"I declare!" Grandma exclaimed. "That's something, all right."

Grandpa's face brightened. "Why, it's a wheelchair."

"Look at this. James even made push handles for it." Auntie Boots rolled the chair back and forth to demonstrate the practicality of the handles. "Let's see if it works." Auntie Boots picked Grandpa up and set him in the rolling chair.

It screeched a bit and barely made it through the door, but it worked. Grandpa tried moving it by himself and was successful.

Grandpa gradually began recovering from his injuries. Two weeks later, the doctor came to the house and removed the cast on his leg but warned him not to put any weight on it. School started for Jeanne that Tuesday, and Auntie Boots ruled the roost for a time while Grandpa was healing. She wheeled Grandpa out to the fields to oversee the planting and give directions to the workers from the high school. The experience with the workers wasn't the same for Jeanne this time. The atmosphere was subdued this year without Eli and Billy, and Jeanne did more work in the barn instead of in the field.

Maggie came, but she was depressed because she hadn't heard from Eli. Jeanne and Maggie had lunch together each day, and the conversation was always the same.

"Have you heard from Eli?" Maggie asked.

"You know I would tell you if we had," Jeanne said. "I would love to hear from him as well."

"You haven't heard from Billy either?" Maggie's mind seemed to always be on romance.

"No, I don't think I'll be hearing from him." Jeanne hoped that her comment didn't lead to other questions. She didn't want to say any more than she already had. The town gossip was aflame with speculation as to why Cindy had suddenly left Readfield. Cindy's mother told everyone that she had gone to help her frail aunt Millie.

"But you had a date with him," Maggie persisted.

"It was just a date. Nothing serious." Jeanne tried to be nonchalant as if the whole date thing was not important. She believed she was convincing.

"I figured you'd be crazy for him," Maggie said. "All the other girls were. I was surprised when he joined up and left town so fast."

"That was all the men talked about last year, going off to war." Jeanne didn't' want to talk about Billy.

"Who's Billy?" asked Auntie Boots. She sat down next to Maggie and unwrapped a sandwich.

"Only the handsomest guy in the county," said Maggie. "Except for Eli."

"And they're all gone, I take it."

"Yep, off to war," Maggie said. "Jeanne had a date with Billy and then he was gone. No letters either."

"Maggie," someone yelled from the field.

"I'd better go and help my group. Can you believe I'm the oldest?" Maggie disappeared around the barn.

When Maggie was gone, Auntie Boots said, "Tell me about this Billy."

Jeanna sighed. "What Maggie said is true. He is handsome, and he charms everyone, but he was not for me."

"Oh, did he call it quits?"

"He really didn't say anything." Jeanne then decided to tell

Auntie Boots what she had witnessed in the Greyhound parking lot.

"You're lucky then," Auntie Boots said when Jeanne had finished. "To find out about the kind of man he is before you really got your heart broken. You may not feel that way now, and it may take time to get over him, but mark my words, you will."

"I'm really glad you're here, Auntie Boots." It was easy for her to confide in Auntie. She listened and was straightforward with her opinions. Jeanne found that she liked hearing the truth. Betty Ann had lied to them so many times that she expected what her mother said to be false.

"I am too, but I'm going to have to leave soon. Claude is getting better. I'm not sure that foot of his will ever be the same again. I've talked with Beulah about it."

"He's in pain all the time. I thought Grandpa's leg would be the problem, or maybe the hip, but those healed right away."

They sat for a while in the quiet midday stillness, not needing to say anything else. What Auntie Boots had said about Grandpa's foot scared Jeanne. How would he do the work on the farm? She believed what Auntie Boots had said about Billy. She had wanted him to be different with her.

"Oh, I nearly forgot," Auntie Boots said. "Your grandma wants you to come help make lye soap. Good luck with that. I'm going out to bring Claude back to the house."

Jeanne found Grandma on the back porch, straining rainwater through a large clay pot full of ashes. The gray water dripped into a pan beneath it.

"Jeanne, take this water jug and keep pouring it through the ashes. I'll finish clarifying the bacon grease."

"Do you want me to boil the water after I finish?" Jeanne asked.

"Yes, bring it in the kitchen."

Jeanne held the container of lye water in her arms and entered the kitchen. She spotted two letters on the table.

"Put that on the back burner," Grandma instructed. "It'll take a while to boil it down."

"Whose letters?"

Grandma faced her, holding a ladle in one hand and a stained cup towel in the other. "One is from your daddy, and it looks like one is from Daniel."

"Oh." Jeanne picked up the envelopes and searched for the postmarks. "They're both military returns. Isn't Daddy too old to join?"

"Go on and read them while I watch the lye," Grandma said. "I've read the one from Robert."

Jeanne grabbed the letters and ran up the stairs to her room. She was glad to hear from Daniel, but she was anxious to find out if her father had gotten her letter, so she read his first. It was addressed to the Bradshaw family.

July 29, 1942

Dear Mama and Pa,

I'm sorry I missed last Christmas. I am now part of the US Navy Construction Battalion. The navy recruited the construction company I worked for. We build airstrips. We will be going to the Pacific to build bases. The nickname for our bunch is Seabees. I'm proud to serve. Maybe it's the first time I've done something I'm proud of. Mama, my pay is coming to you. I know you could use it on the farm. I hope times are not hard for you and Pa. I haven't heard from Betty Ann and the kids for a long time. I think about how they are. Eli is grown, and I wonder if he's fighting too. So many youngsters are here.

Your son,

Robert

Jeanne put the letter down on her cot. The letter she had written to her father was lost in a post office somewhere. Tears spilled down her face. She felt as if she didn't exist. No mention of her or

Robby, and he believed Betty Ann was still around. Jeanne wiped her tears as anger replaced the hurt. She was still determined. She would write to him through the Seabees. There was an address on the envelope.

Now the war had Eli, Daniel, Billy, and her father. The reports they heard every day on the radio were not encouraging. The war was not going to be over soon like the men in town had said. Jeanne expected they were just getting started.

The next letter was thicker. She looked at the front of the envelope. Daniel had nice handwriting. She felt guilty. She had only eked out two letters to him. There was the early one, and a month later she sent another informing him of Grandpa's injury. That letter had been wordy and contained details of the accident. Thinking about it now, she must have needed to share the events of that terrible night with someone. She had asked him not to tell Eli about Grandpa's accident.

October 4, 1942

Dear Jeanne,

Your last letter was a welcome sight. I'm sorry about your grandpa. I have read your letter over and over, and I feel like I am there every time. I wish I could have been there to help you when your grandpa had the accident. I hope he is getting better every day. After our basic training, Eli and Billy were assigned to other ships, and I haven't seen them.

So far, I like the navy. The ocean is the most beautiful blue I've ever seen. We even have dolphins swimming along the side of the ship. They jump out of the water like they're saying hello to us.

I've met men from all over the country. When this war is over, I want to go visit other states, especially Florida and Montana. Not only are the boys from different states, they are from different occupations. There are farmers, but those in the city work at things like being clerks in stores and building things in factories. It doesn't matter where you're from, everybody here is homesick, including me. Maybe this will be over soon, and we can all get back to our lives.

By the time you get this, it will be close to Thanksgiving and Christmas. I hope you are doing well. I miss everyone back home.

Your friend,

Daniel

∽

Jeanne felt better after she had written a letter to Daniel and Eli. She even began writing one to her father. She didn't know what to say to him and stumbled over her words. It was strange knowing that this letter could end up in his hands. She wanted to tell him about Robby and Eli and even Betty Ann. She put her stationery down and looked at the few sentences she had written. Too much, and yet, not enough. She decided to wait and give it more time.

A week later, Jeanne had mailed four letters. Besides the letters to Daniel, Eli, and her father, Jeanne included one to Betty Ann. She wasn't sure she had seen her mother on that day at the bus stop. She certainly had experienced plenty on that occasion. She prayed for strength after the bus pulled out and took the young men of the town away. She did more at the farm and still made her grades at school. Other women and girls did the same. Everyone worked hard for the war effort.

Jeanne hadn't heard much from Sandra since their encounter in the library. She was glad. She didn't have time for that foolishness. She was so tired lately, she doubted she could argue, even a little bit. The letter she had sent to her mama was short. Less to argue about if she saw her again.

Auntie Boots was leaving today. She wanted to be home before the kids got out of school. Jeanne had a Friday holiday and helped her load vegetables from the garden into Old Sacrifice for Uncle James and the kids. They tied a blanket over it all. Grandpa and Grandma had already gone back in the house and left them there to say their goodbyes.

"Remember what I told you about men," Auntie Boots said. "You'll find good ones out there too. They're not the flashy kind. Those will get you in trouble."

"I'll remember." Jeanne hugged her aunt around the waist and cried. "I'll miss you so much, Auntie Boots."

"Why, ol' Boots will be available." She held Jeanne by her shoulders. "You send for me if you need me, ya hear? I'll be here in a flash. You pray to sweet Jesus, and you'll be all right." Auntie let out a howl and laughed her big laugh, jumped in the car, and drove off down the road. Jeanne gazed up at the cloudy sky and estimated Auntie Boots had left in plenty of time to make it home before dark.

Jeanne had learned how to manage school and work at the farm while Auntie Boots was there. She would have enough credits to graduate early. There was a lot for her to consider.

She ran back to the house to get out of the cold. Grandpa had said this was going to be a hard winter. The temperature was dropping fast, and the icy wind froze her skin through her thin cotton dress. Jeanne backed up to the fire and warmed her arms and legs. The house was somber and depressed without Auntie Boots in it. She tried to shake the glum feeling, and as soon as she was warm, she grabbed her coat and went back outside to gather an armload of firewood.

While Jeanne was bringing in the third load of wood, she saw a car approaching. At first, she thought Auntie had forgotten something. As she peered through the dark afternoon haze, she could make out a shiny black sedan driving slowly down the drive. Jeanne was mesmerized. Not blinking, she held the stack of wood and wondered who was coming to their house. Maybe they're lost. That fancy car surely couldn't hold up on these rough country roads. One thing for sure, it wasn't Auntie Boots.

The car rolled to a stop in front of the porch. Eli got out dressed in a fancy suit. "Hello, sis. Let me help you with that wood." He grinned from ear to ear.

"Don't stand there gawking, Eli," a woman with yellow hair yelled from inside the car. "Come open this door and help me out." She pulled on a fur-trimmed coat as she climbed out of the sleek sedan.

Chapter 25

"I'm coming, honey." Eli waved at Jeanne and hurried around the car to help the lady out.

"Don't drop my fur in the dirt!" she shrieked. "Do you know how much that cost my daddy?" The woman wobbled to the front steps in her matching black leather high heels and clutched the newel post while Eli scrambled to her vacant side.

Jeanne finally came to her senses and walked over to greet them. "Eli, it's so good to see you. Are you home for good?" She looked at the stranger and then at Eli. Her stack of firewood blocked access to her brother, but at the same time provided a barrier to the woman.

"He's on leave, and we're here for a short visit before he ships out," the woman said. Her words dripped with familiarity and ownership.

"I'm his sister, Jeanne." She felt compelled to establish her territory. After all, this was her home.

"Yes, I know, dear," she snipped. "He's talked of nothing else except you, Robby, and this farm. Of course, his grandparents too."

By this time, Eli had opened the front door and the woman had walked into the house. Jeanne followed with the armful of wood and saw the shocked look on the faces in the room.

"Let me take the wood." Eli took the bundle and stacked it by the fireplace.

"You must be Mr. and Mrs. Bradshaw. I'm Gloria. Gloria Putnam of San Diego." She didn't wait for responses but went to Robby and spoke slowly and looked straight at him. "And you are Robby." Gloria reached out with a gloved hand and patted him on the head.

Old Dog began to howl. Gloria jumped back but tried to pet him anyway. Old Dog continued making a ruckus. Jeanne tried to corral him, but he would have none of it and ran into the kitchen.

"Have a seat, Miss Putnam," Grandma said.

Grandpa stood and nodded at the woman. Eli made the rounds, giving hugs and smiling. He then sat on the hearth and looked around the room.

"How are you, son?" Grandpa asked, still standing.

"I'm home for a couple of days. Then I report back. I'm shipping out next week."

Jeanne was too nervous to sit. She studied each face, trying to take in what was happening. She could see the disappointment on Grandpa's face. It didn't seem that Eli had even noticed that Grandpa had been sitting in a wheelchair. She saw Eli and Gloria exchange looks. Gloria nodded to Eli, urging him to continue.

"I wanted Gloria to meet my family because when we get back, we're getting married."

Jeanne was stunned. In this short time, Eli had changed his life completely. Grandpa sat down at that announcement, but Jeanne let out a gasp and said, "What? What do you mean?"

"Put on the kettle for tea, Jeanne, and get out those cookies," Grandma said. "Let's serve our guest."

Gloria beamed and took Eli's hand, but when Jeanne picked up Robby and carried him with her, Eli followed her into the kitchen. He took Robby and put him in his high chair. Jeanne waited for her big brother to start a conversation as she went about boiling water and getting the nice cups and saucers out.

"Isn't she something?" Eli said as he absently patted Robby on the shoulder. Then he took Robby's small white hand in both of his huge ones. "I'm going to marry her, Jeanne, and I probably won't come back here except to visit."

"How long have you known her? Why are you doing this so fast?"

"Gloria says it's not so fast if you consider that I may not come back from the war."

Jeanne turned away and tended to the water on the stove. "We didn't write to you about it, but didn't you notice that Grandpa is sitting in a wheelchair? He had a terrible accident right after you left." This exchange didn't seem real to Jeanne. It felt like they were in two separate rooms carrying on different conversations. Her brother was not a part of her world.

"I was so caught up in what Gloria wanted me to do, I didn't notice." Eli jumped up, embarrassed and worried, with an uncharacteristic frown.

"Don't go back in there now," Jeanne pleaded. She clutched his sleeve and pulled. "No need to upset things more. I'll catch you up on what has happened since you left." By this time Jeanne was distraught. She wanted to settle down and get control of her emotions. *How will we make it on the farm? What am I to think of this strange woman in our living room who's going to marry my brother?*

Eli faced her. "What are you going to do now that Pa is hurt?" He sat back down and put both hands on the tabletop—the familiar position he had taken when they were making the decision to leave Deep Creek.

"We were going to hang on till the war was over and you came home. You tell me what we can do." Jeanne tried not to show the bitterness she felt in her gut. *Yet, what would I do if I had the same chance Eli has?* "He's getting better every day, and Auntie Boots came for a month to help." The finality of his announcement was a vise squeezing her life. Jeanne struggled to breathe.

"The government was supposed to be sending people to help with the crops," Eli reasoned.

"They still are, but Grandpa supervises them while I'm in school." Jeanne filled the teapot and fixed the tray, trying to focus on the mundane. "The tea is ready. We'll talk more later." She left both brothers there and pushed her way into the living room.

Gloria was red-faced when Jeanne set the tray down on the hearth. Grandpa was quiet, and Grandma was fanning her face with her apron.

Eli walked in, oblivious to the surrounding tension. He sat in the chair by the radio and put Robby in his lap. Jeanne had seen Eli ignore Mama's behavior before to avoid conflict. A fight brewed inside of Jeanne. Silent screams surged in her throat, but no one noticed. All the attention was on Eli. She swallowed her anguish. She loved her brothers. There they were, Eli cradling Robby protectively, Robby's face glowing with complete trust. Jeanne felt shame at her anger. She remembered then what Jesus told his disciples: Love one another as I have loved you.

"Let's listen to music," Eli said as he clicked on the radio. Static sputtered, and he fiddled with the knobs with great interest, avoiding eye contact with anyone in the room.

Jeanne was relieved to have a distraction. Eli had to know how much he had turned everything upside down. Jeanne busied herself serving tea while Eli tuned in Tommy Dorsey's orchestra. It gave them time to recover, and for the first time, she had a good look at Gloria. Her blond hair hung to her shoulders in a stylish pageboy. It was parted on the side and held back with a mother-of-pearl clasp. She wore beautiful black leather pumps and, of all things, silk stockings. That was unheard of since the war started. She wore an elegant white blouse that tied at the neck and was neatly tucked in the tiny waist of a red pleated skirt. She was a breathtaking younger version of their mother. Jeanne couldn't believe she hadn't noticed the striking resemblance when Gloria came through the door. Her brother was not the only one not paying attention. What she wouldn't give to have Auntie Boots here at a time like this.

Jeanne settled down with her cup of tea and listened with the others to the Tommy Dorsey band play "Let's Get Away from It All."

Gloria sang along. "Let's take a boat to Bermuda."

Eli answered, "Let's take a plane to Saint Paul."

They finished the song together and laughed at a personal secret only they knew. Robby clapped his hands and smiled, always happy and loving. Jeanne prayed she could endure the remainder of the evening. She looked at Grandma and Grandpa. Their faces were passive. They were trying to take in the scene before them.

Jeanne didn't know how, but Grandma fixed supper and managed sleeping arrangements. She put Gloria on the cot off the kitchen and made a pallet for Eli on the floor by the fire. Jeanne stayed awake for a long time that night until the sounds in the night settled. Even Old Dog crawled under Robby's bed and stayed there till dawn.

"Oh, good morning," Gloria greeted the four Bradshaws sitting around the breakfast table. She wore a heavy robe, and her hair was still fastened with bobby pins. "Excuse me." She scooted past the table and ran out the back door to the privy.

"Is she going to be all right?" Grandpa asked.

"I showed her where it was last night," Jeanne said. "She seemed okay then. She did say it was the first time she had been outside to use a toilet. I believe she called it quaint."

"Maybe you better check on her, Jeanne," Eli said, his voice edging closer to alarm.

"She's a grown woman," Grandma chimed in. "Jeanne, you stay put. I'm sure she will make it just fine by herself."

"She's not used to the ways on a farm," Eli explained. "I tried to tell her about how hard it was before we came." His voice trailed off, ending his weak excuse.

About that time, Gloria rushed through the door and made

a beeline for the sink. "At least you have running water in the kitchen," she said as she took the bar of newly made lye soap and washed her hands. "What is this?"

"Lye soap," Grandma responded. "There's no need to try to get a good lather. It's not store-bought soap."

Gloria dropped the triangular gray bar in the sink and joined them at the table. Grandma placed a large plate of eggs, bacon, and biscuits in front of her.

"Oh, my," Gloria said, still wiping her hands on her skirt. "You do eat well. You don't happen to have a grapefruit or orange juice? I don't eat much until noon."

"Try your best, hon," Eli encouraged. "It'll be a long day. Oranges don't grow here."

Gloria smiled at him and pinched a morsel from the biscuit. She continued to pass bits to Old Dog, and he showed more tolerance for the visitor when his leftover meal had doubled in size.

The day was a lark for the blond woman in their home. Gloria giggled and smiled and complimented Grandpa. She tried to help Grandma by washing dishes. She attempted girl talk with Jeanne, but Gloria's social life was a far cry from what Jeanne had experienced. For a while they talked about hairstyles and how hard it was to find decent stockings, but most of the time Jeanne simply listened.

That evening before everyone went to bed, the conversation turned to the war following the nightly news broadcast. Fear gripped everyone in the room as the realization dawned that Eli was going to fight in that war. There was no doubt he was going away this time. Everyone's future was in limbo—Eli because of the war, Gloria because of Eli leaving, and Grandma and Grandpa tending the farm without Eli. Jeanne and Robby were connected to their grandparents, so whatever they decided, she and her little brother were bound to that decision.

Grandma was the first to speak. "So, are you coming back here after the war, Eli?"

Jeanne could see she wanted to hear it for herself. She was

going to force the topic. Grandpa said nothing but stared directly at Gloria. Jeanne was silent as she waited for the answer.

"I'm not sure what I'm going to do," Eli stammered. He was struggling. No wonder Gloria had come with him. He never would have done this on his own.

"He may get a good job with my daddy's company in San Diego," Gloria said. "It's a really good opportunity. Much better than here on the farm. Eli's smart, and everybody loves him. He might even get to go to college and get a degree. He couldn't do that staying here." She slowly looked around the room and took in her surroundings as if for the first time. Gloria's evident disdain spoiled her lovely face and settled over the room, leaving them without any air to breathe.

Jeanne bolted outside and stood on the porch in the cold. She still heard muffled conversation inside. She moved away from the voices and finally found herself in the stall with Polkadot. She stroked the cow's back until she calmed down.

When Jeanne finally slipped through the front door, Eli was asleep on the floor. Old Dog sniffed her leg and trotted off to Robby's cot.

"He looks so innocent lying there," Gloria said in a hoarse whisper. "I understand why it's hard on you. He's special. I knew it the minute I met him."

Jeanne followed the voice to find Gloria huddled in a quilt, sitting in the shadows by the radio. She, too, stared at Eli, noting the similarity of both brothers' peaceful sleeping countenances. She was the one honed by cruelty. Gloria's words were true. Eli was special. Everyone loved him.

Gloria motioned for her to follow her into the kitchen. Jeanne tiptoed around her sleeping brother and sat at the table opposite their newest guest.

Gloria began at once. "Eli has told your grandparents he will come back here after the war. He couldn't bear to see them disappointed."

"What?" Jeanne exclaimed. "I thought—"

"I know." Gloria's eyes flashed. "That's why I'm telling you this. Not only will he not come back here after the war, he will never come back to this hovel. Ever. He has a chance in life, and I will see to it that he gets it."

Jeanne's heart had swollen with joy and broken with pain in that miniscule moment. God help me, she prayed. This was her mantra till she was waving goodbye the next day.

Chapter 26

Jeanne, wrapped in her favorite quilt, listened to tidbits of the New Year's Eve program through the static on the radio. She reached across the arm of the sofa, clicked the knob off, and walked to the fireplace. She didn't feel like celebrating. After Eli's visit, Thanksgiving and Christmas had slipped by uneventfully with a mere hint of Christ's coming. She was simply going through the motions. If it hadn't been for Robby and his delightful childlike wonder, the entire holiday time would have lost its magic. Grandma and Grandpa slipped into the hard routine that came with winter days.

Jeanne studied the patchwork quilt draped over her shoulders. Each square had been a piece of clothing someone in the family had worn. Grandma Biddy had pointed out the squares of material that had belonged to her father. She felt closer to him when she pulled the edges together and became a cocoon of memories. It was 1943. *Am I ready for what this new year will bring?*

"Wake up, child." Grandma gently shook Jeanne's shoulder. "You'll catch your death on the floor like that."

"I fell asleep waiting for the new year. It was warm here by the fireplace."

"The new year will come whether we wait for it or not," Grandma said. "You need to get dressed. The cooperative will be here this afternoon, and then we'll see what's really going to happen this year."

"Do I hear Robby coughing?" Jeanne asked as she folded the quilt.

"It's not bad," Grandma replied, "but I want you to stay in the back with him when everyone gets here today. I don't want him exposed to something the men might bring into the house."

The meeting lasted longer than Jeanne expected. In the next room, voices rose and fell with a steady rhythm. If they were discussing the war, she was sure opinions were flowing freely. By the time she heard the men filing out the door and saying their friendly goodbyes, Robby was asleep.

Jeanne slipped into the kitchen to watch the last of the cooperative members leave. Instead, she found her grandparents sitting in the living room talking with Mr. Ledbetter, the lawyer go-between.

"Come in, Jeanne," Grandma Biddy called. "You need to hear this too."

Jeanne hesitated, but went to her grandma. "What is it?" She sat down softly and edged close to Grandma.

Grandma patted her on the knee while she looked stoically at Mr. Ledbetter. He had been talking but had stopped to wait for her.

Grandpa bent forward with his elbows balanced on his knees and his hands clasped together. "Jeanne, Mr. Ledbetter has engaged another family to move here and take over running this farm for the cooperative."

"How can they do that?" Jeanne sat up and glared at Mr. Ledbetter. "How could you do that?"

The lawyer's neck turned red that crept up his face and

disappeared into his hairline. His gnarled hand rubbed his forehead, and he looked back at Jeanne with a pained stare.

"This really isn't a surprise," Grandpa confessed. He leaned back and folded his hands in his lap. "This was bound to happen. I can't work the farm like I used to. I'm grateful we had this time after my accident. It makes sense."

"When do we have to leave?" Grandma asked.

"You'll have till the end of February, before spring planting." Mr. Ledbetter paused and addressed Grandpa. "You'll get paid for the winter wheat."

"We'll have more questions, but we have to talk amongst ourselves first." Grandpa stood for a handshake.

"Of course. Come by my office anytime." Mr. Ledbetter shook Grandpa's hand and walked out the door. He donned his coat and hat as he hurried down the front steps.

The three of them watched the lawyer leave. Jeanne looked at her grandparents, but her grandpa turned away from her. He walked through the kitchen and out the back door with Old Dog trailing behind.

"I'll make us tea." Grandma went to the sink and filled the kettle. "Check on Robby before we talk."

Jeanne peeked in the bedroom to find a still-sleeping Robby. She tiptoed to his cot and touched his forehead. He was cool and dry. When she backed away, Robby stirred but didn't wake. She slipped back through the door and left him sleeping peacefully. When she returned to the kitchen, Grandpa was sitting at the table with a steaming cup of tea.

"What are we going to do?" Jeanne sat to calm herself. She felt betrayed and angry for herself and for Grandma and Grandpa.

"The Lord will provide," Grandma reassured. "I know that. I've been thinking about this, and I can sew for the public. Of course, we'll have to move to town."

"Town? When do we have to move?" Jeanne was amazed at Grandma's calm as well as her belief that God would provide. *How is that possible?*

"I'll talk to Mrs. Watkins at the dry goods. She'll send customers my way. She's wanted me to sew for her before, but I couldn't with the responsibilities here at the farm."

"But that is *you*, Grandma, not God," Jeanne said. The words had flown out of her mouth, but she did not regret it.

"Oh, dear child, God gave me the talent to be a fine seamstress. He gives me the hope and the strength to face this life in the hard times and the good. Most of all, he put love in my heart. You must not be angry with God, for it rains on the good and the bad."

"What does that mean?" Jeanne knew what Grandma meant. She couldn't let go of the bad news.

"I believe you know what it means." Grandma looked at Jeanne. "It's hard to accept right now. You want to blame someone."

Jeanne nodded. Grandma was right. She needed to think of what to do, not who to blame. She wasn't ready for another move.

"Take time to be by yourself," Grandma advised. "Talk to God."

Her grandparents walked out of the room together and left her there to contemplate the new events. As they left, she saw Grandpa take Grandma's hand, and Grandma pat Grandpa's arm. Her heart broke and filled with love at the same time.

She left the table and walked outside. She wanted to feel the cold air on her skin. She didn't want to pray. Instead, she walked down the front drive and past the mailbox. She stopped thirty minutes later and looked up to find herself on the road to the church. She continued until headstones greeted her behind the church with their quiet serenity. She read the family names on the tombstones as she wandered among the graves. The markers were old and faded, and she couldn't make out the writing. Jeanne traced a beautiful cross on a prominent headstone and wondered if what she had learned in church would help her now.

She sat in front of a tall stone and leaned against it, letting her tears fall. The wind danced through the bare branches, leaving a soft clatter around her. Listening to the strange rhythm led her to acceptance and onward to determination.

When the afternoon light began to fade, Jeanne rubbed her arms to erase the chill, then ran the entire distance back to the farm. She arrived full of grit and her heart nearly bursting with the love she felt for her family.

∽

Three weeks came and went, and Grandma found a house in town.

Jeanne was packing the pickup to transport a load of belongings to the new place. "The pickup is full," she shouted as she slammed the tailgate shut.

"Carry this sack on your lap," Grandma instructed. "I'll put Robby on mine. You'll have to straddle the gear shift."

Jeanne took the soft sack that molded to her lap and held the bundle secure under her chin for the trip. Finally, Grandma and Grandpa slid into the cab beside her, and they drove off to see their new home.

"It seems like it's taking forever to get there," Jeanne complained.

"I'm taking it slow on purpose," Grandpa said. "I don't want to jostle our furniture in the back."

"This is a long journey for all of us," Grandma said. "I'll be glad when the move is finished."

Robby patted the glass and said, "Town."

"Yes, it is," said Grandpa. "Yes, it is."

"Turn here." Grandma pointed to a white two-story home with gingerbread trim on the front porch. The house looked worn but cozy. Evidence of rosebushes grew in the front along the walk, and trees lined the street. Jeanne thought they were oak, but she wasn't sure with the leaves gone.

Grandpa pulled into a narrow driveway that ran beside the house and led to a garage in the back. The door to the garage was open and filled with someone else's boxes. The structure leaned vicariously to the left and looked as if any moment it would fall, had it not been for those boxes inside. Jeanne hoped the house was in better shape.

The backyard was big and overgrown. Even in winter, it looked a mess. Grandpa walked around the garage and stepped off the backyard as if measuring it for a project.

"Grandpa is fencing this back part for Polkadot," Grandma said. "The lot goes back much farther, and we can keep our cow and chickens here."

"Is he going to fix up the garage?"

"That and repair the house," Grandma said. "We got the house cheaper because it needed work."

Jeanne took a quick look at the outside and saw that the backyard, although narrow, went back two hundred feet. A shed was at the end of the lot. There was enough space for their animals and a good-sized garden. The neighborhood yards had the same accommodations. Only one had a cow, but they all had gardens. Grandma was already talking to the lady next door. Maybe we will make it in town. They would have to keep up with the house payments. She remembered what had happened to their home in Deep Creek, but Grandma certainly wasn't Betty Ann.

"Come on, Jeanne, let's go inside. Your grandpa will be out here all day."

Jeanne ran up the stairs to the back door in answer to her grandma's call. She looked around the empty screened-in porch. There were no pots or tools, and it looked like the place had been vacated for a long time. When she closed the screen door, the top hinge broke and the door fell at an angle.

"One more thing for your grandpa to fix," Grandma noted.

"It sure is." Jeanne tried to balance the door against the wall, and it kept falling. Finally, she propped it up in the doorframe and locked it so it would stand upright.

"Come see the kitchen."

In the center of a wooden drainboard was a large sink with a window above it. A stove and oven sat to the right of it.

"It's big enough for us to do canning and have the table," Jeanne observed.

"The best part is the indoor bathroom. Just look at this!"

Grandma walked down a hall and into the bathroom. With Robby balanced on her hip, she turned and looked at the tub, the sink, and the toilet.

Robby clapped his hands, sensing the good mood.

"This is great, Grandma." Jeanne grinned. "Let me take Robby, and let's look at the rest of the house."

Jeanne was happy that her grandma would enjoy the more modern appliances in this house. She had had these conveniences in Deep Creek. *Maybe I wasn't as thankful as I should have been then.* Betty Ann filled up the house with her presence and effectively eliminated Jeanne's thinking about anything else. It was up to her to change her attitude about Betty Ann and not let her mother control her feelings. She was pleased with this new house.

Jeanne and her grandparents stopped at the mailbox when they returned to the farm that evening.

Jeanne hopped out and waved them on home. "I'll walk the rest of the way in."

The pickup chugged down the drive toward the house.

Three letters rested in the mailbox. She could tell in the dark they were military. Maybe one each from Eli, Daniel, and her father. Jeanne slid the thin envelopes into the large square pocket of her coat and walked down the road, hoping for good news from the writers.

"Did we get anything?" Grandpa asked.

"Three letters."

"Come to the kitchen," Grandma called from the stove. "You can read them while I fix supper."

"They're from military addresses," Jeanne said as she looked at the envelopes in the light for the first time. "One is addressed to me. It's from Daniel." She shuffled it to the bottom. "The next one is to the Bradshaw family. It's from my daddy." Jeanne moved it to the bottom to see the next letter. "This one's to me as well, but it doesn't have a return address. Maybe Eli has written."

"Read the one from Robert," Grandpa requested.

Jeanne carefully opened the letter and began to read it out loud.

Folks,

It's hard to believe that I am somewhere in the Pacific. I can't tell you where. We are constructing landing strips for our boys. I keep thinking Eli could be one of them. Maybe he's in the army and will sleep in one of the barracks I've had a hand in building. So many of the soldiers I run into are his age. We must be alert because the enemy could attack us at any time. I hope all is well.

Your son,

Robert

Jeanne handed the letter to her grandma. "I want to go upstairs and read my letters. I'll let you know if one is from Eli. It's probably from Daniel too." She didn't wait for an answer. She was disappointed in her father's letter. Still no mention of her or Robby.

It was toasty in the tiny attic room. She had left the door open, and the heat had traveled up the stairway. She didn't have to worry about privacy and could leave her door open. The new house had two bedrooms upstairs, and there was a fireplace in each of them. She would be able to have a fire in her bedroom when it was cold.

She sat back on her cot and opened the mystery letter first. She checked the date and saw it had been mailed first. If the letter was from Daniel, she would read them in chronological order. She quickly shuffled the pages to look at the signature page. It was signed, With love, Billy.

Chapter 27

Jeanne dawdled in her room on the last moving day, reading her letters. Daniel's letter was sweet, but Billy's letter was shocking. He told Jeanne he loved her and that if she had heard what Cindy had said that day, it was a lie. She folded Billy's letter and stuffed it in her pocket. She wanted to believe him, but she had to believe her own eyes instead. Billy's words sprawled across the near-transparent paper conveyed volumes. In Daniel's letter, he wrote about the great guys on his ship, but Billy wrote about how terrible Cindy was. Daniel was kind, and Billy was harsh.

She felt the letter in her pocket. She wanted to write to him and get answers. Even her best friend, Becky, had told her about Cindy. It couldn't all be Cindy's fault. She had seen her face contorted and in anguish, and she didn't want to become that girl. The town had almost forgotten she had gone to the movies with Billy not so long ago. *I should forget Billy altogether*, she thought as she packed her belongings into a box.

"Come on, Jeanne," Grandpa said. "Grandma and Robby are waiting on us in town, so don't tarry."

"I'm coming." Jeanne clutched the pillowcase, then decided to look once more at the picture of the blond boy, her half-brother. Was he fighting in the war, as well? She returned the picture and Billy's letter to the pillowcase. It was heftier now that she had added so many others, including from Auntie Boots and even one from her mother. Jeanne wondered if her mother was in El Paso. Had she really seen her that day at the bus station? The same day she saw Billy and Cindy? Daniel did tell them in his letter that Eli had married and shipped out, but they had heard nothing from Eli.

"Jeanne."

"Coming." She ran down the stairs of the farmhouse for the last time.

Grandpa had loaded his tools and the animals and taken them to the new house while Jeanne was at school. The farmhouse was vacant now that she had finished packing her room. They had slept in the town house for a week. This was the last load. The move would soon be finished, and she would be a townie again. She didn't look back. Grandpa was quiet, so she didn't speak of leaving and watched the cedars pass by in a green blur.

School was only half a mile from the house, and Jeanne enjoyed walking every day. At least three days a week she arrived early and spent time in the library. Miss Beatrice usually unlocked the door for her. Today, Jeanne sat at her table in the back and stared at her English textbook while she absently ran her fingers over the envelope in her pocket.

"Jeanne, you have ten minutes before the bell," said the librarian. "You better start packing your things."

Jeanne waved from the back. "Yes, ma'am." She picked up her heavy books and hurried to class.

Jeanne's schedule was packed. Six courses with no study halls kept her focused. She was considering graduating early as she sat alone in the cafeteria, waiting for her friends to join her. This year she didn't share academic classes with her friends. She only saw them at lunchtime and at PE, the last period of the day. Jeanne opened her history book and began to study the Civil War. She already knew the material, but it gave her something to do.

Senior girls were talking and laughing at the table behind Jeanne, but their noise didn't bother her. She was in her own world until she heard someone mention Billy's name.

"I don't know how, but Cindy got Billy's address and wrote him about the baby," said the girl.

"How did she ever have the nerve?" another girl whispered.

"How could she not contact him? Everyone knows it's his baby."

"That doesn't matter. You know it's her fault. He did what boys do. Cindy knew what a playboy he was. It's her own fault."

Jeanne recognized the last voice as her nemesis, Sandra. Of course she would say something salacious about Cindy and Billy. Jeanne forced herself not to turn around and give the senior girls the satisfaction of seeing her face, which she was sure showed her feelings.

"I'm sorry we're late," Becky said. "We had to stay and help put up the gym equipment. Mrs. Doris is in a state, so we helped her."

Jeanne's friends crowded in and filled the table where she was sitting. Soon the chatter drowned out the gossip coming from the other girls.

"Come to my house this afternoon after school," said Barbara. "We're planning prom."

"I can't today," said Jeanne. "I have something after school." She didn't want to tell her friends that she was talking to Mr. and Mrs. Watkins about an after-school job until she had it. Grandma had taught her a lot about sewing and fabric, and she loved the dry goods store despite her terrible confrontation with Sandra there. Besides, the money would help at home. She was happy that she would be able to contribute.

After school, Jeanne walked the short three blocks to the dry goods store.

"Good afternoon," Mrs. Watkins greeted her.

Mr. Watkins walked toward her with his hand extended and a big grin on his face. "Welcome, Jeanne. We're glad you're here. Mrs. Watkins has needed help. Welcome, welcome." He pumped her arm with a strong handshake.

"That's enough now, Walter." Mrs. Watkins gently put her hand on his arm.

"Well, I'll leave you two ladies to work out the details."

"We'll go over the types of materials, their costs, and how to display them this afternoon, dear." Mrs. Watkins ushered her to the display table and explained the finer points of cottons and linens. "That's enough for today. I'll show you how to inventory and track supplies tomorrow."

"Does that mean I have the job?"

"Yes, it certainly does. I think you'll have the hang of it in a week."

"May I ask what the pay is?" Jeanne needed to know so she could tell Grandma and they could plan their budget.

"Of course you can. We'll pay you twenty-five cents an hour. You can work two hours after school and eight hours on Saturday. That's four dollars and fifty cents a week. After you have worked for a while, we'll talk about raising your pay."

"Yes, ma'am. Thank you." Jeanne had hoped for more money, but she was grateful, nevertheless. She worked the rest of that day to earn her first fifty cents. She was thrilled.

⤳

Supper was on the table when she got home. A fire crackled in the fireplace, Grandma Biddy was smiling, and Robby was in his high chair.

"I got the job, Grandma. I'm making twenty-five cents an hour."

"All right, now. Look at you. My working girl."

"I think she hired me because of you. She wants you to sew for her customers."

"You'll make a fine clerk, and you already know about fabric," said Grandma. "You're good with numbers, and personable too. Now hurry and get freshened up for dinner. I have news for you too."

"News? What is it?" Jeanne was anxious. With the war, she could have all sorts of news, but Grandma wouldn't be smiling if the news was bad.

"Go on, we'll talk about it over the supper table."

When Jeanne sat down, she looked at Grandma and stuck out her hands. "I'm ready. Look, all clean, and from the running water in the bathroom."

They all laughed for the first time in quite a while. The lines on Grandpa's craggy face turned up and brightened his whole countenance.

"Indeed, you are," Grandma said. She patted Grandpa on the arm. "Tell Jeanne your news, Claude."

"I got a part-time job at the feedstore today," he said. "It's in the office. I'm helping with the books. Starting tomorrow, I'll work three days a week."

"That's such good news, Grandpa. That will still give you time to take care of the milking."

"It couldn't have worked out any better," he said. "Let's bless this food and eat. I'm starved."

By summer, Jeanne had nearly taken over the women's department at the dry goods store. She was even ordering piece goods and sewing supplies. The women and girls in Readfield looked to her as an expert, and Grandma Biddy's custom sewing business was growing. School would start in a month, and she would officially be a senior.

Jeanne climbed the ladder to retrieve bolts of material from the top shelf to rotate them in the stacks on the show tables. She wanted to have everything ready for the back-to-school sale.

"Hello, Jeanne. I see you're sensibly employed." The familiar voice rang in Jeanne's ears as she stretched for the last bolt.

"Betty Ann," she said as she turned her head. Jeanne had to tug on the recalcitrant cloth to make it come loose from the shelf. She held on to the bolt and slowly descended the ladder to face her mother.

"Well, you look all grown up," Betty Ann commented.

"You look well," Jeanne answered. She moved on to the floor table and began arranging the materials. She saw that Betty Ann's hair had been freshly done, and she wore a fashionable dress. Her shoes were sturdy but not worn. She didn't seem as flashy as Jeanne remembered. "Is there something I can find for you?"

"Don't treat me like one of your snotty customers."

Jeanne inched to the other side of the table and looked at her mother. "What do you want, Betty Ann?"

Her mother steadily paced around the counters of the store, running her fingers over the cloth. She stopped at the cash register and began tapping her nails on its metal top. Then she whirled around to face Jeanne, her implication clear.

Jeanne waited for her mother to ask for money.

"How is Robby?" Betty Ann said. "Does he miss his mama?"

Jeanne didn't answer at first. She kept her reply as short as possible. "He's fine."

"Have you heard from Eli? Tell him to write his mama. I need to hear from him. He gives me money."

"We haven't heard from him lately. He's at sea."

"Doesn't he send money home? That money should be coming to me. I'm his mama."

"Eli is married. His money goes to his wife."

The color drained from Betty Ann's face. She sucked in her breath as one hand clutched her throat. "What do you mean, wife? A floozy has taken him from me. My beautiful boy. How could he do this to me?"

Jeanne turned her back on her mother and continued arranging the table. "It was his choice. He's a grown man. Furthermore, his wife, Gloria, told me she would never let him come back to this place."

"You talked to her?" Betty Ann sounded shocked. "What did you say to her to make her take him and never come back?"

"I believe it was the farm. They visited us there. She's a city girl with money." Jeanne was calm talking to Betty Ann without red anger burning in her. She was glad Eli was out of this conflict. She should have known Betty Ann would turn up again. A twinge of fear gathered around her, a familiar old enemy that made her scared of what her mother would do.

At that moment a group of girls came in who wanted to browse the sale fabric. Jeanne showed them their choices, and when she looked up, Betty Ann was gone.

When Jeanne walked home that evening, she met the telegram man coming from her house. Alarmed, she ran up the stairs and burst through the door. Grandma and Grandpa were seated facing each other and holding hands. Grandpa's head was bowed, and silent tears ran down Grandma's face. The yellowed telegram was crumpled in Grandma's lap. When she saw Jeanne, she handed over the message from the War Department.

Jeanne's stomach twisted in knots. She tried to read the words, but her vision was blurred through her own tears.

"It's your daddy," Grandpa lamented. "Robert was killed during an attack on the airstrip they were building."

Jeanne slumped in the chair and let the wad of yellow paper fall to the floor. She didn't want to read the carefully typed letters that spelled death. Every day after school, she had pictured her father at home and sitting at the kitchen table when she opened the door. "I thought he would be safe. I never imagined he would get killed."

"The airstrip was bombed," said Grandma.

"How can they be sure? How can we be sure it was Daddy? They make mistakes sometimes."

"His body will be sent here by train," Grandpa told her. "They'll let us know when."

Jeanne bent over, picked up the ball of paper, and smoothed it flat in her lap. She couldn't read through her tears, so she stood and carried the telegram to her room. The hope of seeing her father again was gone.

Chapter 28

A month later, Grandpa and Jeanne drove to the Snyder train station to pick up her father's body. The stationmaster and his clerk helped Grandpa load the casket in the back of the pickup. Grandma had made special arrangements to bury him in the cemetery behind the Methodist church. Their family plot on the farm wasn't an option since moving to Readfield. Grandma and Grandpa had purchased four sites at the cemetery. Jeanne couldn't bear the thought of who else would be buried there, but deep down she knew.

"Who will come to the funeral, Grandma?"

"Not many. Your daddy had been gone a long time, and he didn't live in Readfield."

"The funeral director is coming up the walk," Jeanne noted.

"Tell him we will come in the truck," Grandma said. "No big black car for us. We'll see him at the church."

When Jeanne delivered the message to the somber little man at the front door, he hesitated, then returned to his black sedan parked in front of their house. Little US flags fluttered from the front fenders, and the windows were covered in black satin to hide the faces of the grieving. Grandma had been right about not taking the car. It felt pretentious, especially for Readfield.

Grandma had predicted correctly that only a few would attend the service. However, it was nice to see Mr. and Mrs. Watkins, Jeanne's high school friends, and a couple of their new neighbors attend, even if they didn't know her daddy. The sealed casket kept Jeanne from seeing his face, so she could almost pretend this was all a dream and this wasn't her daddy. But he wasn't coming to get them and take them to live in a big house together. That was only a little girl's imagination.

∞

"Holy, Holy, Holy . . . ," the choir sang.

Jeanne drifted in thought as the familiar opening hymn called the congregation to worship the Sunday following her father's funeral. She missed the family atmosphere of her country church, but she was becoming accustomed to the more formal services at the First Methodist Church. Her friend Becky attended here as well and called the services "High Church." Jeanne liked the title. She thought it suited the beautiful building with its colorful stained-glass windows and intricately carved altar. The sanctuary had a quiet serenity that surrounded her with peace. She felt she was truly in the presence of God there.

Robby snuggled close to her side when they were seated, knowing he could go to sleep as soon as the pastor began his sermon. Grandma lifted his feet and put them in her lap. Jeanne stroked his hair until he closed his eyes.

Brother Smith always prayed for the men and women at war. Jeanne was especially touched by it today with the funeral of her father fresh in her mind. She had mailed letters to Eli and Daniel and was still trying to compose an appropriate response to Billy. She tried to listen to the sermon but to no avail. Her thoughts lingered on her early graduation, working permanently at the dry goods store, and Billy.

"Jeanne, come with us this afternoon," said Becky.

Jeanne realized church was over and Becky was standing at the edge of the pew. She wasn't sure what Becky was talking about.

Grandma responded instead. "Go ahead with your friends to the choir concert. It'll be fun."

"It's not until two o'clock," Becky said. "Meet us at the school auditorium."

"All right." Jeanne smiled and made her way down the aisle. She waved to Becky as she ran out the side door.

Grandma and Grandpa were at the door shaking the minister's hand by the time she reached them. Cindy was standing outside on the church lawn. Jeanne searched the area for a baby, but instead she made eye contact with Cindy standing next to a young man in uniform. Another woman who looked like Cindy's mother stood beside the couple. There was no baby in sight, and the soldier did not look familiar. He put his arm around Cindy's shoulder and drew her close to him. Cindy's mother beamed up at the young man.

Jeanne walked with her family but glanced over at Cindy. The look on her face was not as pleased as her mother's. The whole group seemed stilted and false. Jeanne felt Cindy's anguish even across the churchyard. The damaged girl turned away from Jeanne with her eyes cast down.

When the group walked away, Jeanne picked up Robby and carried him home for lunch. Cindy's story was a familiar one around town. Her family had sent her to her aunt's till the baby was born. Jeanne hoped she was happy.

❧

After lunch, Jeanne had to hurry to make it to the auditorium in time. Becky and Nancy were talking about Cindy when she walked up to them.

"Her mother told me she got tired of living with her aunt and decided to come home," Becky said.

"She looks all right to me," Nancy commented. "I mean, if she had a baby, you can't tell. My sister gained fifty pounds and hasn't lost it yet."

"Everybody's different," said Becky. "Not everyone gains that much. Besides, your sister has always been on the pudgy side."

"That's true, but you're eating for two, you know. And what about that boyfriend? I wonder if he knows about the baby."

"Come on, let's get a seat," Jeanne interrupted. "Stop talking about having a baby. Enjoy the concert."

Jeanne had heard all she needed to hear about Cindy's situation. She would write Billy, but she wasn't sure what to say to him. She didn't want to hear from him again, but she wanted to say it in a kind way. He was fighting in the war, after all. It made her sad. She had really liked him, but she was over him. *It must have been a crush, not the real kind of love everyone talks about.*

∞

On the way home from the concert, Jeanne decided to go by the church cemetery and visit her father's grave. As she rounded the holly bush on the corner of the building, she saw someone standing by her father's fresh grave. The blond hair shone in the afternoon light. It had to be Betty Ann.

Her mother's shoulders sagged with a deep sob. Although Jeanne stepped closer, she let her mother express her grief in solitude and waited behind the trunk of a large oak until her mother had gone. Betty Ann stopped farther down in the cemetery to kneel at another grave. Jeanne didn't move until Betty Ann rose and walked to a waiting car. Her mother's grief was real. She had always known that Betty Ann had loved her father, but who was in that other grave?

Jeanne searched dozens of headstones in the area and found

nothing. Finally, she made her way back to her father's grave and sat in the quiet.

"Jeanne, Jeanne," someone called. "I thought I might find you here." Becky hurried through the cemetery gate and ran toward Jeanne. Her face was contorted.

"What is it, Becky? What's wrong?" Jeanne's heart started racing.

"Your grandma is looking for you!" Becky exclaimed. She bent over, gasping, with her hands on her knees. "Something's wrong with Robby." She looked up and blinked. "They took him to the hospital. You're supposed to go there." Becky waved her on.

Jeanne didn't wait to hear anything else. She took off running and left Becky in the cemetery still catching her breath. The hospital was a three-story brick building on the other side of the square less than a mile away. She would not be impeded by traffic or pedestrians late in the afternoon on Sunday, so Jeanne cut across the empty courthouse lawn and kept running down the middle of the street till she reached the front steps of the hospital. The building looked ominous in the evening shadows.

She took the steps two at a time and burst through the front door. The garish white room inside blinded her at first, and she shaded her eyes to look for her grandma. The first floor was the waiting area where she and Grandma Biddy had stayed when Grandpa was in surgery.

Jeanne walked directly to the reception counter at the back. "Excuse me, ma'am. I'm looking for Mrs. Bradshaw. She's my grandmother. She came in with my little brother, Robby Bradshaw. Are they here?"

"Oh, dear. Yes, let me see where they are. They came through the emergency door, so I may not have the information." The receptionist kept turning through papers on a clipboard and finally looked up at Jeanne. "He's been moved to the second floor, room 261. You'll have to take the stairs."

Before the lady had finished her directions, Jeanne was running up the steps to the second floor. She bumped into a nurse when she rounded the corner at the top of the stairs. "Where is room 261? Robby Bradshaw."

"That's at the end of the hall."

Jeanne skimmed the numbers as she hurried past. When she got to room 261, she found the door was open. Grandpa stood by the window, and Grandma was sitting in a chair by the bed where Robby lay. Jeanne burst into tears and covered her face with both hands.

"Come sit on the bed." Grandma motioned Jeanne in.

Jeanne walked over to the bed and picked up Robby's limp hand as she had dozens of times while he slept. He looked so helpless, so vulnerable. He always had. "What did the doctor say?" Jeanne whispered.

"Robby's had a stroke."

She stared at her grandma, shaking her head from side to side. Jeanne looked back at Robby and waited for his chest to move. Finally, she saw a slight rise and fall. He was breathing.

Grandpa walked over to Jeanne. "The doctor said the first hours are critical. He may recover if he makes it through tonight."

"He's paralyzed on the right side of his body," Grandma said. "The embolism traveled to his brain. You know he's always had a weak heart."

Because of the critical nature of Robby's condition, the hospital staff allowed them to have extra chairs moved into his room. Grandpa paced, and Grandma stayed in the chair by Robby's side. Jeanne fidgeted and kept bending over him and giving him a kiss. The night dragged on, and Robby's status didn't change. Dawn was secretive in its approach. A cloudy sky dulled their awareness of the new day, but Grandpa's internal clock had them awake.

"I have to go tend to Polkadot and feed Old Dog and the chickens," Grandpa said.

"You have to go to school, Jeanne," Grandma added. "You've missed several days already this month."

"I know, but how can I go?"

"Your being here won't change what will happen. I'll send word if anything does."

"Beulah, I'll be back after I tend to the animals," Grandpa said. "Then you can go home and rest for a while."

Jeanne kissed Robby one more time and reluctantly left with Grandpa to go home and change clothes for school. Old Dog was fretful, roaming around the house looking for Robby, so Grandpa took him to the barn to help settle him. Jeanne dressed but didn't remember putting on her dress.

By the time she got to school, Jeanne realized it was a mistake. Everyone asked her a million questions, and after first period, she stopped in the office to check out.

"Jeanne Bradshaw," Miss Rayburn said. "You look terrible, and I know you were up all night. Becky told me what happened. I'll see to it she brings your books and homework to you."

"Thank you, Miss Rayburn."

"I'll tell the principal. Don't worry."

Jeanne went straight to the hospital so she could relieve Grandma. Robby's condition hadn't changed, and he looked the same to Jeanne. Two of the chairs had been removed.

"They said only one person could stay with him in the room from now on," Grandma said. "We can have short visits when we are all here to see him, and the nurses come in here to check on him often. I think his color is better."

"Why don't you go home so you can rest," Jeanne said. "I'll be fine staying here tonight. You can come back in the morning."

"Fetch us if something happens."

"I will." Jeanne tried to reassure Grandma.

When the nurses entered the room, Jeanne walked to the waiting room to stretch her legs. The odd collection of chairs in the waiting area stared back at her, unchanging in their obvious indifference to the raw emotions expressed there every day. Jeanne couldn't even consider life without Robby. His unconditional love was her transfusion for survival. She had long known that Robby was an angel on Earth, her direct contact with God. Of course, she believed God was always there for her, but her baby brother gave her real hugs and pats and told her he loved her in his special language. He was a river of love and affection and kindness she could feel deep in her heart. People thought Robby needed her, and she did take care of him. However, the reality was that she needed him.

Back in Robby's room, Jeanne sat in the lone chair throughout the night and looked at the tiny frame under the sheet, barely moving. She periodically touched Robby's hand or forehead. She was exhausted and anxious at the same time. A nurse from the midnight shift brought her a pillow, and near dawn that bit of extra comfort eased her into sleep.

Jeanne jolted awake. She felt someone had touched her on the shoulder. Daylight was filling the window, and she jumped up to check on Robby. He looked as though he was still sleeping, but when she touched him, his hand was cold.

"No!" she cried and gathered Robby in her arms.

"I'm sorry, Jeanne," the nurse said. "He passed in his sleep. Let us take care of him. You go let your grandma know."

"I can't leave him." Jeanne shook her head and rubbed Robby's hand. He was angelic in death, perfect features that had a glow of happiness.

"I promise we will take care of him," another nurse said. "We need to prepare him before the morning shift comes in to take over."

The nurse put her arm around Jeanne's shoulders and led her out of the room to the nurse's station. They called a neighbor to take the news to Grandma Biddy. Jeanne let the nurse deliver the message to Mrs. Boyd next door.

Jeanne waited for her grandparents in Robby's room. The nurses had gone, and she was alone.

Chapter 29

"Jeanne Bradshaw," Superintendent Dandridge called out. "Jeanne graduates with honors. Congratulations, Miss Bradshaw."

Jeanne walked across the stage and shook Mr. Dandridge's hand as she grasped her diploma in the other. She looked across the auditorium to find her grandparents clapping with big smiles on their faces.

It had only been three months since Robby's death, but choosing to graduate early seemed the right choice for Jeanne. However, Sandra Crawford had not graduated on time last May, and sat next to her on the stage. As always, Sandra managed to be the center of attention, and she kept waving at someone in the audience and causing a commotion. Jeanne tried to ignore her antics but did notice she had an engagement ring on her finger. Sandra had shoved her sleeve up her arm so people wouldn't miss it. In fact, she flapped her hand in Jeanne's face until Jeanne glared at her.

After the ceremony, an excited Becky and Nancy ran to her.

"Congratulations!" Becky said. "A bunch of us are waiting outside to celebrate with you. Come out when you've finished visiting in here. Don't be long. It's cold. It's January, you know."

Becky was gone in a flash, and when Jeanne turned around, she found Sandra talking to Grandma Biddy. In the crowd, Jeanne and Sandra were civil in front of their families. They had had a silent truce for a while. Sandra had even come to Robby's funeral. Now, Sandra was more interested in getting married than harassing Jeanne. She flitted from one group to another and flashed her engagement ring. Though the diamond was tiny, the importance of it was enormous.

"What did Sandra want?" Jeanne asked. "I guess you heard she's getting married this summer."

"Yes, I just heard," Grandma replied. "She wants me to make her wedding gown."

"What did you say?" Jeanne didn't know how she felt about Sandra coming to her house for fittings. Grandma didn't know the history between her and Sandra.

"I said yes, of course. She's going to have five bridesmaids, and I will get those jobs, as well."

"Good," Jeanne declared. She could avoid them. Fittings were done in the living room, and she would make a habit of coming and going through the back door. The less she saw of Sandra, the better for everyone.

Grandma gestured toward her outfit. "I'll take your cap and gown, and you can go with your friends. You should enjoy your special day. They're waiting outside for you."

There were only seventeen graduates for the winter ceremony, and five of them were boys who wanted to join the military and run off to war. They still had visions of glory instead of the cruel reality that rained on families of dead heroes. Jeanne couldn't understand why her classmates were so excited about the prospect of fighting and ignored the likelihood of dying.

In the pharmacy's soda shop, Jeanne gazed at the bright faces laughing too loudly and carrying on like there was no other time but this one. This could be the happiest time in their life. Jeanne pretended to be happy with them, donning a smile and patting them on the back with hearty congratulations.

Eventually, Sandra sashayed in with her fiancé and made the rounds, showing off her ring and introducing her future husband, Timmy. The rude fellow was bored and looked away from them during introductions. He was on the way out the door with Sandra in tow when she stopped halfway to the door and turned.

"Jeanne," Sandra called over the heads of her friends. "I guess you heard that Daniel's back in town. He came in today."

Jeanne stared at Sandra, her mouth half-open and her mind racing. She caught the look of satisfaction on Sandra's face.

"Daniel came in on a stretcher," Sandra announced to the entire group. "He's been terribly wounded. I think he lost a leg in an explosion on his ship."

"Is he at the hospital?" Becky asked.

Dozens of questions flew around the room.

"You were the one writing Daniel." Sandra taunted Jeanne. "How come you didn't know?"

Barbara put her hand on Jeanne's arm and gave her a slight tug. "She's not worth it."

"You're right, Barbara." Jeanne turned away from the hateful girl who was never satisfied unless she was hurting someone. She refused to be her target today.

Sandra turned away from the crowd. "I'm coming, Timmy. Let's go to our own party." Her heels clicked on the tile floor as she and her fiancé exited the pharmacy door.

Daniel is home and wounded. The aggravation of Sandra's performance dissipated quickly as she digested the information. Jeanne had to go see him. It was almost dark, but she didn't want to wait till morning.

"I'm going home, Becky," Jeanne said. "I want to go over to Daniel's house. I'm sure his aunt and uncle won't mind."

"Do you want me to go with you?" Becky asked.

"Not this time. First, I need to go tell Grandma Biddy where I am."

⌘

In less than an hour, Jeanne was standing on the long front porch of Daniel's uncle Fred and aunt Cheryl. A swing swayed in the cold north wind. Its slight squeak made the house feel deserted. Jeanne eyed the two front doors, trying to decide which one was the main opening. She had been in such a hurry that she hadn't thought of what she was going to say to Daniel. *Has the war changed him?* He had been so easy to talk to before he left. She prepared herself and knocked on one of the front doors. She would find out soon enough.

Jeanne finally saw a flickering light come to the door. She heard the lock click and the door being pulled open. The white door screeched in protest and stopped with only a small opening.

"Oh, hello, Jeanne," Cheryl said through the crack. "This old thing won't budge." She pushed and rattled the door and finally gave up. "The other door is just as bad. Come to the back door, dear. That's where everybody comes anyway."

Cheryl held the back door open, and Jeanne walked into a warm kitchen. The smells of fried chicken and cabbage lingered in the air. Bowls and plates of food sat on the back of the stove, covered with dish towels.

"I hope I'm not keeping you from supper," Jeanne said.

"Don't you worry about that. I'm so glad you came."

"I was anxious to get here. Thank you for letting me see him this evening."

"I'm grateful. Daniel has barely said two words since he came home and hasn't eaten a thing. You'll be good for him. We've made a room for him downstairs. Come this way."

Cheryl walked through the kitchen and opened a door. Daniel was half-sitting in a bed set up in the dining room. He was sleeping when Jeanne came in.

270

"Daniel, Jeanne is here to see you."

Daniel stirred, then opened his eyes and looked around the room, confused at his surroundings. Jeanne almost didn't recognize him. He was ghostly and emaciated. His skin was tight against his jaw, and his head had been shaved. His eyes blinked and darted from object to object around the room.

"Daniel, it's me, Jeanne. I've come to visit you." She stood by the bed until he looked her in the eyes, and she saw recognition. "I'm glad to see you." Jeanne struggled to keep from crying. The tragedies in her life were crushing her. She had to be strong.

"Jeanne? You're here." Daniel struggled to sit up straighter, and Jeanne noticed his difficulty getting into a comfortable position.

"You're home now." Jeanne glanced at his lower body and saw the outline of two legs under the blanket. Sandra had exaggerated.

"Yes, Aunt Cheryl and Uncle Fred came to the train station to get me. It's not the first time they've rescued me."

Jeanne wanted to reach out and touch him, hold his hand. However, he hardly looked at her. It didn't take long for her to realize that the war had changed her friend drastically. She felt awkward standing there, so she pulled up a dining-room chair and scooted it close to the side of the bed. If she didn't look directly at Daniel, he might relax and be more comfortable.

The door from the kitchen opened. "Here's supper for you two." Aunt Cheryl set plates piled high with food down on the dining table that had been pushed against the far wall. "Put the plates in the sink when you're finished." She cast a meaningful glance at Jeanne and left.

"You have to admit that was a pretty smart move," Jeanne teased. "Now you have to eat something because I'm starving. I haven't eaten all day, and I left my root beer float on the counter at the soda shop when I heard you had come home."

Daniel smiled for the first time that evening. "So, you've become a social butterfly since I've been gone. Who were you with at the soda shop?"

Jeanne laughed. "It's not quite like that. My fellow graduates and I were celebrating today."

"You decided to graduate early then."

"Yes, I did. I can go to work next week full time at the dry goods." Jeanne went to the table and got a plate for Daniel. "This looks great. How about a bite of mashed potatoes?"

"I can feed myself, thank you. Hand me that plate." Daniel rested the plate on his outstretched legs and ate. Although a bit unwieldly, the potatoes stuck to his fork, and he managed the fried chicken with his hands.

All in all, Jeanne was pleased. Daniel needed to gain weight, and he ate as long as she was eating. She did most of the talking. Even when she asked about his friends, he avoided saying anything of significance relating to his time in the navy.

Going home that night, Jeanne went over their conversation. She had told Daniel about Robby, her father, and even seeing Betty Ann at the gravesite, but she had not mentioned Billy. Daniel had not mentioned his injury. *I guess he'll talk about it when he's ready.*

∽∾

Jeanne truly felt she was an adult going to a job every weekday and on Saturday. Her full-time work guaranteed they had enough money for their house payment. They were also paying off the hospital bills and the funeral costs. They needed every penny.

Days were getting warmer, and Grandma and Grandpa were putting in a garden. In a couple weeks they would have the first fresh vegetables. Trees were budding, and the bluebonnets were beginning to bloom. Jeanne could already taste the onions and green beans. She was tired of pinto beans.

Walking through the giant cedars in the cemetery was calming after her hectic day in the store. Everyone was buying fabric for Easter dresses, especially since the new pastels arrived. Jeanne sat on a cement bench close to Robby's headstone and touched the angel wings carved near the top. A twig snapped behind her.

"You didn't tell me my baby was gone," Betty Ann accused her. "I had to read it in the papers."

Jeanne's mother quietly sat beside her on the hard bench and looked at the father and son plots. Rain had settled the dirt, and the graves did not look as fresh as they once had. Jeanne's wounded heart wasn't as raw as it had been either. Even her mother sitting beside her did not shatter her.

Jeanne leaned back against a tree and looked at her mother. She was surprised to see Betty Ann wearing a large hat that hid her face. Her dress was neat enough, but her mother must have felt Jeanne's scrutiny, for her demeaner changed. Jeanne could see cruelty taking form, and she quickly told her mother, "He died peacefully in his sleep."

"Were you with him?"

"I was."

"You didn't tell me. You wanted me to suffer. People should have come to see me. He was my baby."

Grief had brought them to the bench, but anger separated them. Jeanne could feel resentment emanating from her mother. The fury sitting next to Jeanne burned the skin on her arm and face. Jeanne reached up and touched her cheek. A fever seared her fingers. She didn't recognize her own body. It was betraying her. Her mind was under control and not responding to her mother's paranoia, but her body was out of control. She had to leave.

She got up and ran to the opposite end of the cemetery and kept running. She went back to the dry goods store, unlocked the back door, and slipped out of sight. Jeanne sat in the dark of the closed store until the streetlights came on. Sitting in the corner near the sewing equipment, she looked out at the darkening sky. Friends walked by and looked at the window displays.

Suddenly, Betty Ann appeared at the storefront and banged on the window. "I know you're in there. Don't think you're so grown I can't fix you, missy." Betty Ann grabbed the doorknob and rattled the door.

Jeanne moved back into the shadows. She could confront her

mother, but the whole town would be a witness, and Betty Ann had already attracted a crowd. If she walked outside, the confrontation would escalate.

"Come out here! You better obey your mama, right now." Betty Ann turned around and shouted to the people in the street. "What are you looking at? What do you think you're looking at? Get the hell outta here. This is none of your business."

Jeanne started for the door. This had to stop. She would finally confront her mother, even if it was in front of the town. As she approached the door with the key, Betty Ann began to beat on the window. Sheriff Brown drove up with lights flashing and parked in front of the store, blinding Jeanne through the glass front. Before he could get out of the car, Betty Ann started yelling at him.

"What are you doing here?" she shouted. "This is none of your business either. Don't you understand? My baby died, and she's responsible. She didn't tell me."

"It's not anybody's fault, Betty Ann," Sheriff Brown responded as he took her arm. "It was God's will, and there's nothing anyone can do." The sheriff put Betty Ann in the squad car and drove away.

When the crowd dispersed, Jeanne let herself out the back door and walked home. She felt like a coward. She felt guilty. She wanted to talk to Daniel.

Chapter 30

"Jeanne, you're off somewhere else gathering wishes this morning," Mrs. Watkins said. "I need you to take inventory so we can get our orders in for the fall material. I received the new patterns last week, and we can calculate the amount of cloth we'll need."

"Yes, ma'am." Jeanne couldn't get the clash with Betty Ann out of her mind. The day felt like an eternity as it dragged on, and she counted bolts and bolts of fabric. Jeanne unwrapped bolts with less than a yard of material and folded them into squares. She had forty squares marked and ready for the sale tables when a middle-aged man walked through the door.

"Excuse me, miss," he said. "I'm Binford Jennings, the editor for the *Readfield Examiner*. You know, the newspaper."

"Of course. How can I help you?" Jeanne asked. "I didn't know you were the editor."

"I've been away in the military and have just returned. My father's been running the paper while I've been gone."

It was then Jeanne noticed the large burn on the right side of the man's face.

"I know I look a fright, but I really am harmless. My wife says she doesn't even notice it anymore."

"No, I just . . . It's . . . Can I help you?" Jeanne finally sputtered. She was horrified that she'd been caught staring at the man. He certainly looked harmless. She remembered him from a visit her journalism class had made to the paper. They had met both Jennings generations. This man had been in the printing room. The older Mr. Jennings had come out to talk to the students.

"I'm looking for Jeanne Bradshaw."

"Oh! I'm Jeanne." *Why in the world is he looking for me?*

"I understand from my cousin that you're a writer. She showed me articles that you wrote for your high school newspaper, and I like your style."

"Thank you. I've written a few pieces, but I haven't thought of myself as a writer."

"You should," he encouraged her. "I may have work for you at the paper. It won't interfere with your work here."

"I could only work after five and on the weekend."

"I think we could work something out. Can you come by the office after work today so we can talk about it?"

"Yes, I think so."

"I'll look for you then." Mr. Jennings nodded, smiled, and left the store.

Jeanne took a deep breath. She'd forgotten to ask what the job was. A writer! She had only dreamed of writing. She had her poems and the school newspaper articles, and of course her letters. Mr. Jennings could have her do something else. It would be exciting to be at the paper, whatever the job was.

☙

Mrs. Chaney, her English teacher, was standing behind the long counter and greeted her when she came through the door of the *Readfield Examiner* headquarters. *Mrs. Chaney must be Mr.*

Jennings's cousin. One question answered. The printing machine running in the back made it hard to hear. Mrs. Chaney pointed to the office to the right and motioned her to go on back. Jeanne waved at Mr. Jennings through the glass door.

He motioned for her to enter his office. "Have a seat, Miss Bradshaw. I'm glad you decided to come. The paper has suffered because of the war like every other business. I've lost my only reporter. Mrs. Chaney is helping me with writing and ads after school, but I need a reporter to cover the social happenings here in Readfield. I can't do it all myself."

"Do you mean like funerals and weddings?" Jeanne asked.

"Exactly like that. There will be other things, but I'll give you those assignments. The first one is the Crawford-Miller wedding. Can you cover that event?"

Jeanne sat back in her chair and started laughing. She saw Mr. Jennings's puzzled stare, but still she laughed. She held her sides and kept laughing. She deserved this irony for her first assignment.

"Are you all right?"

"I'm fine, Mr. Jennings." Jeanne hiccupped. "I would be happy to report on Sandra Crawford's wedding."

"Good, that's settled then. I will pay you by the article, and I want you to work with Mrs. Chaney." Mr. Jennings stood, continuing to look at her with raised eyebrows. "She'll teach you what you'll need to gather for the articles. As you progress and learn the business of reporting, you'll have other assignments."

"Yes, sir." Jeanne's head was spinning. She was excited and a little frightened. She wanted to do well.

Mr. Jennings stepped around his desk and opened the office door for her. The interview was over, and she had her second job. Outside the small office, the roar hit them like a blow from a heavy weight. Mrs. Chaney took her to the back and introduced her to the typesetter, Bill. He worked at the keyboard of the Linotype machine. Fascinated with the operation, Jeanne stayed until Mrs. Chaney motioned for her to come outside.

"That's better," said Mrs. Chaney. "I think I'm losing my

hearing in there. Congratulations, Jeanne. Now you're a reporter. A lot of job opportunities have become available for women since the war. Make the most of this job, and maybe you'll keep being a reporter when the men come back."

"Yes, ma'am." Jeanne would be glad when the war was over, even if she didn't get to keep her job at the paper. For now, she wanted to enjoy learning the newspaper business.

❧

Jeanne visited Daniel every weekend and a few weekdays after work. On a Sunday afternoon, she walked into the makeshift bedroom to find Daniel standing alongside his bed, balancing on crutches.

"Daniel!" Jeanne exclaimed. "What a surprise!"

"I know. It is to me too. The doctor brought them to me today. Said I should get out of bed and start using these to get around. I think he figured I'd been a slacker long enough."

"What did he say about how long it would take you to walk with them?"

"He said it was up to me. The doctors in San Diego said I might never use my left leg, but I'm getting some feeling back in it, so maybe."

"You told me shrapnel cut your leg to the bone. Do you still have a lot of pain?"

"No more than anyone else." Daniel hobbled over to the bed and sat on the edge. His pajama leg scrunched above his knee, and Jeanne glimpsed the terrible purple scar that ran the length of his calf. Daniel quickly pulled the sheet over his leg and sat back against the stacked pillows.

Jeanne could see the pain on his face. "Are you pushing too hard?" she asked.

Perspiration beaded on Daniel's forehead. "I want to get ready to spend time outside the house. The weather is warm. Ever since I was little, I've loved being outside. That's what I remember about my dad, being outside with him."

"Daniel, tell me about your parents. You always talk about your aunt and uncle, but never your parents."

"I remember them mostly through Uncle Fred's stories. Dad was his youngest brother and they were close. Aunt Cheryl said we were happy as a family, but Uncle Fred had to help us out during the Depression times. It seems my parents had a hard time making ends meet."

"What happened to them?"

"My mother died in a house fire. They think it was a grease fire on the stove. That's where they found her, on the floor in front of the stove."

"That's terrible. How old were you?"

"About six. I don't remember any of it. Only what they've told me, but it's real enough since I've heard it so much. Then my father died in a factory accident. His sleeve was caught in the machinery, and it crushed his arm. He bled to death before they were able to get him to the hospital. I don't remember much about that either. Aunt Cheryl told me about it."

"I'm so sorry, Daniel."

Silence fell between them for a moment. Then Jeanne glanced at the clock on the table. "I'd better go. I need to get home before it gets too dark."

"Can you come by tomorrow?" Daniel asked.

"I will. I have good news to tell you. How about six o'clock?" Jeanne smiled and went to the door. Tomorrow she would meet with Mrs. Chaney, and she could tell Daniel about her first assignment.

"Wait, how can you leave a person like that? What good news?" Jeanne smiled. "Tomorrow."

She hurried to make it in time for her visit to Robby's grave before the light faded completely. Since her last encounter with Betty Ann, Jeanne kept watch at the front gate to be sure she didn't get a surprise visitor. Grandma told her the sheriff had escorted her mother out of town and that she didn't have anything to worry about, but Jeanne was never at ease. Betty Ann would show up again. She was sure of it.

Wind rattled the oak leaves above her and dotted the cemetery floor with fleeting shadows, making Jeanne more anxious than usual. The constant movement in the trees made her think someone was moving about in the cemetery. She slowed her pace and carefully scanned the rows of tombstones. Nothing. Jeanne stopped. The evening light shone on a headstone in front of her. It said *Karlson*—Daniel's last name. She walked closer. The monument marked two graves. One was Daniel's father, David F. Karlson, but the other was for Harold James Karlson. Jeanne bent closer to see the dates. *Born 1919, died 1926*. She was perplexed. *Who could this be? Did Daniel have a brother, or did this child belong to his aunt and uncle?* This was obviously a large plot for a family. Other sites were already laid out and had his aunt and uncle's names on a separate monument with just their birth dates. Jeanne looked again. Daniel's father and this child were buried side by side with the same monument. There was a connection. The encroaching darkness kept her from seeing any more.

Jeanne had become so engrossed in her discovery that she had forgotten to look for Betty Ann. She decided she would come back tomorrow. This boy had been born the same year as Sonny. Jeanne searched the cemetery to get her bearings. This plot was in an obscure place. She had found it because she entered a gate coming from Daniel's house. She would have never found it otherwise.

She hurried to leave. Grandma Biddy would be worried. By the time she had walked across the cemetery and was opening the gate near the church, she remembered the Karlson headstone was near the spot where Betty Ann had stopped. She wasn't sure where exactly, but it was in that area.

⤋

Sandra fanned continuously as she described in minute detail her wedding plans. Jeanne sat opposite her in the soda shop listening to Sandra get louder and louder to be heard by every passerby. Jeanne dutifully scribbled notes and appeared official. She had enough information to fill the entire paper, but she let Sandra talk. Jeanne was beginning to wonder if she would finish before the soda shop closed and they had to leave.

"Remember, Jeanne, pink, pink, pink," Sandra said. "Bridesmaids' dresses, flowers, and cake are all pink. I love pink, you know."

"Got it, pink. I have it in my notes." Jeanne flashed her notebook with pink underlined and circled in front of Sandra. "See you at the wedding." Jeanne left Sandra at the ice cream table, still fanning herself.

Jeanne ran down the sidewalk. She was having dinner with Daniel and his aunt and uncle tonight. She didn't want to be late. The cicadas had begun their whirring and comforted Jeanne on her walk. Their wings stilled when she turned and went up the steps to the Karlson house. Daniel's uncle had repaired the front doors so they opened without trouble.

"Hello, Jeanne," Aunt Cheryl greeted. "Come on in. Everyone's in the parlor."

Daniel was sitting on the sofa. "Come sit by me," he said. "We have something for you. It's for your reporting." Daniel handed her a package wrapped in white tissue paper.

She was stunned. "You didn't need to do anything for me."

"We wanted to," said Daniel.

"Go ahead," Aunt Cheryl urged her. "Open it, dear."

Jeanne tore into the thin paper, opened the box, and pulled out a leather bag with a wide strap that fit over her shoulder. "Oh my, how beautiful. I've never seen anything like it."

"Put it on," Daniel said. "Let's see how it looks."

Jeanne slipped the strap over her shoulder and across her chest. "It's perfect. I can carry everything I need in it. Thank you!"

"Then put this in it." Daniel passed her notebook to her.

Jeanne buckled the clasp and patted it. "Perfect."

"Let's eat dinner," said Uncle Fred. "Daniel forgot to tell you. He's coming back to the store next week."

"You are? That's wonderful!"

"I am," Daniel confirmed. "The doc said it's all right. I can only work two days in the beginning, but it won't be long before I can work full time. Now tell us. How did your first interview go?"

"Funny you should ask. Here's a clue. It's a color and it rhymes with stink."

Daniel laughed. "Pink?"

Chapter 31

"Wait!" Sandra screeched. "I'll let all my breath out, and then maybe you can zip it."

"You'll ruin your dress if I zip it any further," Grandma Biddy said. "I can let the bodice out under the arms. That will be the best choice. The seams are big enough, and you won't even be able to tell it's been altered."

"Can you have it ready in time for the wedding?" Sandra asked.

Grandma soothed her. "Of course, dear."

Jeanne listened from the kitchen. She could see through the half-open door that Sandra was standing on a stool like an overstuffed sausage in her lace wedding dress. Grandma stood behind her with her hands on her hips, waiting for the girl to get off the stool. Sandra's crew of followers sat on the horsehair sofa like three bright flamingos. They looked on with glassy-eyed boredom.

"Don't just sit there," Sandra yelled at the entourage. "Help me get down from this death contraption."

All three of the bridesmaids jumped up from their perch and grabbed an arm. The stool skidded across the hardwood floor, but the girls eventually lifted Sandra and the wedding dress to the floor. She began wriggling out of her dress when Jeanne decided to ease into the hall and sneak upstairs to her room. She had heard enough about the wedding already and had written a draft of the article. However, she was waiting to attend the wedding before she finalized the story.

A letter waited for Jeanne on her nightstand. *Grandma must have put it there*. She hadn't heard from anyone for so long that she couldn't imagine who it could be. The letter had a military address and was addressed directly to her. The mewling group in the fitting room was soon forgotten as Jeanne sat on her bed and carefully opened the thin envelope. Eli could have written, but the signature said, *Your father, Robert Bradshaw.*

She checked the envelope again. There was no date on it, but the letter itself was dated the week before he died. Jeanne took a breath and pressed the tardy pages to her heart before she read words she had waited for her whole life.

June 21, 1943

Dear Jeanne,

I don't know how much you remember about me, but you were always such a sweet little girl. I guess you're grown by now and could even be married and have a home of your own. When you were little, you had the prettiest bright brown eyes and silky chestnut hair. I'm sure you grew into a fine-looking woman. I'm writing to you because so much can happen in each minute that this may be the only chance I'll get to write to you. I know it's been a long time, and when this war is over, I hope I will get to see you again. You need to hear from me. First, I'm sorry. Sorry for not being there, and sorry I left like I did, but I do love you and your brothers. Tell Robby I love him. One more thing you need to know is that you have a half-brother. Betty Ann will never tell you about him, but she had a son who is two years older than Eli. You may never find him or even know who he is, but you needed to know. I would tell you his name if I knew it, but I don't. I only know him by Sonny. I'm sorry I let you down all these years.

If I don't make it home, I hope you have a good life.

Your father,

Robert Bradshaw

News about Sonny would have been a shock to Jeanne if she hadn't already read her father's letters to Grandma Biddy. Her father must have known the danger he faced in the war and the possibility he could die.

Jeanne folded the letter, put it back in its envelope, and held it in her lap. She looked out the window and drew comfort from her cozy room. She rubbed the line of spools on the footboard of the double bed. Somehow, Grandma had found a Jenny Lind bed and a feather mattress for her. She smiled every night before she fell asleep to have something so luxurious and different from a cot. Her tidy desk no longer displayed schoolwork, and the drawers were bursting with stories she had written. Everything she had published in the school newspaper was tucked away in a folder. Soon, she wouldn't have any space left in the small desk. Mr. Watkins had let her have two wooden crates from the dry goods, and she had stacked them against the wall for bookshelves. She had tied her letters together by the person who had sent them and used one of the shelves to store them.

She slipped this last letter from her father in the stack tied with a blue satin ribbon and put it away. Jeanne looked at the collection and remembered her fear of her mother on the farm and her anxiety when she sat alone in the dark at the store. That last conflict had been in January, and now the warm days of June and her crate of memories put her at ease.

⌒∞⌒

"This is the news CBS received from a German radio broadcast earlier today," the newsman announced. "They have proclaimed the British and Americans have launched an invasion of Normandy. The American War Department has stated they do not know anything about this German broadcast. We'll hear more after a word from our sponsor, Maxwell House."

Jeanne sat by the radio, listening for news of the war. She had friends who had gone to fight Hitler in Europe, but most of those she knew had gone to fight on the Pacific front.

Grandpa leaned closer to the speaker to hear. "Sounds like we've done something in Europe."

"Maybe Mr. Roosevelt will come on later tonight," Jeanne said. "He didn't say anything about any action last night, though."

The announcer interrupted the commercial. "The president of the United States will be speaking to the nation in two minutes."

"Beulah, the president is on!" Grandpa yelled into the kitchen as he turned up the volume.

Grandma came in drying her hands on her apron and sat on the same sofa the three bridesmaids had occupied earlier. While this was the fitting room during the day, it was their living room at night.

"The president of the United States," the announcer said.

Mr. Roosevelt's words broke the absolute quiet in the house. "My fellow Americans: Last night, I spoke with you about the fall of Rome, I knew at that moment that troops of the United States and our allies were crossing the Channel in another and greater operation."

Jeanne unwittingly clutched a cup towel to her chest as she listened with hope.

"It has come to pass with success thus far," he continued. "And so, in this poignant hour, I ask you to join with me in prayer: Almighty God: Our sons, pride of our Nation, this day . . ."

Jeanne looked at her grandparents' bowed heads, grieving for the loss to her family and all the others in her country.

Later that night, she said her own prayers for healing and hope.

She had given the letter to her grandparents to read. All this hate and fear and anger drained her of energy. *Was the letter too late or just in time?* Jeanne didn't know. She was so tired. She fell asleep talking to God, asking him for strength and an end to the war.

⌘

Daniel folded Jeanne's letter and handed it to her. "Jeanne, I know you're stunned by this."

"I am. Grandma and I have talked about it. Did Eli ever mention Sonny to you?"

"No, never, but he didn't talk about your dad either."

"Eli wouldn't talk about Sonny to me, but I want to find him. I think Betty Ann came to Readfield to see someone when she took Sonny away from the farm. I think she gave him to someone. Maybe his father."

"Do you have any proof or a name?"

"I have a picture. A photograph fell out of an envelope when I was reading letters my father sent to Grandma." Jeanne took the picture from the envelope and handed it to Daniel. She was sure he would see something familiar about the little blond boy in the picture, but there was no recognition. She didn't know if she was relieved or disappointed. For a long time, she believed she and Daniel could be related. She had kept their relationship platonic because of it.

"He doesn't look like you or Eli," Daniel observed. "Ask my aunt. She might have an idea."

"I'm going to search records at the courthouse. I thought I could use my reporter status to talk to the clerk. Do you think that would help?"

"It might," Daniel replied. "You can try."

"What are you two cooking up in here?" Aunt Cheryl asked. "Here's iced tea for you." Two tall glasses clinked as she set them on the table. "You may want to take it to the porch where there's a little breeze."

"Let's go outside," Daniel said. "I think I can manage these crutches."

Jeanne carried the tea glasses and let Daniel lead the way. She let him take his time while she gained the courage to ask him about the boy buried next to his father.

A soft breath of cool air brushed against Jeanne's face as she and Daniel drifted back and forth on the porch swing.

"This is nice and peaceful," Jeanne said. "I'm glad you wanted to come out here."

Daniel smiled. "You have something on your mind."

"How did you know?"

"I've known you for a long time, Jeanne Bradshaw."

Jeanne hesitated. "I wanted to ask you something."

"Sure, what is it?"

"I stumbled upon a headstone in the cemetery. Who is Harold James Karlson?"

"Is that all?" He smiled. "Did you think you had the Sonny mystery solved?"

"Well—"

"Let me put your mind at ease. Harold was Aunt Cheryl's and Uncle Fred's little boy."

"How did he die?"

"I believe pneumonia. He died soon after my mother died in the fire."

"Where did you say the fire was? Where did you live before you came here?"

"I lived in Deep Creek. I went to the site where the house burned when I was working and living in Deep Creek so I could see it for myself."

"I remember you helping us in Deep Creek when we moved to the farm," Jeanne said. "I was so embarrassed. I didn't have any shoes on my feet."

"I remember it too. Like it was yesterday. You were so brave and beautiful standing there by that wagon, daring me to say anything to you at all."

"My life changed that day, Daniel."

"So did mine. I always hoped we would be together. I just had to wait for you." Daniel took her hand in his, and peace lingered there on the porch as they listened to the evening sounds.

Jeanne put her head on Daniel's shoulder. "I'm glad you waited."

Chapter 32

"Tie this around your face," Mrs. Chaney instructed as she handed Jeanne a large white handkerchief she had pulled out of her desk. "Since you seem determined to read through all these archives, you might as well protect yourself from the dust you're stirring up, and I'm shutting the door to this room. Mr. Jennings won't want the machines clogging."

"Yes, ma'am," Jeanne replied as she dutifully tied the kerchief, cowboy-style, around her face. She had plaited her long hair into a thick braid to keep it out of the way. The style and the jeans she wore made her look years younger, but it was the best way to dress for this task. Editions of the war years were kept in Mr. Jennings's office, but earlier ones were here in the archive room. She searched for evidence of the house fire where Daniel's mother had died.

Reporting for the *Examiner* and working for the dry goods store had kept Jeanne busy throughout the summer and fall of 1944. Daniel began working at his uncle's grocery, and between their two schedules, they had been spending less and less time together.

She was a week into sorting the old newspapers when she finally reached the year 1925. Daniel hadn't told her the month or the time of year the fire occurred, so she was combing through each edition beginning with January. The papers were nearly twenty years old, so Jeanne wore thin white gloves to protect the pages. Even with those precautions, yellowed pages sometimes crumbled in her hands.

She had made it through June when the door banged open.

"Jeanne, the war report is on," Mr. Jennings said. "Come on, let's listen. MacArthur is back in the Philippines."

In the outer office and printing room, Jeanne joined the *Examiner* staff surrounding the radio just as General Douglas MacArthur spoke. "People of the Philippines: I have returned. By the grace of Almighty God our forces again stand on Philippine soil . . ."

"Does this mean the war could be over soon?" Jeanne asked when the short speech was finished.

"I think the war is turning in our favor," said Mr. Jennings. "We're getting reports of more victories on both the Pacific front and the European front."

"At great cost," Mrs. Chaney sobbed. "The casualties are terrible. The battle at the Siegfried Line with the Germans is raging. We get reports of hundreds of American casualties every day. When will it stop?"

"We can pray from this end and support our men and women with sacrifices," Mr. Jennings said. "I have news to report. I think 'MacArthur Returns' is a good headline, and next week we'll have a presidential election to cover."

"Roosevelt will surely be elected again," Mrs. Chaney said. "We can't change leadership now."

"I expect that's what most folks will think," Mr. Jennings said. "Mr. Roosevelt will be elected, but he's not in good health, you know." He rubbed his forehead and grimaced as his fingers traced the burn on his face. "Let's get back to work."

Jeanne sighed and pulled the kerchief up to cover her nose and mouth. She hoped to finish reading the papers for 1925 by the end of the day. She picked up the first July edition and placed it on the small tabletop. The headline read *King and Queen Crowned.*

Jeanne had covered the same royal contest for the Roadrunner Festival contest winners last July herself. Now she was getting more meaty stories. Last week she'd covered a robbery trial at the courthouse. Mrs. Watkins had let her go during work hours. Granted, it hadn't lasted long with the robber being caught on his climb out the window by the homeowner. The thief was held at gunpoint until Sheriff Brown arrived, sirens blaring. It turned out to be an interesting little story on the second page. The front page was reserved for news about the war. Unfortunately, they had plenty of that.

The days were getting shorter, so Jeanne decided to leave early and get home before dark. She was responsible for locking the doors, since she was the last to leave. She pulled her coat tightly around her and tied the belt to protect her from the vicious north wind that had blown in earlier that afternoon. With her leather bag secure across her shoulder, she could hold the door and lock it. She needed both hands to align the door with the latch for the key to turn.

"Can I help you with that, pretty girl?"

She spun around to find Billy standing there with his hands in his pockets.

"Billy!" Jeanne stepped back and bumped against the door.

"In the flesh," he said. "Is that any way to greet a hero home from the war? Don't be afraid. It's only me, your Billy."

Jeanne realized her reaction to Billy must have seemed odd. She moved away from the door and took out the key. "I was startled, that's all. How are you?"

"Who, me? I'm always fine. This little thing took me down a notch, though." Billy pulled his left hand out of his pocket. It was wrapped completely in white gauze. Jeanne saw that three of his fingers were missing.

"I'm so sorry, Billy. What happened?"

"A landmine surprised me. I still can use my thumb and index finger, which is not so bad, considering the boys who are far worse off than I am."

"Are you home for good? I mean, do you have to go back?"

"I'm home for good." Billy's face was unexpressive. This unusual silence coming from Billy unnerved Jeanne. His crisp uniform stood there wearing him. Jeanne noticed the sharp edges to his thin face and the deep hollows around his eyes.

"Come to dinner, Billy. Grandma and Grandpa will be glad to see you." Jeanne regretted the invitation as soon as she said it, but she was committed. His countenance had elicited a sympathy that Jeanne felt for all the military who sacrificed for their country and her freedom. She would have invited a stranger.

"That'll be nice. I didn't think you would ever talk to me again."

Jeanne started walking down the sidewalk, and Billy fell in step with her. Gusts from a norther blew against them on the way and silenced their meaningless platitudes.

Jeanne stopped in front of the church. "I always make a visit to the cemetery before I go home. You can come with me if you wish."

"Sure, I'll come."

"It's near twilight when I usually make my visits here," Jeanne said. "Let's sit on this bench. It's out of the wind and not so cold. That jacket doesn't look so warm."

"I'm all right."

"Why did you come to see me?"

"I wanted to . . . I wanted to make it right with you."

"Someone else needs to hear that, not me. I wrote you that I didn't consider us together. That we were only friends."

"I know," he said. "I had to see you. I couldn't forget the look on your face that day behind the bus station. You looked hurt and horrified all at once."

"I was," she admitted.

"I wanted to see if there was a chance for us, before . . ."

"No, Billy, there isn't. That incident at the bus station was a long time ago, and we're both different people now." Jeanne had to admit to herself that when she first heard his voice, she felt some excitement, and when she saw his maimed hand, her heart melted. She couldn't still be attracted to him after what he had done to Cindy. The more he talked, the more confident she felt in her decision to have nothing to do with him. Being a part of Billy's personal gossip was enough to deter any girl from getting involved.

"I had to check before I made a hard decision."

"What about Cindy and your baby? It is your baby. Cindy's not the kind of girl you said she was." Jeanne had said it out loud. She wanted him to be accountable for how he had treated Cindy and her. She was duped the same as all the other girls.

"I wanted to see how you felt about us first."

"So, you're going to see Cindy?"

"Yeah. My mother is at home crying. I can't get around it. She says I have to do the right thing."

Jeanne stood up. "Go home, Billy. There is no us."

"You'll be sorry about this," Billy warned. "Your life would have been great with me. Other girls beg me to take them away from this boring life. You're the only girl to say no to me."

"This is not a contest!" She couldn't believe she was a prize to him. It made her sick to think she'd felt sorry for him a few short minutes ago. She had asked him to come home with her for dinner. *What a fool I've been.*

"Old habits are hard to kick," he said. "I may marry her, but I won't be around, I can tell you that for sure. Men are like that, baby. They can't be tied down to one woman."

Billy didn't deserve a response from her, so she left him standing in the cemetery with a bewildered look on his face.

⚭

"Daniel came by to see you," said Grandma Biddy when Jeanne walked in the door.

"What did he want?"

"He saw you and Billy walking away from the paper, and he

thought you might be home."

"We went by the cemetery," Jeanne said. "I wanted to visit Robby. Billy went with me."

"How'd that go?" Grandma asked. "Apparently he didn't walk home with you."

"Don't worry. He won't be coming here." Jeanne began setting the table for supper.

"I don't worry about your decisions, Jeanne," Grandma said. "Why is Billy home? I heard he was hurt."

"He lost three fingers from a landmine explosion, but he'll manage just fine."

"Did he say anything about the Cindy situation?"

"He did, but I brought it up first. I wanted to get it in the open."

"Is he going to marry her?"

"Sounds like it, but he didn't seem all that committed."

"Maybe they can go somewhere and get a fresh start."

"Maybe." Jeanne was sure Billy wouldn't stay around for anyone for long.

"Daniel was only using a cane when he came by, and he didn't seem to need it all that much," Grandma said. "He did seem a little upset about Billy."

"What did he say?" Now Jeanne was worried. Daniel must have thought she and Billy had feelings for each other.

"He said he would be back later, but he did leave in a hurry."

"I'm going to comb my hair and change then. I'm a mess after digging through the archives all afternoon."

"Dinner is almost ready. Don't tarry."

In her room, Jeanne loosened her braid and began to brush out the tangles. She stared at the neatly tied bundles on her shelves and picked up the pack of letters from Daniel. She had pulled out his last letter to read again when Grandma called her to supper. Conversation was intermittent, and Old Dog settled down to sleep under the table at Jeanne's feet.

After supper, her grandparents left to go to a church meeting. Soon after, a knock at the door startled Jeanne out of her thoughts.

She pushed back her chair, picked up her plate, and took it to the sink. She would wash the dishes after Daniel's visit. She and Daniel had a lot to talk about. She hurried to open the door.

"Don't stand there gawking," Betty Ann demanded. "Move aside and let me get in out of this cold."

Chapter 33

Betty Ann brushed past Jeanne and pushed her against the door as she stormed into the room. She marched to the fireplace to warm her hands.

"You're not welcome here." Jeanne stood there with her arms crossed and glared at her unexpected visitor.

"Can't I talk to my daughter?" Betty Ann continued to soak up the heat. "Don't you worry, I won't be here long."

Jeanne suspected the worst, but she was ready to face her mother on her own. Grandma and Grandpa wouldn't be back for another hour. She slowed her breathing and walked away from the front door. "All right, what do you want?"

"That's my girl." Betty Ann smiled and left the hot fire to walk across the room. She patted Jeanne on the arm. Condescension oozed from her knowing smirk.

Jeanne recoiled from her mother and tried to rub the invasive touch from her skin. She wanted to scream. She wanted to rant and accuse. Anger consumed her.

Satisfied with her handiwork, Betty Ann returned to stand in front of the fire. With her hands clasped behind her back, she rocked forward, her chin down and her eyes staring upward. Evil shimmered across Betty Ann's face as she fixed her gaze on Jeanne.

For the first time, Jeanne understood Betty Ann to be someone other than her mother. She was able to withdraw her emotions and analyze the reality of the woman who stood before her. Jeanne's anger subsided.

Her mother's shoulders slumped, and her demonic countenance melted away. She had spent her last scrap of energy battling her daughter.

Taller by five inches, Jeanne stared down into Betty Ann's bloodshot eyes. Her mother wavered and squeezed her hands together to hide her trembling. Jeanne had never seen her mother shriveled to this thin emaciated body.

"Let's sit," Jeanne said. She led the way to the chairs angled against the radio.

Relieved, Betty Ann sank into the chair. Their knees would have touched if Jeanne hadn't been sitting so rigidly straight. Her mother, on the other hand, was swallowed by the large wingback. "I see you're working at the paper now."

"Where have you been?" Jeanne asked, ignoring her mother's attempt at small talk. She wasn't going to discuss her job. She knew her mother would twist the information and tell her that her life was pitiful and she fell short of what her life should be.

"I don't answer to you. You're all grown up, but I'm still your mother. I ask the questions."

"It has to be something for you to show up here at Grandpa's."

"I've been under the weather a little." Betty Ann smoothed her skirt over her legs and pulled her flimsy coat sleeves down to hide her hands. She reached up and pushed her scarf around her neck. She was in constant motion as her eyes darted around the room.

"What do you want, Mama? Why did you come here?"

Betty Ann rubbed the tops of her legs back and forth. She repeated the same motions over and over. "I came to see you. You're my daughter. I can see you if I want." She slid her feet back and forth on the carpet as if she were going to stand, but she never did.

Jeanne could not conjure words to placate her mother's needy demands. Her walls had gone up the minute she opened the door and saw Betty Ann standing there. She could not run away this time. She was in her home, and Betty Ann was the intruder. This woman had silenced her for long enough. She had to speak up for herself.

"What do you want?"

"You're so cold, Jeanne Bradshaw. Not like either of your brothers." The familiar pattern of abusive criticism had begun. "They are sweet and love their mama." Betty Ann couldn't help herself. She had to berate Jeanne.

Silence had become Jeanne's response, her way of coping with Betty Ann's habitual abuse. "They're gone now, Betty Ann, and don't you mean all *three* of my brothers?"

Betty Ann glared at her and jumped up with her hands balled into fists at her chest. "I didn't come here to talk about him," she hissed through rotted teeth.

Spittle fell on Jeanne's hand, and she wiped at it absently while she rose to face her mother. "No, you came to see your daughter. Isn't that right? When have you ever wanted to see me or cared a whit about me?" Jeanne leaned in, her face inches from Betty Ann.

"Your daddy and I talked about what trouble you were," Betty Ann said as she drew back. "I told him he spoiled you. Why did you defy me? You made me whip you. You behaved whenever I showed you the belt."

"I don't believe you about Daddy, but he's dead now and can't refute what you say. You will never convince me. You spew lies wherever you go."

"You always accused me with those eyes," Betty Ann shouted. "I hated those eyes looking at me like they are now. Who do you think you are?"

"Nobody made you beat us. You did that. There is something eating you up from the inside, and you blamed me for it because you couldn't face yourself."

Betty Ann lunged toward her, bony hands grasping Jeanne's

throat. "I hate you! You ungrateful liar. Liar! Liar! You have no right to judge me!" Nails dug into Jeanne's flesh, and a thumb pressed against her windpipe, choking her.

Jeanne grabbed at the hands on her throat and peeled Betty Ann's claws from her neck, easily overpowering her mother. Jeanne held tight to the attacking woman. She pushed her screaming mother into the chair. Jeanne stood over Betty Ann, gripping her wrists until she stopped screaming and went limp. As she released her hold, Jeanne realized how much stronger she was than her mother. She could have snapped Betty Ann's fragile bones. *No, I won't be like Betty Ann, else I'll become the abuser.*

Tears streamed down her mother's face as she curled into a ball. Jeanne backed away, and she began to tremble. Her mother tugged on her coat sleeves to cover her hands again.

Jeanne was shocked at herself. *What have I done? What am I capable of?* "You're right, Mama. I don't have the right to judge you, but I do know how you treated us. I'm not a liar." Jeanne took long, slow breaths. She did not want to carry this resentment any longer. The burden of it was too heavy.

Red eyes glared at Jeanne.

Jeanne ignored the glare. She would have her say. "You left us alone to fend for ourselves more than once, and the last time we only survived because of Grandma and Grandpa. You know that isn't a lie."

"You and Eli were old enough," Betty Ann countered. "You made it all right. Look at you now. You're better off than I am."

Jeanne heard the mother she knew emerging from their confrontation. Betty Ann's voice cleared and filled with vindictive bile.

"Why did you stick around at all?" Jeanne asked. "Why didn't you give us away like you did Sonny?"

"I won't answer such hateful questions!"

"What was my brother's name, Mama? Where is he?"

Betty Ann looked down at her lap, where clenched fingers revealed her struggle. "His daddy gave him a different name, but I still called him Sonny."

Jeanne leaned toward her mother. Her voice was hard. "But you know, don't you?"

"I've told you already, I didn't come here to talk about Sonny." Betty Ann stood up. "That was a long time ago."

"Why *did* you come? It wasn't to see me. You made that clear. You hate me, remember? What do you want from me?"

Betty Ann didn't look at her. "Can you loan me five dollars? I'll pay you back."

"I should have known. It had to be money. It's always the money."

"Just this one time and then you won't see me again."

Jeanne shook her head. "I don't have five dollars to give you."

"Maybe you could ask your grandpa."

"I would never ask Grandpa or Grandma. You're unbelievable. Don't you have any pride left at all?" A knock at the door startled Jeanne.

"Anybody home?" Daniel called as he poked his head inside the front door and stared at Jeanne and her mother. In one hand he held a nicely wrapped gift while he held his cane in the other. "Hello, Betty Ann," he said as he closed the door. "I haven't seen you in a while." Daniel took his time while he propped his cane against the door jamb and put the gift on the sofa.

"She was just leaving," Jeanne said. She helped Daniel out of his coat. "Please have a seat, Daniel." Her heart was pounding, but Jeanne walked over to the front door and opened it, still holding Daniel's coat over her arm.

Betty Ann stood by the chair and glared at Jeanne. "We're not finished here. What about the five dollars? That would be a big help to your poor old mother." Then Betty Ann stared at Daniel with the same expression she had used with Eli all those years.

"You need to leave," Jeanne said. "I don't have five dollars to give you."

Daniel reached in his back pocket and pulled out his wallet. He handed Betty Ann a five-dollar bill.

She smiled up at him and patted him on the chest. "You were always a good boy and a friend to my Eli too." Betty Ann took the money, stuffed it in her pocket, and stopped in front of Jeanne. She sneered at her and stormed out of the house.

Nothing had changed. Betty Ann was victorious. Her mother had gotten what she had come for in the first place. Jeanne felt defeated—not because of the five dollars, but because she had lost control. She had let her mother manipulate her again. At least she had not run away, but now Daniel was involved.

"Daniel, you shouldn't have given her money. She'll be back again for more."

"Let me worry about that. I was there when she used to come to the store and get money from Eli. He would say he had to help her because she was his mother. I'll always remember that. I felt sorry for Betty Ann and Eli."

"Eli did always have a soft spot for Mama," Jeanne admitted. "I suppose he was right to help her. She thinks I'm judgmental, but it's hard for me to forget what she has done to us."

"Do you think you could ever forgive her?"

"I'm working on it." Jeanne felt the coldness in her heart. Her mother had seen it. She had never told Daniel about the beatings and the dozens of times Betty Ann had left them alone without any food. "For now, I'm trying to hold on to something Auntie Boots told me. 'If you can accept your mother for who she is, then you can forgive her.' I've always wanted her to love me, but if she is who she is and doesn't change, then she will never love me. I have to accept that too."

"I came tonight to talk about taking you somewhere special for your birthday tomorrow."

That managed to bring a smile to her lips. "I had forgotten it was my eighteenth birthday. Thank you for reminding me. Betty Ann must have remembered. She called me a grown woman."

Chapter 34

Franklin Roosevelt had been elected for a fourth term on November 7, 1944, the Battle of the Bulge had begun, and Christmas was only two days away.

Jeanne checked the time on the watch Daniel had given her for her birthday. She understood the extravagance of his gift, and she had accepted it. She had strong feelings for Daniel, but part of her held back. She rubbed the face of the delicate Bulova. She would make it to the dry goods store on time. An early ice storm had blanketed Readfield in the night, and she didn't expect many customers this early.

Jeanne slid into the front door on a patch of ice and caught the doorknob to keep from falling.

"Watch yourself!" Mr. Watkins greeted her. "I'm heading out front to put salt on the walkway. We don't want people falling, especially in front of our store." He was bundled to his ears and held a sack of salt. He looked like a giant walking gingerly on the icy sidewalk.

"Good morning, Mrs. Watkins," Jeanne said. "I didn't see you there behind the counter."

"I'm trying to block that cold air when someone opens the door. I think we'll have a busy day this afternoon when this ice melts. You wait and see. This is the last shopping day before Christmas."

"Do you mind if I go over to the courthouse during the slow time? The clerk is researching records for me."

"Oh, for a story you're writing?" Mrs. Watkins asked.

"Something like that."

"The earlier the better. How long will it take?"

"Less than an hour. If she hasn't found anything, I'll be right back."

"Run along then. I can handle it here for a time."

Jeanne wrapped her scarf around her neck and pulled her knit hat over her ears before she headed to the courthouse. The trees were covered with ice and clacked in the wind. She avoided walking under the branches in case they broke off and fell on her. Her shoes slid across the steps, and the handrail stuck to her gloves as she negotiated her way into the courthouse. A blast of warm air struck her when she opened the giant wooden door.

The clerk's office was down the hall and toward the back of the courthouse. Miss Gertrude ran the records department and was known for her rigid rule, but Jeanne had made friends with her. She discovered that Miss Gertrude loved to get her name in the paper, and Jeanne assured her at every visit she would mention her in the *Examiner* as a named resource.

"Hello, Miss Gertrude."

"Come on back, Jeanne. I've found the book you were looking for, births in 1919 for the entire county. You must remember, not everyone registered births here at the courthouse. Babies were born at home without a doctor, and parents didn't bother to come to the courthouse. More than likely, they wrote it in the family Bible, and that was enough for them. Here you are."

Jeanne sat at a table piled high with record books. She understood why a book could be hard to find. The shelves were crammed with volumes of land plats and probated wills, not to mention births, marriages, and deaths. No doubt this was a treasure trove of information.

"Use this. It will help you keep track of an entry." Miss Gertrude handed Jeanne a wooden ruler.

This was worse than the search through the archives at the newspaper. She had fifty minutes left to search the records. By the end of her time, she had forty names for boys, and three were named Sonny.

Jeanne folded the paper and put it in her bag. By the time she returned to the store, three customers were standing around tables inspecting cloth. One of the women was Cindy.

Jeanne's heart sank as she slowly approached the group. "May I help you?"

Cindy was looking directly at her. "Can I talk to you for a minute?" Cindy left her companions, and Jeanne reluctantly followed her to the opposite side of the store.

"What can I do for you?" Jeanne relied on her clerk persona to manage the situation.

"Don't talk about me, I suppose," said Cindy. "Although, it doesn't matter now. The damage has already been done. You're the one who heard Billy and me that day behind the bus station."

"I haven't said a word." Jeanne could see how it looked to Cindy, but the gossips in town had the news about Cindy before she had even left town.

"Billy came to see me. He told me he had already talked to you and that you had turned him down."

"He told you that?" Jeanne couldn't believe his arrogance. "What else did he say? He was angry when I left."

"He offered to marry me for the baby's sake." Cindy wasn't hiding anything from Jeanne. She seemed tired of pretending. She had been bold to come back to Readfield at all.

"What are you going to do?" Jeanne asked. The entrance bell rang, and five more ladies walked into the store. "I have to go. I'm sorry."

"Wait, I wanted to ask you something," Cindy said. "I'm marrying Bob on Christmas Day, the soldier you saw with me. He says he loves me, and he wants to have someone to write to when he ships out."

"What do you want to ask me?"

"Will you come to the church and write about the wedding in the paper? That's what you do, isn't it? I want everybody in the county to know I got married. I want to put it in the paper. Will you do it?"

"Jeanne, you're needed at the cash register," said Mrs. Watkins.

"Yes, ma'am," Jeanne answered. "I'll be right there." She turned to Cindy. "I have to go."

Cindy grabbed Jeanne's arm. "The wedding is at eight o'clock in the evening. Will you be there?"

"All right, I'll come. Eight o'clock."

The dry goods store stayed open late, and Jeanne didn't get a chance to make her usual visit to the Examiner. Instead, she found herself knocking at the Karlsons' door.

"Come in, dear," Aunt Cheryl greeted her. "Daniel and Mr. Karlson are still at the grocery. I'm afraid they'll be pretty late tonight."

Jeanne stepped into the warm house. A small pine tree was decorated in the living room corner, and the scent of it permeated the house. "Your tree is lovely, and I love the Christmas fragrance."

"Thank you. Why don't you stay and have a cup of holiday tea with me? I have the kettle already on the stove."

Jeanne followed Aunt Cheryl into the kitchen for a cup of tea before she went home. They sat at the table, sipped their tea, and exchanged niceties.

It was Aunt Cheryl who brought up the topic Jeanne had on her mind. "I heard from Daniel that you wanted to know who Harold was. He was our son. He died when he was six from pneumonia. He was always frail, such a lovely child. I still miss him so."

"I'm sorry, Aunt Cheryl. I saw his tombstone on one of my visits to Robby, and I was only curious."

"I understand. You're trying to find your brother. I would want to know if I had a missing brother."

"I know they called him Sonny. I don't know if that's his real name or not. I've asked my mother, but she won't tell me his name."

"Lots of folks call their little boys Sonny until they start school, and then they use their full given names."

"I'm not making any progress in finding him. I've searched the birth records at the courthouse, and it's like you said. Several boys in the records were named Sonny. I think I'm at a dead end."

"Sometimes we don't get answers," Aunt Cheryl said. "We can't let that fact rule our lives. We have to move on and accept that's the way things are."

Aunt Cheryl sounded as if she were talking about her grief over losing Harold. But Jeanne was not ready to give up and accept that she would never find her missing brother. She was still struggling with the loss of Robby. Her father's death was sad, but she hadn't seen him for so long that her grief for him was different. Robby was a part of her very existence. She woke up every morning missing him. She had an emptiness inside her. She was trying to fill the void by finding Sonny.

"I have a picture of Sonny," Jeanne said. "Would you look at it and see if you remember anything?"

Aunt Cheryl looked surprised and didn't have a chance to comment before Jeanne took the picture from her valise and handed the photograph to her. Aunt Cheryl let the picture rest in her palm. She stared at it for a few moments and gently passed it back. "I don't recognize this child."

Jeanne looked closely at the expression on Aunt Cheryl's face. She saw warmth but no recognition or grief. Neither was there any fear or guilt. It really was a dead end.

Jeanne left Daniel's house even more distraught than when she had come. She didn't stop by the cemetery. The evening was cold, so she hurried on. She would find no comfort there tonight.

∽

War news intensified. Word of the battles on the European and Pacific fronts flooded the wires daily. Local events seemed insignificant by comparison. Mundane everyday life was dull. She had mentioned this to Mr. Jennings, but he had assured her that the town and county news was essential to the well-being of the people. He told her the horror of the war had to have something to counteract the sadness.

Jeanne finished searching the *Examiner* archives with no results. There was no article about Daniel's house fire, so she began to check the names of the boys born in 1918 through 1920. Most were in the military and could be verified. Tracking down the names in her limited free time was slow. It didn't take long for Mr. Jennings and Mrs. Chaney to find out about her project.

During the week following Easter, Mrs. Chaney approached Jeanne at the *Examiner* office late one afternoon. "How many names are on your list?" she asked. "I have an idea for a feature article about your boys."

"I'm down to five. I've located the others. They all have families, but I haven't been able to talk to them yet."

"You could report on the men from our county who are serving in the military," Mrs. Chaney suggested. "You have plenty of information, and it would give you a reason to talk to the families."

"That's a wonderful idea. I'll get started right away."

"I've already talked to Mr. Jennings. He's approved the story. This is your chance to have an article on the front page."

"I can have it ready for the next edition," Jeanne said.

"That will be in plenty of time. Right now, you need to go see Jill at the Majestic about the new movie coming. I hear it's that new Bing Crosby one, *The Bells of St. Mary's*."

"I'm on my way." Jeanne slid the strap of her bag over her head and was out the door. Her mind was jammed with ideas about her first feature article.

Jeanne spent the next two days writing. She finished the article in time for the next edition of the *Examiner*, but when she opened the door to the office, the atmosphere was somber and quiet. Mrs. Chaney stood behind the counter, crying.

"Here's my article, Mr. Jennings," Jeanne said as she placed it on his desk. "What's happened?"

"President Roosevelt died," he said. "Your article will have to wait."

Chapter 35

"Ouch!" Jeanne jerked her hand back. "Eating dewberries is heavenly, but picking them is tricky. These yellow jackets like them too." Jeanne rubbed her hand where she had been stung.

Thickets of dewberries by the shed were black and juicy and ready to be harvested. Jeanne and Grandma Biddy were determined to battle the insects and birds to get their share. Neighbors were out behind their houses, taking advantage of the bumper crop on this warm May afternoon. The vegetables and fruits beginning to ripen would ease the food crisis. Rationing had taken its toll on the home front. Shortages of sugar, canned goods, clothing, rubber tires, and fuel were part of everyday life.

Jeanne and her family were fortunate. Readymade clothes were in short supply, and fewer ladies came in the dry goods to buy fabric. They had sold the last of the men's work boots just last week. Mr. Watkins worked part time at the store and spent most of his time on their farm planting.

Polkadot had continued to give them plenty of milk, and the chickens laid eggs for them to sell. Even with ration stamps, many didn't have the money to buy what they needed. With Jeanne's two jobs, Grandma Biddy's sewing, and Grandpa working part time, they got by and made the payments for the house. Jeanne had seen her grandma giving eggs and milk to those in need.

"As long as we have food, we'll feed the hungry," Grandma had told her.

Jeanne took her bucket of dewberries and stepped over the brambles, avoiding the thorns and the grass snake underfoot. Her hand had begun to swell. "I'll take this batch to the house and wash them, then I'll be back."

Grandma poured her pail of berries on top of Jeanne's. "Put bluing on the sting," she advised. "And get your grandpa's gloves when you come back. Then you won't be barehanded."

⚯

Jeanne didn't know why she bothered to apply the bluing to the sting. It didn't seem to hurt any less, but she poured it over the spot anyway. She was standing on the back porch screwing on the bluing lid when Sandra walked around the corner of the house.

"Is Miss Biddy here?" Sandra asked. "I need to talk to her about a dress." She held up a sack. "I bought this cloth in Abilene. It's much finer than what they carry at the dry goods store, and I want a dress made right away."

"She's out by the back fence picking dewberries." Jeanne pointed toward the shed.

Sandra tiptoed through the damp grass for a few steps and stopped. "Well, I'm not dressed to go traipsing through gardens and cow lots."

"You can come back in a couple of hours," Jeanne offered. "She'll be through by then."

"Go get her now," Sandra demanded. "I don't have time later. I have other things to do. I'm a married woman, and you wouldn't understand."

"Why don't you try again tomorrow," Jeanne suggested. She

was exasperated with Sandra's insipid mewling about a new dress when most women hadn't had a new anything in months. She walked down the steps and started to the dewberry patch with a bucket in hand.

"It has to be finished by next Saturday for the church picnic. Now that the war is over in Europe, I want to wear it in the parade to celebrate. She won't have time if I wait till tomorrow."

"Is it that important to you?" Jeanne shaded her eyes and looked at Sandra.

"You can't imagine how important." Sandra looked at her feet, quickly glanced toward Jeanne, then looked back down at her feet again. There was no hateful quip this time.

Jeanne mulled over the request and put down her bucket. "Let me go talk to her. I have on my boots." She reached for the sack. "She'll need to see the material."

Sandra handed it to her, looking both puzzled and relieved. "Why would you do this for me after all the things I've said and done to you?"

Jeanne was shocked. People must be comparing her to her mother. She felt guilty after what she had thought about Sandra's request. "It's good of you to bring work to my grandma. She really is a wonderful seamstress."

"My wedding dress was perfect, and what you wrote in the paper was nice."

"Do you have a pattern? She'll need that so she can tell you how long it will take her. I guess being in the parade is important to you."

Sandra sucked in her breath, then burst into tears. "I can't seem to do anything right. My cooking is terrible, and I try to keep our apartment clean, but my husband leaves things everywhere. I can't keep up, and he gets so mad about it. He goes out every night and doesn't come home till midnight. I was hoping this new dress would help. We're supposed to ride in the mayor's car in the parade. Tim will wear his uniform." Suddenly, Sandra put her hand over her mouth. "I shouldn't have said that. Mama told me to never tell anyone what happens behind closed doors. You can't tell anyone."

"Don't worry," Jeanne reassured her. "I won't say a word."

"You're easy to talk to. I never knew that. You're not like your mother at all."

Jeanne didn't know what to say to that. "I'll be right back with an answer for you."

Sandra stood there wringing her hands.

The nasty girl from high school had changed into someone scared and unsure of herself. Jeanne was thankful she had not lashed out at Sandra. She felt better about herself when she was kind. She had listened to the scriptures many times about clothing yourself in compassion and kindness, but she truly experienced it for the first time today. Sandra had helped her too. One of her greatest fears was that she would be like her mother. *I am my own person.*

Even in the early morning hours, the July heat was suffocating. Jeanne fanned her face as she waited for courthouse employees to arrive. Finally, the huge front door swung open, and the building security guard nodded for her to enter.

"Good morning, Miss Gertrude," Jeanne said as she entered the records office. "You sent word that you had information for me?"

"Yes, dear. I found old adoption records. I don't know if you're interested or not."

"Yes, ma'am, I'm interested."

Miss Gertrude looked through piles of folders on her desk and stacks of papers on the counter to no avail. She continued into the back room and came back holding a thick folder. "Here we are. These documents date all the way back to 1915. That should cover the time period you're researching. You'll find only the adopting parents' names. The birth parents' names are covered over or marked out."

"Why would the birth parents' names be hidden?"

"Well, a few of these births are under, let's say, embarrassing circumstances, if you know what I mean," Miss Gertrude whispered.

"Oh, I see," Jeanne said.

Miss Gertrude placed the papers on the counter. "I'm afraid you'll have to look at the documents out here. That's the rule. I must be in the room with you. You can use the stool around here, if you want."

Miss Gertrude stood behind her as she sat on the stool and opened a file to read the first document. *Joseph Paul Reynolds* was the name written at the top. The adoptive parents were Delbert and Carol Reynolds. At the bottom of the page, a yellow half sheet of paper had been glued to the adoption certificate to hide the names of the birth mother and father. Jeanne traced the edges with her fingertips. The truth underneath was secure.

For a while, Miss Gertrude played the role of an official courthouse clerk. She stayed close by and watched Jeanne read the records. Eventually, Miss Gertrude went back to her own paperwork at her desk. Jeanne relaxed and quickly scanned each document. Occasionally, a yellow sheet was loose, letting her see the names of the birth parents. A few records had no father's name.

Then the name *Daniel Lee Karlson* was printed on the next file. Jeanne quickly scanned the page and saw the adoptive parents were Fred and Cheryl Karlson. One of the yellow corners was torn loose. Jeanne could get a fingernail between the two documents, but she dared not chance Miss Gertrude seeing her.

"Jeanne," Miss Gertrude said, "I have to take papers over to the judge. It'll only take me a minute, and I'll be right back." She hurried out the door and across the hall.

Jeanne didn't hesitate. She checked the paper and worked the tip of her finger in between the pieces of paper. She had to be careful not to rip the yellow cover. One side easily parted as she slid her finger upward. The bottom of the document was not so easy. Jeanne inched along, only getting halfway before Miss Gertrude came huffing back into the office. Jeanne put her hand over the spot where she had been working. She had not gotten far enough to check the names underneath. The clock on the wall showed she had five minutes to get to work.

"Miss Gertrude, do you mind if I come back tomorrow?" Jeanne asked.

"I won't be here tomorrow. The records office will be closed. You'll have to come back on Monday."

Jeanne's heart sank. She was so close, and she could have seen the names under the yellow paper. She reluctantly closed the folder.

"Let me take that." Miss Gertrude got up from her desk and picked up the heavy folder. "This will be right here. I promise. It's not going anywhere."

"I'll be back at lunchtime. Thank you, Miss Gertrude."

Jeanne moped about all morning, wondering about the names on Daniel's adoption papers. At lunch she ran to the cemetery to check his name for the spelling. She wanted to be ready when she went back to the courthouse. Miss Gertrude had the folder on the counter waiting for her. Jeanne had brought a letter opener with her to help with the stuck yellow sheet. She was even left alone while Miss Gertrude worked in the record room in the back. Everything was as she had left it.

When she found Daniel's adoption papers, Jeanne inserted the letter opener and easily lifted the yellow flap to see the information. *Evelyn Gail Braxton Karlson (deceased)* was written in the birth mother's space. Jeanne wrote the name on a piece of paper and tucked it inside her valise.

⤞⤝

Late afternoon was busy at the *Examiner*. Jeanne had written two war articles, and she had learned she was going to Abilene next month to report on a visit from the governor.

"Governor Stevenson is going to be in Abilene to ride his horse in the Victory Parade," Mr. Jennings said. "You'll get to meet Mr. Texas himself, so ask him a few questions for us."

"Are you sure you want me to go?" Jeanne was nervous and excited at the same time.

"Of course. It will be a great experience for you. You'll have to go to Snyder to catch the train to Abilene."

Jeanne left the paper thinking about going to Snyder. She would have to go by bus from Readfield. At the grocery store, she found Daniel in the back, unloading produce.

"Hey, Jeanne. It's a surprise seeing you here," Daniel said as he set down a crate of cabbages. "Sit over here." He pointed to an overturned wooden box. "Is everything all right?" He wrinkled his brow and looked at her with concern.

"I wanted to tell you about my new assignment," Jeanne said as brightly as she could. "Yes, everything is all right."

His face changed and was happy and without worry. "What's your new assignment?" Daniel asked as he picked up another empty box for himself.

As soon as Jeanne faced Daniel, she said, "Next month, I'm going to Snyder to report on Governor Coke Stevenson's visit." It even sounded important to her when she told him.

"Congratulations!" Daniel smiled his beautiful smile. "That's great news."

Jeanne decided not to ask what his mother's name was. Daniel was special to her, but she still had nagging doubts about his mother's identity. She had never found a report about the fire in Deep Creek, but Daniel and his aunt were matter-of-fact about him being David Karlson's son.

That evening when Jeanne walked into the kitchen, Grandma Biddy was reading a letter.

"We've heard from Eli," Grandma said.

"At last," Jeanne breathed. "What does he say?"

"You can read it, but he and Gloria have a baby girl named Anita."

"Who's Anita?" Grandpa asked as he came into the kitchen.

Jeanne and Grandma started laughing.

"What is it? What's so funny?" Grandpa asked.

"Nothing, Claude. We're just happy. We have a letter from Eli, and he and Gloria have a daughter named Anita."

Chapter 36

Jeanne had written Auntie Boots asking if she could spend the night on her visit to Abilene.

"I hope we get a letter from Bootsie today," Grandma said. "We need to know if you have a place to stay or not."

"Perhaps it will come in the mail today," Jeanne said as she opened the screen door and headed to work.

It was another August in the Texas heat, and the dry goods was busy selling fabric for back-to-school clothing. The beginning of school was a month away. Grandma Biddy was sewing school clothes, and Jeanne was needed to help as ladies crowded the store to get a free pattern Mrs. Watkins was giving away.

"Jeanne, Jeanne, the phone is for you," called Mr. Watkins from the counter. "There's a lady who says she's your aunt."

Jeanne hurried to the phone. "Hello?"

"Jeanne, is that you? It's your ol' Auntie Boots."

"I wrote you a letter. Did you get it?"

"That's what I'm calling about, girly girl. Of course you can stay here. I'll meet you at the train."

"You're the best, Auntie Boots. I can hardly wait to see you and

Uncle James and the kids."

"Us too, honey. Bye-bye now."

Jeanne stood there smiling after hanging up the phone. She would be glad to see Auntie Boots. She had so much to tell her.

❧

The day before her Abilene trip, Jeanne finalized the last of her plans at the Examiner office.

"Here's your bus ticket," Mrs. Chaney said. "This is a round-trip ticket. Don't lose it for your trip back."

Jeanne carefully tucked away the ticket in her valise.

"You are to be careful in Abilene," Mrs. Chaney said. "Are you sure your aunt will be there?"

"Oh, yes, ma'am. She'll be there."

"Good luck, Jeanne," said Mr. Jennings. "Bring back a zinger of a story. Mr. Stevenson is a cowboy on his own ranch south of here. That's why he's riding his horse in the parade."

"Yes, sir, I'll do my best."

"I know you will. Good luck." Mr. Jennings waved and walked back into his office.

Jeanne finally left the *Examiner* office so she could go home and finish packing. She had to be at the bus station by 6:00 a.m.

It was still dark when Daniel knocked on the door the next morning. He insisted on walking her to the bus station. She had told him she would be all right, but Jeanne didn't mind. She was happy to have his company.

Daniel carried her suitcase on their way to the bus station in the relative cool of the early morning. "It seems strange to be having a parade when we're still at war with Japan," Daniel commented. "I wonder what Governor Stevenson will say about the war."

"Surely, the Japanese will surrender soon. It seems to be quiet since the second atom bomb has been dropped. The Japanese are admitting that there was considerable damage."

"President Truman had to get British approval before they dropped the bomb," Daniel said.

"Yes, but the damage is horrific. They are predicting the death toll to be at a hundred thousand, and it's climbing. Think of it. Whole cities flattened; people seared instantly."

"I guess that's why I needed to see you this morning. I'm fearful of what could happen. I'll be glad when this war is over."

"We all will. Shortages are getting worse, and too many of our men and women are losing their lives."

"I want you to make the most of this trip and seeing your family in Abilene."

The bus had already pulled into the station, and the driver was inside the tiny café drinking a cup of coffee. Jeanne stood beside Daniel, watching other travelers arrive until it was time to go.

"Is this your suitcase, miss?" the driver said.

Jeanne nodded, and the man loaded it in the baggage compartment.

Daniel took Jeanne's hand and pressed it to his lips. "Take care, my brave Jeanne. You're very important to me." Then he gently lifted her chin and softly kissed her. The light touch of his mouth made her lips tingle.

The feeling of that kiss lingered as the Readfield buildings passed by and were replaced with fence posts and plowed fields. Jeanne sat by the window and began to relax after the rush to the station. An elderly woman sat beside her, but they hadn't spoken. The gray-haired lady spent the entire time searching through a tote bag. *She must have forgotten something.*

Jeanne looked through the windshield ahead and saw a bank of dark clouds on the horizon. The bus was moving directly toward it. The storm front moved fast, and within ten minutes of leaving the bus station, rain pelted the side of the bus. Immediately, the driver slowed from the deluge of rain and the darkness that surrounded them.

Soon the bus was hitting giant patches of water that had collected in the hollow places on the road. Jeanne clutched her leather bag to her chest as the bus jerked and tossed the passengers from side to side. She thought about the time when she clung to a tree in just such a storm on the farm—one that had fostered a tornado. The rain pounded the window from the side. Light and landscape disappeared. There was nothing but rain streaking across the window. Jeanne felt the bus turn as the driver pulled into a roadside park and stopped. Wind rocked the bus, and the trees beside them thrashed from side to side. Jeanne listened for breaking branches. Instead, a trash barrel broke loose and rolled down the road.

"We'll be here for a few minutes, folks," the driver said. "I'm sure this will pass."

"I need to catch a train," a man in the front seat said. "I can't be late."

The driver walked down the aisle to the back, turned around, and walked back to the front. "We'll have plenty of time," he said. "We always plan a few extra minutes in the schedule for anything unforeseen."

Jeanne was calmed by his words, but her thoughts went back to her God experience in the tornado. She closed her eyes to pray. She stayed that way until the rain subsided, and she opened her eyes.

"Are you a believer?" the old woman asked. "I saw you was praying." The woman looked straight ahead while she clutched the front of her dress as if buttons were missing and she needed her hands to keep it closed.

"Yes, I am," Jeanne said. After seeing the old woman's spotted hands clenching in fists, Jeanne relaxed and put her bag in her lap. Her actions prompted the lady to turn loose of her dress and begin smoothing the front.

"I've seen people pray and pray, and it comes to nothing," she said. "Why do you bother?"

"God's answered my prayers—in a storm like this one. I hung on to a tree when a tornado hit. That tornado destroyed everything around me except that tree. I prayed for help and God saved me."

"Did your prayer stop this storm?"

"I didn't pray for that. I only prayed for God to be with me. My grandma told me that it rains on the good and the bad. I needed God to be with me no matter what."

"Was your prayer answered?"

"Always. He is always with me. That's his promise."

"Looks like our prairie storm has passed," the driver said. "Let's move on to Snyder." He started the engine and drove out of the park and onto the highway to the bus stop near the train station.

Jeanne boarded the train in Snyder and changed to a train in Roscoe that took her on to Abilene. Auntie Boots was waiting in her old jalopy. She leaned back against the driver's door, smoking a cigarette underneath a ten-gallon Stetson. She had on jeans, a purple shirt with fringe on the sleeves, and, of course, fancy high-topped cowgirl boots.

When Jeanne stepped off the train, Auntie Boots took off her hat, swung it around her head, and whooped, "Hello, Jeanne."

The crowd at the train station all turned and looked at Auntie Boots and then at Jeanne waving back. Crowds of soldiers waiting in the station joined in the fun, whistling and whooping right along with them. Jeanne couldn't help but grin. There was no one like her Auntie Boots.

"What a lady you've become. My, my, my," Auntie Boots said as she walked up to Jeanne. "Come on over here and give your ol' Bootsie a hug."

Three of Bootsie's kids were with her. Jeanne talked louder to be heard above her cousins, who laughed and shouted, "Howdy," then Auntie Boots got even louder. They all piled in the jalopy and drove across Abilene to their house.

"It's about time you came to visit," said Bootsie. "How's your grandma and grandpa?"

That started it. Jeanne and Auntie Boots didn't stop talking until they went to bed that night. Jeanne talked about losing the farm and the adjustment of moving into town. They caught up on the latest about Eli and his new baby. She talked about Betty Ann and the last time she had seen her when the sheriff kicked her out of town.

It was late that night before she brought up Daniel. Saying her fears out loud helped her understand her feelings more.

"What is the woman's name you found in the courthouse records?" Auntie Boots asked. "Maybe I know her."

Jeanne pulled out the slip of paper and handed it to Auntie Boots. "Her name was Evelyn Gail Braxton."

"I knew a Braxton family who lived in Deep Creek. Had a girl they called Evie. It rather fits, but I don't know who she married. We had moved to Abilene by the time we were grown."

"Can you describe her?"

"She was a towhead. I don't remember the color of her eyes."

"Daniel is blond, and so was Sonny when he was little."

"That's no proof of anything, and you've had Daniel and his aunt tell you who Harold is. Cheryl would have told you the truth about Harold when she knows how Daniel feels about you. She wouldn't have kept that from you knowing you two could become involved. It wouldn't make sense. Sometimes, Jeanne, you must trust people, especially when it's someone you love."

"What do you mean?" Jeanne had been guarded with her heart, afraid because of Sonny's identity. Her aunt made sense. She didn't know why she hadn't seen it.

"Don't look so surprised." Auntie Boots chuckled. "I've listened to you talk about Daniel. Take your time and come to terms with how you feel. You're still young, and look at you, a reporter. You have your whole life ahead of you." Auntie Boots stood and patted Jeanne on the shoulder. "We'd better get to bed. That parade is early in the morning, and we're *all* going."

Jeanne snuggled in the quilts on the floor, too sleepy to think anymore tonight.

By eight o'clock the next morning, Jeanne, Auntie Boots, and the kids lined the streets of downtown Abilene, waiting for the parade. As expected, the governor, Coke Stevenson, rode down the street on his horse, a paint. Jeanne made notes about his cowboy hat, the bandanna he wore around his neck, and how he rode with the ease of a man who felt comfortable on his horse.

After he passed by, Jeanne left the cousins and made her way to the bandstand that awaited Stevenson's arrival. Here he would make a speech, and it would be a chance for Jeanne to meet him.

It wasn't long before the governor made his appearance. Jeanne was one of the first to be there near the podium. The crowd increased and began to push forward, making it hard for her to maintain her position for the speech. She was swept along with a group of reporters and found herself in the auditorium for the governor's reception.

When the governor arrived, a crush of people surrounded him and made it impossible for Jeanne to ask him a question. She did manage to reach over a woman's shoulder and shake his hand, but that was as close as she could get. At least she could say she had officially met him, and she had plenty of notes for her story.

Jeanne slowly worked her way out of the auditorium and back to the jalopy to meet Auntie Boots. It was one o'clock by the time she rounded the corner where Auntie Boots and her kids were sprawled around the car. When they saw her, they jumped up and started talking at the same time.

"Did you get your story?" Auntie Boots asked. "We were about to give up on you."

"I did! I'm sorry. I was mashed in the crowd, and it was hard to get away, but I did get lots of information."

"Let's go, I'm hungry," one of the boys complained.

"Yes, let's go," said Jeanne. "I can fill you in on the way."

"Well, don't just stand there, kiddos," Auntie Boots said. "Load up."

∽∾∽

Four other people were sitting in the passenger coach on the train to Roscoe. Two were animated in their conversation—intense and interested, but not angry. The other was a lone man, asleep and oblivious to his surroundings.

Jeanne scribbled notes, trying to put ideas together for her Governor Stevenson article, but her concentration splintered. Daniel, Betty Ann, Sonny. She gave up and let the herds of cattle and blankets of mesquite flicker by as she gazed out her window. The rhythm humming from the tracks hypnotized her.

She smiled as she thought about her visit with Auntie Boots. Her hurricane of an aunt always instilled confidence. She had accepted the fact that Daniel was not her lost half-brother. She smiled about that too. She was grateful for her grandparents, but she missed her brothers and longed for Betty Ann to be the mother she imagined most people had. Jeanne tried to remember her mother nurturing and loving them. Betty Ann had always adored Robby. She sensed his perfect innocence. He loved them all that way, unconditionally.

Lurching forward in her seat, Jeanne braced herself as the train slowed coming into Roscoe. She put away her tablet and prepared to disembark. With an hour layover in Roscoe before she changed to go on to Snyder, Jeanne gathered her suitcase and stepped off the train. She checked her bag at the depot and headed to the tiny diner next door.

When Jeanne entered the narrow diner, everyone was crowded around the radio, listening to the latest war news. The only place available was a stool at the counter. She inched her way toward it, pushing through men standing around and discussing the atomic bomb dropped on August 9 and whether Truman would drop another one. Her personal problems shrank by comparison to what she was hearing.

"The Japanese have to give up," one man said as Jeanne squeezed through the crowd.

Finally, she reached the stool at the counter. A fan mounted on the wall above her head made it hard for her to hear.

"Whatcha want, hon?" the woman behind the counter shouted.

Her voice vibrated with the blowing air. "We don't have much. These boys have eaten just about everything we have." She pointed her pencil around the room.

"A glass of iced tea, if you have it."

"Sure 'nough."

The woman was back in no time. She deposited the tea and left the ticket in one smooth motion. The supposed iced tea was tepid at best, but Jeanne quenched her thirst, nevertheless. She looked at the door and dreaded threading her way back outside. She regretted coming to the diner.

She wove her way between the stools and the booths against the opposite wall. She was turning sideways to slip between a chair and a table edge when she came face-to-face with Betty Ann. Her mother sat alone, crouched in the corner of a wooden booth. Jeanne stopped and stared at her. "Hello, Betty Ann."

Her mother's hands shook as she sipped a mug of coffee. "What are you doing here?" Betty Ann clutched the hot coffee close to her chest. "I thought you were in Readfield."

"I've been on a trip to Abilene." Jeanne rested her valise on the empty seat. "How are you, Mama?"

"I'm all right. Only a little tired."

Jeanne could see that her mother wasn't all right. Her face was gray, and her blond hair was limp and stringy. There was nothing evil here, only a needy human being, alone and desperate.

"Are you going to order something or not?" snapped the floor waitress. "We've got lots of folks waiting for this booth."

"What do you have left to eat?" Jeanne asked.

"Donnie can cook you up a burger or a grilled cheese, but that's about it," she said.

"Bring a burger with fries," Jeanne said.

"Are you payin'?" the waitress asked. "I ain't got paid for that coffee yet." She pointed at Betty Ann with her order pad.

"Yes, I'm paying, and bring a piece of pie, whatever you have." Jeanne pushed her shoulder bag over and slid into the seat opposite Betty Ann.

"Why'd you do that?" Betty Ann asked.

"You looked like you needed to eat something."

Betty Ann sipped more of her coffee, and they sat in silence, curious about each other. Jeanne tried to take in her mother's appearance. Over the years, Betty Ann had been living high one day, and the next time Jeanne saw her she would be destitute like this.

Finally, Jeanne asked, "Where are you living?"

"I'm on my way back to El Paso. I have a place to stay there. I have lots of friends, you know."

"Are you working there?" Jeanne asked. "How do you live?"

"Oh, I get wife benefits. I'm married again. He's in the army over in Germany." Betty Ann fumbled in her purse, brought out a cigarette, and lit it. She inhaled and picked stray pieces of tobacco off her lip and tongue with her ring finger and thumb. Jeanne had seen the familiar habit dozens of times. The intimacy of the gesture shook Jeanne. So many arguments had started with her mother smoking a cigarette. "You didn't think I could catch me another man, did you?"

"Mama, you can get any man you want. I only hope you're happy."

"Here you go," said the waitress as she set the food on the table.

Betty Ann picked up the hamburger and began wolfing it down. Jeanne handed her a napkin and looked out the window. She tried not to watch her mother eat. Her heart hurt. How Jeanne had wanted her mother to love her. She had seen the warmth in Robby's eyes when he saw Mama. She saw the pain on Eli's face with each disappointment. And here Betty Ann sat, a sad, bitter spirit beaten to the ground by her own choices.

"All my beautiful boys are gone," Betty Ann lamented. "Did you know that, Jeanne?"

"Yes, Mama, I know."

"Robby, my baby is gone to heaven, and Eli, my handsome son, won't come back to me." She began to cry. "Little Sonny, I'll never see him again. Jeanne, you're the only child I have left." She wiped her eyes and blew her nose with the napkin.

"I'm sorry. I miss them too."

"I know," Betty Ann said. "I know." Tears splashed on her empty plate and made yellow rivulets in the smeared mustard.

"What was Sonny like?" Jeanne whispered.

Betty Ann pulled more napkins from the metal holder and wiped her face. Jeanne waited and silently hoped her mother would talk to her. A train whistle pierced the diner buzz, and for a second everyone stopped talking, then just as quickly, the buzz started up again.

"Sonny was a miniature of his daddy," Betty Ann related. "Those sparkling blue eyes and wavy blond hair highlighted his sweet nature. I've made a million mistakes in this wretched life, but he wasn't one of them." Her admission told of her torment.

Jeanne's judgment shattered. It was clear Betty Ann suffered her own punishment. "Is Sonny still alive?"

Betty Ann hesitated. "I don't really know for sure. I think I would have heard if anything had happened to him." Her mother attempted to smooth her hair as she often did when she felt threatened. "Sonny grew up a fine young man. I heard he married."

"Where is Sonny?" Jeanne kept her voice soft.

"The last I heard; his daddy moved to Fort Worth. I don't know if he's still there."

"Do you think Sonny is fighting in the war?"

"He's the right age, but no telling what's happened to him."

"What's his name? How will I know if he survived this war if I don't know his name?" The train whistle blew, and Jeanne looked at her watch. "I have to catch my train. Here, take this." Jeanne put a five-dollar bill and change on the table and stood to go.

Betty Ann grabbed her arm. "John Williams." She exhaled.

Jeanne caught her breath. Betty Ann had said Sonny's name. There it was. The anguished look on Betty Ann's face verified the secret. Jeanne believed she was telling the truth.

Betty Ann bowed her head and held Jeanne's arm in a fierce grip. "I haven't always done right by you," she whispered.

Jeanne's response flowed instinctively from her heart. "It was hard growing up, Mama, but I have forgiven you." She heard her own words in stunned relief.

"You're strong. You were always strong." Betty Ann released Jeanne's arm and picked up her fork. She no longer looked at Jeanne.

Jeanne left her mother eating the apple pie, and glanced back in time to see Betty Ann slip the five-dollar bill into her bedraggled purse.

As Jeanne was weaving through the tables, working her way toward the door, a roar erupted from the crowd in the diner. It began with the folks crowded around the radio. The uproar swept the diner and onto the surrounding depot.

Men and women alike began shouting, and the mountain of people erupted into pandemonium. "The war is over! The war is over!"

The train whistle blew over and over, and Jeanne was transported with the mass of people celebrating onto the platform. Some were jumping up and down, crying, while others were shouting. It was a frenzy of joy, laughter, and relief.

A man picked Jeanne up and swung her around, both of them laughing. When he put her down, he ran off yelling to the world in general. People were patting her on the back and hugging her. Jeanne hugged them back, and for the first time, she cried happy tears. She had never felt anything like this and knew she would not experience it again. Her country had held together, fought together, and loved as a people, and she was part of it.

Jeanne picked her way through the revelers to the depot, retrieved her suitcase, and headed to the train. She passed the ticket window, stopped, and stared at the train schedule. She looked down at her ticket, which read *Snyder*. She was eager to go home and share the war victory with her family.

But she took a deep breath, stepped forward to the ticket window, and said, "One ticket for Fort Worth, please."

Minutes later, Jeanne boarded the eastbound train and found

her seat. Her hands shook as she sat alone near the window. She hugged her satchel tight against her chest and wept. The terrible world war was over. Her war was over.

Epilogue

September 3, 1945

Dearest Jeanne,

I am still reeling from your visit. I can't believe you found me with the number of John Williamses living in Fort Worth. My family and I talk about you every day. I think I knew you from the moment I saw you at my front door. I have always had an empty space in my heart, and now I know why. To think I actually have a sister and a brother as well is overwhelming. I am writing you this letter to let you know that I want to come and visit you in Readfield. We have a lot of catching up to do. My uncle, my father's brother, will run the bank while I'm gone. I can come next month. Please let me know if this visit is convenient.

I have also written to Eli, but I haven't heard from him yet. I sent it to the San Diego address you gave me. If everything works out with Eli, I want to go visit him as well. Please consider accompanying me and my family on that journey. Jan and I think it would be a nice family reunion.

I look forward to hearing from you. God bless you, my dear sister.

Your loving brother,

John Foster Williams Jr.

Questions
and
Topics
for
Discussion

1. Abuse, abandonment and neglect of children exist in our society today. How do you think each differs in Jeanne's time from what is happening today? How is it the same?

2. How did Jeanne's fear of becoming like Betty Ann manifest itself? How did she manage her behavior? How would you manage avoiding or changing your behavior?

3. When did Jeanne experience God moments? Do you think it changed her life? If so, in what ways did it change her?

4. Jeanne wrote poems to find peace when she felt threatened. In what other ways did Jeanne cope?

5. Who were the people in Jeanne's life who gave her encouragement, and how did they support her? Have you had people in your life who have been there for you as a mentor or guide? List those who are no longer in your life. What did they do or say that helped?

6. How did Jeanne feel about God when she lived in Deep Creek? How did her feelings change over the next five years? How have you changed in your beliefs in the last five years?

7. Have you known of someone who has been abused as a child? As an adult? What resulted in the abuse cycle? Did it continue? If not, how was the cycle broken?

8. Auntie Boots was a bigger than life character who gave Jeanne some sound advice. Did you agree or disagree with Auntie Boots? Why or why not? What advice would you have given Jeanne about boys?

9. Why do you think Jeanne was shy around boys and shocked by Jameson's actions?

10. What reasons do you think Jeanne wouldn't admit her feelings for Daniel for such a long time?

11. Jeanne was abandoned more than once. Which time had the most impact on her life? Why?

12. Did Jeanne think God answered her prayers? How? When? Was she aware of God's answered prayer? Do you feel God has answered your prayers? Have you been disappointed in His answers? Why or why not?

13. Jeanne's grandparents played a significant role in her life. What did they do for the three children? Discuss why extended family is important. Do you know of someone who has depended on an extended family? How were their lives changed?

14. Do you think Jeanne forgave her mother, father, brother? Why or why not?

15. Do you think Jeanne held resentment in her heart? Why or why not?

16. Jeanne experienced a powerful love for her little brother, Robby. How was her life influenced by this love? Have you ever experienced love in this way? How did it change your life?

17. Why do you think the cicada was used as a symbol in Jeanne's story?

18. Whisper Jeanne's prayer. Do you think asking for help is sometimes all we can say?

The Author

Experiences and stories from Sylvia Hornback's own childhood in farming country and small-town Texas inspired the story of Jeanne. Readers will follow this resilient young girl from days of abandonment and sorrow to become an irrepressible young woman. After being left alone by both parents, Jeanne and her two brothers walk miles to find help from their Grandparents. With her older brother injured and her little brother suffering with a heart defect, Jeanne is left with the responsibility of providing for them all. Having no choice, they leave their home hoping to find food, shelter and love with their grandparents. Jeanne endures the hardships of West Texas farming and the agonies resulting from World War II. Through her turmoil she discovers she has a missing half brother she has never met. Jeanne is a story of a girl's journey from abandonment and abuse to forgiveness and truth.

On the next page is a picture of Cary, my little brother at age six with his giant Christmas peppermint stick. I patterned Robby in *Jeanne* after him. Cary was an angel here on earth for twenty-three years. He brought unconditional love into our family. I tried to convey that special love through the character, Robby.

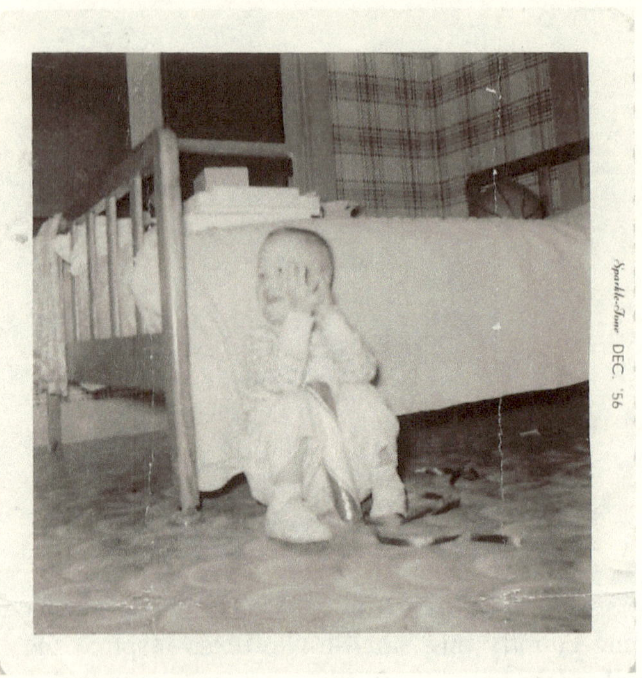

In *Jeanne*, the facility referenced in Austin was the first state home for what then was called the feebleminded. Children were boarded there under lock and key for fear of them developing criminal tendencies, and their families were not allowed to visit often. In the 1940's when the story takes place, Robby's condition was known as Mongolism. This label didn't change until the 1970's when the term was replaced with Down Syndrome. Today, services and opportunities for special needs children have dramatically changed. Over the years, parents, teachers and communities have come to understand and accept children of special needs. We are blessed to have them in our lives.

www.ingramcontent.com/pod-product-compliance
Lightning Source LLC
Chambersburg PA
CBHW031614100726
47898CB00006B/1789